MAXIM JAKUBOWSKI was born in England but educated in France. Following a career in publishing, he opened London's famous MURDER ONE bookshop. He has published over 70 books, won the Anthony and Karel Awards and is a connoisseur of genre fiction in all its forms. His recent books include eight volumes in *The Mammoth Book of Erotica* series, as well as *The Mammoth Book of Pulp Fiction* and more recently *The Mammoth Book of Pulp Action, The Mammoth Book of On The Road* and *The Mammoth Book of Future Cops*. Other well-received anthologies include: *London Noir*, three volumes of *Fresh Blood, Past Poisons, Chronicles of Crime* and *Murder Through the Ages*. A regular broadcaster, he is the crime columnist for the *Guardian*, writes for *The Times* and is the Literary Director of London's National Film Theatre Annual Crime Scene Festival. His fiction includes *Life in the World of Women, It's You That I Want to Kiss, Because She Thought She Loved Me, The State of Montana, On Tenderness Express, Kiss Me Sadly* and *Confessions of a Romantic Pornographer*. He lives in London.

THE MAMMOTH BOOK OF

Best
New Erotica

Volume 3

Edited by Maxim Jakubowski

CARROLL & GRAF PUBLISHERS
New York

Carroll & Graf Publishers
An imprint of Avalon Publishing Group, Inc.
245 W. 17th Street
11th Floor
NY 10011
www.carrollandgraf.com

First Carroll & Graf edition 2004
Reprinted 2005

First published in the UK by Robinson,
an imprint of Constable & Robinson Ltd 2004

Collection and editorial material
copyright © Maxim Jakubowski 2004

ISBN 0–7867–1287–2

Printed and bound in the EU

Contents

Acknowledgments   ix

Maxim Jakubowski
INTRODUCTION   xv

Michel Faber
THE TWO HELLOS   1

Cara Bruce
FOR SALE   10

Mark Ramsden
TRULY SCRUMPTIOUS   18

Rich Logsdon
SWEET, SWEET ANNIE   27

Dawn O'Hara
LONDON DERRIÈRE   39

Andy Duncan
THE HOLY BRIGHT NUMBER   52

Debra Hyde
ON HALLOWED GROUND   60

M. Christian
THE COLOUR OF LUST   69

Mary Anne Mohanraj
WILD ROSES   80

Nicholas Kaufmann
THE VIP ROOM   88

Cheyenne Blue
CACTUS ASS   108

Maxim Jakubowski
THE SHAPE OF CITIES   115

Adhara Law
THE DEATH AND LIFE OF EDWARD GRABLE   121

Morgan Hawke
ALCHEMICAL INK: SHATTERED ANGEL   129

Lilian Pizzichini
MAKING WOOFIE   146

Michael Crawley
SIX BEFORE NINE   151

Jacqueline Lucas
MOTHERING   159

E. M. Arthur
DIVER'S MOON   166

Sage Vivant
THE LITTLE AMERICAN   179

Bianca James
FUGU   190

Mike Kimera
DESERVING RUTH   200

Anya Wassenberg
CAT   210

Cole Riley
IF IT MAKES YOU HAPPY   221

David Surface
GOING OUT WITH ANGELA   234

Renée M. Charles
DIVING INTO OCEANS OF AIR   243

Michèle Larue
THE WATER HOLE   259

John Grant
THE ADVENTURE OF THOMAS THE ROCK
    STAR IN THE COURT OF THE QUEEN OF
    FAERY   266

Justine Dubois
SAN SEBASTIAN   280

Karen Taylor
WANTING THAT MAN   286

Madeleine Oh
LA DÉESSE TERRE   294

Sacchi Green
TO REMEMBER YOU BY   306

O'Neil De Noux
DEATH ON DENIAL   320

Tara Alton
THE SWEATER   332

Jennifer Footman
TRYING IT ON   344

Claire Tristram
TOMATOES: A LOVE STORY IN THREE PARTS 352

Lisa Montanarelli
THE WHORE GENE   357

Julia Peters
SHOW TIME   368

Alison Tyler
PROGRESSIVE PARTY   379

Tom Piccirilli
HORSEPOWER   386

Lee Elliott
ENGLISH LESSONS   398

Lisabet Sarai
BUTTERFLY   407

Rachel Kramer Bussel
LAP DANCE LUST   423

R. Gay
A COOL DRY PLACE   428

Susannah Indigo
BACON, LOLA AND TOMATO   441

Mari Ness
THE SWING   452

Anne Tourney
THE BLOOD VIRGIN   463

Diane Kepler
SAKURA   475

Christopher Hart
DRIFT   490

Acknowledgments

THE TWO HELLOS by Michel Faber, © 2002 by Michel Faber. First appeared in THE EROTIC REVIEW. Reprinted by permission of the author.

FOR SALE by Cara Bruce, © 2002 by Cara Bruce. First appeared in BEST FETISH EROTICA. Reprinted by permission of the author.

TRULY SCRUMPTIOUS by Mark Ramsden, © 2003 by Mark Ramsden. Reprinted by permission of the author.

SWEET, SWEET ANNIE by Rich Logsdon, © 2002 by Rich Logsdon. First appeared in SUSPECT THOUGHTS. Reprinted by permission of the author.

LONDON DERRIÈRE by Dawn O'Hara, © 2002 by Dawn O'Hara. First appeared in BEST WOMEN'S EROTICA. Reprinted by permission of the author.

THE HOLY BRIGHT NUMBER by Andy Duncan, © 2002 by Andy Duncan. First appeared in POLYPHONY. Reprinted by permission of the author.

ON HALLOWED GROUND by Debra Hyde, © 2002 by Debra Hyde. First appeared in SCARLET LETTERS. Reprinted by permission of the author.

DIVER'S MOON by E.M. Arthur, © 2002 by E.M. Arthur. First appeared in TOUCHWORD. Reprinted by permission of the author.

THE LITTLE AMERICAN by Sage Vivant, © 2002 by Sage Vivant. First appeared in PEACOCK BLUE. Reprinted by permission of the author.

FUGU by Bianca James, © 2002 by Bianca James. First appeared in THE BEST OF THE BEST MEAT EROTICA. Reprinted by permission of the author.

DESERVING RUTH by Mike Kimera, © 2002 by Mike Kimera. First appeared on the EROTIC READERS AND WRITERS ASSOCIATION website. Reprinted by permission of the author.

CAT by Anya Wassenberg, © 2002 by Anya Wassenberg. First appeared in GRUNT AND GROAN. Reprinted by permission of the author.

IF IT MAKES YOU HAPPY by Cole Riley, © 2002 by Cole Riley. First appeared in CLEAN SHEETS. Reprinted by permission of the author.

GOING OUT WITH ANGELA by David Surface, © 2002 by David Surface. First appeared in SLOW TRAINS. Reprinted by permission of the author.

DIVING INTO OCEANS OF AIR by Renée M. Charles, © 2002 by Renée M. Charles. First appeared in MIND AND BODY. Reprinted by permission of the author.

THE WATER HOLE by Michèle Larue, © 2003 by Michéle Larue. First appeared in France as JE D'O. Reprinted by permission of the author.

THE ADVENTURE OF THOMAS THE ROCK STAR IN THE COURT OF THE QUEEN OF FAERY by John

Grant, © 2003 by John Grant. Reprinted by permission of the author.

SAN SEBASTIAN by Justine Dubois, © 2002 by Justine Dubois. First appeared in THE EROTIC REVIEW. Reprinted by permission of the author.

WANTING THAT MAN by Karen Taylor, © 2002 by Karen Taylor. First appeared in BEST BISEXUAL EROTICA. Reprinted by permission of the author.

LA DÉESSE TERRE by Madeleine Oh, © 2002 by Madeleine Oh. First appeared in WICKED WORDS 6. Reprinted by permission of the author.

TO REMEMBER YOU BY by Sacchi Green, © 2002 by Sacchi Green. First appeared in SHAMELESS. Reprinted by permission of the author.

DEATH ON DENIAL by O'Neil De Noux, © 2002 by O'Neil De Noux. First appeared in FRESH BLOOD: DARK DESIRE. Reprinted by permission of the author.

THE SWEATER by Tara Alton, © 2002 by Tara Alton. First appeared in SCARLET LETTERS. Reprinted by permission of the author.

TRYING IT ON by Jennifer Footman, © 2002 by Jennifer Footman. First appeared in FOR WOMEN. Reprinted by permission of the author.

TOMATOES: A LOVE STORY IN THREE PARTS by Claire Tristram, © 2002 by Claire Tristram. First appeared in CLEAN SHEETS. Reprinted by permission of the author.

THE WHORE GENE by Lisa Montanarelli, © 2002 by Lisa Montanarelli. First appeared in BEST FETISH EROTICA. Reprinted by permission of the author.

SHOW TIME by Julia Peters, © 2002 by Julia Peters. First appeared in CLEAN SHEETS. Reprinted by permission of the author.

PROGRESSIVE PARTY by Alison Tyler, © 2002 by Alison Tyler. First appeared in GOOD VIBRATIONS. Reprinted by permission of the author.

HORSEPOWER by Tom Piccirilli, © 2002 by Tom Piccirilli. First appeared in BEST FETISH EROTICA. Reprinted by permission of the author.

ENGLISH LESSONS by Lee Elliott, © 2002 by Lee Elliott. First appeared in CLEAN SHEETS. Reprinted by permission of the author.

BUTTERFLY by Lisabet Sarai, © 2002 by Lisabet Sarai. First appeared on the EROTIC READERS AND WRITERS ASSOCIATION website. Reprinted by permission of the author.

LAP DANCE LUST by Rachel Kramer Bussel, © 2002 by Rachel Kramer Bussel. First appeared in BEST WOMEN'S EROTICA. Reprinted by permission of the author.

A COOL DRY PLACE by R. Gay, © 2002 by R. Gay. First appeared in SHAMELESS. Reprinted by permission of the author.

BACON, LOLA AND TOMATO by Susannah Indigo, © 2002 by Susannah Indigo. First appeared in THE BEST OF THE BEST MEAT EROTICA. Reprinted by permission of the author.

THE SWING by Mari Ness, © 2002 by Mari Ness. First appeared in TONGUES OF FIRE. Reprinted by permission of the author.

THE BLOOD VIRGIN by Anne Tourney, © 2002 by Anne Tourney. First appeared in SUSPECT THOUGHTS. Reprinted by permission of the author.

SAKURA by Diane Kepler, © 2002 by Diane Kepler. First appeared in WET. Reprinted by permission of the author.

DRIFT by Christopher Hart, © 2002 by Christopher Hart. First appeared in THE EROTIC REVIEW. Reprinted by permission of the author.

Introduction

Maxim Jakubowski

And so THE MAMMOTH BOOK OF EROTICA series moves into its tenth year already. And it just feels like yesterday! Trust erotic matters to keep you eternally young . . .

When I wrote the introduction to the first volume in 1993, the erotic shelves in bookshops worldwide were thinly stocked, and in the majority of stores there wasn't even an erotic section per se. In the previous couple of decades, there had been less than a handful of anthologies published, generally of an historic nature and explicit short stories in mainstream magazines were few and far between. Erotica was hiding, so to speak. Now, as cybersex is already becoming a thing of the past itself, the bookshelves are groaning under the sheer weight of new books in the genre (and I daresay the Mammoths contribute to this by being the longest, and also the best value books!) and anthologies on offer cover every theme and sexual orientation under the sun – or should it be the moonlight, for those who prefer their sexual entertainment to be concealed under a relative cover of darkness. In addition, the cyberworld has taken a leaf from the real world and a wonderful community of web magazines are flourishing and proving an invaluable training ground for so many new writers.

Long may this flourish.

Sexuality is at the core of our beings and the act of writing, of self-expression, must reflect this essential part of our psyche. Explicitness in writing about sexual matters need not be vulgar or downmarket, and there is more titillation in an elegant phrase or original storyline than there is in a picture or photograph in my humble, if prejudiced, opinion. And that's the difference between eroticism and pornography. Yes, our Mammoth authors wish to arouse your dormant senses but it's all in a good cause.

This year's volume encompasses some of the best short stories I managed to come across published during the course of 2002 in a variety of places. There are familiar names for veteran readers of the series (all previous volumes are still in print and available, so go and complete your set and improve your sex life accordingly!), as well as new discoveries, many of whom, I hope, will become future regulars and will graduate to doing books of their own one day.

The stories hail from Great Britain, the USA, Canada, Australia and France and all evoke a rainbow of emotions and sexual feelings with talent and empathy to spare. There is still too much erotica that comes in the form of pseudo readers' letters describing a particular sexual encounter or ersatz poetic memories attempting to raise the mythic consciousness of a past tryst, but the majority of the authors here transcend these bonds and treat their characters with humour or even darkness, and hence make their fictional creatures of flesh, blood and genitals even more believable. That is the art of erotic writing at its best.

So, get ready for an exciting ride with some of the dirtiest and shrewdest minds in the business, and explore combinations, positions, variations and possibilities beyond even your wildest imagination. And, should you need reassurance, no bedsheets were harmed during the writing of this book.

Maxim Jakubowski

The Two Hellos

Michel Faber

She didn't phone him directly after she got off the coach, because she was hungry and her bum was very sore. She phoned him about an hour later, after she'd had some breakfast and wandered around the city for a while.

"Hello?" she said, into a public telephone receiver that was cold and damp with other people's breath.

"Yes?" he said back, having no idea, apparently, whose voice it was – as always.

In the pause before she identified herself, she felt that little prick of irritation which is merely the tip of a giant hypodermic full of fermented hatred. They'd argued about this so many times.

"Why don't you ever know it's me?" she would exclaim when she got him alone.

"For Christ's sake – what do you expect when all you say is 'hello'?" he would say, or (even worse): "Look – in the course of a day I'll get calls from any number of women . . ."

"But I'm your wife," she'd insist.

"I know that," he'd assure her. "But what happens if I say 'Hello, darling!' and it turns out the woman on the line is a client for data management software?"

"If you knew my voice, it wouldn't ever happen."

"Look, lots of women sound . . . uh . . . similar. Especially on the phone."

"No more so than lots of men. And I know your voice."

"OK, so you're better at recognizing voices than I am!" he would offer, as a concession that was at once exasperated and sarcastic. "Microsoft should develop you as a piece of voice recognition software."

Such comments would enter her through the softness of her flesh, and harden inside her – in all the wrong ways.

"When Carol calls, you don't hesitate: you instantly respond."

"Carol's my sister."

"OK, then: Patricia."

"Pat's an old lady. She has a very distinctive voice."

"Maybe I should take lessons from her."

"I didn't say her voice was a particularly nice one – just distinctive, because she's old and she's got a mouth like a . . . like a . . . uh . . . an old person." (Similes – or indeed anything creative – were not his forte.)

"OK," she would say at this point, if she felt compelled to push the argument to its climax. "What about the times I phone you up, and I say 'Hello', and you say 'Yes', and I don't say anything, and eventually you say, 'Is that you?' "

"What about them?"

"If you know it's me, why don't you just say so first off?"

"I don't know . . . I can't be sure . . . I have to think about it."

She could never win, precisely because she always won. On the defensive every time, he was more reasonable than her, kept things in proportion, observed the rules of debate, only ever raised his voice if she did it first, tried to keep emotions out of it. In the absence of an impartial adjudicator, his expression was her only mirror, and it showed her a reflection of herself behaving irrationally, unfairly. He would stare at her, hurt and at a loss for words, like a quiz show contestant who's been led to believe he would be questioned on Roman history, and was suddenly being interrogated about the human nervous system.

Yes, she was being unfair. Probably. But it had happened more than once, that in the middle of this same stupid argument about recognizing voices, the telephone had rung and he'd answered it, caught one second's worth of distant greeting, and immediately replied, "Oh hi, Lynne!" or whoever. The bastard just couldn't help it.

"It's me," she said to him now. "Your wife."

"Where are you?"

She couldn't tell yet whether he was worried or angry about her being fourteen hours late.

"Princes Street. Near the station."

"Well, I'm sorry but I can't pick you up now." He still didn't sound unequivocally worried or angry, merely pained. "I have to leave for work in a few minutes."

"I know," she said, secretly pleased that she'd timed her call so well.

"I met the plane you were supposed to be on yesterday evening," he said. "It came in bang on time, but you weren't on it. Where were you?"

"Still in London," she said. "My handbag got stolen at the airport, just a few minutes before the plane was due to leave. Some teenage kid just ripped it off my arm. I chased him, but I was still in the same shoes I wore to the wedding, so it was pretty hopeless."

"Why didn't you get on the plane anyway?"

"My ticket was in that bag, my credit cards, mobile, everything."

"It's an e-ticket. The number is just for your reference. Your name is in the computer system, that's all that matters."

"I was flustered. They'd already started the boarding calls. I didn't feel I could just talk my way through."

"You could have phoned me then."

"Will you listen to me for once? My handbag was stolen. It had my mobile in it; everything. I didn't even have change for a public phone."

"I – I'm sorry, it just didn't click for a moment . . ."

"I'm a woman," she reminded him bitchily. "I don't walk around in a dark-blue suit with wallets and phones in the pockets." She knew her bitchiness was uncalled for, but she forgave herself because she was sure he would say something equally insensitive to her any moment now.

"Hang on . . . You had about . . . God, how much money did you lose?"

"About £500," she replied. "In cash."

There was a sharp intake of breath at the other end.

"You said you'd put it straight into your card account!" he reminded her accusingly.

"I know. I didn't. I forgot. And didn't feel like it, anyway."

"I told you not to carry that sort of money around."

"Well, I did, and it's lost. So what?"

"I don't work for nothing, that's what."

"You insisted on giving me the money. Another few days of my card being overdrawn wouldn't have killed us. I could've taken it out of my wage next week."

"We agreed: your wage is for the house repayments."

"Fine. So are you happy now?"

There was a pause while he digested the fact that they'd once again proved their ability to cook up an argument in three minutes or less, using only minimal ingedients. Then he said, "I have to go to work now."

"Fine," she said. "I'll see you this evening."

"Are you going to work yourself?"

"How can I?" she said. "I've just spent all night sitting on a bus, I've had no sleep." She knew she'd perhaps forfeited her right to any sympathy from him, and she also knew she wouldn't value it if he showed it, but she wanted it anyway, if only because she was angry that he lacked the imagination to figure out how she must have got back to Edinburgh in the circumstances.

"On a bus?" he exclaimed, as if she'd just told him she hitch-hiked back, clinging to the tarpaulin of a lorry.

"Yes, on a bus," she sing-songed. "Do you think I'd ask my sister on the first day of her honeymoon if she could lend me the dosh for a private jet?"

He sighed; the whole affair still didn't quite make sense; but he was smart enough to bite his tongue on further demands for explanations.

"You could at least have rung me. I was worried about you." Ah! Here it was, at last – too late as always, a whole argument too late.

"I tried," she said. "Several times."

There was another pause, while he decided whether she deserved to be felt about any differently from the way he was currently feeling about her. When he spoke again, she noted he was aiming for a neutral, tolerant tone.

"So you're not going to work. Do you want me to ring them for you?"

"I can ring them myself, thanks. I've got 70, maybe even 80 pee. The kindness of strangers . . ."

"And . . . uh . . . You must be tired. Do you think you'll be able to sleep today?"

"I don't think so. I've got a pile of washing. If I don't do that I'll have nothing to wear."

"What are you talking about? You've got wardrobes full of clothes."

"No, I don't mean that sort of clothes. Underwear. I used up all my underwear during the trip – I've got my period."

He laughed, attempting to repair their disharmony with a good-humoured expression of shared intimate knowledge. "Say no more," he said.

"Fine. See you later," she said, and hung up. If he thought she derived any comfort from his intimate acquaintance with how copiously she bled and how usual it was for her to soil her panties at the gusset edges, he was mistaken. Again. Nor did she get any thrill out of the other little details he knew about: her creamy discharges mid-cycle, the yellow stains she sweated into the armpits of her spencers, the pale brown stains caused by farts whose constitution she'd misjudged, and so on. She could live without his knowing these things, though being married to him made that impossible. For a week every month, by mutual arrangement, she would sleep in the guest room, to spare the expensive linen on the double bed.

"I've married one that leaks," he'd commented once, as a sort of mawkishly well-meant joke. They'd argued about that one, too, until she started leaking from the eyes.

On the bus home, she dozed over her suitcase, her matted hair falling over her face. She hadn't had time to have a shower before leaving London. She must have a shower when she got home – but not right away. First things first.

She walked in the front door of her house at a quarter to nine, dumped her suitcase next to the living-room sofa, and got the call to her boss over with. It was painless. Concern was expressed about the shock and outrage she must have felt at the theft, the inconvenience of her all-night trip, and the loss of the

£500. There was even some suggestion that this day off might be treated as sick leave, a possibility which did not interest her just at the moment, though she made an effort not to sound too blasé.

"Thanks, see you later," she said, and hung up.

On the dining room table she found the remains of her husband's breakfast: dregs of orange juice in a tall glass, an empty coffee cup, a bowl plastered with bits of milky cereal. She cleared these things away, washed them properly in detergent and hot water, dried them and stored them in their appointed cupboards. Then she filled the blue plastic laundry tub with warm water, poured in some pink liquid described on its label as a "super dirt dissolver" and "stain shifter", carried the tub into the living room, and set it down in front of the sofa.

Her bum was still sore: she noticed it especially as she leaned over from her sitting position to pull her dirty clothes out of the unzipped suitcase. Not one of the garments was bloodstained, of course, because her period was only starting now, or to be more precise, it had started last night on the bus.

Out of sudden curiosity she rocked back on the sofa and pulled off the panties she was wearing. She tossed the lightly soiled pad aside without even bothering to roll it up; it was the crotch of the panties that interested her. She had been certain, when she'd first settled into her seat on the bus, that she had felt another little trickle of come seep out, but had decided it wasn't possible: it must be some sort of nervous tickle.

Now, in the warm light of mid-morning, she held the gusset of her panties taut and stared at the uneven, elongated diamond-shape of semen, like a primitive painting of her own cunt. She held it up to her nose: it still had a smell, though nowhere near as strong as the smell she'd got on her fingers when she had pointed her rear at him and, in lifting the cheeks of her arse for his easier penetration, had found her flesh slippery with his come from earlier on.

Dropping the panties into the tub, she rummaged in her suitcase for the slip she was wearing when she'd first hugged his prick inside her. She had observed the delight on his face when he felt how wet she was for him, and as she had guided him into her she'd laughed and said, "You've been getting me wet for hours."

It was true. Foreplay had begun virtually the moment they'd been introduced to one another at the wedding reception, even though they had stood at a demure distance from each other and done nothing but talk.

And talk, and talk. Their talking was like nothing she'd ever been able to do with anyone else: free of pretence, free of condescension, free of dilution. There were things she was able to say to him that she'd ceased attempting to say to other people years ago, and he not only understood these things, but understood the way she felt about being able to say them as well. Some of the things he said to her, although she took them in with more intellectual attention than she'd given to just about anything ever said to her, had the additional effect of a warm middle finger sliding up between her labia.

After a couple of hours of this, she'd excused herself for a minute to dash up to her sister's toilet, and, as she parted her legs on the toilet seat, she had heard (above the murmur of the reception downstairs) her cunt make a sucking noise. She'd decided then that she had to make love to this man.

Alone now in her house in Edinburgh, she held up her cotton shift. The stain on it was in the shape of a phallus, but that was coincidental, of course. The shape was actually created by his come being squeezed out, little by little, by the contractions of her own orgasm, and spilling into the cleft in her arse as she moved it beneath him. Similarly, the stain on her spencer was caused by her lying belly-down on a wet spot as he eased the head of his prick into her arsehole. He had moved too gently at first, until she'd begun to buck to give him the idea.

On the bus many hours later, sitting on the arse she had urged him to fuck deeper, she had almost regretted it, but later still, in her house in Edinburgh, she squirmed experimentally on the sofa and took joy in the vestige of pain and the memory of his hoarse cry as his pelvis fell against her buttocks for the last time.

It was her impression that he knew exactly what to do when they were fucking, though perhaps she was constantly letting him know what she wanted without really being aware she was doing it. If his hands were on her nipples just when she wanted them there, how did her breasts get uncovered in the first place? He wanted all of her, so she gave him what he wanted, but in the order she wanted it taken, perhaps. She couldn't be sure. There were things he had done that she hadn't been aware she wanted done to her, which she'd craved instantly and desperately as soon as she felt him begin.

It didn't even occur to her to decide whether or not he was a good lover; that would be like a four-year-old child wondering if its sibling was a capable playmate.

She had just wanted to keep fucking and talking and laughing all night and all day, and (looking back at it now) she liked to fancy that at 7.35 pm yesterday afternoon, when her plane lifted off the runway on its way to Edinburgh without her, she'd been coming hard against his warm, wet fingers, cradling his head on her shoulder.

Pushed down into the tub of sudsy water, her underclothes relinquished their hold on his stains and hers. The house was quiet around the swirling of the water as she rubbed and wrung the submerged garments. Detergent and grey-brown water dissolved the difference between the sweating she'd done on the plane to London and the sweating she'd done while fucking her man. She would put these things in the tumble-dryer and they would come out dry and pale, while she herself would have a long shower and wash the last of his smell off her body until she, too, emerged dry and pale.

Later that day, very sleepy from the warmth of the shower and the hairdryer, she went out again, to the local shops. She could still feel him, ever so slightly, in her arse, if she walked really stiffly. She walked that way every now and then, when she thought no one was looking.

She bought a new handbag in the first shop she walked into. It was not even as expensive as her old one (which she still had with her), but she liked it better. She transferred a few things from the one to the other, things her husband would lack the imagination to be surprised had not been in her handbag when it was "stolen". The rest, including her e-ticket confirmation and her credit card, she destroyed. She'd already thrown away her mobile phone in London, afraid of her husband catching her out making calls on a gadget she claimed to have lost. The empty, flaccid handbag she now deposited in a charity shop collection bin.

The post office had telephone cubicles outside, two in a row. She entered one of these and extracted from her new handbag one of the things she had not discarded: her address book.

Leaning against the side of the cubicle, she dialled the newest number with its 0207 prefix, getting as comfortable as she could in preparation for a long conversation. Running out of money was not a worry: on the cubicle shelf she'd put a small handful of pound coins. If they ran out, she had another four hundred-odd pounds' worth she could convert to coin, and that was an awful lot of talking.

His telephone, six hundred kilometres south of hers, rang about eight times before he answered it.

"Hello," he said noncommittally.

"Hello," she replied, as fresh sweat prickled into her newly-laundered underwear. "This is –"

"I know who it is," he said at once, in the same warm, teasing tone with which he'd told her, such a deliciously short time ago, that he was about to come inside her. "It's so good to hear your voice."

For Sale

Cara Bruce

The red, overstuffed chair sat on the dying lawn like a throne in an overrun kingdom. Marlo could not take her eyes from it. The yard was cluttered with scuffed leather shoes, stupid knick-knacks, chipped glass lamps the colour of burnt amber, and torn paperbacks, mostly romance novels. A rack of brightly printed shirts stood proudly on the outer edge of the lawn. Marlo ran a single finger up the arm of the chair. She could feel the wooden skeleton underneath the worn red fabric. It wasn't the shape of the chair, or the feel, but the colour. Marlo had a proclivity for the colour red.

It had started when she was young. She would lie in her parents' big king-sized bed and watch as her mother flitted back and forth in her bright red nightie. It was a slip-type thing with dainty, clever lace at the top and a scalloped edge at the bottom. Marlo remembered admiring how the slip hugged her mother's ample bosom and rear, hoping that she would have a body like that someday too. Then her memories shifted to sorting through her mother's closet, looking for something to bury her in. She took the red slip out and held it up to her own body, noticing how she still didn't have the body of her mother. Her own frame was tall and straight, muscular and almost boyish. Lesbians loved her. Men were curious, but standoffish. She usually didn't mind. The slip was worn thin, almost threadbare, and the lace at the top was torn, shrivelled, like tiny, dying flowers.

The second instance of red Marlo remembered was a bra and panty set that she had found discarded in the woods in back of her suburban apartment complex. The panties still had a wet stain in the front and Marlo had squatted down in the patch of dead, fire-ready leaves and sniffed them. They smelt like sex. Marlo had sat cross-legged with the bra and panties in her hands, rubbing her thumb and forefinger over the silky material. She made up stories about what the woman who had been wearing these had been doing. She had been a waitress or a bartender – jobs Marlo had always thought were glamorous back when she was young – and some man had come in and swept her off her feet. Marlo imagined the young woman gingerly slipping her long, sculpted arms out of the pretty bra. Marlo was too young to wear a bra back then and wasn't quite sure how big the woman's breasts would have been. She slipped it over her powder blue Camp Little Rock T-shirt and left the back unhooked and dangling behind her. The panties she just held carefully, not wanting to wipe off the fresh scent. It was the closest she had ever come to sex. She wasn't even sure what sex was, but she compared it to kissing Jimmy Thomas, the boy with two first names, in the coat closet of their first grade classroom. He had asked her to pull up her shirt so he could take a Polaroid and she had done it. He passed it around to all the other kids in their class until her teacher saw it and gave it to her Mom. Her Mom held it limply in one hand and cried, shaking her head, looking down at the photograph and up at her face. Marlo had been confused, concerns about her body implanted in her mind.

Marlo had the red bra and panties, the wet spot long since dried, and her mother's worn slip in a box in the back of her closet. There were other red objects in it as well: a red toothbrush that she had used the handle of when she first learned to masturbate; the tight red T-shirt she had stolen from the very first girl she had had a crush on; a tiny, red nylon backpack that this club kid had given her after they had had the most amazing sex on Ecstasy.

"Go ahead, sit in it." The owner of the chair motioned for Marlo to sit down. His voice was salty and smooth, rumbling over her like an earthquake. She jerked, arrested in her reverie of hungry thoughts and spilling memories. The man smiled. Marlo's mouth made a tiny "o" – as if she wanted to say something but then thought better of it.

"It's comfortable," the man said. "I used to spend almost
every night in it," he continued wistfully, "but my new
girlfriend is moving in and she hates it. She thinks it's tacky.
She doesn't like red much. Well, it's not like she doesn't like
red as much as she thinks that red should be used only for small
things and kept away from big objects."

The man finished his soliloquy and pressed Marlo's shoulder
forward a bit. She was surprised by his foray into the territory of
red, having spent all these years thinking that she was the only
one who thought about it. She was tired as well and sank
comfortably into the chair. The chair opened up and took her
in. It felt like a gigantic hug and she leaned back against it,
hoping to glean all the love from it and soak it up into her own
beating, red heart. She shut her eyes and leaned into it. When she
opened them the man was standing there smiling at her.

"You like it," he said, beaming. Marlo blushed, a deep pink.
The man took one finger and brushed it across her cheek. She
thought of scratches, welts, menses and bloodshot eyes. The
man cocked his head and looked carefully at her as Marlo
caught her breath. It was like he could read her thoughts, as if
her mind was strewn with construction paper hearts and
strawberry sauce.

Her obsession with red had swirled into a crescendo the year
she had graduated from college. It was the first apartment she
had ever had by herself. She had painted the walls red. She had
cross-stitched her monogram on the pillows in a bright fuschia;
her dresser and desk set were a rich mahogany. It was in that
room that Marlo had spent nights alone wildly masturbating
and nights with strangers that had accompanied her home. It
was in this apartment, the one with cherry magnets on the
fridge, that she had learned how to have multiple orgasms and
what she really liked about sex.

Every sexual memory she had was related to the colour red.
If it wasn't available when she was having sex she would make
it available – shoving her nail into a white shoulder and letting
the red rise up to the milky surface of the skin. Without red,
she didn't feel sexy. As if the colour alone jerked something
alive, she mentally compared herself to a sex puppet, with red
holding the strings. The sexiest she would ever feel was when

she put on her mother's slip. She would get into bed wearing it, hiking it up around her waist and sometimes rubbing it between her legs. The first time she did this she felt sinful, as if she was participating in incest just by the use of the article of clothing. Often, that made her cunt even wetter, her heart beat faster.

The man was helping her get out of the chair. The long sleeve of his work shirt pulled up to reveal a tight, red undershirt underneath. Marlo swooned.

"I have to go," she mumbled, pushing off him and hurrying away from the chair. The chair that this man had probably spent hours upon hours jerking off in, pulling on his long, hard cock until he reached nirvana.

"I'll be out here tomorrow," the man called after her, "eight to three."

Marlo rushed down the street with her head held down. The man had been cute and she had been attracted to him but he had a girlfriend. It wasn't something that Marlo liked to do. A young Mexican girl stepped around the corner, her white, plastic bucket full of thorny red roses leering up at Marlo like a demented clown with his grin smeared by the back of his oversized white gloved hand. It felt as if the world was closing in on her. Everywhere she looked there was a sign in red, a car, a flower, an apple. She bit the fleshy part of her palm, leaving red teeth stains and a smear of lipstick.

Her cunt was throbbing and her breath was shortening. She wanted to duck into a bathroom and get herself off, thinking about the man who fucked in a big, red chair.

The next day Marlo woke up early thinking about the chair, which starred in her dreams. It played the part of that couch in that commercial – where the cute guy photographs it thousands of times in thousands of different scenes. She played the part of the woman sitting in it. She imagined where she would put it in her apartment and how she would lie back on it, one hand moving furiously between her legs, the other gripping the arm as she clenched and came. She dressed, thinking of the man as she flipped through her closet – a black skirt, sweater and sandals, red lingerie set underneath.

She had thought long and hard about what she would do if the man asked her to go upstairs. Or better yet, if he had moved the chair into the garage, so they had to go someplace private to see it. Surely, he couldn't have left it out on the lawn all night! If the man wanted her then that was his business. It had been months since she had gotten laid and the last night had gotten her more than ready for it.

As she walked up to the house she saw the familiar garage sale memorabilia. It was nine in the morning and she wondered where all these garage sale fanatics came from. She would never have gotten up for a normal sale.

She walked shyly up to the chair, then circled it, performing a lop-sided tango. The man saw her from across the lawn and smiled. Marlo's stomach somerassaulted her as he approached. She didn't see any way that they would be alone, and she had decided that she wanted to have him in this chair. Maybe if she bought it she could invite him over to visit it, but that was stupid, nobody visited a chair.

"You're back," he proclaimed triumphantly.

"Yeah," Marlo nodded her head shyly. "I was wondering . . ."

"Come with me," the man interrupted like an excited child, tugging on her shirtsleeve. "I have something to show you."

Marlo followed hesitantly, she didn't want to leave the chair, lest someone else bought it, but she did want to see what the man had to show her. She wondered where his girlfriend was.

"Who's watching the sale?" she asked.

"My neighbour. We're co-selling," he grinned, his tongue flicking against his teeth. Marlo melted and followed him inside.

He pulled her into a room that had been made into a library. Inside were three of the exact same chairs – all different colours. Marlo gasped.

"Great, huh?" the man asked, excited.

Marlo wondered why he was showing her this. But then he pulled off his shirt to reveal a bright red T-shirt underneath. Marlo staggered backwards a step. And the man caught her.

"I knew you would love it," he whispered, heavy in her ear.

Marlo felt his strong arms wrap around her as she sank into a kiss. She opened her eyes to watch the man's shoulders heave under the red shirt. He pulled her down into one of the chairs so she was sitting on his lap, facing him. His hands were quickly on her tits, his mouth on her neck. He began to take off his shirt but Marlo put her hands on his, "No," she said firmly.

He looked at her, a bit puzzled, but shrugged in agreement. When he went to remove her shirt he met with no resistance. Soon they were almost naked, minus the man's red shirt and Marlo's crimson underwear set. Marlo slid off his lap and knelt down between his legs. There she stroked his long, thick cock before deftly placing it in her mouth. One hand massaged his balls as she continued sucking his cock. He pulled lightly on her hair, tugging harder when she moaned.

Marlo felt the man growing rock hard before she pushed herself up and rejoined him on the chair. She straddled him gleefully. Again he tried to remove his shirt; again she wouldn't let him. He went to unhook her bra, confusing Marlo when he took it all the way off. But once he began sucking on her nipples she didn't mind. His tongue flicked them gently until they were hard as cherry pits. Marlo slid her panties over to one side and the man slid on a condom.

Soon she was lowering herself on top of him, slowly opening for him. She was tight and he opened her. He slid one hand up her back, supporting her as they began to rock, their momentum increasing as they moved back and forth, up and down. Marlo looked down to watch his large cock slide in and out of her wet pussy, framed by the silky red panties, so dark they looked like blood. The sight alone got her going. She pressed down harder on his shoulders and used her stair-stepper leg muscles to push her up and down, harder, faster. The man began to pant; both hands were helping her move up and down, like a piston in an engine.

He thumped her harder, deep inside. Marlo screamed. A blood-curdling current of wavy red passion. Her cunt clenched, her thighs shivered, her back arched. Marlo came, her eyes squished shut so all she could see was white dots on a black background. The man came as well, pushing so deep Marlo thought he would surely spurt up into her stomach.

She collapsed on top of him. He brushed back her sweaty hair.

She slowly climbed off him. He groaned audibly as he pulled out of her. She got dressed silently, as did he. They both stood in that awkward after sex moment, looking at their feet, playing with shirt sleeves and rings.

"Well," Marlo said slowly, "I want to buy the chair."

"The chair?" the man repeated blankly.

"The one for sale. On the lawn. The red one."

"Oh," the man brightened, "that's not for sale."

"What?" Marlo exclaimed, her eyes widening, her brain spinning.

"Oh, my girlfriend let me keep it. I love these chairs. It's the only place I can . . . you know . . ."

"What?" Marlo asked, suddenly feeling used and offended.

"The only place I can do it," the man said quietly. "I thought that's what you wanted too," he added as an after-thought.

"The chairs?" Marlo asked incredulously. "These ugly old things? I only liked the red one. I don't care about chairs," she spat, exasperated.

The man looked as if he might cry. Both walked out through the house, shame-faced and confused.

When they stepped out onto the lawn they immediately noticed one huge difference: the red throne chair was gone, four indentions in the grass were the only sign it had ever even existed.

The man and Marlo walked as if asleep to the spot where the chair had been. The man choked back a sob and Marlo closed her eyes and shook her head, already missing the hot nights she never had.

The man's neighbour walked up, wagging two crisp hun-dred-dollar bills. "I got two hundred for that crummy old thing," he bragged. "Can you believe it? Some woman almost orgasmed when she saw it. She told me that she always wanted a red chair, paid two big ones on the spot and hauled it off. What a freak . . ." The neighbour handed the dumbstruck chair man his bills and walked away, shaking his head and mumbling about weirdos and good luck.

The man and Marlo stood silently, mourning the loss of what could have been. The man handed Marlo one of the hundreds. As she took it she swore she saw a tear in his eye.

Truly Scrumptious

Mark Ramsden

It is not that socially acceptable, yet, to talk about male domination of submissive females. It still looks a bit nasty to the uninitiated – because many educated people are still in thrall to the 1970s idea that men are all secretly Jack the Ripper. They seem to think, because of some bad-tempered college girls, that the hand-spanking of a willing female leads inexorably to torture and murder. And I've just breathed further life into what should be a rotting corpse by now. Never mind. I was a lettuce-eating liberal myself once, before reality reasserted itself. Even I need to have a disclaimer before I can tell you about gently warming Truly Scrumptious's tight little bottom cheeks with the palm of my right hand. While slowly insinuating the fingers of my left hand into her moistening cleft until . . . but that would rob the moment of why it was so interesting in the first place. If we don't know who Truly Scrumptious is, none of the other stuff would matter particularly. And it's not the same if you're not just a *little* bit in love, now is it?

Her real name is Holly but I wanted to give her a new name; Truly – as in Truly Scrumptious. My son had recently forced me to watch *Chitty Chitty Bang Bang* far more often than was good for me. The name of the attractive nanny seemed to fit her very well – as she was and is gorgeous – although I didn't learn the "true" significance of "Truly" until later. Her habit of telling the truth, always, no exceptions, was refreshing but sometimes made you long for the traditional system of saying whatever caused the least grief.

I lost my heart to Truly on our second meeting.

I was already smitten the first time I saw her, when she walked on stage during a slave auction at an S/M club. She had short black hair cut any old how. Her smile was wide and salacious, full-lipped with a cute little gap in her front teeth. Some of the others were arranged in the traditionally haphazard British manner. I found this honest and endearing, like her charity shop clothes. I might have a shaven head and some serious tattoos but I'm an old hippy at heart – like my wife, Katrin. And like Truly. Although they are younger and considerably easier on the eye.

Even in a night club Truly wore almost no make-up and her only accessory was a school prefect's badge on her jacket lapel. The lettering read "Perfect" instead of "Prefect". I couldn't argue with that.

Her blue eyes seemed to be saucers full of nourishing liquid. Or were they shot glasses full of some ferociously strong hooch? I had been off the hard stuff for some time, being married. But you never really get over the craving, you just decide life's smoother without it. Or you keep telling yourself that till you believe it . . .

After my wife and I had bought her company for the price of a few pints of foul British beer we had the option of some lewd chastisement – to which she had already assented as part of the auction. But instead we talked about what it felt like to offer yourself to strangers. Even in the safe confines of a fetish club it was still an edgy thing to do.

Then we talked of her recent romantic entanglements. She preferred sex with other women's men. It seemed to me that this bizarre preference was in order to shield her from commitment, although she dressed it up in a lot of nonsense about breaking the shackles of conventional morality and no one being anyone else's property. Fine. But not everyone believes in what used to be called free love. In fact, very few people do. Not only is there no such thing as a free lunch there may not be free love either. Although you probably have to be over a certain age to find that out.

Later that evening I dipped my head between her legs and licked and nuzzled her for what seemed an eternity – time having melted due to some pure MDMA powder, a substance that had yet to drive me mad with overuse. That would come later . . . or was it the loss of Truly Scrumptious that pushed me over the edge? This was long before the blizzards of e-mail, the endless phone calls, the hopes, the wishes, the dreams.

The day after the auction Truly Scrumptious turned up at our flat. She looked different in daylight, but still warm and cuddly and smart and cute and lovely in a manner that was hers alone. There can sometimes be nasty surprises when you meet people who have bewitched you in the flattering light of night clubs. Especially with the aid of Ecstasy. Luckily she was still beautiful. Her features were still fine enough to stand being foregrounded by the scruffy student haircut. I was already very fond of her by the time she had sat her bejeaned bottom down opposite me.

Over freshly ground coffee we discussed, briefly, bands I had never heard of, politics I had long since abandoned and why consumerism meant the end of the planet. I had lived long enough to prefer central heating to squats with broken windows so I let her talk. And I had thought the same at her age so I couldn't really complain.

She might have disdained consumerism but seemed to like trying out whatever new therapy had just been invented – the more the merrier. Although they didn't seem to fix whatever it was that was wrong with her. She worked for a charity but played very hard indeed – sex, drugs, fags, booze. Truly had a light Northern accent but appeared to have a vaguely genteel background. Just like me. And she was actually scanning her way through our many bookshelves.

"You're a writer!" she said, eyes shining.

"Not any more," I said. But not so retired that I don't want people to read what I have already produced. My books are left where our visitors can see them. No one ever picks them up. But Truly had found one of the novels and was flicking through it avidly.

"What are you writing now?" she said. She actually wanted to know. I was already lost – not yet "in love" – but afflicted with something or other. Something heart-shaped anyway.

"I packed it in," I said. "But *you* write." She raised her eyebrows.

"How did you know?"

Probably because anyone other than an aspiring writer would have ignored the book. She was looking a little awe-struck. I was obviously psychic. It is amazing what you can do with a bald head and a bit of enigmatic silence.

"You keep a journal," I said. It seemed a safe bet.

"Wow!" she said. I had passed the audition. I would be able to sort out her life.

"Where's Katrin?" she asked. "I really like her."

"She's whipping an old tart called Ernest," I told her. Although I didn't mention that this was an entirely financial arrangement. Or that Ernest still wore fishnet stockings at the age of 72.

"You have an open marriage?" asked Truly, surmising correctly.

"For S/M play, yes. And we discuss everything. No secrets. Playing is fine. I don't do intercourse. You have to keep something for your primary partner. But playing lasts much longer anyway. So it's not so much of a sacrifice, anyway."

A wicked little smile slowly spread as she sees the logic of this.

"She's out?"

"Yes. Till tonight."

"And she won't mind, then?"

"No," I said. For this is what Katrin had said that very morning. Although she may not have actually meant it, of course.

"I can be a slut, then?" she asked. She was easing into her minx persona. The bad girl who was about to use her body in ways that would have broken her mother's heart. I blame Roman Catholicism myself. Although, as it produces a regular supply of especially wicked women, perhaps we shouldn't complain *too* much.

Her eyes widened. Her lips were moist. After a flirtatious shake of head sideways she gave me the full moon eyes back again. They were big and blue, although the whites were strewn with red wreckage. This was a reminder that she had a plentiful supply of her own demons. Perhaps she didn't always like what we were about to do. But was driven to do it anyway.

She stood up and kicked her red Converse sneakers off. Then eased her jeans and knickers down. She laughed as she threw her T-shirt in a corner and unhooked a bra that was never going to feature in a lingerie catalogue. But with firm, full breasts like hers she did not need to spend money to look stunning.

Naked, she stepped into my space. The warm scent of her breath sent the blood racing around my body. Something bigger than the two of us was setting this in motion. The force that impels sperm to impregnate a fertile womb. Well, not on this occasion, Grandma. Mother Nature was just going to have to wait. But the Devil himself was coming out to play.

"I've been bad," she said, taking her voice back some decades. And jutting her lower lip out.

"You've been wicked, my dear," I told her. "You need firm handling. Someone to take care of you."

I don't always feel comfortable mouthing these shop-worn lines. But it was what she needed to hear. Besides, I can credibly personify authority in short, sharp bursts. Particularly when there is a flawlessly pert bottom to be unveiled. With a rapidly moistening, slitted pouch peeking out from between her long, lean legs.

"Do I need a spanking, sir?" she asked, her eyes twinkling, though her voice seemed anxious.

"You certainly do," I said. "It's the only language you understand."

She laid herself over my lap and sighed gently as she made herself comfortable. Some think you should start a spanking with outstretched fingers, gauging the required force of the slaps by the sighs of gratitude or the squeals of pain. I prefer a multi-disciplinary approach myself, a little of everything. A cupped palm here, a little pull and prod there. Tweaking the springy bottom flesh between finger and thumb made us both sigh. With so much moisture coagulating in her pussy cleft it seemed a shame not to put a thumb inside her. Soft sighs of satisfaction mingled with my own less than graceful groaning. We both needed this. Badly. A few more taps with my fingers and it was time to cup my hand. And strike where the curves were at their roundest.

Part of me was thinking it would be always be like this: the lover's fallacy that strikes when the blood first drains from the head to more erogenous zones. Perhaps that's why the rational part of the brain ceases to function. We never did get to repeat this peak moment often enough for me, but the memories still remain.

Sometimes, when lost in lust, she would turn around and pull the cheeks of her bottom apart. Do me. Do me now. I found this sort of thing passed the time quite adequately. It was an absorbing hobby. One I never got tired of. Although Truly was infuriatingly unreliable when it came to arranging our diary. Understandably enough, she was looking for a life partner and not someone to do sex with occasionally. And then there was the new age tripe. "I am choosing to experience life on a higher plane," she would tell me, when cancelling dates to which she had only just enthusiastically assented. Still, there's nothing like spirituality, is there? "Choosing to experience life on a higher plane", indeed!

Even on the first day she offered herself to me I was irritated by her recommendation of some new age twaddle called "Conversations with God", which had, needless to say, sold several million copies.

My own "Conversations with My Lord Lucifer" was unlikely to sell a similar amount, even if I ever got around to writing it. Thinking of this particular idiocy I smacked her squirming bottom three times in quick succession, hard enough to hurt the palm of my hand. I'll give her "choosing to experience life on a higher plane", I thought, starting to warm to my task. An indignant "hey" soon disabused me of the notion that this was acceptable behaviour.

Well, sometimes you have to do what is good for the person over your lap rather than what they think is good for them. And the warm glow spreading from her chastised cheeks appeared to be bucking her up no end. But I slowed down anyway, as the customer is always right, once they have placed their trust in you. In any case, just watching her get lost in the moment was exciting enough to make my heart pound.

"Yes! Yes! Yes! Oh, thank you! Thank you!" she said, giving sincere thanks for something for which she had waited too long. I was beginning to feel a little blessed myself. Fortunate to have found her. I stroked her slowly, front and back, until a note of desperation entered her voice.

She flirted and squirmed, finding postures that would encourage me to penetrate her. Or slap that impudent little rump of hers just a little bit harder. I was in no hurry. Although Truly appeared to disagree, urging me on by performing some frankly indecent contortions.

This may be one of the reasons Truly preferred father figures. Most young men would have come by now and be halfway out the door to boast about it in the nearest pub. Whereas, being forty-something, I don't have the energy to scamper anywhere except here, where everything is set up just the way I like it.

While Truly got deeper into her trance I patted the reddened flesh for a while, still hardly able to believe my luck. Then a scratch of a fingernail here and there reminded her that into each life a little rain must fall. And that a little vinegar mixed with oil makes a fine combination. The sour-sweet tang of her scent was heavier now and her posture inelegant to say the least – thrusting her rump up in the air and kneading the bed-sheet with her outstretched fingers. Well, we all have needs and I've often done what she was doing. Tarting around on all fours demanding to be serviced. Fill me up. Fuck me. But it's best not to answer these prayers too quickly. Stroking up and down the divide of her bottom with my left hand while keeping the soft slaps coming with my right seemed to be doing her a lot of good.

The soup was simmering nicely now. I thought boiling would spoil it. Truly seemed to disagree. She straddled my body, face down towards my feet, legs wrapped around my stomach, backing herself up towards my face as I continued to pat her with cupped hands. Harder smacks seem to be finally answering the question she posed some time ago. Her skin was rosy red, the heat spreading where it was needed most. The scent of her twin openings was a mingling of the sacred and the profane; heavenly, yet grounded on earth.

"Go on! Do it!" She was getting impatient. Coming to the boil. I kissed and licked her as she urged me on. Now the surface of her hot red bottom was moist with saliva the slaps had more effect. A mewl of distress told me to tone it down. Which I was happy to do. It was just as nice stroking and kissing the warm velvet flesh for a while before a different sort of urgent moan and upward thrust of her hips was telling me to pile on the pressure again. As I resumed the gentle but firm pitter-patter of slaps and smacks, the sounds she was making were closer to those of a hungry beast. Once she unzipped me I was no longer so aloof, not so much in control as I perhaps should have been. But, as my old Zen master used to say to me, when you are hungry you should eat. And with a hot dish in front of me, and with the chef urging me on, it was time to tuck in.

I buried my face in the cleft in her beautiful bottom while Truly took my hardness in her mouth. The sounds of guzzling and slurping competed with our grunts and groans. Once her teeth had caught my piercings once too often – which was once, actually – I yelped and withdrew. She took me in hand, rubbing me slowly up and down. Meanwhile it seemed appropriate to form the fingers of both hands into wedges to press gently inside each of her openings. Once I had done that her eyes screwed up and her mouth opened to its fullest extent. One thing that was bothering me was my wedding ring slipping off inside Truly's warm, wet pussy. But it was too late for that now. And it would have been nice if that astral image of a disapproving Katrin could have disappeared but you can't have everything.

Now my right hand was inside her pussy it was easy enough to wiggle my first two fingers down onto the spongy tissue which some chap claimed to be the G-spot – naming it after himself, as if Grafenberg was ever going to be a sound you would want to associate with pleasure zones.

And then there was no more time for talk. The storm enveloped us. We came. Then came to our senses, both starting to feel guilty in different ways.

Should young ladies really behave like that? And what about married men? Who were old enough to know better?

My phone alerted me to a voice message withdrawing permission for what had just happened. Although my wife had been keen enough – or apparently apathetic enough – to agree to it that very morning.

"What's the matter?" asked Truly.

"Katrin," I said. "She's gone off the idea."

I didn't have to explain. Truly was used to the anger of wives and significant others. Was it even part of the thrill for her? Kicking Mummy out of Daddy's bed?

I breathed in her Body Shop soap and hints of her innermost secrets still on my fingertips as she dressed, looking for ways to remember her. Just before she left she put both hands on her still glowing bottom and pushed her lower lip out. She stood with her feet turned inwards, regressing back to some time she must have felt cared for, secure.

"You're very . . . thorough," she said.

"Any time," I said, making detailed plans for a number of futures that never happened. At least I still have her cheeky smile. Even though I had thought it was the start of something. The start of everything perhaps. Instead of a few years of near-misses and misunderstandings and trying to ignore primal urges while dealing with tearful goodbyes and endless arguing about relationships. We did have our wild moments together. Now and then. But less times than you could count on the fingers of one hand.

She's driving someone else mad now. There isn't a cure in sight, just yet. She rang to say she was pregnant the other day. But she couldn't quite get her head round the concept of marrying the father just because society expected her to. So she had assented to a marriage then decided not to go ahead. After all the arrangements had been made.

When I stopped laughing at that I wondered if her parents sometimes regretted that she was now too old to spank. Or whether her new bloke took care of her in that way. Someone should, anyway. It's the only language she really understands . . .

Sweet, Sweet Annie

Rich Logsdon

I

Christmas Eve, and here is Annie, my sweet angel of the night. A small, thin and beautiful Asian girl, she is dancing topless in animal splendour to incessant, pounding music. Dim stage lights cast a glow over her, and my eyes feast upon this delicious woman. She's changed, I think: though her eyes are still dark slits, her hair has a reddish brown tint and is tied in pig tails; and while the rose tattoo (which I bought her) remains below the belly button and small golden rings pierce her nipples, she has put on needed weight and enlarged her breasts.

But I've changed, too, and I'm sure she senses that. As she dances, eyes darting at me, her nipples are erect. I can smell her sweetness. Her back against the pole, she slides down to the stage, spreads her legs, and massages herself through her light blue, semi-transparent panties. She never takes her eyes off me.

"That's my Annie," I say.

In the smoked-filled club, I grin, stick my tongue out, and wiggle it obscenely, hardly an appropriate gesture for a professor known for scholarship on Nabokov and Pynchon. She laughs, pulls away from the pole and, on hands and knees, crawls over to me.

"How ya doin', Jerry?" she purrs, leaning forward and licking my forehead. Wrapping her arm around me, her hand cradling the back of my head, she puts her face inches from mine.

"Merry Christmas," she says in a seductive whisper. "Long time, no see."

"Same here," I respond. I can't imagine another place I'd rather be than with Annie. It's like standing at the gates of paradise. She smells like a rose garden, and I want to stick my tongue between her legs and taste her juices. Through sweat and smoke, she leans forward and kisses me lightly on the lips.

"Missed you," she says, slowly pulling back. "You still taste good?"

"We'll find out if you want," I say.

Aroused, I hesitate: though I've finally found her after months of searching, I'm now not really sure that I want to start up again with this woman. Annie can be a mixed blessing. An unusually sensitive person who will allow me to fuck her any time and any place, she has the ability to pull me from the black hole in my soul. But there's another side. Once, several years ago on Christmas Eve, when we were playing in the front room just after dinner and just before church, she grabbed my dangling manhood in her teeth. (Please understand, of course, that we had been drinking.) When I didn't respond the way she hoped, she bit, at first gently, then harder and harder. I tried to push her away when, with an angry snarl, she gave a hard yank, a dog tearing a piece of meat. Pain shot through me like a hundred lightning bolts. Immediately seeing that she had wounded me, Annie panicked, wept apologetically, grabbed my manhood and tried to stop the wound with her tiny hands. "Get a towel from the kitchen!" I shouted, visions of John Wayne Bobbit bouncing in my brain. As she ran to the kitchen, I looked between my legs and saw blood dripping down my legs and onto the carpet. "Hurry, you little cunt!" I screamed. Instead of calling a physician, Annie drove me, bundled in a light green dishtowel, to the ER where some young smart ass right out of medical school stitched me up.

This is what I remember as I now watch this gorgeous little beast dance. Once again, it is Christmas Eve, and in my bones I ache for Annie.

"Hey, Merry Christmas, you little dickbiting bitch," I tease her, placing my hand on the back of her head and pulling her lips onto mine. As I kiss her, I run my free hand over her nipples, and she reaches down, places a hand between my legs, and grabs my hardness through my pants. When Annie finally draws her hand away, I tell her that I'll be sitting at one of the tables under the big stage across the room.

"Come and join me when you're done," I say. She nods and smiles. For old times' sake, I want once again to spend the night with her and enter her savage garden of delights.

II

I met Annie years before in another joint. At the time, five years out of high school, she had taken several classes at the college and had a two-year-old daughter, whom she left with her mother. She didn't know who the father was. "One of hundreds," she told me. She danced at Cat's Place, a purple and pink one-story topless nightclub located in the industrial area of Vegas and just behind Stupak's Tower, the tallest building on the Strip.

The place had the best dancers in town. Many were university or community college students trying to make a little extra cash. I had been invited to the club by two of my students. In their papers and out-of-class, they had alluded to this specific club, and at the end of spring semester had asked me to come, all promising at least one free dance. Expressing my preference for another club located downtown, I had politely refused. But finally, late in August of the same year, my girlfriend having flown to Seattle to attend her sister's wedding, the fires of desperation exploded within me and I agreed.

I sat at a table in the back of the club with Angela and Marci; I forget their stage names. Angela wore a thin black net top revealing large tanned breasts while Marci was dressed in a small white blouse, open at the top, and a plaid schoolgirl dress. No sooner had they excused themselves to go to the back room when a small Oriental girl pulled herself away from the bar, walked over to me and asked if she could sit. "Be my guest," I said, gesturing her to sit in the chair next to me. She gently sat on my lap, her left arm around my neck, gazed longingly into my eyes, and smiled coyly. It wasn't the me-

chanical smile you might expect from a dancer whose chief
means of livelihood is stripping in front of gawking men and
making them hard; this one was warm and teasing, the kind
you get from someone who likes you and wants to know you
better. Her eyes were dark brown, almost black in the dim
light, and her raven hair was swept back out of her face and
flowed down to the small of her back.

"What's your name?" she cooed. While she had a tinny,
singsong accent, there was laughter in her voice. Before I could
answer, she kissed me lightly on the cheek.

"The professor. Call me that for now," I responded.

"Don't play games with Annie," she said, reaching between
my legs and feeling me through my slacks. I was already partly
hard. "I know who you are," she added.

Slightly over five feet, she had an engaging manner. When I
pulled her blouse open, admired her nipple rings, and then
kissed one of her nipples, she commented, "I like that." When
I slipped one of my hands into her panties and found her
already wet, she purred.

I don't know what happened to my students. I didn't much
care. I bought Annie drinks, talked, asked her to dance, and
finally slid inside her as she sat on my lap. It was a darkly
glorious moment: with people wall-to-wall, dancers performing on each of the four stages, Annie pulled the crotch string of
her panties to the side as I unzipped and then slowly, gracefully
eased herself on top of me. She took all of me. To a casual
observer, she must have looked as if she were performing a
normal, slowly pulsing dance.

III

That night, I left the club with Annie. We didn't go right to my
place as I had planned. Hungry for steak, Annie suggested we
stop somewhere and get a bite to eat. Because she lived on the
west side, she named a small family restaurant miles away from
the Strip on Sahara. At the time, I had no idea that Annie's
wildly passionate nature went beyond her sexual desires; I had
no idea that mine did as well. At the time, I didn't know
myself.

I still can't remember the name of the place: a cozy Italian restaurant located in one of those new shopping centers with squat, stucco buildings that age in five years. Across the street was a soccer field, and several adult teams were practising under the lights. While I ordered something typically Italian – spaghetti, I think – Annie asked for a steak, done very rare.

"Your steak will be very bloody, almost raw," the waitress said. "Did you know that?"

Sitting next to me in the booth, her hand between my legs, Annie smiled and responded, "That's the way I like it. The bloodier the better."

As we waited in a semi-dark corner for our salad, Annie looked at me, asked, "Ready for a little fun?"

"Always ready," I said, heart pounding.

Swiftly, she unzipped me, reached her small hand in through my fly, and grabbed me.

I laughed at Annie's boldness. The waiters stayed in the other room, so I figured we could do pretty much what we wanted. When I unbuttoned Annie's blouse, she put her head between my legs and slid her warm, moist mouth over my cock.

"That's my girl," I remember saying.

Visions of angels dancing in my head, I leaned back, and as I did I glanced across the restaurant. When we had first come in and sat down, I really did not see anyone else in the restaurant. But now, my eyes adjusted, I glanced across the room and noticed, in a far booth, a couple about our age, maybe a bit older. They were both shooting glances our way between, I suspect, mouthfuls of lasagne or chicken Marinara or whatever they were eating. I remember remarking to myself that the woman, a beautiful, stacked blonde with blood-red lips and long red fingernails, looked good enough to eat.

"Whatsamatter?" Annie mumbled, raising her head.

"We're being watched," I said. I didn't enjoy the sensation of being watched as I do now.

"So?"

"That couple over there keeps looking our way."

"They don't know what we're doing."

"Sure they do."

"Well, fuck them," Annie said. She lowered her head.

"Annie," I said, pushing her head back gently, "let's do it later. I can't enjoy this with them watching." I looked across the room at the blonde, who was no longer looking our way.

Annie sat upright, arranged her hair and blouse and stared across the room.

"People should just fucking learn to live and let live," Annie commented. At that moment the waitress brought our salads.

Dinner went well. Annie ignored the woman, and as we ate we talked about everything from Annie's job to baseball in Korea. Annie even hinted that, recently, she had been marginally involved in a triple homicide for which three of her family members went to prison.

"Would you ever kill someone, Jerry?" she asked, studying me between mouthfuls of raw steak.

The thought made me queasy, and I chokingly responded, "Not on your life."

We finished with the house specialty for dessert and, after paying, rose to leave. Heading for the door, Annie glanced over her shoulder at the blonde, who was staring back at her.

"Forget it, Annie," I said, pushing the glass door open for her.

We walked out of the restaurant, hand-in-hand, two love-birds, and I figured then that the rest of the evening would consist of porn, sex, and maybe mild stimulants.

When we got into the car, just as I was starting the ignition, Annie reached over, grabbed my arm and said, "Wait, Jerry." She pointed.

"What?" I said.

"Look."

When I glanced up, I saw the other couple walking toward a green Mercedes in the parking lot on the east side of the restaurant. The man walked with short, mincing steps.

"I see," I said. "So what?"

Annie laughed. "Wanna have a little fun?"

"With them?" I asked.

"Sure," she said. "Why not?" Normally a staid, retiring type, Annie's question aroused something in me. I realized that I would enjoy a little excitement.

"Why not?" I agreed. Having some fun at the other couple's

expense would bring back memories, I told myself, recalling how in junior high and high school my friends and I routinely tormented neighbours and school mates.

I started the engine and waited. Just before the Mercedes reached the exit, I hit the gas. My car shot forward, blocking the way. As I put my car in neutral and pulled on the emergency brake, Annie threw open her door, walked around my car, and positioned herself outside the Mercedes passenger door, shouting and gesturing obscenities at the young blonde. I got out and stood behind Annie.

Almost coolly, the woman got out, closed the door, and faced Annie while her boyfriend remained inside. This gave me a chance to see this woman more closely, and my heart almost stopped. She wore a blouse tied just above the navel and in a manner calculated to reveal her breasts, and skintight blue pants that left nothing to the imagination. She was gorgeous beyond words, and, as she faced Annie, licked her lips and gave me a seductive look.

"Think I'm a cunt?" Annie hissed, standing sideways, a posture a friend of mine used to assume just before he hit someone in the face.

The woman was not intimidated. "Of course you're a cunt. You're a disgraceful little tramp, is what you are." Apparently a tough type, she was probably from New Jersey or Brooklyn.

Annie stepped forward and shoved the woman backwards against her car. I'd seen women fight only on film.

It was a beautiful night, I'll confess that much in retrospect, and at the time I wondered what the woman's boyfriend, still sitting in the car, was thinking. There was a cooling breeze, and we were far enough beyond the strip that I could see thousands of stars overhead. The moon was brilliant.

There was a long, almost predictable pause before the action began when the two women called each other things like "bitch", "whore", and "cunt." My legs trembled in anticipation. After Annie said something in Korean and started to walk away, the blonde stepped forward and grabbed Annie's hair in both of her hands. Annie turned and, in windmill fashion, swung back with closed fists, striking her adversary several times in the face.

Then Annie stumbled and, with little effort, the blonde bore her to the ground. I watched as Annie, one of her arms held and on her back, was slapped repeatedly. Annie shrieked and fought like a wildcat and did rip open the left side of the woman's blouse. An enormous, well-shaped breast hanging out of her blouse, the blonde went into a rage and hit Annie in the face again and again and, while I wanted to step in, I decided it would be safer and just watch. Besides, as far as I was concerned, Annie was to be no more than a one-night stand.

For a moment, the women stopped, the stars seeming to spin slowly overhead. I could hear Annie gasping and lightly sobbing as she looked up at her adversary. Then as Annie struggled weakly, the blonde tore off Annie's blouse, exposing small but beautiful breasts. Annie's nipple rings glowed in the moonlight.

With surprising ease, the woman pulled Annie's shorts off, revealing that Annie wore nothing underneath. Pulling Annie's legs apart, spreading my angel's pussy, the blonde looked at me. "This is the fresh meat you're after, right?" she asked. I could see that the woman had a small cut over her right eye. She patted Annie's pubic area gently as I kept my eyes on the beautiful pink slit between Annie's legs. Then, making sure that I was watching, the blonde slowly inserted one finger into Annie, who offered no resistance and moaned like an animal. It was almost more than I could bear.

As the couple drove away, I retrieved Annie's clothes and then walked her back to my car. As she sat in the front seat, brushing her hair out of her face, I wondered how she would handle the humiliation she had just suffered. "Well," she said, sniffing, "I got my ass kicked that time."

"Yeah, you did," I said.

The fight didn't seem to faze her much, and she used a Kleenex to dab the blood from her mouth, nose, and chest. I figured that she'd been in fights before.

Curiously, the night turned out well. By the time we got to my apartment, Annie had apparently put the fight behind her. As we undressed, face and body bruised and cut, Annie attacked me savagely, first grabbing me in her mouth and then allowing me to fuck her in any way I wanted. I learned that every hole in her body was an avenue to bliss. We never slept that night, and one week later Annie moved in with me.

For six months, we lived together and feasted off each other. I tasted every inch of her, and she tasted every bit of me. Pudding and pie became our favourite desserts because they're easy to lick. It was a period of unrivalled sexual frenzy and delight, and often, when Annie had three straight days off, we never left the apartment. After the Christmas Eve accident three years ago, Annie moved out without an explanation, and I was left horribly alone.

IV

And now, here she is, and here I am. Sitting at the table, awaiting Annie, I think over the past three years when I became addicted to a savage, even occasionally violent kind of sex. As one might suspect, I finally did meet up with the parking lot blonde, who could fight but failed nonetheless to rise to Annie's standards. The blonde disappeared just six months before this night.

Top still off, Annie approaches, smilling hugely, and I have put all hesitation aside. I can't wait to resume our frenzied, anything-goes sex.

After her shift ends shortly after midnight, I drive Annie through the desert and into the mountains. When she asks where we are going, I tell her to a special place. It's a very cold Christmas Eve, the temperatures in the low thirties, and I've heard that it's been snowing in the higher regions just outside of town.

Just above the lodge, I turn to the right and slowly drive the slick road up to a small cabin; as the moon temporarily breaks through storm clouds, we can see that the ground is white with snow.

"This is my cabin," I say, and in this I tell the truth. It's a cabin I bought last year with the inheritance from my parents' estate.

"Oooh, how pretty," Annie says. She's moved by the Christmas Eve winter wonderland.

"Do you want to come in and see?" I ask, moving into the gravel driveway and turning off the engine.

"Do you want me to come in?" she asks, coyly.

"I have a surprise for you."

Annie doesn't hesitate. She loves surprises.

After we enter through the front door, I flick the switch and the room softly explodes in soft, almost ethereal light. The living room looks like something right out of a magazine: wreaths over the window, a soft brown couch with the stairs behind it, three lamps, a coffee table made of cypress, and two soft leather recliners. Norman Rockwells hang on the wall.

"God, it's beautiful, Jerry," she gasps, removing her black leather coat. Underneath, she's wearing a Green Bay Packers T-shirt.

"You want it?" I say, walking over to the stereo and putting in a Christmas CD.

"Of course," she purrs.

My heart soars as I walk to Annie and, putting my arm around her shoulders, say, "I want you to see one more thing."

I guide her through the pantry to the storage room in back. The room is cold, and when I flick on the dim overhead light she sees the padlocked freezer across the room.

"There's something here I want you to see," I say, guiding her across the room.

Tense, Annie is frightened, but I keep one arm firmly around her waist as I slip the key in the padlock. As I lift the top of the freezer, I pull her closer and tell her to look in. She shrieks and resists, and I can feel her whole body trembling. Suspecting some diabolical trick, Annie collapses and, with both arms, I pick her up, hold her over the freezer, and force her to look inside.

It takes her a moment to realize that I am not going to shove her inside and close the lid. Her body becomes merely rigid as, stunned, she sees that the long rectangular block of ice contains the body of a nude woman: the blue-green eyes are wide open, the face has a slight blue tinge, her nostrils are flared (odd for a freezing), and her blood-red lips part in eternal bewilderment; the woman has large tanned breasts whose shape has been preserved. Even now, six months after her disappearance, the blonde's features are quite recognizable.

Numbed, Annie shakes her head as if to clear it of thought and stares at the corpse as I put my arms around her, kiss her on the neck, and whisper, "Merry Christmas, my sweetest angel."

As "Silent Night" fills the air, Annie breathes deeply, laughs very nervously, relaxes even more, and says, "Jerry, you are one sick son of a bitch, you know that? I think you've changed a bit."

I have to admit, albeit silently, that Annie is right: I've changed.

"This is your gift, Annie." Holding Annie, my cock pressed hard against her small ass, I tell the brief story of my relationship with Joan: how I met her at a supermarket maybe a year after her fight with Annie outside the restaurant, began dating her, actually lived with her in order to gain her trust, and then asked her to join me up here where, lured by the thrill of ropes and bondage, she actually allowed me to strangle her to death.

There is a long pregnant pause, and the player switches to the next CD.

"Did you fuck this bitch on the night you killed her?" Annie finally asks, almost offended by the prospect that I might do such a thing. The tone of the question tells me that, outward appearance notwithstanding, Annie really has not changed; she's still the delightfully possessive slut that I used to live with. It's a question she would have asked years ago, and I am ready for it.

"No goddamned way," I say. "I'm not that crazy. But I figured I had to do something to get you back after you left – I went fucking nuts when you weren't there – and I figured that this would work."

For a long time, Annie says nothing, and I know that she is considering asking me to take her back. If she asks, I will oblige. Annie is my angel, and I shall never harm her.

Finally, she turns, puts her arms around my neck and, before I have time to say anything, kisses me on the mouth. I remember then how much I enjoy how Annie tastes.

"It works," she says, slowly drawing back. A few years back, as I'm sure she recalls, she wanted this blonde bitch dead. "I won't leave again."

In my bedroom, "O Little Town of Bethlehem" playing softly in the background, we slowly undress each other, taking precious time on the parts that have become significant. Delicately, I part her legs and slip my tongue inside her. When Annie takes my manhood in her tiny hand, I can feel her touch and then lick the scar. The sensation is euphoric.

"Bite me, Annie," I request, looking back at her, and she begins giggling. "But not too hard." This is as close to true love as I have ever been.

As Annie gently takes me in her teeth and gives me an easy tug, I lie back on the bed, listening to the Christmas music; I put a hand between her legs and insert a finger into her asshole. I remember that Annie has a fondness for anal sex.

It doesn't get any better than this, I tell myself, hard as a rock. Annie and I will surely be inseparable from this night forward.

London Derrière

Dawn O'Hara

Never perform with your back to the audience, Orlando taught his rare music students (he took on such a commitment only when financially desperate). Shaking your booty works if you've got Jon Bon Jovi's ass, he instructed, worthy of leather encasement and admirable even from the back row of an arena. But if you are a mere mortal crooning in a local pub, best to face the fans.

How, then, did Orlando come to find himself bent over a barstool on the stage floor – nothing more than a bar corner cleared of tables – with Isabella's dick up his forty-one-year-old virgin ass? His back to the audience, indeed.

Orlando now sang a different tune than the melodic ones he'd played for the small audience of late-nighters. His voice lost its smooth patina. His words contained no witty double entendres, looping rhymes, or seductive repetitions. He abandoned his lyrical search for meaning in a complicated world of misunderstood words. His fingers no longer picked at intricate chord progressions on the six-string or the electric keyboard. They clawed at the air. He growled and shouted, his words incomprehensible, pushing back against Isabella's thrusting thighs. But before he descended into passionate, guttural urges, his words were clear.

Orlando feared the peculiar combination of words he shouted. He was terrified that, once uttered, Isabella would have what she wanted and would leave him. Again. Only this tiem she would desert him for speaking the irretrievable, and not for silence.

Hold something back, Orlando taught. Leave them wanting,

so the fans return, or, better yet, purchase the compact disc you've peddled for years, stacks of them stashed in your attic. The whole song can't be a repeating chorus, he instructed. You've got to build up to the consummate word at the end of the line. A literary crescendo to a word so perfect that the audience thinks they could have guessed it, but a word so unexpected they never do. They echo it once they've heard the song, and then forget the wonder and surprise of it. Like this word he just enunciated as clearly as the *Rain in Spain* before deteriorating into whimpering gibberish. A word that all-too-often atrophied, stalled, and lost its meaning through overuse. A powerful word that dulled and tired. Coveting words, understanding their potency and deception, he had refused to utter it all these years.

Now that he'd said it, held nothing back, Isabella would leave him with his cock dancing in the air. Something prevented him from seizing his straining dick, which beseeched the stale bar-room air like a blind man extending his cane over a bluff. One clench of his fist and Orlando would add to the stains on the floor, he hovered that close to the edge of primal fulfilment. Isabella hadn't told him not to touch himself, though she often commanded him in bed. Orlando himself was never comfortable articulating what he wanted done to his body, and he graciously accepted what was offered. But right now he wanted his satisfaction – if she planned to give him any – to come at her hands, the gift of her body. He'd had enough of his own fist since she kicked him out a month ago.

As Isabella brought up the rhythm section behind him, the logistical success of this joint venture amazed Orlando. But, then again, they'd always enjoyed the challenge of different body sizes. He tended to forget how small she was. Her ass gave her such solidity, a gravity-hugging mass – like a steel girder that holds up a delicate bridge, one of those impossible pieces of architecture that tourists traverse the world to see – that he often forgot that his long fingers could nearly span her petite waist. Sometimes when he spied her tiny shoes kicked off at the front door, he wondered who'd come to visit.

Isabella's ass. Now there was a show fit for stadium concerts. Forget the rules about facing the audience. Her magnificent flesh danced in multiple directions when she moved. Some law of physics or aerodynamics caused one hemisphere of her buttocks to return from movement while an opposing quarter gained momentum in the opposite direction, the way two stones tossed in a pond throw concentric circles into delirium. Her gluteals were like tectonic plates beneath the earth's surface, the mountains above them trembling and quaking when they shifted.

When Orlando was still a young man, years before Isabella backed her ancient Cadillac into his Toyota, one of his dates had blubbered over the televised royal wedding of the worthless second-in-line son to the worthless British throne. Somewhere in her tears Orlando saw the crushed belief that even though the first-born prince had escaped her, the second son had still roamed in her fantasies as a distinct possibility. She, an American. From Detroit. He had waited impatiently for the "I Do's" so they could head to dinner. And then he'd caught sight of the bride's well-padded ass behind an oversized satin bow. He could have watched the princess march up the aisle for miles. He wanted to reach up inside her gown and caress those buttocks, to crawl after that fanny through the church and into eternity with his hands groping. Her ass wasn't even *that* big, except in comparison to Barbie dolls like her new sister-in-law. When radio deejays made cruel Mount Everest and Twin Peaks remarks about her behind, Orlando knew that not one of those men voicing loud derision over the princess's flanks would turn down the chance to feel her ass bouncing against his belly, his cock lost in the valleys only mountains like hers could provide. A guy's dick could seem awfully small and insignificant rutting around a generous ass, and Orlando suspected their taunting was born of that insecurity. Orlando thanked whatever cosmic force had blessed him with the long and narrow cock ideal for such excavating, a highly evolved instrument honed for intricate manoeuvres.

Orlando and his date never did get to dinner that night. They ordered in, and he had barbecued rump roast right in her bed. It wasn't the start of a fetish, exactly, or even an obsession. Orlando liked women of all sizes – but big-hipped women became synonymous with royalty in his plebeian mind. That bow on a princess's palatial behind tied a permanent knot around his preference, and he remained married to the idea of someday finding his own monarchical mounds to worship.

But Orlando soon learned that these splendid endomorphs didn't crave worship of the twin-buttressed cathedrals on their backsides. Rather, they wished to crush these sacred temples, as ancient peoples had smashed shrines glorifying opposing religions. They wanted to destroy these icons of femininity, praying for the holiness of honed and toned hind-ends. They wanted him not to pay homage to the bouncing, mirrored embodiment of his faith, but to ignore them, converting to a belief in lean and inhospitable flanks.

When the princess crash dieted later on and became the spokesperson for a diet product, Orlando composed a dirge. Her lost flesh symbolized the war waged upon the tortured landscape of women's asses, a genocidal campaign for the extermination of something holy. His lovers all felt rotten about not being Twiggy. He craved the sight of their haunches wriggling, but these ripe, succulent women extinguished the lights and crawled under the covers, face up in the dark. Which is why, with the passage of years, he seldom followed through on his attraction for them. He swore them off, a gluteal abstinence, the way friends with wheat allergies had given up gluten. Their constant need for reassurance wore him down. They vacuumed up his repeated compliments, and then ceased to believe them precisely because of their repetition. Ah, the trickiness of words.

Then Isabella had climbed out of her mammoth automobile a few years ago after reversing into his hatchback. When she leaned across the seat to dig her insurance card out of the glove box, her derrière sticking out of the car door, Orlando swooned. Such an ass could sing opera. No little Mimi or Butterfly pining for her straying dude, either, but a ferocious and tender Turandot demanding the severed heads of unworthy suitors. Orlando stuttered so ferociously when she approached that Isabella thought he'd had a concussion from the minor accident. He'd bruised his forehead on the steering wheel with her lurch into reverse, yes – but all he wanted was to smash his face against those cheeks, just the way his hood had crumpled under the staggering weight of the Cadillac's trunk. He wanted bumper imprints ground into his deliriously smiling front grille. He reminded himself that he had given up on these women, swore them off in a permanent Lent. The simplicity of a glorious derrière had too often trapped him in complicated and ugly arguments. When he wanted a fistful of those mounds, he usually got an earful about his inability to understand. He didn't blame them for their insecurity; they were the victims of a modern witch hunt for body fat. But despite his devotion to their ample order, Orlando could not resurrect a religion based on his cock alone, and so went on a flesh fast.

He could have abstained, he lied to himself, if Isabella hadn't spoken in that damned accent, refined aristocratic education crossed with Monty Python crass in her Oxford gutter mouth. A dethroned British queen had backed into him, and he wanted her to keep backing up, rolling her glorious bulldozer of a behind right onto the cock pulsing in his lap. He bulged so prominently that he refused to get out of his squashed bug of a car. She feared that he couldn't extricate himself from the interlocking, twisted metal of the two cars, and it was true in a way, his heart remained trapped by her rear end. His lustful frame of mind was permanently bent to her shape.

The dreadful sound of the two vehicles wrenching apart, Isabella with her foot on the gas, this time in first gear, was not as painful as the silence after she drove him out the front door last month, suitcase and guitar in hand.

She drove him home that first afternoon, but said she was so rattled she needed to stop for a drink. She declared he looked like he needed one, too. She drank her double whiskey in regular cola, "None of that diet crap," she warned the bartender.

After three beers himself, Orlando couldn't help it: he began to hum *Londonderry Air*. Making the words up on the spot, the revised *London Derrière* began spilling out. She might have socked him in the jaw, but instead she laughed, delighted. She dragged him onto the dance floor and gyrated, her back against him. This time he could not hide his eager gear shift behind a bent steering wheel. They hooked together like a tow-hitch and its load. He wrote her a new song on each anniversary of their crash. *Do the Locomotive With Me. Fanny Fandango. Mother Goose Your Caboose. Let's Cause a Rumpus.* The songs were for her only, hymns performed during private services to her body. But on their fifth anniversary, she didn't want a song. She wanted a three-word sentence.

He admired the way she dressed – or didn't. Not attired in a flowery potato-sack to hide her figure or a blouse tight on the boobs to distract from the rest of her. No obvious and generally futile attempt to disguise the fact that she wore a jeans size in double digits, twice her blouse size. "Vertical stripes aren't going to fucking fool anybody," she said, not that she cared to. She wore bright, bold colours and patterns, and snug fits. Not tight or restrictive, but contoured to her shape. Mostly, though, Isabella went naked, stripping with relief as soon as the front door closed behind her.

Isabella didn't need convincing or wooing to bend over for him. After cocktails, she took him to her house without asking where he wanted to go. Bedroom curtains open, Isabella offered herself like one of those monkeys on the Discovery Channel. He approached the twin celestial planets that orbited around her fiery core with reverential hands. Just as he had once caressed Jimi Hendrix's left-handed guitar, the curves so like Isabella's; as he had stroked the Buddha's belly in China; as he had held his first erection in wonder and terror. He spread her cheeks apart. He broke Lent. He lost his cock in her cosmic folds, a tiny spaceship careening through her vortex. The puckered crater of her asshole winked up at him from between her double moons.

With the lights blazing, he got to watch his fingers digging into her hips, circles of white spreading from his grip. It was like denting a tender peach, or watching the impression of his foot haloing out on wet sand. He seized that jiggling ass to hang on, like a roller coaster handle, wanting to bruise it with the force of his grip. He reached around to lolling breasts and thighs spread just right for easy access to the magic spot so many men, apparently, ignored. Why? It was so easy. He'd seen the way women worked over his dick, with mouth, hand, or body. Jesus, making him come took *effort*. But he could just lay back, one arm under his head, and move a single finger. Even a pinkie. Even a goddamn toe positioned just right, though it tended to cramp up on him if she took awhile – and Isabella was never one to hurry. Yeah, sometimes it was an afterthought – face it, he could be as quick and eager as the next guy, he was no god – but the gesture was one they sure appreciated.

Orlando carefully kept one of his fingers uncalloused. His love digit, Isabella christened it. All it takes is one, his first girlfriend had taught him, a piece of knowledge that had served him better than anything he'd learned in college. Keep it clean and well-trimmed, she'd said, and that way you can put it just about anywhere. Later, after he'd picked up the steel-string and welts of protective skin cropped up all over his hands, he left one fingertip smooth. Only good for picking his nose, he told his vapid-eyed music students. It hampered complicated riffs, but the sacrifice was worth it.

Like the perfect lyric, Isabella continued to surprise him. Unlike the girdle-ish contraptions he found other women trapped in, Isabella wore thong underwear – when she wore any at all. She claimed panties wouldn't fit her, other than the suffocating type she had no interest in wearing. Instead of plucking at elastic that climbed uncomfortably, she let it all hang out. Her undies were no more than a swatch of fabric that cupped her *mons*, and a string that nestled where Orlando wished his tongue could take up permanent residence.

Isabella let him watch her shower, the soap disappearing between the cleavage of her thighs. She bathed belly-down in the oversized tub she'd remodelled the house around, her ass mounds looking like twin atolls rising out of the bubbly deep. Amelia Earhart's plane could vanish in that landscape. Isabella declared she would never need a tattoo, since Orlando's ass hickeys permanently decorated her. He couldn't help nibbling his devotion, a taking of the sacrament. As soon as one love bite faded, he replaced it with another. She backed up to mirrors, contorting impossibly as she tried to find Rorschach meaning in their patterns.

On the rare occasions when Orlando refused to be distracted from practising by her undulating waves of desire, Isabella practised naked yoga in his line of vision. Her wide-hulled boat continually capsized during the balancing poses. His will power couldn't surmount such a tidal effect, and before she'd toppled over a third time, he gave in to temptation and righted her with his sturdy mast.

He'd been surprised when she'd packed his things a month ago. (There was no question as to who would stay, as he could never ask her to give up the bathtub.) She abdicated the throne he'd constructed beneath her. Left him a country-less peasant, an expatriate wandering through the pages of disappointing swimsuit issues. All because of one word. One stupid word. What a tragic irony, fit for an opera, that his song lyrics had wooed Isabella to him, but his silence in response to her demand had driven her away.

Dumping him looked good on her. He couldn't take his eyes off her once he'd spotted her precariously perched on a barstool. He wanted to metamorphose into that stool. She looked like she'd swallowed the goddess she always sprinkled into casual conversation. She looked powerful. She looked like trouble. Dressed to kill in a red Empire-waist dress that cinched her bodice but flared out at the hips and fell past her knees, she looked like the Great Pyramid. Not one of the Egyptian queens mummified inside, no, but a live monument pulsing with desert sunlight, stretching to the sky yet rooted on earth, radiating heat.

Isabella always looked damned hot walking away. Trailing behind her at the mall or the market, admiring her bouncing globes, Orlando often felt he would have been a better student with such visual aids.

But Isabella looked even better coming towards him.

"Isabella." He spread his hands when she approached him after the last song. She needn't have waited so politely – she was an audience of one.

"You're an asshole," she said in her irresistible accent.

"I know." He would do or say anything tonight to get her back.

"No, you don't. I'm going to make you *feel* the meaning of asshole. So that next time you'll think twice before using it on someone else."

"Hey, I did *not* shit on you."

"No, because you're emotionally constipated." She seemed surprised by her own wit.

He spied the crack in her slammed door, the thin moment where he could sneak in and make her forget her anger. "Can I use that in a song?"

"Always a joke. Always your music." She hung on to her resentment, levering herself against the other side of the door, her side of the argument. "Always detachment. Reserve. Calculation. Tonight I'm breaking your barrier. Drop your pants, asshole." But she lifted her skirt, exposing herself to the waist.

"Jesus." His mouth dropped open, not his 501s. Instead of damp and minuscule panties, curlicues of wiry hair escaping along the creases of her hip, Isabella had sprouted a penis. It seemed as if their entire courtship had been a build-up to the lyrical surprise of the pink and white swirled cock *springing* from beneath her uplifted dress. Strapped on with a complicated series of belts and buckles, the cock appeared lifelike in shape, if not in colour. The straps looked damned uncomfortable, cutting into her generous flesh. He admired her ease with the contraption. Most women of her build wouldn't be caught dead in a bikini, much less this get-up. Her thong was proving entirely inadequate to the task of restraining the hungry beast.

"Isabella, what the hell do you want?"

"I want your hymen."

Hi, men! His mind spun spellings and alternate definitions. His mental word play always got worse when he was nervous, a subconscious tic he couldn't control. "Whoa, whoa, whoa."

"I want your cherry. Your maidenhead."

He stepped backwards, away from the threatening member. "This is a joke, right?"

"You're looking at the punch-line." She took the hefty pink cock in her small fist. "Take a good look while you can, because you're not going to be seeing much of it the rest of the night."

Ironically, Isabella had never seemed less womanly than with this jutting member thrusting forward from her thighs, her queenly power visibly concentrated in this vengeful scepter. Orlando was hot. Inflamed. Also terrified.

"Isabella. Christ. Here?" He glanced around the deserted bar. The bartender had started to set the chairs on the tables halfway through Orlando's last set. His mediocre and distracted performance once he'd caught sight of Isabella in the audience had encouraged few to remain through to the last number. The bartender had waved goodnight before Orlando's last note faded, calling out for him to lock up on his way out, adding that he'd mop in the morning, unless Orlando wanted to do it for extra cash.

"All the better if someone sees you for the asshole that you are," Isabella said.

"Fine! Fine." Orlando tore at his belt buckle and thrashed his pants to his ankles. "I'll play your little game. Whatever you want, Isabella." He turned his back to her before lowering his boxers, so she couldn't see the eager state of his cock. Orlando didn't know if he was angrier at Isabella or at the betrayal of his own dick, which rose up in direct opposition to what he thought he didn't want. But he did know that he wanted her to stay, to connect with her. On any level. He bent over the barstool he'd perched on for his show and reached around to spread his ass cheeks. "Come and get it."

Her dress rustled as she stepped close behind him. He smelled her, an oasis of bubble bath clean in a stale swamp of cigarette smoke and beer.

"You know what I want," she said, the tip of her dick hovering in his delicate pucker.

"Why is it so important?" he shouted over his shoulder. "Christ, you *know* how I feel. Isn't it more important that I *show* it? *Express* it? Don't I do that?"

She pressed deeper, the tip of her cock just kissing the tight fist of his asshole. "I want you to say it."

He grunted. "It can't possibly mean the same thing to different people."

"You're holding back out of fear. Just like with your music. You won't commit the last three per cent. That's why you're still playing dives like this."

"We've been over this a thousand times. It's worthless to say it."

The tight bud of his asshole opened at her nudging insistence. "I know it's what you feel. Just say it."

"It's meaningless if you have to ask."

"It's everything."

He made an incoherent noise as she slipped in a centimetre, then another. Isabella still worked with metrics.

"It won't kill you," she said. "Don't be afraid."

"I'm done talking. You . . . uhn, you just do what you have to do to make your point."

"I'm not stopping till you say it."

Crafty Isabella had just thwarted herself. Her cock crept its slow, methodical way into his body; Orlando didn't want her to stop. Considering his preoccupation with rear ends, it now struck him as odd that he'd never considered his own. His morning post-coffee toiletries and a vigorous scrubbing were all the attentions he'd ever thought of bestowing upon it.

"You're pressuring me," he quipped, disguising his level of enjoyment with the sort of response that had incited her to this in the first place.

She slapped his ass. "Say it."

Orlando was silent.

Slowly Isabella worked her slippery dick in. She was being careful, he could tell, cautious not to really hurt him. His ass now pressed firmly beneath the swell of her belly. The front of her thighs nudged the back of his. Her high-heeled feet, calculated for the height she would need for this manoeuvre, were wedged between his scuffed cowboy boots, swathed with his jeans and boxers like the base of a Christmas tree. The hem of her dress tickled his lower back. Orlando had never experienced the blindness of having someone make love to him from behind, never felt the surprise of every touch by their hands or body. Isabella often mounted him while he lay on his back, telling him to hold still until she'd used him for her own friction, but he could still participate, teasing between her legs or massaging her breasts, communicating with facial expressions. This was powerlessness of another order. Total abandon, at her mercy. An absolute trust and giving of oneself. And she had done it so boldly, so baldly, so often.

She grabbed fists full of his scant hips, and leaned over to whisper in his ear. "Say it."

Orlando pushed back against her.

Isabella began to fuck him in earnest. Her breath changed to short pants of hot steam on his back. Her movements became more calculated. She had gone from anger to arousal. He sensed her surprise, that this fucking would afford her pleasure, too. She picked up her pace, forgot the metric system and took a quantum leap. Isabella gave him her last three per cent, going deep.

She grabbed his hair. "Say it!" She punctuated her repeated demand with the insistent sound of her belly slapping against his ass. If someone had peeked through the steamy front windows into the dim bar, all they would have seen was the flapping red tent of her dress, the spread wings of an exotic bird.

Orlando opened his mouth but couldn't catch his breath.

"I love you," Isabella said softly. She broke through his barrier with her thrusts.

"I . . . Damn it, I love you," Orlando half sobbed. She had burst some dam within him. Some massive, concrete structure that had allowed only trickles of truth to get through, leaving those on the other side thirsty and parched. The granite crumbled, and years of pent-up, churning water deluged the desert. "I do. I really do."

Isabella abruptly stilled.

"Don't stop! Don't."

"Say it. Say it."

"Jesus," he bit his lip. "I fucking love you. I fucking love you. Oh, God, fuck me, I love you. Christ. Let me love you."

She was right about his music, about everything. He had cassette tapes crammed with serious songs. Lyrics that expressed his ache and longing and, yes, his love. But he feared they were sappy, that he would be laughed at, and so he made laughter at his humorous songs a certainty. No risk. Isabella's thrusts knocked those tunes loose, setting free a flock of singing birds in his head. Stored up inside him for years now, they tumbled out.

"I love you, I love you, I love," he said, in time with her

thrusts. She arced. He knew her sounds, could tell how close she was. She slapped against him, harder and faster. He was so full of her, to the depths of his core, that he could hardly stand it. And he couldn't believe it, but he was coming. Without a touch from her on his cock, he was coming, too. He cried, and came, shouting that he loved her. She burst, and he burst, and they stood shuddering. The red dress shimmered with the trembling of their joined bodies.

She played with his hair and nibbled on his shoulder, her arms tight around his belly, her breasts smashed against his back. He didn't want this moment to end. He didn't want her to ever pull herself out of him. He wanted her to take up residence in his guts. Except that then he would never have another good look at her ass.

The Holy Bright Number

Andy Duncan

Once a high-yellow business girl named Clarissa lived in a dead cropper's place at the head of a trail in a hollow up Tobaccoville way. The trail was made by deer and widened by men and narrowed again by the mountain itself in the years after the last cropper died and burley leaf dropped cheaper than souse meat and the bank let the fields go to laurel and huckleberries, so as she picked her way up the hollow the first time, she must have been walking on faith that the way led anywhere at all. Or maybe instead she had no faith, and walked into the woods for that reason instead, which is another kind of faith and one often borne out in the hills. But walk she did, and was surprised or not by the one room cabin she found at the head, and that very evening the folks on the other side of the ridge saw smoke pluming up from the dead cropper's chimney and resolved to coon hunt elsewhere for a spell, for the dead have been known to kindle a fire. Soon the trail started widening up again, as fear of the dead lessened or grew, either way leading men all over the country to tramp the trail to pay their respects to Clarissa. On a chestnut stump at the edge of the clearing she set an unopened box of Red Devil Lye: on its side meant please abide; standing straight, no need to wait. Those who waited stood several trees apart, smoking, not speaking, each imagining himself alone between the great black woods and the lighted window.

One new moon night when only a granddaddy coon could have found his way from the turnpike to the head of the hollow, a stranger named Charlie Poole sauntered up the trail whistling, banjo in one hand and bottle in the other. As he passed the Red Devil he kicked it over. When he reached the front door he kicked it open. "Whoa, now," said Clarissa as he plucked her up dripping and kicked the washtub a-slosh across the floor. Her wet cat shot onto the stove, snarling.

Later Clarissa said, "I got a good notion to gate that trail. How'd you find me in the pitch black dark?"

He fought free of the friendship quilt, grabbed the back of her head and said, "This dowsing rod here."

Later she said, "I purely hate a banjo."

"For the rest of your life on this round Earth," he said, "whenever you hear a banjo, that'll be me, talking."

Still later Clarissa padded naked as a jaybird through the dewy gray grass, snatched up the Red Devil box and carried it back to the porch. A groundhog watched her from the garden patch.

"Look, then," she told it, and went inside, slamming the door.

Months passed. Visitors got no farther than the stump, where, confused, they turned back. No one entered, no one left the hollow.

(Many years later, a young woman writing notes by hand amid a stack of books and records at a little desk in the college library in Chapel Hill asked herself what Charlie Poole could possibly have been doing for four and a half months in the spring and summer of 1924. The answer occurred to her even before she set pen to paper to record the question, and she snorted with laughter at herself, a sound that so emboldened the young stranger at the adjoining little desk that he peered over the partition and spoke to her. Whatever he said wasn't much, but it was enough.)

One afternoon in the cabin in the hollow, Charlie Poole was laughing fit to bust. Clarissa's tabby had decided his bouncing pecker was a play-pretty and was trying to jump up and bat it as Charlie galloped from one end of the cabin to the other, daylight breaking through the floorboards each time he landed, Clarissa's arms around his neck and her legs around his waist and her lips against his ear murmuring giddyup. But Charlie's laughter faltered and died as he slowed to a canter and then to a walk. Clarissa had to lick him to get his attention.

"Charlie! I said, let's fetch that tick and straw from the yard and get this bed back together. It's aired enough, and there's thunder coming."

"You hear it, too?" Charlie said, standing still.

When his pecker quit bobbing, the cat lost interest and went to wash itself under the stove. Clarissa slipped off Charlie's back and knelt beside the water bucket, drank deep from the dipper. "God damn, it's hot in here," she said. "Wish that storm would come on. Might break the weather a little."

"Ain't no storm," Charlie said. The way he said it made her look at him.

Another *boom boom boom* sounded, closer now, as if just the other side of the ridge. The canning jars rattled.

The cat yowled as Charlie trod on its tail in getting to his clothes. The rocker righted itself a little at a time as Charlie relieved it of britches, brogans, shirt.

"Charlie," Clarissa said. "Charlie?"

The *booms* were in the hollow now, continuous and evenly spaced, like a heartbeat or a funeral march.

Charlie's gaze met hers for a second as he slipped on his braces. "You ain't dressed yet?" he asked.

One more deafening *boom*, then a silence painful to the ears. A voice rumbled from the front yard.

"Charlie Poole, come out and be known to the Lord."

Clarissa stood, mouth open, arms at her side, staring at the door, heedless of her nakedness, of the dress Charlie was trying to thrust into her hands. He finally draped it over her shoulders like a shawl.

"Charlie Poole, come out."

A heavy *thump* like a body flung down made the porch boards groan and jumbled the knick-knack shelf. A souvenir dish from the Natural Bridge fell to the hearth and smashed. Another *thump*, then another, coming closer. With each one a bit more daylight appeared beneath the door.

Clarissa was trying to put on the dress, really she was, but in her terror and her focus on the door her arms were leaden, and her fingers wouldn't work. It was like trying to button when she was a girl, while watching the contrary Clarissa in the head-to-toe mirror at the Federated store in Winston.

Behind her, someone pounded on the sash, but she didn't look around. The whole floor of the house now sloped toward the door. Off balance, fearing she would pitch into the arms of whoever was now turning the handle, she instead fell backward onto the sagging ropes of the bed frame, where she clawed for purchase like a spider as the dress slithered to the floor.

The sudden breeze as the door swung open smelled of summer mud and honeysuckle. Filling the doorway, stooping to peer inside with deep-set ice-blue eyes, was the largest man Clarissa had ever seen.

He wore a bluish-white seersucker suit, jacket buttoned, pants creased as sharp as the ridge line, shirt collar hooked tight but no tie. His neck was as thick as Clarissa's waist, his jaw ponderous, his mouth wide and crooked like the glancing blow of an axe, his rectangular head made more so by his terrible haircut, razored so close that he was patchily bald. His nose and brow were lumpy, too much in them. Meeting his steady, shadowed gaze, Clarissa thought of two miners' headlamps deep down in the seam.

The well-dressed giant bared his teeth and said, "Evening," so loudly she flinched and so low in pitch that her bones vibrated.

The giant stepped inside, massive shoulders hunched, buzz-cut head sweeping dust from the ceiling. The little cabin rocked like a cradle as he moved about, gazed at the dime store gifts that cluttered the shelves, the few dresses huddled in the chiffarobe, the stove battered as if clenched in a fist and unfolded again. Clarissa suddenly hated her whore's nest, and all it contained, and herself.

"No, you don't," the giant rumbled, his back to her. She gasped, the answer to her unspoken thought more invasive than this uninvited hulking presence among the scraps of her life.

The giant knelt and began picking up the shards of the Natural Bridge, piling them in a calloused palm. They clicked together like a cricket's legs. "You don't *hate* nothing, Clarissa," the giant said. "You're just *ashamed* of a right smart of it." He drew one last shard from between two floorboards, topped off the pile, then cupped his palms together and rocked them. "Afraid this plate here has been to breakfast," he said, looking mournful, but in his hands the bits looked less like fragments of something broken, a ripped jumper, the insides of a jack-o'-lantern, and more like fragments of something yet to be made, the squares of a quilt, kindling. The cat twined around the giant's ankle, purring, and rolled onto her back to present her belly.

"He lay down as a lion, and as a great lion," the giant recited. "Who shall stir him up?"

He closed his eyes, brought his cupped hands to his mouth and blew into them, his cheeks inflated like a child puffing out a candle. "Restore unto Clarissa this geegaw, O Lord," the giant said, and blew again, then opened his eyes and his hands. The smashed bits of plate were unchanged. The giant's whole face wrinkled as he beamed at Clarissa. "Indeed, the Lord's work is ever marvellous to behold," he said. "You got any glue?"

Sitting on the edge of the bed frame now, a rope burn streaking across her thigh, she shook her head.

The giant grunted and stood, shoved double handfuls of plate into his jacket pockets like a bashful suitor. "My name's Ralph Poole," he said. His smile faltered on "Poole."

Since the giant entered, Clarissa had not been studying about Charlie. But now, with a pang of guilt, she looked for him. She, the cat and the giant were alone in the room. The tatty curtains in the open window billowed in the rising breeze.

"Gone, of course," said the giant Poole, shaking his head just as she realized, with something like nausea, that Charlie Poole was never coming back. "No matter," the giant continued. "He ain't no harder to find than cigarettes and beer." He reached for the dipper, one huge hand enfolding the battered tin handle all the way to the bowl. He peered into the bucket as he stirred, the dipper clanking against the sides. "I reckon you know, Clarissa, that my little brother stinks like blinky milk. He is a varmint and a rake-hell and a hard, hard man."

"I know him," Clarissa said, enraged – *I could have gone with him but you stopped me, somehow you stopped me* – and blinking back tears. "But I don't know you."

The giant Poole lifted the streaming dipper, swung it toward her. "Drink," he said.

The dipper rasped across her cheek once, twice, leaving a damp trail.

Still furious and sick at heart, she also was suddenly thirsty. She parted her lips. She drank the hot, metallic well water that had come to taste like home, looking into the giant's eyes as he gauged her throat movements and tipped the dipper steadily, unerringly, as if his arm were hers.

When she was done he dipped more water and poured it onto her upturned face, onto her shoulders, her chest, and somehow she felt calmer and less naked, not more. The water was colder now and she shivered, her body awakening despite herself, as the rivulets coursed down her arms and back and backside and legs. Empty dipper still in hand, the giant Poole regarded her nipples without expression, a look Clarissa knew well.

She weaved a bit as she stood. Wanting to hurt him, she spread her feet a bit farther apart for balance, put her hands on her hips and said, "It'll cost you."

The giant Poole's high-pitched chortle made Clarissa flinch and sent the cat streaking beneath the bed. "You think I don't know that?" the giant asked.

He scooped her dress off the floor one-handed and tossed it at her. She tried to snatch it from the air but her body caught most of it, the fabric plastering to her damp skin. She had no trouble putting it on. Then the giant handed her the cat. It lay draped across his hand, purring.

"Where are we going?" she asked.

"To get some glue."

Outside, the sun was past the ridge line, and a cloud was rolling through the hollow, spattering rain as it brushed the tops of the chestnuts and poplars. On the porch, leaning against the woodpile, were a gnarled walking stick and a double-headed, leather-handled drum. The giant reclaimed these as he passed. Clarissa held the cat close for warmth as she stepped from the porch onto the flat, mossy, rain-hollowed rock that served as a step, a puddle already collecting at its green centre, and then onto the clover that long since had taken the grass. Splintered locust wood, then water and stone, a

damp cushion of green – she stood for a moment on each, her
bare feet digging imaginary toeholds to mark the place as hers
forever, and then walked forward, following the mist
enshrouded figure of the giant along the path.

Entering the woods, the giant began to beat the drum one-
handed with the stick, the steady *boom boom boom* flushing
quail and squirrels and larger creatures, too, that crashed and
slid and plopped out of sight as he advanced. Clarissa quickly
saw that however she hurried, inviting stumbles over roots and
thrashes among clinging, clammy leaves, the gap of twenty feet
between her and the giant never closed, so instead she took her
time, content with the drumbeat and the purring mass against
her chest and the familiar underfoot treacheries of the trail. She
tasted the rain and filled herself with the bullfrog-scented air.

In the thickest woods, just as Clarissa could only hear, not
see, the giant before her, she heard another, more distant
music: a banjo.

The drumbeats stopped, and Clarissa knew the march had
stopped, too. She stood, swaying amid a copse of honeysuckle.
She had not been lying when she told Charlie she purely hated
the banjo and all the tunes he and Satan could commit with it,
but he *would* play them, so she couldn't help but recognize this
one – "Budded Rose," Charlie had called it.

"Too damn many notes flying out of this thing," he once
said, sitting drunk on her porch wearing only his bowtie and
picking the evening away. "Better catch 'em, now. Hear that?
Here they come. That's *one* for your pocket, and *one* for your
stove, and *one* for when you wake up hungry at night."

At first she thought this "Budded Rose" was coming from
that very porch, but then it was ahead of her, and then off to the
side toward the rock fall, and then downslope and sharing a
laugh with the water in the branch. It was everywhere; it was
nowhere. Nowhere. Hungry at night, indeed. She wept into
the cat's fur, feeling as if she had awakened from the saddest of
dreams.

Up ahead, the drumbeat resumed, and Clarissa walked
forward again, though she was no longer following the giant
but coincidentally walking along behind him. Clarissa was
done following Pooles. The second had broken the spell of

the first; now the first had broken the spell of the second. One day Clarissa would cast a third spell herself, and not on any damn Poole. Now if only Charlie's banjo would hush.

To her relief, the giant, with more volume than skill, at this point began to sing.

I want to join that holy bright number
I want to join that holy bright number
I want to join that holy bright number
And turn some ransomed one home.
They number one hundred and forty-four thousand
They number one hundred and forty-four thousand
They number one hundred and forty-four thousand
Oh, turn some ransomed one home.

The song was easily learned, and Clarissa sang along as she trudged down the hollow. Her voice grew louder, the giant's, fainter. By the time she reached the turnpike, a rutted silver scar leading into a gloom only deepened by the distant lights of Tobaccoville, the giant and his drum and his voice had melted away as if they had never been, and any trace of "Budded Rose" was temporarily lost in the rattle and snarl of a pulpwood truck labouring up the grade. Clarissa held the squirming cat tighter as she stepped forward and stood, proud and ready, in the middle of the road. Standing straight, no need to wait. She listened to nothing, squinted into the glow of the headlamps cresting the hill.

On Hallowed Ground

Debra Hyde

It would probably surprise you to learn that a graveyard sits smackdab in the middle of a small New England city. You'd never know, to drive by on either one of the two highways that skirts Hartford. But it's there, nestled between the Gold Building and a massive urban church, shadowed by the Travelers tower, first phallic symbol of this old Puritan outpost.

If you were to wander into the cemetery – the Ancient Burial Ground, as it's called – you'd find tombstones as old as Hartford's first residents and as young as American Federalism. And if you felt you were being watched as you strolled the grounds, it might be the angel-heads staring at you from their timeless perches atop their tombstones, visages like some happy-faced renaissance sun met with a pirate's skull, then morphed into something only director Tim Burton would love.

And if you still felt yourself being watched – well, maybe the street culture's checking you out. Maybe the beady, withdrawal-plagued eyes of a street person, just waking up under the cemetery hedges, have spied you out. Or maybe it's the disaffected gaze of folks just outside the grounds, people curious enough to watch you because you're new to their tired old routine of watching and waiting for the Q bus. Then again, maybe you hit it lucky and found a group of overexcited schoolchildren, field-tripping their way through Connecticut history.

But chances are, you won't find Mark or Ramona there. They already had their moment in the sun – well, under moon, really – and they're not likely to repeat their offence. Not after narrowly escaping the watchful eye of the HPD.

It started with Mark. A lover of trivia, he stumbled across the fact that Hartford's founder, one Thomas Hooker, Puritan minister and pioneer, probably was not actually buried at the tombstone that honoured him. As a humble pilgrim, Hooker didn't believe in frills, and because a tombstone was as frilly to him as a lace collar, he swore off the concept of hallowed ground. So the man's buried somewhere in there, Mark realized, but he could be next to an illustrious lawyer, a poor pilgrim, or a very early-American slave.

Unlike Hooker, Mark believed in hallowed things, but only for the sake of sacrilege. He lived in an arrested state of punkhood and still looked for new ways to transgress against the status quo, especially now that the status quo included former drinking buddies who had long ago settled down to lawns, kids, and SUVs. How to transgress, however, had become problematic with age and he was always on the prowl.

Ironically, Mark's idea came to him during one day during a boring jack-off. In a brief mental epiphany – the best of which always happened when it involved his dick – the word sex led to hooker, which led to Thomas Hooker. That was followed by the vision of Ramona's face, followed by his familiarity with her tight ass, followed by a quick tension, a long release, and a thick glob of come which oozed onto his belly.

Knowing a good idea when he had one, Mark dipped his fingers into this creamery-thick pool, then reached for his nightstand phone and put his goopy fingers to dialling Ramona.

"Hey, baby," she cooed when she recognized Mark's voice.

"How about dinner and a trick?" Mark inquired.

"It'll cost you," she warned.

"It always does." His voice sounded like a shrug of the shoulders.

Dinner was a hoot. On the surface, they looked like a stylish couple consuming peasant chicken and micro-brewed beer at City Steam. Men would think Mark lucky to have such a doe-eyed, lush-haired, pouting-lipped beauty while women would ruffle territorially. But when the hordes on the happy-hour make looked closely, they would see a hint of masculinity where none should have existed and an aggressive glint in eyes that should've shown demure and inviting. Which suited Mark just fine. He liked freaking the mundanes.

But not Ramona. "This place is a fucking meat market," she complained.

"That's how straight men cruise, Sugar."

"Pigs!" she decided before amending her judgment with a *present company aside* codicil.

Mark simply smiled. He loved Ramona's feisty ways and if the straight men and women around them found themselves challenged by her presence, all the better. He had known Ramona for four years and, while he had never had the pleasure of meeting the Juan that once was, he'd seen enough of the remnants of Juan to make him adore Ramona all the more. That his relationship with Ramona always included a cash-and-carry exchange only made her more attractive to him. After all, how many straight men could say they forked over good cash for a piece of tight ass and to fund a favourite fuck-buddy's lifelong dream of gender reassignment?

"I don't like this place," Ramona protested. As she glowered her way through coffee and dessert, Mark reminded her that the day she got her pussy was the day she'd have to start living straight.

"After all, how much of gay society's going to be there for you when you give up your dick?" he asked.

Ramona huffed and feigned indifference but Mark knew that beneath her haughty veneer sat an appreciative girl. No matter what she threw his way – fuck fees, bills for her hormone treatments, conflicting schedules due to her slavish clients, even the occasional temper tantrum – he stood by her without complaint. She knew he had earned the right to be her Sugar Daddy, even if he was wrong about her gay friends.

As they left the restaurant, Mark remarked, "Time is money." To which Ramona answered, "So what do you have in mind?"

Mark smiled slyly. "You'll see." He took her by the arm and briskly walked her down Main Street. When they passed Asylum Street and the parking garage that sat on that block, she knew they weren't about to leave the city. As they breezed past the Gold Building, she started to complain, "Slow down. It's hard in these heels."

Mark chuckled. "I'll get you off your feet soon enough."

When they rounded the corner of Gold Street and headed into the Ancient Burial Ground, Ramona crossed herself as she said, "You fucking pervert."

"Not yet, I'm not."

Slow dining had afforded Mark and Ramona with the cover of dark and with the city now void of activity, the burial ground afforded them some privacy. Mark took Ramona deep into the cemetery, past the back of the old church, and practically centre square to the burial ground's Main Street entrance. Had he done so during daylight, they would've never escaped notice, the spot was so public, but now, at night, only the occasional glint of a streetlight through the trees cast any light.

Darkness didn't keep Mark from knowing where he was and what he wanted. He had Ramona kneel before the tombstone of his choice, and, as he unzipped his pants and freed his dick he read, "In memory of the Rev. Thomas Hooker who in 1636 with his assistant Mr Stone removed to Hartford with about 100 persons where he planted ye First Church in Connecticut. An eloquent, able and faithful Minister of Christ, He died July 7th, 1647."

"Now," he added "make yourself eloquent and minister to my dick."

"Teeth or no teeth?"

It was a classic Hartford whore statement, but Mark opted to "make it middle class". He didn't need a taste of Ramona's early days, where she could charge more for a blowjob by virtue of a no-uppers grin? Not this time, at any rate.

Ramona sneered, called him a pervert again, and took his dick into her mouth. She crossed herself as she did. Whether it was over the teeth or the setting, she didn't say, but whatever distaste she displayed evaporated when she tasted his dick. She loved how it bulged when it felt her mouth slip over it. She inhaled deeply as she took it, thinking that if she couldn't actually have his balls in her face, at least she could enjoy their scent.

As she sucked, Ramona swooned, not because she worshipped Mark's magnificence but because she conjured up a pussy in her head and longed to know how it would feel to have a cock swelled inside her. She wondered how it would feel to finally have a dick on the inside instead of outside.

In all honesty, she wasn't sure she'd really let Mark's dick inside what would be a $30,000 sculpture, but that didn't stop her from giving good head. She tongued Mark's dick with enthusiasm, working up and down its length and paying special tongue attention to that tender spot just below its head

Mark groaned in hearty appreciation but he wanted more: he wanted to face-fuck her. He leaned forward and, bracing himself hands-first against the top of the Honourable Hooker's tombstone, began to push-up himself in and out of her mouth. Briefly, Ramona's teeth scraped over his head and, flinching, he wondered if he should've gone for the lower class accommodation.

But his dick throbbed, his balls grew tight, and Ramona made little sex sounds – the whimpers of a good bottom getting done – and other than that one scrape, her mouth felt oh so good. It was a wet and wonderfully open thing, made all the more delicious by the rumbling groans vibrating up from her throat.

However, as much as he might like to, Mark didn't want to come this way. He had other plans, just as morbid as doing a hooker over Hooker's marker and they didn't conclude with a blowjob. He pulled his cock from Ramona's mouth, uttering a moan as she let it pop free.

"Get up," he rasped. He helped her up, giving her time to get steady on her feet, before moving her over to another grave.

Unlike Hooker's tombstone, this grave had a tablestone – a tombstone laid flat atop several walls of stone, meant to mimic a sarcophagus. Mark patted the tablestone's top, motioning to Ramona. "Time to bend over."

"You're going to keep me in confession for a month, you know that?" Ramona complained.

"At least you have a priest for your private demons, honey," Mark replied. "Me, I want my demon exorcised."

Ramona huffed, "Enough with the clichés," as she bent over

the tablestone. She laid a hand to each side and held herself there, just like she was at the kitchen table. She felt Mark lift her skirt and pull down her panties just enough to expose her ass. She heard the snap of a lid and then felt Mark's lubed fingers at her ass. "At least you're generous," she opined. Mark smiled. If only Ramona knew that she was pressing her tits against an ancient, morbid poem that warned *Death is a debt to Nature due/Which I have paied & so must you*, she might insist on the convent.

Mark kept that esoteric knowledge to himself and slathered Ramona's hole instead. Then, he slipped his finger inside, as much to claim his territory as to ready it. He loved Ramona's ass and he financed her well enough that she only had to do out-call domination. That ass was his and someday Ramona's cunt would be as well.

"You have the perfect hole," he told her.

For the first time all evening, Ramona giggled and, looking over her shoulder, smiled broadly at Mark. His words were manna to her ears, especially when she fast-forwarded into the future and applied those words to her cunt. However, the here and now was a riskier place, and she knew from her street days that one only had so much time in which to conclude business.

"You better get to it, if you want to fuck me before the cops show up."

Mark grunted in agreement, took his cock in hand, and aimed it at that perfect hole. Slowly he pushed. Ramona's hole resisted ever so slightly before it acquiesced and let the head of his dick in. Ramona moaned lusciously; she liked the feel of his cock making headway as much as he liked the feel of her hole giving way. Mark pushed a little more and felt himself slip in further.

Normally, Mark would've slowly inched his way in and out and up Ramona's ass. He liked taking his time in encouraging her to open up to him, but when he looked up from her round ass, the cold stone memories of the long-ago departed jutted up from the ground all around him as if they were watching. The grounds were quietly eerie and only the sounds of leaves rustling in a tree top breeze and the occasional late-night vehicle punctuated the silence. Mark was glad for those sounds of urban normalcy; they kept him from imagining the dead rising up to watch him.

Which would've kept him from Ramona and her willing ass. He took her by the hips and began a slow but firm reaming. Ramona groaned again as his cock went to work on her, then threw back her hair and arched her ass to show she liked what he was doing. And her response – sexy, defiant, willing – sent Mark right into frenzy mode. His slow reaming went straight to merciless ramming.

Ramona grabbed the tablestone when Mark slammed into her and clutched it for dear life. An abject moan escaped her lips every time Mark rammed his dick up her, and her whole body reacted every time he pulled back. His dick was relentless in its pursuit; swift and selfish and something else.

And swift, selfish fucks don't take long. Between Ramona's perfect hole and his hungry dick, Mark felt his climax approach in no time at all.

But not before Ramona got to issue her own selfish complaints. Mark's fury had pushed her right up against the tablestone, pelvic bone first, and she had just issued her fourth expletive when Mark pulled out of her and pushed her aside. He barely uttered "move!" when, pumping his dick with his hand, he came, spurting a stream of come over the tablestone. Gasping as his orgasm raged through him, he caught the last bit of spunk in his hand.

Next to him, a vexed Ramona declared, "You bastard!" as she rubbed her crotch and lowered her skirt.

But the scene wasn't over. Not yet it wasn't. Not until his orgasm subsided, until his panting returned to quiet breathing, and until he had the presence of mind to put his dick in his pants.

Then and only then did he conclude the scene: he took that last bit of spunk and returned to Hooker's grave where he wiped it over the dead man's name. He looked to Ramona. "Now I'm a fucking pervert."

Ramona, pointing to her crotch, hissed, "You shithead! You rubbed me raw!"

"Is there a problem here?"

It doesn't take a big stretch of imagination to know those are the words of a cop on duty and, sure enough, one of Hartford's finest had finally caught up with Mark and Ramona. Rising from Hooker's grave, Mark answered, "Not really, officer. I just wanted to take in a little history after dinner. She's miffed that I dragged her in here after dark."

Ramona turned to face the officer, said nothing but crossed herself like the good Catholic girl she always wanted to be.

"Next time, visit before dinner," the cop said curtly. "These grounds are closed after dark." He scrutinized Mark and Ramona as he spoke, trying to assess just what they might've been doing. He hadn't seen the scramble typical of people trying to hide drugs and paraphernalia as he approached, neither did he smell pot or alcohol on them. All he'd really witnessed was a woman apparently scolding a man so quietly that he couldn't detect any clues.

"We'll leave," Mark offered. "Sorry to have been a nuisance."

As the cop nodded, Mark took Ramona by the arm and headed back towards Grove Street. The cop, meanwhile, turned his attention to the hedges, looking for vagrants.

When Mark and Ramona hit the relative safety of the street, Mark said, "That was close."

Ramona laughed. "That wasn't close. Close is when you've just lifted your head up from a john's lap and he barely gets zipped up before the cop's at the window, asking for his ID and your smile."

Mark smirked. He knew Ramona was right and he wasn't about to argue with her. But he was also satisfied. He'd left his mark on Hooker's grave. He had completed his perverted little goal and it was easy to be charitable in the flush of accomplishment.

As they walked down the street, he let Ramona harangue him for his thoughtless treatment of her crotch. He let her carry on about how she wasn't going to let him anywhere near her pussy when she got it, if he continued to treat her with such disrespect. But he also knew what kept them together and, as he planted an affectionate peck on her cheek, he knew that depositing an extra twenty-five per cent above and beyond Ramona's exorbitant fee into her pussy bank account would redeem him. And no matter how much she ranted otherwise, he wanted to stay in her haughty but good graces. After all, she was hallowed ground and he intended to make sure she knew he worshipped that which he loved to defile.

The Colour of Lust

M. Christian

POOL, the sign said, and BILLIARDS, in typography that some-how managed to be early 40s without any of that period's style.

Below TEVIS'S POOL & BILLIARDS was a tobacconist's, a dark little corner store with displays of musty boxes lined with greasy old cigars. Next to it a door stood open, showing a heavy green runner on a narrow flight of stairs. The banister was polished to a dark, mahogany glow from endless palms.

A row of narrow smoke-stained windows, once gold-trimmed, ran around the second storey. Islands of threadbare rugs and strips of matted oil-stained carpeting were cast adrift the ancient parquet floor. A cage stood against the far wall containing an old black man in a crisp white cotton shirt and simple black dress tie. His eyes were too sharp and clear for him to need protection. Daisy imagined him as a dapper tiger, kept locked away for the safety of the hall, and not as a precaution against the half dozen sharks circling lazily around the tables.

Standing next to her, Eddy's hard, narrow face slipped into a wry grin. TEVIS'S was a heavy place, burdened by architecture, sagging from decade after decade of a meticulous game played by tough, desperate people. It was a place that didn't know joy or ecstasy, only winning or losing in a game played with sticks and little round balls. Eddy was there, Eddy was on, Eddy was in her place and pool was her game.

Daisy also knew what her role was supposed to be. "Eddy –" she said with an exasperated little sigh, "– there's not even a fucking bar."

"We can get a drink later, doll," Eddy said, walking away

towards the dapper man behind the bars, the narrow leather case swinging gently in her long, thin hand. "I promise."

"Yeah, right," Daisy said, catching up to Eddy with a quick dash. Her own thin hand clutched at his sleeve. "Come on, Eddy, let's go get something to eat, OK?"

Eddy turned to her, looked straight in her pale blue eyes. Daisy was small, like a model. Sometimes, when Eddy kissed her, when she held her in her arms, a bitter surge of guilt swept up from deep inside her. She was small, like a child. But the feeling rarely lasted more than one or two heartbeats. Eddy had been around, had kissed – and more than kissed – a lot of girls. None of them, even the ones with the leather and the rock-solid attitudes, had been as much of a hurricane in bed. Yes, she was small; but concentrated would be a better word. "I've got to do this, doll," Eddy said.

"No, Eddy, you don't." Daisy aimed fiery eyes up at the taller woman. "You don't have to do anything but go back to the hotel room with me." In her little blue and white cotton dress with her long blonde hair hanging straight down, Daisy looked every inch like Dorothy or Alice, stepped right out of their native pages. But the heat in her eyes revealed the edge that hid under her candy and silk.

"Baby, you know I gotta," Eddy said with firmness, certainty. "You know this is something I have to do."

"No, Eddy you don't. You have to eat, you have to drink, you have to fucking breathe, but you don't have to play pool. You don't have to."

Eddy stood and looked down at her, the narrow leather satchel still in her long-fingered hand. Daisy's eyes flicked, and Eddy knew she was right. It was a game played with a stick and a few coloured balls. It wasn't life, it wasn't love. It was just a game. Life was many small hotel rooms, a Gideon in a drawer, a blue plate special for dinner, and Daisy.

Daisy standing naked in a beam of merciless sunlight, her little body graceful and fine. Her nipples were red kernels on breasts as luscious as her thighs; her thighs were as soft and tender as her breasts. The gentle swell of her belly, the tight blond curls just below, the shocking pinkness of her cunt, the sweet taste of her juice. The way her tongue danced with

Eddy's as they kissed, mingling hot breaths; and the way her tongue danced between Eddy's thighs, always with the right tempo, the right steps. Other lovers had stepped on her clit's toes – too much, too little, not enough – but Daisy knew ballet, she knew just the right steps. She was light and strong, and had a perfect sense of rhythm.

It was a good life. But there was something missing; it all seemed too simple. They were dancing in an empty hall to a predictable tune. There was lust, but it was a lazy, easy lust. Eddy absently stroked the handle of the case with her thumb, feeling the worn smoothness of it and the way the leather warmed under her touch. There was something thundering and powerful in the game: skill, risk, reward . . . a reward not as spectacular as when Daisy danced her tongue between her thighs, but sweeter because Eddy won with her own talent.

Eddy was possessed by two different kinds of lust. Lust for the green felt, the cue, and the coloured balls, fighting roughly in the back of her mind with that other lust: lust for Daisy in a cheap hotel room, her skin a patina of hot sweat, her small breasts tented, tipped with tight, hard nipples, her legs spread gently apart, her lips pink like Georgia O'Keefe's flowery labia.

A solid click, the hollow sound of a ball falling home in a pocket. Eddy shook her head, clearing her eyes and mind. "I have to do this, Daisy," she said, turned back to the man in the cage. "I just have to."

Daisy just glowered, the fire in her blue eyes only burning brighter.

"I hear you've got quite a pool player here," Eddy said to the man behind the bars.

The little man gazed at Eddy for a long time. When he was done sizing her up, he drawled: "So who's looking?"

"Just someone interested in a game of pool, that's all. Just someone looking for a game," Eddy said with a sly grin. Out of the corner of her eye, she caught Daisy heading towards a chair at the edge of the hall. Her little ass moved like poetry when she walked.

The man in the cage smiled, showing two porcelain teeth

and many more of tarnished gold; then in a shockingly loud
voice, he yelled, "Hey, Fats, some guy named Eddy wants to
shoot some pool."

The place had four walls. Two of them had narrow windows,
two were banked with chairs. Eight tables. The cage. The
stairs. From somewhere Eddy hadn't looked, Fats appeared.

It was as if a smudge of night stepped out into the cool
twilight of the pool hall. Big and round, she walked – she
didn't lurch, she didn't struggle, she didn't roll. Fats had a
grace that froze Eddy in her tracks and made her incapable of
doing anything but watch as Fats materialized from her
hidden corner of TEVIS'S POOL & BILLIARDS. She moved
as if on oiled bearings, as if she'd discovered the pure beauty
of what walking could be, and was now demonstrating it to
Eddy.

She was middle-aged, her dark face a play of round cheeks
and dark, hooded eyes. Her hair was the purest black, cut so
short that the shape of her perfectly round skull was showing. Fats wore an immaculate white cotton shirt, perfectly
pressed and buttoned up tight to her dark throat. No tie, but
instead a tiny cross hanging from a thin gold chain. At her
wrists she sported gold and onyx cufflinks. Her pants were
black, almost invisible in the shadows of the hall. She wore
black and white men's shoes that looked brand-new. The
room was warm and getting warmer in the growing day, but
Fats looked elegant, refined, immaculate, and cool. "Yes,
Winthrop?" she said in a deep, drum-roll voice, naming the
black man in the cage.

"Girl here is interested in a game of pool," Winthrop said,
with a tilt of his head to Eddy.

"Is that true?" Fats said, turning her dark face towards
Eddy. Suddenly she smiled, showing a row of perfect white
teeth.

Before Winthrop could answer, and before the allure of
Daisy and another soft hotel bed could change her mind, Eddy
said: "I heard you're one of the best, Fats. I heard it in
Oakland, I heard it in Chicago, I heard it just the other day
on the train. I just want to see if it's true."

Fats slowly measured her, looking Eddy up and down as if

sizing up a lobster in a tank. Under her dark-eyed gaze Eddy felt a surge of heat in her face and chest. She felt herself shrink under her scrutiny.

Someone put a small, very strong hand on Eddy's shoulder. "Come on, Eddy. Come on back to the room with me," Daisy said, her voice edged with tired anger. "It's just a game, Eddy. Come on, it's just a game."

Eddy felt the anger thrill up her spine, tension bloom in her long arms: "Come on, fat girl. You wanna play or not?"

The smile returned to Fats's face – but it was worse, much worse than her cool scrutiny. "Let's play pool, Eddy."

Eddy put her case on the table and carefully popped the tiny latches. "What we shooting for, Fats? Hundred a game?"

Fats nodded, a long, slow motion as if she had all the time in the world. "Let's see your roll first, girl."

Eddy smiled, showing sparkling, perfect teeth. From a deep pocket she pulled a fat roll, tossed it down onto the velvet. "Ten grand, Fats. Count it if you want to."

Fats picked up the roll, weighing it in her chubby, dark hands, her face suddenly cool and earnest. Then she smiled, tossed it neatly back to Eddy. "Looks good, girl."

They rolled to break; despite her humming nerves, Eddy got the opening. In her hand the cue was steady, a part of her body. Languishing before the virgin balls, she cocked and slid the pale pine along her fingers, driving the cue in a perfect strike – just enough, and no more, to snap the eight and four balls away to bounce gently against the cushions and return to the pack. No quarter taken, none given.

"Deal with that, fat girl," Eddy said with a note of bravery she barely felt.

Fats smiled, showing the sparkle of a gold tooth. There is a mastery that disguises itself as bored, casual actions. Without looking, with a careless stroke, she smashed the pack – sending the right two balls into side and right corner pockets with hollow sounds of perfection.

Eddy could do nothing but watch her clear the table.

As the next to last ball fell neatly into a side pocket, a hand suddenly rested on Eddy's shoulder, and a firm but soft voice whispered in her ear: "Come on, Eddy, let's go back to the room."

Eddy wanted to shrug off Daisy's pity, her simple answer of a soft bed and a hot cunt, but she didn't. The first burn of failure was too hot. Instead, she patted Daisy's hand and said, "Maybe – but not yet."

During their words, the last two balls had sunk neatly into pockets. Winthrop had emerged from his cage, swimming lazily through the murky depths of the hall, and had quietly racked them up.

"You're good, fat girl," Eddy said, stepping away from the wiry energy of her lover to peel off some bills from her fat roll, slap five of them down on the table. "You're damned good. But you're not the best."

"Are you going to talk, or shoot pool, Eddy?" Fats said, her coal-dark face calm and inscrutable.

"I'm going to do what I came here to do, Fats; I'm going to show you the best damned pool player there is."

With that, leaning into the shot, pine slick and fast between her fingers, Eddy made the first break – sinking the right two balls, neat and clean.

"I already own a mirror, Eddy," Fats said with a frighteningly cruel smile as she signalled Winthrop for a cold beer.

Despite the deep sting, Eddy cleared the table and won the game. Then the next, and the one after that. She was on, she was there; right there, in that hall and in that game. Every ball obeyed her will, every shot was sweet perfection. It wasn't the body scream of orgasm, or the thrill of Daisy's nipple in her mouth, but it was the climbing glory of winning.

A hand, again on her shoulder. "I want you, Eddy," the sultry voice, low and deep, whispered in her ear. "I want you, back in our room. Your fingers deep inside me, your lips on mine, my nipples hard, yours as well."

"Not yet, not yet," Eddy said, chalking the tip of her cue and smiling slyly at Fats.

"Eddy, you've won. Please, Eddy, come back to the room with me. Lick me, fuck me, suck me, put those sweet fingers in my cunt, my ass. I want you to come with me; I want to come with you. Don't bathe, don't shower, just spread your legs for me – I love the smell, the taste of your sweat, the perfume of your cunt. I want it all. I want it now."

Eddy hesitated in the game to look down into Daisy's burning, hungry eyes. There was so much hot and steamy stuff. But then she looked at the table, saw the balls still in play. "Not yet. Maybe later."

Eddy won the next game – making it ten to six – but her edge slipped away in the middle of the one after that and Fats ran the table clean. Then the big black woman won the next, and the next after that. Eddy felt the world slip away, felt it vanish like chalk between her finger tips, like one of Fats's balls falling into a deep, dark, bottomless pocket.

"Come back to the room with me," Daisy said, whispering again in her ear. "Make my clit hard, make my juices flow. Make me scream and cry. I want to lay in bed half asleep and watch you, naked, walk to the bathroom for a drink – I love to watch your ass jiggle, your neat little tits jiggle when you walk. You're so beautiful."

She did okay with the next game. But as the seven ball sped towards the cushion Eddy felt the edge fade again; the ball bounced just short of the pocket and lazily rolled away, giving Fats the perfect opportunity to run the table.

"Come with me, Eddy," Daisy said, arm wrapped around her, holding Eddy close. "I want you, warm and soft in my arms. I want you in me, on me, I want to hear the way your voice changes when you come, the way you breathe quicker and quicker till it just bursts out of you in a great, wonderful sigh of release. I want to feel your cunt grab my fingers, your muscles holding on tight as the come surges up and out through you. Come on, Eddy, this is only a game."

Eddy stared at the table, hypnotized by the way Winthrop racked up the balls; nestling them together in momentary perfect geometry, waiting to be shattered apart and scattered across the table.

A game . . . only a game? Absently, Eddy chalked her cue as she walked over to the table. She could just put the cue down, shake Fats's hand and walk out into the fresh night. Maybe a cup of coffee, a cheeseburger in some diner, then back to their cheap room. A kiss, Eddy's hand cupping Daisy's small, firm breast; Daisy reaching down, pulling her cotton dress up and off, standing in the cool night air of the room in bra and panties. White cotton below and yellowed nylon above, holding Daisy's perky little breasts like deep secrets. With a sly smile, she'd reach behind her back, unsnap and reveal herself – two neat puddings, pale and silky, yet firm and upswept. Nipples burning pink, like they'd been lipstick-painted.

Then, reaching down, she'd step out of her simple cotton, revealing the uncommon beauty of her golden-coloured curls. Then she'd stand, naked in the dim light, a lithe nymph, a Kansas goddess, a strong little wheat and plains sprite.

They'd kiss, they'd suck nipples, they'd lick clits, they'd come. Eddy was the easiest, the quickest to scream, shout, with Daisy sometime thereafter. It would be wonderful; and then they'd do it the next morning, the next afternoon, the next night.

The table was green felt, a deep verdant green – like the Amazon must look from high above. An impenetrable green. Just a game?

"Come on, Eddy," Daisy said with firm exhaustion, determined tones in her voice. "Come on."

But this wasn't about winning and losing. It was Eddy's way, her real passion; the green of the felt was the colour of her special lust. Her lust to be the best, to be better than anyone. "Go back to the room, Daisy. I have a game to play." Then, not waiting to see if her lover had left, she turned to Fats and added in level tones: "Let's play some pool."

Eddy lost the next game, and the one after that, but the pain of losing wasn't there. Instead she was building up speed, accelerating to where Fats was steadily cruising. She wasn't there, not yet; but she could feel the groove, and knew that catching it was just a matter of time.

She won the next game but, like the loss, the win wasn't hot. Eddy wasn't there yet, not yet.

After she won the next game and the last ball sank home in its pocket, she knew she had the edge. She could taste it, she could hear the prolonged low note in her ears, there was a new clarity to everything. She almost put her cue away, almost shook Fats's hand and walked out. She knew she had it, and she knew she'd win every game. The edge was there.

But she didn't leave. Just knowing she had it wasn't enough. She won the next three games; with each sinking ball her game grew clearer and more perfect until the cue was more than just an extension of her body, it was an extension of her will – a part of her mind. It was 15 to 12.

The sun had set a long time ago, and would rise soon. Time had become nothing but a way to measure the game. That she'd played through the whole night, that she hadn't slept or eaten in over twelve hours, meant nothing. Only the game mattered.

It was good. It was very, very good.

Suddenly Fats's voice broke loudly through the edge to reach Eddy: "That's it, Eddy; You've won, you've beaten me."

Eddy blinked away the glamour, saw Fats for what seemed like the first time. The gleam was gone from her gold tooth; her hands were bilious green from the velvet and the chalk, her skin was gleaming with sweat, and her shirt was sticking to her stomach and tits.

Eddy smiled, wide and true, and shook her damp hand. "Thanks for the game," she said.

"Thank you, Eddy," Fats said. "You play a damned good game of pool."

Which Eddy knew meant she was the best. The best there was.

Daisy didn't know the girl's name and didn't care. All she did care about was that the girl was there in the bed.

She was fresh, maybe too young, but eager and willing. They'd started flirting earlier in the night, just an hour after Daisy left the pool hall. She was behind the counter in a place called, simply, EATS. Young, plump – soft skin billowy and yielding under Daisy's fingers – but best of all willing. It just wouldn't do, to have such a perfect opportunity and have no one who wanted to play with her.

The girl had actually blushed when Daisy had taken her coat, hanging it behind the hotel room door: "You're so gorgeous. I wanted to kiss you the instant I set eyes on you."

Then Daisy did, and the girl's blush deepened even more. "Th-thank you –" she'd stammered gently when the kiss ended. Was it for the compliment or the touch of her lips? Daisy didn't know what the girl was thanking her for.

It didn't take long. Her dress buttoned up the back, easy pickings. As they sat on the too soft hotel bed, kissing meekly and then with growing passion, Daisy's knowledgeable fingers neatly popped one, two, three, then all of the girl's buttons.

Weakly protesting, she'd tried to hold the dress together, only giving Daisy an excuse to tickle and nibble her mercilessly. When the tears had stopped and the laughter had died down the girl was in her bra and panties. Daisy looked at her for a long moment, savoring her plumpness: the way her breasts pushed up and around the confining bra, the twin little mounds of her nipples, the scratchy hairs peering around the elastic of her everyday panties, her gentle little swell of belly. "Tasty," she'd mumbled as she took the nameless girl in her arms, and kissed her long and deep as her fingers explored the seams of those panties.

Wet – a marvellously pure wetness greeted her hunting fingers. A wetness of legend, a hungry virgin's kind of wetness. Looking the girl in the eyes, she withdrew her hand to taste and murmur delighted sounds at the girl's savoury cunt. Then she pushed her back onto the bed, knelt between her legs, gently pulled aside her so-wet panties and kissed, then licked her into a quick, shuddering orgasm – one of many.

The girl was young, juicy, and naïve. When it was time for her to return the favour her tongue slipped and missed, her fingers gripped Daisy's thighs too tight, and her thumb and forefinger were too meek with Daisy's nipples. When Daisy did come, it was more from her own quick fingers showing the way than from the girl's timid explorations of Daisy's body. Still, it was a good come. But simply coming wasn't what made Daisy smile like a kitten that feasted on cream.

"I should be going," she said as Daisy let her hands roam over her luscious body. When Daisy found a plump nipple and gently teased it into rubber hardness she whistled softly in excitement. "Don't you have a girlfriend?"

"Yes," Daisy said, dropping her mouth to the nipple, sucking and nibbling it into even further firmness. "I do."

"What if she comes back?" the girl said with sudden fear.

"Maybe she will, maybe she won't – not for a while yet anyway. Not if I played it well, that is."

"I should still go," the girl said, but Daisy pushed her back on the bed, resting a firm hand on her still wet cunt.

"Stay. I want to come again, and I want to make you come again, too." Daisy bent down to part her fat labia and lick – once, very fast – making the girl whistle with a quick intake of breath. "I think I played it perfectly well; just the right amount of tantrum, the right amount of ego stroke. No, she won't be back till dawn, at least. She won't be back till she sweeps the table. We've got hours."

"I don't . . . understand," the girl tried to say as Daisy licked her harder, longer, circling the throbbing bead of her clit.

"My Eddy has her game, and I have mine. And mine is to keep her busy while I fuck you at least five more times. Eddy's good –" Daisy said with a wicked smile as she absently rubbed the girl's hard clit "– but I'm the best there is."

Wild Roses

Mary Anne Mohanraj

It started with a phone call. Sarah had been expecting the call, but it was still a shock. She had learned over the last few years, as friends succumbed to old age, and to one or another disease, that there were limits to how well you could prepare for death. It was usually cancer, of one type or another. Cancer had gotten Daniel, too. It was hard when it was someone you'd loved.

"He's gone."

"I'm so sorry, Ruth."

"Can I come out? Tonight?"

"Of course."

"The next flight down arrives at 8:30."

"I'll meet you at the airport."

Sarah put down the phone, meeting Saul's calm eyes as he walked out of the studio, wiping paint-stained hands on his pants. She bit back brief irritation at his calm. He and Daniel had never quite gotten along, though they had tried, for the sake of the women. Saul had been quietly pleased when Daniel's career had taken him to Seattle, though not so pleased when Ruth joined him there, a few months later. Saul had locked himself up in his studio and painted huge dark canvases, ugly compositions in a dark palette: black, indigo, midnight blue. But Ruth had been happier with Daniel than she had ever been with them, happier married and with children on the way. Eventually Saul had bowed to that truth.

Old history.

Sarah said, "I'll pick her up. You go ahead and finish."

Saul nodded, stepping forward and leaning down to kiss her forehead gently. "You OK?"

Sarah managed a smile. "I'll be all right. Ruth didn't sound good, though."

"No." He opened his arms then, and she stepped into them, heedless of drying paint. She rested her cheek against his chest, wrapped her arms around him, desperately glad that he was healthy. Some arthritis, a tendency to catch nasty colds; nothing that couldn't be fixed by keeping him out of the studio for a few days. After this many years, she could manage that, at least, even if she had to scold like a shrew to do it. She rested in his arms a moment, breathing in his scent, cinnamon sugar under sharp layers of paint and turpentine. He kissed the top of her head, and then let her go.

"I'll make up the bed in the guest room," she said.

Saul nodded, turned, and walked back into the studio, quietly closing the door behind him.

Sarah waited at the Alaska Airlines gate window, her face an inch or two from the cold glass. It was raining outside, a cold hard rain, typical for Oakland in January. The baggage handlers drove their little carts back and forth, luggage covered by dark tarps. The plane had been delayed, leaving her with nothing to do but wait and remember.

The last time she had made love to Daniel, they had been alone. He was leaving in the morning; Ruth had already said what they all suspected would only be a temporary goodbye. Sarah knew her own would be a final one, and so she had taken this last night alone with him. She had planned for it to be tender, sweet and slow. That had seemed appropriate for a goodbye. But instead, Sarah had found herself biting his neck, raking his back, riding him until they were both exhausted, until she was trembling with tiredness. Daniel hadn't been gentle with her either, had dug his fingers into her ass, had bitten her breasts. They had left marks on each other's bodies, dark and brutal and bruised. They had kissed until their lips were puffed and sore. And it was only in the morning, with the long night giving way to a grey sunrise, that their pace had slowed, that they had settled into a hollow of the bed, his hand

stroking her dark hair, her fist nested in the curls on his chest.
He had asked her then to come with him to Seattle. She had let
silence say no for her, and he hadn't asked again. Sarah had
gone to Saul the next night with Daniel's marks on her body.
He had been gentle with her that night, and for some time
afterwards.

The passengers were walking off the plane, some into the
arms of family or eager lovers. Ruth walked down, wearing a
dark dress, her eyes puffy and red. She had been crying on the
plane. Ruth had never cared what people thought about little
things. She cried freely in public. She had occasionally tried to
provoke screaming fights in parking lots and malls. She had
been willing to have sex in the woods, in open fields, had teased
and persuaded them all until they joined her. It was only in the
big things that she was at all conventional.

They had once travelled east together, two couples in a car,
perfectly unremarkable to all outward eyes. They had stopped
in Wisconsin, had decided to camp that night instead of staying
in a motel. Two separate tents, and the night sky overhead.
While Daniel and Saul finished washing the dinner dishes in a
nearby creek, Ruth had taken Sarah by the hand and led her
into the woods, searching for fallen branches to build a fire.
Sarah had dutifully collected wood until Ruth came up behind
her, lifting her skirt, kneeling down on dirt and twigs and
grass. Sarah wore no underwear in those days, at Ruth's
request. So when Ruth's mouth reached for hers, Sarah had
only to shift her legs further apart, to try to balance herself, a
load of wood resting in her arms, eyes closed. Ruth's tongue
licked under her ass, tracing the delicate line at the tops of her
thighs. Ruth's tongue slid up over her clit, then back again,
sliding deep inside her. Ruth's hands held onto Sarah's hips,
her fingers gently caressing the sharp protrusions of hip-bones,
the skin that lay over them. Sarah was usually quiet, but in the
middle of the empty woods, she let herself moan. Ruth's
tongue flickered over and around, licking eagerly until Sarah's
thighs were trembling. Her heart was pounding, and just as she
began to come, waves of pleasure rippling through her, as the
wood fell from her arms, Saul was there with her, in front of
her, holding her up – his mouth moving on hers, his chest

pressed against her breasts, and his hands behind her, buried in Ruth's hair. Then they were all falling to the ground, Saul and Ruth and Sarah and Daniel too, a tangle of bodies, clothes discarded, forgotten, naked skin against dirt and moss and scratching twigs. Leaves and starlight overhead, and Ruth laughing in the night, laughing with loud and shameless delight. It had always been that way with her.

Ruth paused at the bottom of the walkway, eyes scanning the crowd, passing right over Sarah. It had been over a year since they'd seen each other last. Between Christmas and New Year's, Sarah had gone up to Seattle for a few days. Saul had originally planned to come as well, but had gotten caught up in a painting and changed his mind. Sarah had come alone into a house full of children and grandchildren, a house full of laughter. Ruth had cooked a feast, with her daughters and sons helping. The grandkids had made macaroons, and each one of them had begged a story from Auntie Sarah. Sarah had left their house a little envious; Ruth had built exactly the kind of home that she'd dreamed of. And while it wasn't the kind of home Sarah herself had ever wanted – still, it was lovely. It wasn't until the following March that the cancer had been diagnosed. Sarah had always meant to go up and see Daniel again – but she hadn't, in the end.

She stepped forward, raised a hand to Ruth. There was the blink of recognition, the momentary brightening of eyes. Ruth looked lovely despite puffed eyes, slender and fair in her button-down dress, a raincoat over one arm. Her hair had gone entirely to silver, a sleek and shining cap – like rain in moonlight. Ruth came down through the thinning crowd, paused a few steps away. Then Sarah held out her arms, and Ruth walked into them, her eyes filling with tears again. Sarah held her close, sheltering her in the fragile privacy of her arms, until the crowd had entirely dissolved away.

Saul met them at the door. He'd changed out of his paint-stained clothes. Ruth dropped her raincoat, letting it fall in a wet puddle on the floor, and threw herself forward, into his strong arms. She had calmed down in the car, had been able to talk about the last week with Daniel. He'd gotten much weaker towards the end; in the last few days, he hadn't really spoken. Sarah's chest had ached a little, with various regrets. Ruth hadn't cried for most of the ride, but now she was sobbing, great gasping sobs, catching the air in her throat and letting it out again. Saul held her, looking helplessly at Sarah over Ruth's head. Sarah shrugged, put down Ruth's bag, and bent to pick the raincoat up off the wood floor. She turned and hung it neatly on the rack, while Saul gently led Ruth into the living room. Sarah waited in the hall, listening to them walking across the room, sitting down on the sofa. Slowly, Ruth's sobs quietened again. When it was silent, Sarah walked into the room. Ruth was nestled in Saul's arms, her eyes closed. His eyes were fixed on the doorway, and met Sarah's as she entered. She hadn't expected that, that he would be looking for her. She should have known better.

"Do you want some coffee, Ruth?" Sarah asked.

Ruth shook her head, not opening her eyes. "It would just keep me awake. I haven't been sleeping much this last week. I'm so tired . . ."

"Dinner? Saul made pot roast for lunch – there's plenty left."

"No, I'm OK. Just bed, if that's all right?"

"That's fine, dear. Come on – I'll get you settled."

Ruth hugged Saul once more, and then got up from the sofa. Sarah led her into the guest bedroom, turned down the sheets, closed the drapes while Ruth pulled off her clothes and slid into bed. She had always slept nude, Sarah remembered. Sarah came back to the bed, and stood over it, hesitating. Ruth looked exhausted, with a tinge of grey to her skin.

"Do you want me to sit with you a bit? Just until you fall asleep?"

"No, no – I'll be OK." Ruth reached out, taking Sarah's hand in hers and squeezing, gently. "Thank you."

Sarah leaned over and kissed her gently twice – once on the cheek, once, briefly, on her lips. "It's nothing, love. Sleep. Sleep well." She stood up then, turned out the light, and slipped out the door, closing it behind her.

They sat at the kitchen table, cups of coffee nestled in their hands, not talking. Just being together. Sarah remembered the day when she realized that she would rather be silent with Saul, than be talking with anyone else. They hadn't met Ruth yet, or Daniel; they'd only known each other a few weeks. They'd just finished making love on a hot July night and were lying side by side on the bed, not touching. It was really too hot to cuddle, too hot for sex. They had both ended up exhausted, lying on the bed with waves of heat rolling off their bodies. Saul was quiet, just breathing, and Sarah lay there listening to his breaths, counting them, trying to synchronize them with her own. She couldn't quite manage it, not for long. Her heart beat faster, her breath puffed in and out of her. But being there with him, breathing was a little slower and sweeter than it would normally be. Being with him, not even touching, she was happier than she'd ever been.

Sarah finished her coffee. "I'm going to go to bed," she said. "Coming?"

"I'll be there in a minute. I'll just finish the dishes."

Sarah nodded and rose from the table, leaving her coffee cup for him to clear. She straightened a few books in the living room as she walked through it, gathered his sketches from the little tables and from the floor, piling them in a neat stack. She walked into the hall, and then paused. To her right was the hall leading to their bedroom. Straight ahead was the hall leading to the library, to the studio, and then to the guest room. She almost turned right, almost went straight to bed. But then she walked forward down the long hall, and at the end of it, heard her. Ruth was crying again. Sarah stood there a while, listening.

When she came back to the bedroom, Saul was already in bed, waiting for her. Sarah stood in the doorway, looking at him. He lay half covered by the sheet, his head turned, looking at her. She knew what would happen if she came to bed. She could tell by looking at him, by the way he looked at her. He would pull her close, and kiss her forehead and eyes and cheeks. He would run his hands over her soft body; he would touch her until she came, shuddering in his arms.

"Ruth's crying." It was harder than she'd expected, to say it. It had been a long time.

His eyes widened, the way they only did when he was very surprised, or sometimes during sex, when she startled him with pleasure.

"You should go to her." That was easier to say. Once the problem was set, the conclusion was obvious. Obvious to her, at any rate.

Saul swung himself slowly out of bed, pulled on a pair of pants. He didn't bother with a shirt. "You'll be all right?" It was a question, but also a statement. He knew her that well, knew that she wouldn't have raised the issue if she weren't sure. He trusted her for that. Still, it was good of him to check, one last time. It was one of the reasons she loved him so. She nodded, and collected a kiss as he went by.

Sarah let herself out of the house, walking barefoot. It was a little cold, but not too much. The rain had stopped some time ago, and the garden was dark and green in the moonlight. She wandered through the garden – its neat paths, its carefully tended borders. Saul took care of the vegetables; she nurtured the flowers and herbs. At this time of year, little was blooming, but the foliage was deep and rich and green. Winter was a good time for plants in Oakland; it was the summer's heat that parched them dry, left them sere and barren. She carefully did not approach the east end of the house; even through closed windows and shades, she might have heard something. She also refrained from imagination, from certain memories. If she had tried, Sarah could have reconstructed what was likely happening in that bedroom; she could have remembered Ruth's small sounds, her open mouth, her small breasts and arching body. Saul's face, over hers. She could have remembered, and the memory might have been sweet, or bitter, or both. But she was too old to torment herself that way. There was no need.

Instead, she put those thoughts aside, and walked to the far west end of the garden, where the roses grew. It was the one wild patch in the garden, a garden filled with patterns, where foxglove and golden poppy and iris and daffodil, each in their season, would walk in neat rows and curves, in designs she and Saul had outlined. But the roses had been there when they bought the house, the summer after Ruth had left. Crimson and yellow, white and peach, orange and burgundy – the roses grew now in profusion against the western wall, trimmed back only when they threatened the rest of the garden. Wild and lovely. She had built a bench to face them, and Saul often sat on it, sketching the roses. Sarah liked to sit underneath them, surrounded by them, drowning in their sweet scent. She went there now, sitting down in the muddy ground, under the vines and thorns.

There were no roses in January, but they'd come again, soon enough. She'd be waiting for them. In the meantime, it was enough to close her eyes, feel the mud under her toes, and remember Daniel. The way he laughed, bright and full. The way he would return to a comment from a conversation hours past. The way he had touched her sometimes, so lightly, as if she were a bird. The scent of him, dark and rich, like coffee in a garden, after rain.

The VIP Room

Nicholas Kaufmann

Flickering oil lamps lined the perimeter of the lake, suspended from wrought-iron stands and casting a radiant glow on the dark water. A welcome breeze eased the warm summer night's air, and the glassy stillness was pierced only by the gurgling wakes of plastic paddle boats.

"This was a great idea," Anna said as they paddled their small boat toward the center of the lake. "It's so romantic here."

"God bless the Quick City Parks Department," Mark replied. "We should have saved this for our anniversary."

"They only keep the boat pond open this late on weekends."

"Still," he said, "it's only two weeks away, and this will be hard to top."

Anna took his hand in hers and kissed it right above the wedding ring. "I know you'll come up with a great surprise. You always do."

"No pressure," Mark said, laughing.

Anna looked at him for a moment, then pointed over to one of the small, wooded islands that dotted the shimmering lake. "Let's go over there."

Behind the low trees of the island, they stopped the paddle boat and floated in place. Before Mark could say anything, Anna leaned across the low plastic hump that separated their seats in the boat and kissed him. His lips were warm and soft, and she felt herself melting against him when he put his hands on her face, the tips of his fingers pressing against her dark blonde hair.

It felt like their lips were meeting for the first time, their tongues touching like long-separated lovers, and she felt a delicious tingle flutter through her.

She finally pulled away from him, leaned back against the low bulwark behind her and reached for the top button of her white blouse. She undid it, then the next and the next, all the way down to her black cotton pants. Anna gently pulled the front of the blouse open.

The day had been stiflingly hot and, in order to keep cool, she'd decided not to wear a bra under her top. All through dinner, Anna found herself getting more and more turned on, knowing she was completely nude under the weave of her blouse, and delighting in the feel of the silky smooth material against the tips of her nipples. She spent so much time fantasizing about surprising Mark at the lake, and about what she wanted to do to him, that she had to restrain herself from sticking her foot up his pant leg at the table.

Mark grinned and twisted to see if any of the other boats were around. He could see some on the other side of the island, through the dark cluster of trees and shrubs, but they were far away.

"Do you think they'll see us?" he whispered.

"Let them," Anna said, stretching and lifting her arms above her head. "Let them look." She let her hands fall to her chest, slowly working their way down to cup her small, pointed breasts. She could feel the skin of her nipples bunching together, becoming erect. She kept her eyes on Mark the whole time.

Anna let her hands continue their journey downward, sliding along her ribcage and grazing over the flat plain of her belly. Then she leaned forward and kissed him again.

"Let's make them jealous," Mark said.

Anna pushed him backward, and reached down into his lap. She took the tag of his zipper between her thumb and forefinger and pulled it down. The stark white of his cotton briefs bulged out of the fly. Putting her hands on Mark's leg, she leaned down and ran her tongue over the jutting cloth of his underwear. The bulge began to grow, and she heard Mark utter that strange noise he always made, something between a gasp and a sigh. She could smell the meaty scent of his arousal as the tender flesh expanded and stiffened under her tongue.

Mark ran his fingers through her hair, and another tingle thrilled through her. She reached through the crowded fly of his pants, pulled his briefs down, and tasted his warm, salty skin against the insides of her cheeks and on her tongue.

From her position, she couldn't look up at his face, or look into his eyes the way she liked to when she was going down on him. In her mind, she pictured his expression: eyes closed, neck tilted back, mouth hanging open.

In Mark's mind, with his eyes closed, it wasn't Anna using her mouth on him. It was Arianna, the boss's secretary at work. She had light brown hair, dark eyes and a body to die for. Mark imagined them in the copy room at the back of the office.

Arianna was on her knees, her full, round tits bared through her open blouse, her back against the Xerox machine. Mark stood in front of her, his hands deep in her thick, long hair, his pants around his ankles, thrusting his cock into her mouth so hard that her head was tapping against the copier.

He began thrusting harder in the boat, too, his fingers tightening their grip in Anna's hair, bucking his hips up off the plastic seat and driving deeper into her mouth. The climax pulled him apart inside, then snapped him back together. Mark, grunting, felt Anna try to pull away. Still gripping her hair, he held Anna's head down in his lap.

The way he wanted to with Arianna.

There were only two people Mark considered himself close to at work: Geoff and Tony. Every day at two-thirty they would take a coffee break together in the small conference room near their desks. The ritual never varied: Geoff drank from the grey mug, and Tony from the marbled black one. Mark couldn't stand using the same mug every day. Today it was blue.

"It's getting bad," Geoff said. "The way you look at her whenever she walks by."

Mark swallowed and put his empty mug on the table. "Is it that obvious?"

Geoff and Tony both laughed.

"Everyone's got the hots for Arianna," Tony said.

"But you're a married man," Geoff added.

"I don't know what's wrong with me," Mark said. "I think about sex constantly, and with all these other women. It's like I need it all the time."

"You're a man," Tony said. "We *do* need sex all the time."

Mark shook his head. "It's not just that. It's like I'm wired differently from everyone else. All my life I had a problem with monogamy. I cheated on whoever I was with, because I couldn't stand the idea of all those women out there that I couldn't have. I don't want to cheat on Anna. She's great; she's the best I've ever been with."

"Yeah?" Tony's eyebrow arched up.

"She's always game. She's up for anything, but she can barely keep up with me."

"She's your wife now," Geoff said, frowning. "Cheating on your wife is a whole new ballgame."

Mark took a deep breath. "I'm keeping it in my fantasies."

"Good," Geoff said. "There's a price on your relationship with Anna, you know. You ever cheat on her, you better make sure the price is worth it. It better be something worth losing her for. Because you *will* lose her."

Later, Tony asked Mark to come to his desk for a moment, there was something he wanted to show him. Tony sat in his chair and started flipping through his Rolodex.

"Geoff is full of shit," Tony said. "Not everything is so black and white."

"Geoff's affair cost him his marriage," Mark replied. "What he said makes sense."

Tony shrugged. "Maybe. Ah, here it is!" He pulled a bright yellow business card out of the Rolodex and handed it to Mark:

> ### WORLD'S LONGEST CONTINUING
> ### ADULT CELEBRATION
> *The Aphrodite Club. Est. 1866. Safe. Private. Discreet.*
> *Couples only. Must be over 21. Call for more information.*

"What the hell is this?" Mark asked.

"You gotta check it out," Tony said, leaning back in his chair and grinning. "It's basically a high-class orgy. It's amazing."

"I don't know," Mark said, looking at the card again.

Tony leaned forward. "Listen, you're a red-blooded American man. You have certain needs that the rules of monogamy won't let you meet. So, this is the best of both worlds. You go there with your wife, you *stay* with your wife, but you're surrounded by all these other beautiful, naked women that you can look at. It's like a real-life porn movie. And believe me, Anna won't be upset about all the other women. She'll be turned on. You both will."

"You've been there?" Mark asked.

"I told you, it's amazing. Listen, you said your fifth anniversary's coming up, and you've been looking for something special to do with her, right? Well, here you go."

Mark looked at the card again.

"Keep it," Tony said.

Mark sat at his desk, absently tapping the card in his fingers. The more he thought about it, the more it sounded like a good idea for Anna's anniversary surprise. Provided, of course, he could talk Anna into doing something like this.

But would it really take that much effort? One of the things that originally attracted him to Anna, and kept him attracted to her after all these years, was her sense of sexual adventure. The escapade at the boat pond was proof of that, and it wasn't the only time.

It was only their second date, with both of them drunk at a local bar, when she went down on him in the women's bathroom, her mouth wet and cold from all the beer. Angry patrons banged on the door, trying to get in, demanding to know what was taking so long, and neither Mark nor Anna cared. She let him come in her mouth, and then she spat it into the sink. Their second date, for God's sake! How could he *not* have fallen in love with her?

Just then, Arianna walked past his desk, flashing him a bright smile. She wore a tight black outfit, clearly defining that gorgeous body underneath. It was too tight for her to be wearing a bra, and Mark was sure he could see her erect nipples poking against the tight black top.

He smiled back, and when she was gone he let his breath out slowly. He didn't want to cheat on Anna. He didn't want to hurt her, or lose her. But the fantasy of Arianna's head tapping against the Xerox machine was turning him on again.

Maybe the Aphrodite Club would be just the thing he needed to simultaneously appease and exorcise the feelings that fought inside him. Maybe the thought of Arianna sucking him off in the copy room would pale in comparison to what he and Anna would see and do at the club.

He picked up the telephone, and pressed nine for an outside line.

Mark worked from home the next day. Anna was away at her office, and Mark was checking his work e-mail when the doorman buzzed from downstairs to say a messenger was coming up.

Mark opened the door, expecting to see some kid with dreadlocks and a bicycle helmet standing in the hallway, holding a battered manila envelope. Instead, Mark found himself almost unable to speak, his jaw frozen open for an eternal moment.

She stood in the outside hallway with the luminous poise of some ancient Greek statue of a goddess, carved with care and grace from a single slab of marble. Long dark hair framed a face of finely etched features and piercing dark eyes, then continued cascading down to touch the spaghetti straps of the tight red dress that hugged the generous curves of her slender body.

She held out a brown leather folder sealed with a gold magnetic snap.

"Thanks," Mark said, finally finding his voice. Her finger grazed his hand as he took the folder from her, and it was like electricity running through his body, sizzling through every limb until it ultimately surged into his loins and stayed there.

She smiled and turned wordlessly to walk away. Mark's eyes traveled down the creamy skin exposed by her open-back dress, down to the provocative swell of her ass.

"Wait," Mark called after her. He couldn't let her go, not yet. He just needed one more look. "Do I have to sign for this?"

She turned back to him, her exquisite lips parting to draw breath. "No, Mr Wagner," she said in a silky voice. "That won't be necessary."

Back at his desk, Mark ignored the waiting e-mails on his computer screen, and opened the folder. The leather was soft in his hands, and the gold snap came apart with a satisfying click. Inside was a thin, perfectly bound booklet with crisp white covers, announcing:

> *WELCOME TO THE WORLD'S LONGEST*
> *CONTINUING ADULT CELEBRATION*
> *WELCOME TO THE APHRODITE CLUB*

The booklet offered a brief history of the club, with large black text and plenty of pictures of the club's interior and the various important people who visited throughout its history; impressive names like Henry Miller, Anaïs Nin, Hugh Hefner, Marilyn Chambers.

> *The Aphrodite Club has been continuously open for business and attended by maximum capacity crowds since its inception in 1866.*
>
> *Founded by a small group of anonymous Greek investors interested in exploring the sensual side of adult life in a safe and responsible environment, and without interference from society's stifling rules, the Aphrodite Club instantly became Quick City's best-kept secret.*
>
> *Today, the club continues in that same spirit.*
>
> *The Aphrodite Club is designed for couples – or more – only. All are welcome in our luxurious and sanitary surroundings. The rules of society do not apply here, but rest assured, the Aphrodite Club maintains the strictest policies of safety and privacy.*
>
> *Call soon to make your reservations!*

Mark looked in the folder again. There was nothing else, no certificates of age verification, no questionnaires, not even directions on how to get to the club.

He checked his watch. Anna would be coming home in about twenty minutes. Mark took a deep breath, then called the Aphrodite Club.

The woman on the phone said they didn't have any reservations available for the next two months. Mark's heart practically sank out of his body. He'd gotten so excited by the prospect of taking Anna to the club on their anniversary that he hadn't even considered they might be fully booked that night.

And there was something else feeding his disappointment, something unexpected: the woman who delivered the package. She didn't look like an ordinary messenger; no, she was involved in the club somehow. He wanted to see her again, and the thought of laying eyes on her once more in the erotically charged environs of the club was almost more than he could handle.

"I was really hoping we could get in," Mark explained, trying to remain calm. "It's our fifth wedding anniversary, and –"

"Please hold," the woman interrupted.

A moment later, another woman's voice came on, a familiar silky voice that said, "No problem, Mr Wagner. We'll see you then."

Mark's heart skipped a beat.

"It's you," he breathed into the phone before he could think better of it. "You came by my apartment."

How did she get back there so fast? he wondered.

"Will you be there?" he continued. "At the club, that night?"

"I'm always here, Mr Wagner."

"Mark, call me Mark." He couldn't believe what he was saying, but he didn't want to stop himself, either. This was all too exciting to be checked.

"I'm looking forward to seeing you again, Mark."

"Me, too." In the reflection of his computer monitor, Mark could see the stupid grin on his face. "What's your name?"

"I'm called Priestess."

"Priestess," Mark said. "I like that." His mind flooded with fantasies of ancient cults of women-priests in sheer flowing robes, naked women tied to stone altars and struggling against their bonds, frenzied lesbian orgies in honour of their goddess . . .

"Admission is paid at the door," Priestess continued. "Three hundred dollars, cash. A copy of the directions to the club will be faxed to you right away."

"Let me give you my fax number," Mark said.

"That won't be necessary, Mark. Have a pleasant evening."

A moment after Mark hung up the phone, the fax machine started ringing.

That night, with Anna sweating and grinding on top of him in bed, Mark closed his eyes and pictured Priestess.

He lunged deeper into Anna, and in his mind his fingers were unhooking the red spaghetti straps of Priestess's dress, and letting the material peel slowly away from her naked body.

Then it was Priestess on top of him, not Anna, moaning as he pushed into her, kissing her slender neck and her beautiful, round, pink-tipped breasts.

"Oh, Mark, yes!" Priestess cried, arching her back and shuddering in orgasm. "Yes!"

And then it was Arianna, taking him in her mouth and sucking so hard her head tapped against the Xerox machine behind her.

"I love the way you taste," Arianna said.

"No!" Priestess was on top of him again, riding him hard. "Me! There's only me!"

He grunted, exploding inside her.

Screeching tyres . . . shattering glass . . . rending metal . . . the smell of gasoline . . .

Mark gasped and opened his eyes, disoriented. His whole body was covered in a sheen of sweat.

Anna was staring down at him.

"Mark, are you OK?"

"You didn't hear?" Geoff asked the next morning at work.

"Hear what?" Mark asked.

"Arianna," Geoff said. "She was driving home last night, and there was an accident. She's dead."

Mark stood frozen, his eyes staring off at nothing, his heart pounding.

"Mark, are you OK?"

The next Saturday was perfect beach weather. Mark and Anna decided to take the train over to Long Island and spend the day in the surf. The beach was crowded, and they were lucky enough to find a place to lay their towels without complaining that their spot was closer to the surrounding woods than to the ocean itself.

Mark looked around as they rested after a swim. Anna was reading a book and Mark, having neglected to bring anything, resorted to people-watching.

Once he spotted the woman in the yellow bikini walking on the sand, he was suddenly glad he'd forgotten his book. She had a perfect tan, and sun-bleached hair that blew behind her in the breeze. Her eyes were hidden behind black sunglasses, but Mark could still see her high cheekbones, thin nose and perfect mouth, highlighted by the dark birthmark near the corner of her upper lip. And her body; he hadn't seen a body like that outside of swimsuit models. She was slender and well toned, the muscles of her tight abdomen glistening in the hot sun, and she generously filled out both the top and bottom of her skimpy yellow bikini.

And then she was gone, lost in the crowds.

Mark let his breath out slowly. He turned to look at Anna – reclining in her blue bikini, the water from the ocean rolling in thin streams off her body – and thought he was going to burst. She met his eyes over the top of her paperback, and smiled.

They disappeared into the woods, deep enough to avoid exposure. Anna slipped off her tight blue bikini bottom, and bent herself over a thick fallen tree. Mark lingered, looking at the dark tangle of her wet pubic hair, smelling the thick scent of her arousal through the salty sea water that still clung to her skin, and listening to the desire in her voice when she said, "I want you inside me."

He slid easily into her, hunching over her back and kissing the nape of her neck. Mark's hands glided along her smooth, wet skin, up her sides and around to her chest, cupping her breasts, the wet material of her blue bikini top crushing under his palms.

His hands undid the clasp of the yellow bikini top as he embraced and kissed the woman from the beach, letting their tongues swirl around each other like snakes. The top fell silently to the forest floor.

Her tits were perfect, mashing against him, her nipples so hard he could feel them pressing into his chest. He kissed her neck and, moving down her body, kissed the hollow between her collar bones and, finally, held those big, beautiful breasts in his hands and sucked at them until she gasped.

He spun her around and bent her over a fallen tree, tearing off the yellow bikini bottom and giving her the fuck of her life.

Mark pulled Anna's blue bikini top off her shoulders and slid it down to her waist, then caressed her small, bare breasts from behind.

The woman from the beach cried, "I'm coming!" and trembled against him.

And then she was gone.

Priestess was bent over beneath him, moving her heart-shaped ass back and forth against his pelvis and moaning orgasmically. She twisted around to look at him, ran a warm hand over his chest and said, "There's only me."

He closed his eyes tight as he came inside her.

Rushing darkness . . . bursting lungs . . . no air . . .

Mark gasped, shaking and sweating, unable to remember where he was. Anna straightened, letting him slide back out of her. She turned around and looked at him, touching his arm in concern.

"Mark? What is it?"

"Nothing." Mark shook himself again. He was burning under his skin. "I must be coming down with something."

It was a small news story, buried deep in the last pages of the *Quick City Sentinel*. A local woman drowned at a Long Island

beach over the weekend, apparently caught by a fierce undertow and pulled under before anyone could help.

There was a picture of the victim, a photograph from her
modeling portfolio. She had sun-bleached hair, a beautiful
smile, and a birthmark by the corner of her upper lip.

Mark did everything he could to convince himself it wasn't
the same woman he saw in the yellow bikini, the woman he
fantasized about. It had to be a coincidence.

Mark straightened his tie as he followed Anna out of the taxi. It
was nine o'clock, the summer sun had set just half an hour ago,
and the sky was darkening quickly. He could tell the smile on
Anna's face was fixed there by sheer will; she wasn't happy
being in this kind of neighbourhood after dark, especially on
their anniversary.

The street was lined with rows of dingy tenement buildings,
their rusted fire escapes casting spiderweb shadows all around
them under the radiance of the streetlights. Garbage was
strewn all over the kerb, walls were brightly spray-painted,
and the street was practically deserted. The taxi sped off as if
the driver feared for his life.

"Where are we?" Anna asked.

Mark put a comforting arm around her shoulders. "We're
almost there."

He led her toward one of the dark tenements, checking the
address to make sure he had the right one. It looked no
different from the other buildings surrounding it – dirty, rusty,
spray-painted – but the address was right. Mark led her toward
the steps leading down to the sunken metal door.

"I'm so excited about your big surprise," Anna said, but her
eyes told him she didn't like being here.

Beyond the battered metal door was a cobblestone courtyard
about five yards long, lit by strategically placed colored flood-
lights, peppered with tall potted plants, and lined with
wrought-iron benches. At the other side of the courtyard
was a red wooden door. There was also a red velvet rope,
and a line of six people waiting behind it.

"Cancellations," one of them said.

"I've got a reservation," Mark replied.

"What is this place?" Anna asked excitedly. The fear was gone from her eyes, replaced with anticipation.

"My surprise." Mark rang the bell next to the red door, and it swung open. A woman in a silk Oriental dress, tight and red and flowered, appeared in the dim doorway.

"Do you have a reservation?"

"Wagner, party of two."

Anna tugged excitedly at his arm.

The woman stepped aside and said, "Come right in."

The door closed behind them. They stood in a short, dark hallway with tastefully flowered wallpaper and a luxuriously deep carpet. Mark reached into his pocket and pulled out three hundred-dollar bills, handing them to the hostess.

"Right through there," she replied, pointing to the gold-rimmed door on the other end of the hallway. "Check all your clothes in the room on the left. There's no charge."

"Check all our *what*?" Anna asked.

Mark locked his arm around hers, and said, "Follow me."

There was another short hallway with a booth in the left wall, and a black door at the far end. Another woman stood behind the booth's counter. She wore only a semi-sheer bra and white cotton panties.

"Your clothes," she said. "They're held under your name, and you can pick them up when you leave."

"What is this?" Anna pleaded, tugging on his arm again. But Mark noticed she was smiling.

"Just trust me," he said, and started to pull off one of his shoes.

Undressing before a perfect stranger waiting for their clothes was not the erotic experience Mark thought it might be. They stripped with robotically slow movements. He could see Anna trying to hide her concern – after all, she must have chosen tonight's outfit with measured precision, and she was probably wondering if her new Italian shoes would be safe in this woman's care – but she was game. She was always game.

By the time they stood naked beside each other and ready to pass through the next door, they were both giggling like children. Anna took his arm again.

"I'm going to stop asking questions now," she said.

They were both utterly unprepared for what they saw

beyond the door: a cavernous room, filled with red wallpaper, gold mirrors, vibrant green plants, plush brown couches, soft deep carpeting, the fragrance of a thousand delicate flowers – and people, so many people.

Everyone was naked. Mark and Anna walked slowly into the room, turning their heads back and forth, and staring in slack-jawed surprise at the debauchery that surrounded them.

To their right, two women were giving a man a tag-team blow job. To their left, a man was kneeling before a seated woman, his face buried between her legs, while two other women flanked her, licking her breasts. They heard a high, whirring sound, and turned to see a man with a woman on his lap, her legs spread wide, with both of them holding a pink vibrator to her clitoris. When the woman started bucking away from her playmate in the throes of passion, Mark could just make out the shaft of the man's penis engorged in her anus.

Mark stopped walking and turned to face Anna. Her eyes were wide, but she was smiling even wider, and he could tell she was getting turned on. He reached out with both arms and grasped her shoulders.

"Surprise," he said.

Then he leaned down and kissed her, holding her warm body tightly against his, feeling the soft press of her small breasts against his chest, and sliding his hands down her back.

"Let's make them jealous," he whispered to her.

She pulled him to her again, locking her lips against his so tight he almost couldn't breathe.

A gloved hand fell on his shoulder. "Mr Wagner?" came a voice from behind him.

Mark turned around to see a short, rotund man in a tuxedo standing there patiently.

"So glad to see you're getting into the spirit of things, Mr Wagner," the man continued. "If you'll follow me to the VIP room."

"The what?" Mark asked.

"It is your anniversary, isn't it?"

"Yes," Anna said.

"Then only the best shall do. Follow me to the VIP room, please. There's no extra charge."

Mark and Anna shrugged at each other, and followed the diminutive butler. He led them through the enormous room, then around corners and through corridors and other rooms, all similar to the first. Mark began to suspect, impossibly, that the Aphrodite Club was larger inside than the tenement could conceivably hold.

I wonder if she's here, he thought. I wonder if I'll see her.

Tony was right; it was like a porn movie come to life. They saw a man ejaculating all over the face and tongue of his girlfriend; a redheaded woman lying on the carpet with a man straddling her torso and thrusting his penis between her ample breasts, while a second woman, a brunette, ran her tongue between the redhead's legs; two moaning women, one on top of the other like a yin-yang symbol; everything Tony said it would be.

Anna leaned toward Mark's ear and whispered, "How do they keep this place clean?" She touched his arm while she whispered, and her hand felt hot on his skin.

"Here we are," the butler said, stopping before a thick oaken door with a polished brass knob. "Inside, you'll find complimentary champagne and chocolate-dipped strawberries, as well as private restrooms."

Mark opened the door, and the butler followed them in.

The room inside was much smaller than the others they'd seen, spanning roughly eight hundred square feet. The walls had the same deep red wallpaper, the floor had the same thick carpeting, but the couches looked bigger and more comfortable. There were a dozen other people in the room, some resting, some making love, and all oblivious to the newcomers' arrival.

A black door stood at the far end of the VIP room.

"Where does that one go?" Anna asked.

"A room designated only for our most special guests," the butler replied. "Certain personalities whose privacy must be maintained. I'm sorry, but you can't go in there. We sincerely hope you enjoy your time at the Aphrodite Club." And with that, the little man in the tuxedo was gone.

"Jesus," Mark said, looking around. "Where do we start?" His eyes went to the nearest sofa, where a man with a blond beard was getting a blow job from one woman while making out with another.

"Let's have some refreshments," Anna suggested, pulling a bottle from a standing silver cooler nearby.

They sat across from the bearded man and, sipping champagne from crystal flutes, watched as he ejaculated in one woman's mouth while kissing the breasts of the other. Mark found himself getting so turned on he couldn't wait any more. He grabbed the glass out of Anna's hand and placed it with his own on the endtable.

Remaining seated where he was, Mark pulled Anna on top of him, letting her straddle him, and slowly lowered her onto his erection. She closed her eyes and tilted her head back, gasping as he penetrated her.

Anna looked more beautiful than ever, writhing and moaning in his arms. Her mouth still tasted of champagne, and her tongue had the slightest hint of chocolate from the strawberries. Mark cupped one of Anna's breasts in his hand and lifted it toward his mouth, kissing the nipple and running his tongue around the small, pink aureole. Anna moaned again, bucking her hips against him.

From the corner of his eye, Mark saw the black door slowly, silently open. At first there was only darkness beyond, but a shape began to materialize out of the shadows, walking forward into the doorway: Priestess. She wore a loose red silk dress, with a plunging V-neck that went all the way down past her navel. She stopped just outside the doorway, looking at Mark with a slight smile, her hand grazing along the exposed skin of her torso and just slightly revealing more of one perfect, round breast.

The moment their eyes met, Mark's body was racked by the most intense orgasm he'd ever had, starting at the base of his penis and moving outward into his entire body. He cried out uncontrollably as he violently ejaculated into his wife. Anna practically screamed in climax, then collapsed against him in a sweaty heap.

Looking over Anna's shoulder, Mark's eyes stayed on Priestess. She didn't break eye-contact.

He finally forced himself to look away when Anna straightened up again and said, "That was amazing!"

Mark nodded, trying to catch his breath.

"I'm going to use the women's room," she continued, getting up off him. There were two doors near where a woman was pouring champagne on her breasts and letting her boyfriend lick it off, and Anna went through the one with the picture of a naked woman on it.

Mark waited until the bathroom door shut, then looked back at Priestess. She was still there, smiling at him. He got up and walked over to her.

"Hi," was all he could say.

"Mark," she replied. "I'm so happy to see you again. I've been thinking about you a lot."

"Me, too. A lot."

She ran her hand idly along her torso again. "You want me, don't you?" Mark couldn't answer that. He looked away, toward the door of the women's room. Priestess took his hand. Her skin was warm and smooth. "Come with me, Mark," she said, pulling him into the dark doorway.

Mark couldn't resist the fire her touch sparked in him. He followed her into a hallway, and the door closed gently behind him. It was dark, but he could still see her. A thick metal door stood in the distance. Everything else was black.

Priestess leaned back against the wall and pulled Mark close. "Will you let me kiss you?" she asked.

Her breath was sweet and cool against his face, and she smelled like flowers. Their bodies were so close together Mark thought he could feel electricity arcing between them.

"I've been waiting so long for someone like you, longer than you can possibly imagine," she said. "I knew it from the moment we met. When our hands touched in the hallway outside your apartment, when I heard your voice on the phone, I knew we had to be together." Her eyes bored into his. "I could *feel* you fantasizing about me."

"I did," Mark said.

"I liked it. So much passion. I can't stand the idea of you thinking about anyone else so passionately. You're not like anyone I've ever met before, Mark. You have so much energy. Raw. Uncontrollable."

"No one understands that about me," Mark said, falling into her eyes. "No one but you. I need constant . . ."

"Variety," Priestess finished. "An endless diversity of partners and positions."

"Yes."

"You're always looking for something new to keep you excited. I'm the same way; it's why I came here from Greece all those years ago. I can give you an *eternity* of satisfaction, Mark, and all you have to do is love me."

Mark leaned closer until all he could see was the smooth porcelain skin of her face. Priestess grabbed the back of his head, pulling him in.

It was like no kiss Mark had ever felt before. It started on his lips, then travelled to his tongue, his whole mouth, down his neck and through his entire body, as if his soul was merging with something divine, something godlike, through the meeting of their lips.

Anna, he thought suddenly. What about Anna?

The one thing Anna had always adamantly refused him was a threesome. She said she didn't want to share him with anyone, and five years ago tonight he had sworn to forsake anyone else.

He could feel Priestess moving against him; could feel the soft flutter of her dress as it fell off her warm body and landed at their feet. She pulled him closer to her, their naked flesh crushing against each other.

Geoff warned him there was a price to pay, that he would lose Anna forever if he cheated on her. Was Priestess worth the price? To be with her meant never holding Anna again when she was sad, never hearing Anna's comforting voice after a bad day, never feeling Anna's hand in his hair on a lazy Sunday morning in bed. Could he live with that?

Priestess looked up into his eyes.

"You're thinking about her," she said.

"It's our anniversary."

"I'm a jealous woman, Mark. I can give you everything you want, but your heart must belong to me."

"She's my wife."

Priestess shook her head. "No," she said. "There's only me."

The bathroom was completely mirrored from floor to ceiling, and Anna found it disorienting as she washed her hands in the marble sink.

The door opened behind her, and Anna glanced into a mirror, expecting to see another woman come in. Instead, she saw the short, tuxedoed butler enter the bathroom, locking the door behind him.

She spun around, trying to cover herself with her arms.

"What are you doing in here?" she demanded.

He didn't answer. Instead, he reached into his tuxedo jacket and pulled out a seven-inch, serrated knife.

Anna screamed as he leapt at her, and caught his arms in her hands. The knife hovered inches from her body. The butler had a surprising amount of strength in his small frame and, as Anna's arms started slowly bending, the knife moved closer to her bare skin.

He sank the blade into Anna's chest, all the way up to the hilt.

The little butler opened one of the mirrored panels in the wall, and stuffed her body into the space behind it.

"There's only me," Priestess repeated, pulling Mark toward her and kissing him again.

Mark knew she was right. No other woman could give him everything he wanted, everything he needed; not Anna, not Arianna, not the model on the beach. He belonged with Priestess. He belonged *to* Priestess.

"Come see," she said, taking his hand and leading him toward the thick metal door.

The enormous room beyond it was black, too. An unearthly green light filtering through the darkness.

A wretched orgy filled the center of the room. Mark was certain the desiccated, spent things writhing like snakes on the floor had once been human. The ravages of time and endless exertion had turned them into dry, withered, furiously copulating mummies.

Their jerking movements told Mark they had no control over their actions.

Their wasted shapes told him they would have died long ago

if someone – some*thing* – wasn't keeping them alive, keeping them fucking.

Their dead eyes told him to run.

But Mark's legs wouldn't respond. He couldn't move at all.

The door slammed shut behind him, and Priestess took his hand, bringing him forward to join the fray.

Cactus Ass

Cheyenne Blue

Susan often joked about cacti. Made innuendo-filled quips about the pricks; big pricks, little pricks. But she had never had a close encounter of the personal kind with one. She was a city girl; she lived in Denver, a western city to be sure, but a city that boasted as many espresso bars and alternative newspapers as it had cowboys and bucking broncs. And the only cactus she knew intimately was the one that grew in a terracotta pot on her kitchen windowsill, resplendent with prints of howling coyotes wearing bandanas.

Geordie Mick was from England, and he was the son of a school friend of her mother's. Which didn't mean much to Susan, except that she was duty-bound to entertain him. He was in America for two weeks, and had an impressive list of things he wanted to see and do. Most of them were garnered from the movies, and an outsider's view of contemporary American life. He also didn't comprehend distances too well, and Susan had to point out that a day trip to climb the Hollywood sign was not very practical from Denver.

So they moved on to numbers 23 and 24 on his list, which were a lot simpler. A visit to a real western town and a mountain hike in the Rockies. Susan had no idea what constituted a "real western town", but she consulted the tourist information and they came up with a suitable candidate that had the advantage of being in the mountains. Best of all, from Geordie Mick's point of view, it boasted several bars in its historic downtown district.

They set out on Sunday, but by the time they had found the "real western town" and Geordie Mick had tried several of the authentic and historic cowboy bars it was far too late to consider climbing any mountain. The altitude was affecting Geordie Mick as well, so they settled for a stroll close to the river near town.

They were a mile or so from town, following the beaten hiking path that ran above the Arkansas River. Below them, the river churned its way through the canyon, a deluge of water, ice blue from snowmelt. Rubber rafts filled with city people like themselves bucked and weaved their way down river.

The two pints of amber ale she had imbibed made her giggly. And she had a bursting need to pee.

"Wait here," she told Geordie Mick, who propped himself against a rock to wait, unencumbered by neither a small bladder nor a woozy head.

She started down the slope to the river, dropped her jeans and panties and peed like a faucet for a minute; a rush, a clench, a gush, a strain. The relief was incredible. She snapped her jeans, and started back up the loose slope to where Geordie Mick waited patiently. She was halfway up, using her hands to steady herself, when she slipped. She landed heavily, on her butt, and slid several feet down the slope towards the river.

Geordie Mick heard the thump and the howl of pain. He came galumphing to the rescue, a big uncoordinated knight with a shining face. His large, meaty hands lifted Susan carefully to her feet.

"You OK?" His hands moved carefully over her body, patting gently. Checking for broken bones, Susan thought in exasperation.

"Kinda . . . sorta . . ." she mumbled. "I landed on a cactus. I've got the spines in my ass." She looked down at her feet, at the barrel cactus.

Geordie Mick stared at her for a moment. "In your arse? Lemme look . . ."

She had no choice. She could hardly walk with several spines jabbing her backside at every step. She turned around, leaned over a boulder, presenting her ass for his scrutiny. He flipped up the loose top she wore and studied her butt. Tentatively he pinched one of the larger spines between his stubby fingers and yanked. It came out, and he displayed it proudly. "Got it."

"And the other few hundred?"

Geordie Mick bent to the task with a will. The spines were shiny and slid away from his grasping fingers. He smoothed the denim, trying to stretch it, get a better lock on the spines. He started to sweat. The sun was hot and the air thin. And that arse, presented in the air for him. His cock twitched.

"Can you get them?" Susan's voice, muffled by her arms and embarrassment, reached him. "I have tweezers in the car. Strong, surgical ones."

"I'll get them." Jeez, and maybe he could have a quick wank on the way back. A woman's arse always did that to him, tight and curvy. Geordie Mick loved that part of a woman, loved the feel of it slapping against his balls as he fucked. And he hadn't had a woman since he came to America. Fucking an American chick was pretty high on his list, number three in fact, right behind a visit to the Coors Brewery in Golden, but he hadn't told Susan that. He thought he better get the tweezers.

"Half a mo," he said.

Susan waited, listening to his shuffling feet and muffled curses as he ascended the hill. Really, it wouldn't be so bad if her ass didn't tingle. The sun on the back of her neck burned a little, scorching fair skin. The river roiled past. If she closed her eyes the sound of it filled her head and she felt encompassed by the outdoors. Nature girl. She envisaged herself spread over this boulder like a sacrifice, spread-eagled on sunwarmed rock. She wondered if Geordie Mick liked to eat pussy. Maybe not. He didn't seem the type. More of a missionary stroke type.

Falling scree alerted her to his return. He came down the slope too fast, arms waving as he fought to keep his balance. "Sod it." He was breathless with the altitude and his rush for the tweezers. "Here we go, love. Let's get them buggers out."

She felt his hand stretch the denim over her ass. The tickle of the tweezers and his grunt of satisfaction. "Got another." He returned to the job. Susan wiggled a little. His paw was almost cupping her ass as he concentrated. When he stretched the denim sideways, his thumb dropped down, brushing between her legs. She tried not to gasp, she didn't think he had noticed, and it wasn't his fault she was getting so horny.

Geordie Mick had noticed though. If she weren't wearing jeans or knickers, his thumb would be brushing through her bush. Just tickling her outer lips. His twitch of arousal had grown to a full erection. He wondered if she would notice if he adjusted himself. He applied himself to the task at hand.

"Last one!" He pulled it out and held it aloft.

Susan sighed, relief surely, but the fantasy of Geordie Mick fucking her here on this sun-warmed boulder was too delicious to let go easily. She moved slightly, stood up. And yelped as the unseen finer spines jabbed her anew.

She couldn't meet his eyes. "There's more of them," she said. "If I drop my pants, can you get the fine ones out of my panties?"

Strewth. Geordie Mick couldn't believe his luck. He averted his eyes as she stripped off her jeans, working them over her sneakers.

"Ready," she said.

He turned back to her. Glorious arse, sheathed in some sort of high-cut bikini pants. Red. He bent his head close to study it, and saw the curling blond pubes peeking out the side. His hands wavered in the air, before he put them decisively down on her arse. She yelped.

"Sorry." He bent to the task. It was easier at eye level. He knelt down on the ground, feeling the sharp little rocks gouging his knees. He kept a wary eye out for cacti. He moved his face closer, the better to see the fine cactus hairs. Jeez, he could smell her. Strong and pungent, blending with sunshine and fresh air. At eye level he could see the goose bumps on her thighs where he touched her, see the small damp patch on the gusset of her knickers. He kept plucking cactus hairs to distract himself, but it didn't work too well. Now his thumb rested between her thighs, a thumbprint into the yielding flesh. Her knicker elastic brushed the palm of his hand as he stretched the cheek of her bottom, the better to grasp the spines. She moaned slightly, a breathy little sound, barely discernible above the noise of the river.

"Am I hurting you?" His voice was raspy, as if he'd smoked

his whole stash of weed at once. Number 14 on his list. Californian weed.

"No." A feathery little sound. He could see her hesitating. "Take them off," she said.

"What?" Obviously he'd misheard.

"My panties. Take them off. You'll get the fine hairs better."

"OK." He rubbed his thumb over the moist crotch of her panties with enough casual disregard that he could pretend it was an accident if she turned and decked him.

"Fuck," she gasped. And pushed her arse back against his hand.

He stood and pulled her panties off. She lifted her legs in turn so that he could pull the panties away. He put them in his pocket. She arched herself over the boulder again. Geordie Mick ran his hands gently down over those white flanks, dipping around to curve under the crease of her bum. His thumbs met in the valley between her legs, lightly brushing the pale pussy hairs.

She shuddered. "The spines, Mick."

Ah, the spines. He bent to the task with a will. Sun-warmed rock, ice-blue river, salty twat in front of his nose. He felt like someone had dropped a coke bottle down the front of his pants, they were that tight. A bit of friction and he would blow like a rocket. He stroked those pale globes, pink pin-cushioned peaches. The spines were gone, but he continued his ministrations. Around and around he circled, each touch between her legs bringing him further to the front, stroking through the moisture. Christ, she was dripping, her thighs were wet, and her clit, when finally he dared to touch it with a finger, was like a bullet. He wondered if she would let him shag her.

She could blame the two pints later, Susan thought hazily. But right now, she wanted to be fucked. A nice solid thumping fuck, no romance, no tenderness. She wanted him to push into her, his fat pecker filling her. She spread her legs further apart and one thick finger brushed past her clit again and inside her. She was close. Geordie Mick had short, thick fingers. She wondered if that meant his cock was the same. One finger was still inside her, his thumb rubbing to and fro over her clit. The other hand pushed on her ass, callused fingers rubbing over the cactus rash. She didn't want to look at him, turn and say the words, but she heard the scrape of his zipper, the rustle of jeans and then the fat weight of his cock against her ass cheeks. She pictured him, bemused-looking probably, standing there with his pants around his knees, his cock dripping on her butt.

She curled her fingers around, embraced the rock and waited. She felt his cock drag down over her ass cheeks, push slightly between. God, he wasn't going to do it to her like that, was he? The tension tightened her cheeks, and he moved away down lower. She felt his erection weaving and bumping its way down to her pussy lips, hesitate and push. Wrong angle, the blunt press pulled her hairs. She tilted her pelvis; he grunted and wedged himself further in.

She stood on tiptoes, he bent his knees, she pressed back, and finally, thankfully, he was inside her. He pulled back, a tentative movement forward. And now, she thought, a good hard fuck.

He obliged. Seesawing strokes of his pecker. His hand crept around her hip, cradling her mound, rubbing her clit. Christ, she was hot and tight. And he could see that glorious bum with each out stroke, see his cock, veined and glistening with her juice, the clench as he thrust into her, the release as he pulled back out. Geordie Mick fucked like a train, just to hear the slap of his balls against her bum, the squelch of an aroused pussy. His fingers burrowed and teased her clit. God, she was wet, and moaning fit to bust.

Geordie Mick threw his head back, saw the wide blue Colorado sky above him, felt the shift and slip of sharp frost-weathered pebbles beneath his feet. Felt the cactus that had got him here in the first place prick his leg through his jeans and heard the race of the river through the canyon. And he was coming. The orgasm started from the pit of his belly, raced up his dick, tightening his balls hard up against his body.

He rubbed faster, got to bring her off too, banged harder, pushing into the heat. His fingers twisted, through the slick creaminess of her pussy, coating his fingers. And finally, fucking finally, she was coming. Clench and release, shudder of internal muscles and a shout to the air. And the jism rose in his cock, up, ahhh the build up, the swelling, until finally, the spurt, the wetness, the release.

"God." Susan put her head down on the rock. Geordie Mick rested his chin on her shoulder. His cock softened, disconnected. She felt his thick seed slide out of her. Her head was spinning from too much beer and screaming, her thighs ached from stretching, her pussy throbbed from the double pounding, rock-hard prick behind, hard rock in front. He levered his crushing weight off her. She imagined him flipping his prick back inside his pants, doing up the zip. She was sticky and wanted to wash, but she wasn't enough of a nature girl to imagine dipping herself in the river and letting the trails of semen float away downstream. Fish food. She found her jeans, held out a wordless hand to Geordie Mick for her panties, and she dressed, bunching her panties to soak up the worst of it. She would be uncomfortable driving back to Denver like this, but what else could she do?

He was one hell of a fuck. Tonight she would invite him into her bed and they could do it again, properly. And she would make him eat her, even if she had to give him a map. Susan wondered what he would taste like, what that turgid cock looked like.

Geordie Mick wondered if Susan would stop at Coors on the way back to Denver.

The Shape of Cities

Maxim Jakubowski

She used to come with me to foreign cities.

The ways of lust were impenetrable as it turned us into involuntary and much incurious tourists. After all, we couldn't quite spend the whole duration of every trip barricaded in our hotel room fucking like rabid rabbits, could we?

So, between the hours of sex, we walked, explored, I dived into any bookshop I would pass and she would buy lingerie (on my credit card), we ate too much, saw movies. The Grand Canal in Venice smelled; maybe it was because we were not in season; in the bay in Monterey the otters were silent; in Amsterdam, we had a *rijstaffel* which made our stomachs churn for hours later; in Barcelona, the Ramblas were overflowing with foreign soccer fans; in Brighton, mecca of dirty week-ends, television cameras were everywhere for a forthcoming party political conference as opposed to a blue movie capturing our sordid exploits, but somehow every city felt the same as it harboured our frantic fucks. They had no shape, just a strange presence dictated by the intensity of sex.

Of course, eventually, she tired of travel, of me.

All I now have left of her is this photograph. Black and white. Of a woman naked against a dark background. A hotel room, no doubt. It's not even her, I am ashamed to say. Just an image in a book that somehow reminds me of her. I never had a talent for photography, couldn't even master the simple art of photographing my lover by way of Polaroids. Sad, eh?

This is the way she looked as she stripped for me in a hotel room.

Maybe it was in Paris, a hotel on the rue de l'Odéon with

wooden beams crisscrossing the rough texture of the walls and
ceiling. Or then again it could have been the Gershwin Hotel,
just off 5th Avenue in New York City, where the smile of a
Picasso heroine illuminated the wall next to the bed and
watched our love-making through the walls of darkness. Or
whenever we also kept the light on. Maybe it was a small hotel
in Amsterdam, windows overlooking a murky canal, with the
noise of drunk revellers and cars parking keeping us awake at
night. Oh yes, we frequented many hotels. Those sometimes
elegant, often sordid last contemporary refuges of illicit sex.
The one in Chicago which was being renovated and where she
preferred to sleep in the second bed because I snored too much
(in fact, the final hotel that harboured our pathetic affair;
maybe the excuse was just an early sign of her fading interest
in me), or the St Pierre on Burgundy Street in New Orleans,
far enough from the hubbub of Bourbon Street, where I forgot
to take her dancing (she only did in Chicago, but it was with
other men).

Or the one whose memories I cherished best. Our marine
and pastel-coloured room at the Grand Hotel in Séte, where
the balcony looked out on quite another kind of canal, where
local jousts on long boats took place at the weekend. A coastal
port where she took a shine to the limping waiter who served us
one evening in a seafood restaurant, and seriously suggested we
should invite him back to the room later. Nothing happened,
but for months on end after that I would fantasize wildly of
watching her being fucked by another man and even got to the
point of lining someone up when we next visited Manhattan,
only to have to cancel it because she had her period that same
week.

In my dreams I wasn't even jealous to see her in the throes of
pleasure as another man's cock slowly entered her and I would
listen to her moan and writhe, and watch in sheer fascination as
her so pale blue eyes took on a glazed sheen. After our first
time, as I walked her back to the train station, she had told me
her partner would know immediately she had been with another because her eyes shone so much. No, I felt no jealousy at
the idea of seeing her perform with another. It would be for my
pleasure and edification. I would position her on all fours on

top of the bed, her rump facing the door and would let my fingers slide across the cleft of her buttocks and dip into her wetness as I would introduce the stranger to the beauty, intricacies and secrets of her body. See how hot she is inside I would say, how that sweet cunt will grip your cock and milk it dry. I would be the director, set it all up, orchestrate their movements, stroke myself as her lips would tighten across his thick penis and take him all in, sucking away with the energy of despair (hadn't I told you how good her blow-jobs were? she sucked with frantic energy as if her whole life depended on it but still retained that amused air of innocence in her eyes as she did so, demonstrating her sheer enjoyment of the art of fellatio, much as I hoped I did when I went down on her and tasted her and shook while the vibrations of her coming coursed through her whole body and moved on to my tongue, and heart, and soul, and cock).

So, she stripped for me in a hotel room. Now down to just her stockings. Delicately undulating, thrusting her pelvis out, shaking her delicate breasts, allowing her hanging arms freedom, her hands caressing her rump in a parody of sexiness, just like a stripper in a movie. No music, just us in the otherwise empty room. A jolt, a jump, a shimmy, there just like Madonna in that video, just a tad vulgar but sufficiently provocative, there exuberant like Kylie Minogue, but never as frantic as Jennifer Lopez or Destiny's Child.

And I drank in every inch of her body. The pale flesh, the moles and blemishes, the deep sea of those eyes which never reached bottom, the gently swaying breasts, the ash-blonde hair now growing down to her shoulders, the trimmed triangle of darker pubic curls through which I could easily see the gash of her nacreous entrance, the thicker folds of flesh where her labia, lower down, grew ever so meaty and protruded, the square regal expanse of her arse which looked so good in the thong briefs we had purchased together at Victoria's Secrets on Broadway.

Then she would look down and see me, no doubt with tongue hanging out and my erection straining against the dark material of my slacks, and she would smile, and my heart would melt. And though I right then wanted to fuck her until we would both be raw and out of breath, I would also strangely feel so full of kindness, a sensation that made me feel like a better man altogether.

This body I have known so intimately that I could describe every minutiae of her sighs, the look in her eyes when she is being entered, the stain on the left side of her left breast, the dozen variations in colour of the skin surrounding the puckered entrance of her anus and the hundred shades of red and pink that scream at me when I separate her lower lips and open her up. And the memories come running back, like a hurricane, rapid, senseless, brutal. Of the good times, and the bad ones too. Of the time we went naked on a beach swept by a cold wind. The visit to the Metropolitan Museum when she felt so turned on by the Indian and Oceania erotic sculptures that we almost fucked in the nearby restroom (I was the one who felt it would be too risky and by the time we had reached the hotel again, the mood had evaporated . . .). The e-mail informing me she had shaved her pussy and then a few days later another terse communication informing me that she had found a new lover and my anger knowing he was the one who could now see her bald mons in all its erotic splendour. The first time she allowed me to fuck her, doggy-style, without a condom, watching myself buried inside her and moving to and fro, our juices commingling. The evening we ate oysters, she for the first time, and she recognised their flavour when she swallowed my come some hours later in the hotel room.

That hotel room where she stripped for my entertainment and amusement, eyes lowered, a sober gold necklace around her slender neck, where once down to her fishnet stockings she slowly moved towards me – I was sitting on the edge of the bed – and, the delicate smell of her cunt just inches away from my face stepped onto the bed cover, towered over me and opened her legs wide, the obscene and wonderful vision of her visibly moist gash just a couple of centimetres from my wide-open eyes, teasing me, offering herself, my naked lover, my private stripper, my nude love.

"You like it, Mister?" she asks, a giggle stuck in the back of her throat.

I nod approvingly.

She lowers her hand and, digging two opposing fingers into her wetness, she widens herself open.

"You want, Sir?" she inquires of me.

I smile with detached and faint indifference. Somehow come up with some relevant joke which I can't for the life of me recall now. She bursts out laughing. Once upon a time, I could make her laugh like no other. I warn her to temper her hilarity and remind her of the time on the Boulevard St Germain when she had actually peed a little in the convulsions of laughter. She hiccups and lowers herself on me. The hypnotic warmth of her naked body against me. I am still fully clothed.

All now intolerable memories, of hotels, of jokes that were once funny.

Now, too much has happened since the times we were together and happy in our simple, sexual way, and she wants us to be friends, and no longer lovers. There has been a Dutch man, married, now divorcing, a Korean with dark skin and God knows who else. And finally I am jealous. Like hell. Surely, she insists, we can still have times together, just be friends, no sex, it's better that way. How, I ask her, but then I would, wouldn't I? How can we spend days in foreign cities, share a hotel room and ignore the fact her body and her eyes and her smell and her words and her cunt just shout out sex to me and I know I couldn't accept that ridiculous compact of just friendship any more.

You can go with other men, I say, and I will not blame you, hold it against you, I understand that I am not always available and that you are young and have needs. But she knows I am lying inside. That I would say anything to have her back.

In hotel rooms.

Stripping for me.

Laughing with me. Laughing at me.

In darkness she moves; I am deaf, can't hear the music she is dancing so sensually to. Maybe a blues, a song by Christine McVie or Natalie Merchant. Or "Sing" by Travis. Or maybe it's Sarah McLachlan's "Tumbling Towards Ecstasy" (the Korean man who later abandoned her for a Russian woman, after breaking her fragile heart, had introduced her to that particular music; ironically a man of melodic taste . . .). Or again that Aimee Mann song from *Magnolia* (we saw the movie together; oh, how she enjoyed seeing movies with me). I hear nothing. Can only try and guess the tune from the languorous movements of her body as every piece of clothing is shed to reveal the treasures of her flesh, her intimacy. The crevice of her navel, the darkened tips of her nipples (so devoid of sensitivity she would always remind me), her throat, the luminosity of her face, her youth, her life.

I open my mouth but I can't even hear myself saying "please" or "come back" or "forgive me".

She dances, my erotic angel, my lost lover.

The silent words in me increase in loudness, but she is lost in the music and no longer even sees her audience. Behind her, the hotel walls are all black and she is frozen like a photograph, her pallor in sharp contrast to the surroundings. Stripper in hotel room. A study in light and darkness.

Like in a nightmare, my throat constricts and words fail me totally. I shed a single tear of humid tenderness, all too aware of the fact that I will never again be able to afford a private stripper. Let alone a hotel room.

The Death and
Life of Edward Grable

Adhara Law

Edward Grable was among the greatest lovers who had ever lived. Were sex an art form, galleries would have devoted entire wings to the master and his work during his lifetime, studies in the evolution of his genius. The aura of artistry surrounded him and people who coveted his secret hovered around him continuously, hoping to siphon some of that genius off of him.

But none of that mattered now, because Edward Grable was dead.

To understand the sexual artistry of Edward Grable's life is to understand his fitting and timely death, and this begins in his youth.

His first lover was a woman almost twice his age. She lived next door to him in a split-level house, the kind that dotted every suburb in the fifties. Her husband paid Eddie – he was called Eddie back then – to take care of the yard, to trim the shrubs and mow the lawn and generally keep the estate ahead of the rest of the neighbourhood in that unspoken-of contest for suburban domination. Eddie had just finished mowing the lawn and was about to start trimming the shrubs when Mrs Carlson appeared in the door, her capri pants and tight pink sweater leaving no curve to the imagination. She leaned against the doorjamb and called Eddie's name.

"How about a glass of lemonade? You must be parched."

Eddie thought that sounded nice. He followed her into her kitchen, admiring the décor on the way – he had never been this deep into the Carlsons' home before – and graciously accepted the cool glass, the condensation dripping over his fingers in tiny rivers. At his last gulp, Mrs Carlson reached for the glass and set it with fluid grace on the counter, then settled a perfectly polished and manicured red nail on his shoulder. She traced the outline of his oxford button placket down the front of his chest. "Eddie," she whispered, "would you like to see the bedroom?"

Eddie gulped.

She led him by the hand to the master bedroom, her swaying hips enticing the young Edward Grable forward the way a snake charmer seduces the cobra out of its basket. In the bedroom, she turned to him and pulled him closer.

"Mr Carlson is away on business," she whispered in his ear as she began unbuttoning Eddie's shirt. She noticed his nervousness in the uneven rise and fall of his chest and said, "Don't be nervous, honey. This is perfectly natural."

They eased onto the bed, Mrs Carlson guiding Eddie's hands to her nipples, Eddie nuzzling the warmth between her neck and shoulder. There was something innate that told him what to do even though he'd had no such experience before. Amidst the sighs and moans of Mrs Carlson, Eddie worked the magic he didn't know he had.

It is said that prodigies are infused with an old spirit that guides them through their art, giving them knowledge that would take them years to learn in school. It is said that Mozart began composing at the age of five.

If Eddie could be said to be a prodigy, then this was his composition.

Mrs Carlson's surprise at Eddie's experience was clear. Watching Eddie through the years next door, she had seen him buffeted by the turbulence of puberty. She had watched him grow up from a shy, awkward, and gawky teenager into a shy, awkward, and gawky young man. She could not recall ever seeing a young woman on his arm.

She watched the blond bristles of his buzz cut as they moved ever so slightly up and down between her legs. "Oh, Eddie," she moaned. "You're absolutely incredible!" And with her back arched and her head thrashing from side to side, she came for the first time in years without the aid of her hand.

And so it began. Composition No. 1: Mrs Carlson.

Though Eddie visited Mrs Carlson as often as time and Mr Carlson's busy travel schedule allowed, he was suddenly beginning to notice just how many women there were out there. Women he had never met began striking up conversations with him on the street. Waiting for the bus downtown, he would be surprised to find himself in the middle of a pheromonally induced circle of femininity, soft hands accidentally brushing against his thigh accompanied by the sounds of, "Oh my, excuse me . . ." He would find himself making apologetic faces to the men who were left standing alone at the other end of the bus stop, scowling at him. He would later learn never to apologize for his gift.

His next composition was a young woman by the name of Marilyn Cullers. Only a year older than he, she'd found a way to sit next to him on the bus downtown every day for the past week. Eddie was oblivious to the wordless catfight that ensued every afternoon between the five or so women who rode the same route home that he did. Marilyn had schemed to be the first on the bus when it came to her stop so that she'd have first choice among available seats. Now as she sat down next to Eddie and smoothed her skirt, she shot a smug smile back at the women who gave her dirty looks as they passed by.

"Hi, I'm Marilyn." She demurely offered her hand to Eddie, who was staring out the window.

"Oh," he said, taking her hand awkwardly. "I'm Eddie Grable."

"Eddie . . ." She said the name as if it was a holy password into some unknown vault of treasures. "Would you like to come home with me?" Her wild whisper sounded almost like a plea for help.

She nearly tore her own clothes off as she dragged him to the bedroom, pulling at him wildly as she fell onto the bed. Eddie's artistry took over and soon he was creating art on the canvas that was Marilyn. His fingers and body moved over her as he watched her face carefully, controlling the moment so as to elicit just the right facial expressions, the right twist of the head and the right parting of the lips. As she moaned, writhed, contorted under him, he waited for the perfect moment and then released the power of his genius.

Her face was a study in angelic, epiphanic beauty.

Composition No. 2: Marilyn Cullers.

At a time when most men of his generation were looking for a woman to marry and settle down with, Edward Grable never even flirted with monogamy. The fifties gave way to the sexually liberated sixties, and though Edward never gravitated toward the hippie lifestyle, his sex life certainly espoused the free love sentiment that surrounded him. Still somewhat shy and socially inept, he didn't have to worry himself with the awkward task of meeting women; they flocked to him. And it was around this period that he learned the technique of slowing time.

He was in the bedroom of his small apartment with a tall, sleek redhead, her form stretched languidly beneath him. As his body slowly brought forth the art that was in her, he studied her carefully. Her eyes were shut, her mouth open in what was about to be a cry out. He realized that the moment was slowed so that he could work the canvas until it was perfect. It was as if he could get inside the moment, crawl around in this little bubble of time and stretch it, compress it, tinker with it until it was absolutely right.

He took advantage of it. He moved his fingers and his body, watching her expression change. There – her mouth was set so perfectly, almost but not quite an O. Now the eyes – he moved and played until they were open ever so slightly, just the way he liked it. She was ready. He let time expand back into regularity and watched as his work of art blossomed like a flower beneath him; he admired the delicate arch of her back as she came, the sound of her cries resounding against the walls of the small room. When the moment had passed, she smiled lazily up at Edward.

Edward Grable developed a photographic memory out of necessity. Where most artists had a gallery in which to display their work, Edward had only his memory and a sole audience of one – himself. Even his lovers, his compositions, could not see the genius in their own faces, being wrapped up in the moment as they were.

Awkwardness and social ineptitude eventually left Edward Grable as he matured through the sixties and into the seventies. In the early part of the decade, he moved to the west coast in a fit of artistic ennui. Word of his arrival had somehow spread prior to his coming, and women of the rich and famous elite were already banging down his door before he'd unpacked the boxes. He realized he had a new challenge: take the faces and the bodies that had been seen all over the world and transform them in his own vision.

He was invited to all the important social gatherings; he was often the only one who was introduced without a title. A simple, "This is Edward Grable" often made the new acquaintance's eyes open wide with recognition. If he was a man, he shook Edward's hand and for the next hour tried to pry Edward's secrets from him. If she was a woman, she used every ounce of her charm to get into his bed before the night was over. "Please," she would often say. "Let me be your next composition, your new canvas. I won't disappoint you."

Sometimes Edward took them up on the offer; sometimes he didn't.

He was getting discriminatory as his art flourished, choosing only those faces that, like a slab of unchiselled marble, told him what new creation lay hidden inside. And he no longer limited himself to a single woman. In the late seventies Edward embarked on what was to become known as his pivotal work – menage No. 1. A group of three women.

By now, people begged Edward to let them see a creation in the making. He only had to say the word and tickets would be sold at exorbitant prices, auditoriums would be filled to capacity. The outpouring of admiration nearly brought tears to his eyes. So he agreed to showcase this most astounding, most daring work yet.

He arranged the women on a soft landscape of velvet and satin pillows, making sure that the lighting was right for each one of them. The players were stunning – a young African-American woman with skin the color of flawless mahogany, a strong Nordic blonde with the bluest eyes he'd ever seen, and a delicate Asian woman whose features were exotic and enticing. The spectators were gathered at a discreet distance, none of them wanting to become known as the one who disturbed the master at his greatest moment.

He began with the Asian woman. They watched as he moved over her, his once awkward and stringy body moving with a fluid ease that was borne of his inherent talent. She writhed and moaned and her hands clutched at him wildly. While one hand worked between her legs, the other hand moved on to the African-American woman. She arched her hips toward him. And as he worked the canvases of these two women, he lowered his lips to the blonde.

The pillows were a sea of writhing limbs and colours, Edward's blond head and long arms moving in an orchestrated dance the way a conductor controls his music. There was not a single part of his body, a single appendage or muscle that was not somehow making these women sigh and moan and weep in almost religious ecstasy. Even the crowd, in a strange kind of sexual osmosis, writhed in tiny movements as they watched Edward bring the symphony to a close.

The moment was right. In that bubble of expanded time that only included Edward and his creations, he watched each woman carefully to determine the right moment in which to bring her to climax. He decided to go with the blonde first, then the Asian woman, and then the African-American woman in a dazzling sexual spectrum. While he moved gently in and out of the delicate Asian beauty, his lips and tongue danced between the legs of the blonde. Edward's art had become so refined that he didn't need to see the blonde to know when the timing was right to release her; he felt it in the core of his being. As her back arched and her eyes closed, he watched her quiver and clutch the pillows by her head in orgasmic ecstasy. In an instant his attention was focused on the Asian woman, her dark hair scattered over the pillow under her head like a halo in shadow. She came seconds after the blonde, her tiny mouth open in a small O. Finally, he moved to the African-American woman, who he had been saving for last, keeping her on the edge with his free hand. He moved down between her legs and watched as she threw her head back with wild shrieks.

The room exploded in raucous applause, shouts of "Bravo!" filling Edward's ears.

It capped off the closing of the decade nicely. Through the early eighties, Edward was often asked to repeat the performance, but he felt that every woman was an individual creation under his body, and any work of art that she was involved in was an extremely limited edition.

As the years wore on, Edward Grable grew tired of his art. In his seventies, he had begun to feel that he'd exhausted all the creative possibilities that sex and women afforded him. He had seen every nuance of the female orgasm, had seen every conceivable contortion of the lips, the eyes and the face. There was simply nothing left.

He had gone to a bar near his small studio apartment in L.A. to try and forget what the passage of years had done to him. As he ordered a gin and tonic and fixed his gaze on the old television above the bar, he heard the most beautiful voice reverberate next to him as its owner ordered a drink.

She was stunning. She looked to be in her late twenties. Her hair was gold without somehow being blonde, and her face held all the images that Edward had mentally collected over the years, all of his most striking compositions. This was a woman who would awaken his muse, he thought.

"You're Edward Grable, aren't you?" she asked politely. He could tell that she knew exactly who he was, but was demure enough not to fawn. "I've heard so many wonderful things about you." She extended her hand firmly.

They talked over drinks, and once again Edward could almost feel that bubble in time, and he tried expanding it and transforming it, not wanting the moment to end for a while. But it did end, and they sat across from each other and stared.

"I think we should go back to your apartment," she said quietly. It was not a question, or even a statement inflected as a question. It was almost an order.

Edward did not refuse it. His seventy-odd-year-old bones felt almost twenty again, almost as young as when he had first walked into Mrs Carlson's house that day and drank her lemonade and saw her bedroom and made her come. He watched this woman's hips lead him forward the same way that Mrs Carlson's hips led him forward as they climbed the stairs to his apartment. And he almost felt the same nervousness that he felt with Mrs Carlson as the young woman removed her clothes in a seductive striptease that elicited a croaking moan from him.

They eased to the bed. Edward instinctively covered the young woman's body with his, but she put a hand firmly on his chest.

"Let me," she demanded.

He gently lay back on the bed and let her.

She moved like a cat above him, her hands and mouth and legs all working in concert. He was amazed. The heavy lids of his eyes closed and he was back in Mrs Carlson's house, in her bedroom, listening to her sugary voice whisper, "Don't be nervous, honey. It's perfectly natural." And he heard Marilyn Cullers ask desperately if he would go home with her, and he heard himself answer that he would. And he saw the three beautiful women he had made sexual art with and heard their sighs of contentment as the audience applauded.

The young woman slid down between his legs and began working her own magic, sliding him in and out of her mouth with fluid grace.

As his back arched in delight, he heard the familiar whisper in his ear. "You were the genius, Eddie," Mrs Carlson cooed, long dead now.

"You gave to all of us, Eddie, but you never took any for yourself," he heard Marilyn whisper.

"You deserve so much," the blonde, the Asian, and the African-American all whispered.

Edward had never experienced the sexual ecstasy that he had elicited in hundreds of women. But as the young woman with him covered his body with hers, all the faces of all the women he had made love to, all the lips and all the eyes and all the arms kissed and embraced and smiled at him, all at once.

Edward Grable died, his face the ultimate work of sexual art, far surpassing any composition that he had ever created.

Alchemical Ink: Shattered Angel

Morgan Hawke

For Grey

The Alchemist was getting ready to close his tattoo shop when the bells on his door chimed. He turned and there she was, a shattered angel. She stood paused, frozen in his doorway, neither in nor out, motionless on the threshold, undecided.

The setting sun bled over the rooftops from across the street, staining her hair and cheek with the illusion of mortal wounds. The empty hunger in the crushed blue of her eyes screamed of lethal injuries haemorrhaging but invisible on the surface of her skin. Her mane was a lank yellow and her dead-pale skin was stretched tight over the finely carved cheekbones of her face. Her features betrayed a story of physical exquisiteness, brutalized to a mere shadow of their original loveliness.

His first thought was that she was too damn young to be so broken. She was what, nineteen? Maybe younger? His second thought was more practical; he really did not have time for penniless, injured street kids. He worked to viciously stamp out the twinges of sympathy oozing into his thoughts.

"I'm getting ready to close shop," he growled. "Are you comin' in or are you gonna hold my door open all night?"

She shook her hair, dispelling the impression of blood streaked across her face. Her glance was both fearful and feral as she hunched into her dirty jeans jacket. She flashed a nervous look about the brightly lit tattoo parlour then speared him with her feverish eyes.

"What?" he asked without humor, his tone telling her: I really don't need this.

With frustrated movements, he turned his shoulder to her. "Damn street kids," the Alchemist grumped to himself. "She's just another wounded pup waiting to be kicked." He locked away his tools and straightened the pages of flash art lying on the counter as he tried to ignore the look in her eyes. "Looks like another walking victim begging to get killed."

"Um . . ." The girl's voice was timid. "I uh, want a tattoo," she coughed.

Yeah, right, the Alchemist thought with annoyance. As if this kid has any money on her to buy a tattoo. She doesn't look like she's had enough to eat in a week.

"Do you even know what you want? I haven't got all night to wait for you to pick something out." He wiped his face with his palm then glared at her. She cringed back from his glower then bravely took a deep breath. Her eyes lit up with a terrible hunger.

"Yeah, I do know what I want." She moved closer to his counter, her steps silent on the tile floor. "I want one of those Japanese letter things . . ." The bells jingled on the door as it finally closed.

"They're called Kanji letters." His frown deepened as he noted that her voice must have been lovely once. Living on the street had burned much of its original beauty to ash. Why am I even talking to this obviously penniless kid? Inwardly he baulked. Shame at the way he was treating her, warred with his practicality. She's obviously had enough shit in her life and here I go, being rude to her.

"Khan-jee letters?" she pronounced carefully. "Yeah," she breathed. "I want one of them." She was almost panting with an unidentifiable, hungry need.

"Sure. What do you want it to say?" he asked then flinched inwardly. There I go again. I'm just a damned bleeding heart. He swore at himself softly and bitterly.

"What do I want 'what' to say?" She blinked in confusion.

He rolled his eyes. "Kanji letters are whole words or phrases in Japanese. What do you want your Japanese word to say?"

"Do you have one for 'beautiful'?" she asked then blushed furiously. "I want to be 'beautiful'," she added then sharply turned away from his gaze. Catching her image in a mirror, she glanced away from her reflection quickly. "Then maybe people will love me," she added in a whisper he could barely hear. Her eyes were suspiciously bright with unshed tears.

"Yeah." The Alchemist flinched as pity stabbed through his heart. He pulled out the page of flash featuring the Japanese letters he had collected. Sullenly he turned the page around for her to see, pointing out the simple but decorative oriental letters, or glyphs.

"Oh, how pretty," she sighed. He watched her eyes come alive with an unholy hunger and a joy too defiant to be as simple as hope.

"It'll be fifty dollars and take one hour." He raised his pierced eyebrow sardonically.

"I want a tattoo, but I'm broke. Uh, can I, um . . . Can I pay you without cash?"

"Pay me how?" the Alchemist asked, crossing his arms on his broad chest. "I don't do drugs so I won't take drugs as payment." He was pretty sure that she was going to offer to blow him or fuck him in trade for the tattoo but he wanted her to spit it out herself.

"Yeah, I heard you were clean," she said then looked down at the floor. "Um, I really want that tattoo." She glanced at him from under pale lashes. "Will you do it for sex?" she offered very softly, folding her arms across her narrow chest.

"You want to fuck me for a tattoo?" His smile was thin-lipped and without humour. I hate this kind of shit, he thought in annoyance. At the same time he felt pity creeping through his heart. It wasn't as if she had much else to offer.

"Yes." She blinked, eyes wide, caught off guard by his deliberate rudeness. "Sex for a tattoo."

"You any good?" he asked, trying to see how far he could push her. If he was lucky, she would leave on her own and he wouldn't have to join the ranks of all the rest of the people who had obviously taken advantage of her.

He cocked his head to one side in slight confusion. For someone who was trying to get something using sex, she wasn't even trying to work it. She didn't flirt and her jacket was closed to the throat. Not a speck of tittie was showing. If he didn't know better, he'd swear she'd never tried to use sex to get anything before. She was acting like she didn't know how.

"No, I'm not really that good," she said through clenched teeth. Her gaze darkened in rebellion then faded to sullen hurt.

Well the kid certainly has guts, the Alchemist admitted to himself. "All right, I'll do it for a fuck."

"Great." She smiled with a slight tightening of the lips. "But no weird shit, OK?" she added, taking a step back from his counter, her gaze defiant. "No hitting or cutting."

"Gotcha, no weird shit, just you, me and my dick in your twat. OK." He smiled ruefully. What the hell have I gotten myself into this time?

"Good," she said. She nibbled on her lip then her lips bowed into a dazzling smile in return. He was knocked flat by her smile's sudden and searing brilliance. He found his heart pounding and his palms dampening in sympathetic anger. And lust. His dick was hardening just looking at her smile alone.

Not that long ago, this little broken doll with her shattered eyes and straggly form had been a spectacular beauty. He could see from the smile alone that not all of her soul had been destroyed. Possibilities still shone, though dimly.

"Right," he said, unnerved, then flipped up the counter. "Come this way."

The Alchemist led her back to the stark white room he used, with its black leather medical table. His counters gleamed pristine with sterile cleanliness. His chrome tools glittered coldly in the harsh overhead light. The walls were covered with immense framed paintings.

"Wow, these are incredible," she breathed as she gazed at the swirls of colour and exotic, esoteric imagery on the massive canvases. "Whose art is this? I've never seen anything like it before."

"It's mine," he said curtly then knelt and opened the cabinets under the counter. "I did all of it." Efficiently he pulled trays of plastic coated, sterile needles and a couple of disposable wells for inks. What the hell am I doing, tattooing this shattered angel for a fuck?

"They're gorgeous." She sighed in awe as she looked at all

the art covering his walls. "I wish I had the cash to get some of your stuff," she said in barely a whisper. Then her smile reappeared like magic. She was transformed, practically glowing with a creative potential, a blinding inner beauty, that shone through her damaged body and refused to die.

Oh, that's why, he reminded himself as his dick suddenly sprang to attention in reaction to her untapped power. I could bring all that a little closer to the surface, he mused. Make it easier for her to utilize . . . Damn it! I am *not* a charity worker. I am gonna get my dick wet then go home, eat a burger, drink a beer and watch TV and not feel guilty!

"Thanks, I'm glad you like them, now take off your clothes." He dropped onto the small rolling stool by the table and rigged some needles together.

He watched her closely as she shrugged out of her filthy jacket then put it on the end of the medical table.

"Do you have to stare at me?" she asked defiantly.

"I'm going to be fucking you in a minute, I wanna see what I'm getting."

She flinched at his apparent coldness then turned her back to him. She toed off her filthy shoes then peeled out of her ragged T-shirt exposing a loose and grayed bra. Neatly she folded her shirt and placed it on top of her jacket.

Jee-zuz, I'm being a real bastard tonight. A twinge of guilt and compassion made him regret his harsh words. He bit his lip. "Actually, I want to find a good place to put your tattoo, so I need to see your skin," he said gently as an apology.

"Oh," she responded, very softly. "OK, sure." She shimmied out of her torn jeans then dropped her panties and worn-out bra on top of the pile. Carefully she collected her things then placed them on the end of the medical table. She was surprisingly clean. He hadn't expected that, from a kid living on the streets.

She turned and stared at him, silently, perfectly still. Bird delicate and fragile as blown glass. She wanted this tattoo awfully bad.

The Alchemist stood up and appraised his canvas of human skin. There wasn't much to work with. She was thin, too thin and made up of sharp angles. Good thing she had chosen a small design. His sharp gaze caught the tracing of old needle marks in the bends of her elbows and knees from drug use.

"What the fuck is this shit?" He felt anger beginning a slow rolling boil from his gut, helpless anger for the beauty that used to be there and had been wasted.

"I'm trying to quit, been off it for a week now." He saw desperation threaded in her wide, faded-blue gaze. "I'm tryin' to stay off the alcohol too."

I can fix that, his inner thoughts whispered. I can make her new again. I can kill her need for drugs and booze, give her a little confidence . . . The Alchemist's thoughts rambled with formula and incantation. I can bring her creativity to the surface so she can get a real job. Unconsciously, an Alchemical spell worked its way to the surface of his mind. Change the symbol, use the special inks . . . he mused.

Damn it. I don't do charity work. He snarled at himself, snapping out of a half-trance, awake and annoyed. I am not some Knight in Shining Armour out to save these kids from themselves. He angrily approached her, fingers outstretched.

"Please." She flinched at the look on his face. "You promised not to hurt me." She crossed her arms over her naked breasts.

Guilt and sympathetic compassion crashed down on his head. His hands dropped to his sides. He couldn't do it. He couldn't just fuck and tattoo this shattered angel. He simply couldn't be one of the animals that ate chunks out of her then spat out the remains. He wiped his hands down his face. She had nothing left to take and already teetered on the edge of the abyss.

He shook his head as he gazed at the floor. If something wasn't done, she'd be dead in a dumpster by this time next week. An image of her lying with her eyes open and lifeless, covered in refuse, flashed like neon before his eyes. Her tattoo wouldn't even be healed yet.

All right, I give up, damn it, he sighed in submission to his conscience. I'll fix this one. He shook his head and glanced up to the ceiling, at the powers that be. Resigned, he turned around and left the room.

"Hey!" the girl shouted. "Where are you going?"

"I'm going to get the inks I need," he tossed over his shoulder, "I'll be right back." Resigned, he went into the back room where he kept his special locker. He whispered three ancient words then tapped his fingers on the metal door over the handle. The magical lock disengaged and the door swung open.

The Alchemist pulled out a blue silk velvet-lined bag where he stored the tools for his Magikal Artes then slung it over his shoulder. Roughly he pulled out his Grimoire, the book he recorded all his incantations and his magical recipes in. He slammed the metal cabinet closed.

The Alchemist stalked back into his workroom towing a rolling table. He dropped his Magikal Artes bag down on the counter then dropped his Grimoire on the rolling table. He flipped open the huge silver buckled and leather-bound book. Thumbing painstakingly through the parchment pages he stopped on a particular page and peered at his list of alchemical sigils. Carefully he chose the magical symbol he intended to use on her.

She leaned against the padded bench, waiting. Critically he eyed her. He could make out every rib. Her hipbones obscenely jutted out over her pubic bone.

"Turn around," he said. She turned obediently. Every vertebra down her curved spine was clearly defined. There at the top of her ass, where the swell of her buttocks began, was the perfect place. Now he needed to check her chakras, the individual energy centers of her body, to see what type of repairs she needed most and what would heal itself with only a little prodding.

"I'm going to touch your skin, so don't freak out on me," he said softly, reassuringly.

"Oh, OK," she said, barely breathing. Her shoulders visibly tensed. He could just picture her with her eyes closed, biting her lip, ready to endure his touch. He stepped behind her and lifted his palms. His fingertips brushed the top of her head then skated down, barely disturbing her hair.

Hmm, intelligent, he thought to himself as the energy of her mind curled like warm mist under his probe. His fingers travelled lower to her throat. Strong currents curled under his fingers spiking with unused talent and true power, informing him of her past training and shadows of former glory. "Did you sing?" he asked gently.

"Yeah, I sang in school. I was, um," her voice broke and shattered. She hitched a breath. "I had a scholarship to the School of the Arts for um, mezzo soprano." Her voice dropped to a whisper. "Um, opera singing, you know?"

"What happened?" he found himself asking as his fingers traced the ridges of her spine. He stopped at a point between her shoulder blades over where her heart was located. The energy around her heart was thin and very weak. There was a jagged hole in her heart energy that looked like someone had ripped a piece of it out.

Ah, broken heart, he thought with a flash of returning anger. Some ass ruined her. His own heart began pounding with a stuttered and almost broken rhythm, as though a portion were missing from his own heart.

"There was this guy that I met," she said. "He told me he loved me." She sniffed but didn't cry.

"Let me guess," he said, growing more pissed off by the second, "this asshole told you everything you wanted to hear then left you high and dry after a couple of months." The Alchemist slid his hand around in a circle and noted that she had actually been in love. The asshole had used that love as a tool to hold her long enough to feed off of her like a psychic vampire.

"I moved in with him and everything." She was shaking. "One day, I came home and he told me to get out." A single silver tear escaped her eye. "He'd moved this other girl in with him." A hand fluttered up and wiped at her eye.

"I see," he mumbled. There was heavy scarring in the power centre of her heart where the asshole had been emotionally abusing her for months. He could tell that she had tried to heal it.

"He told me he didn't know what he ever saw in me." She squeezed both eyes shut and took a deep breath. "He told me he never wanted to see me again."

"And you didn't have any place to go," he supplied. His fingers slid down to the cradle of her hips where her personal shields and spirit normally sat. What the hell? he thought, wincing from the screaming spiritual pain she was suffering.

There it was, a gaping, festering hole where all her confidence and self-worth; her soul, was supposed to be. He could practically make out the individual bite marks where she was being spiritually eaten alive. It sat right under the area where he wanted to mark the tattoo. Apparently his instincts had known where to look before he did.

The Alchemist could see several fresh bites out of her soul, some as new as the past day or so, but some of the bite marks were much older and grey with scarring. There was barely enough of her soul left to keep her from slitting her own wrists.

"I was in school at the time. I didn't have a job," she sighed and took a deep breath, getting a grip on herself. "And I couldn't go home."

"Why not?" he asked. Then a twisted and nasty feeling drifted from her very last and bottom chakra. The boyfriend had nearly finished the job, but the boyfriend couldn't have been around long enough to cause this amount of damage. Some of the nastier, heavier scars were years old. It looked as though someone had been feeding on her soul for decades.

He dropped his hand lower to investigate. There appeared to be major blackened areas that looked like burn-marks on her lowest chakra, where sexual energy was generated. Rape, he thought. These burns are caused by hate sex. Shit, he swore to himself.

"I had stuff at home and I wanted out. That's why I went with this guy in the first place."

"Gotcha," he said aloud. She couldn't go home because a violent and abusive family member was waiting there.

I can still fix her, he thought. She isn't completely gone yet, but she's close. Too close. This job is going to be a bitch, but I can do it.

The Alchemist placed his hands on her naked shoulders. She tensed. Her aura and energy was so low, there was a chill to her skin. Softly, gently, he rubbed. He projected calm and safety from his thoughts directly through his palms into her body. Gradually she relaxed under his hands.

"I got a deal for you," the Alchemist said, and then he lied.

"There's this design I've been working on, one of my pieces of art like what's on the walls. I wanna put it on you."

"Wow, really?" She looked around at his exotic and brilliant paintings. "Sure! That'd be way cool," she said softly.

"I wanna put it right here," he whispered against the cup of her ear and placed his palm on the base of her spine. He leaned forward and pressed his chest lightly against her spine, sharing skin, sharing body heat. Their spirits touched and entwined, sharing energy and sharing desire.

He felt the sexual energy stirring in her and shoved a bit more of his power into her, feeding her essence, her soul, directly from his. Her head came up and she shuddered under his touch but not with fear. A soft breathy moan escaped her lips.

He took his other hand and placed it on her stomach then slid his fingers up between her breasts, over her heart. He watched as her nipples hardened at the tips of the soft under-nourished mounds. He could feel as excitement coiled low in her belly, sparking an answering fire in him through their spiritual link. He felt himself growing harder. The Alchemist took his hands away.

She dropped her head with an expelled breath as though released from a spell. Timidly, she looked back at him.

He locked eyes with her then peeled out of his shirt, exposing his flat stomach, muscular shoulders and the titanium rings that pierced both of his nipples. Swirls of brilliant colour and splashes of stark black marked his skin from his throat down. Esoteric sigils and glyphs, mythical beasts, flowers and flames in every shade swirled and twisted around his muscular torso and banded his arms.

He toed out of his boots, then his hands went to the button of his jeans. Her eyes dropped to where his urgency was mani-festly evident and pressing against the imprisoning denim.

Watching her reactions, he unzipped and skinnied out of his snug jeans. His erection lunged out and up, full and brooding. It was tattooed with a dark red serpent.

She hissed in surprise then her pink tongue darted out to lick her lips. Apparently, he thought, she likes what she's seeing. Her breasts rose as she took a deep, fascinated breath. A delicate flush pinked her skin and her eyes dilated.

"Turn around and lay on your belly across the bench," he said, his voice husky with growing passion. "Put your hands over the edge and hold on to the leather strap there." She took a last look at him then silently obeyed.

The Alchemist went to his Magikal Artes bag and spread the necessary tools and some temporary inkwells out on the small rolling table. He laid the huge Grimoire spell book in the middle. Sealed and sterile needles were placed next to the shining chrome of a filigreed tattoo gun.

Over on the counter he lit a red pillar candle and scattered incense over a hot coal in an ornate silver chafing dish. Thick white smoke filled the room with the scent of exotic resins. He set a CD in the CD-player and hit "repeat all" then "scramble". The entire shop vibrated with brooding instrumental music.

He pulled the rolling table with his equipment over to where she lay across the bench. Carefully he pulled from his Magikal Artes bag several ornate glass bottles with the special inks from his personal collection. The recipes for his inks were hard-won and the ingredients very difficult to come by. Some of the inks glowed through the smoked glass. With steady hands he set to filling his temporary wells with brilliants.

He set everything in place on the table then raised his head, closed his eyes and cleared his thoughts. Latin words rolled from his lips in a guttural whisper. He opened his eyes and stepped directly behind her. She turned her head to look – she seemed to be panting in fright.

"Look at the wall in front of you, not at me, Angel."

She turned away. When he placed his hands on her shoulders, she jumped. He moved his palms in slow, relaxing circles down her back, petting her. He caressed her soft surprisingly delicate skin as he would stroke a cat to calm it. Her breathing slowed and deepened as she relaxed under his touch.

"I need to shave the area I'm going to be working, so don't freak, and don't jump, OK?" She nodded and he reached for an antique, ivory handled, straight razor that sat next to his book. He brushed the base of her spine with the palm of his hand then lightly used the razor with quick deft strokes to clean her skin. He wiped the fine hairs from the blade on a clean rag then closed the blade and put it back on the table.

Moving carefully so he wouldn't alarm her, he leaned over and into her, pressing his thighs and his fierce erection against the softness of her buttocks.

She widened her stance, opening her thighs and her soft vulnerable flesh to the coming invasion.

"Now comes the fun part," he murmured to her. "I need you to hold very, very still. Don't move, no matter what. Got it?" He shifted his cock under her and against the soft curls of her mound.

"Uh, huh," she sighed and her body tensed under him.

He pressed his palm to her lower back then gently slid the fingers of his other hand down her spine to the seam of her buttocks then in and further down. Deeper his fingers slithered, past and over the tight rose of her anus until he touched intimate curls then damp pouting flesh. He moved his fingertips, nestling between the damp folds to dip gently into the opening of her well, touching moisture. She stiffened and a hiss escaped her lips.

"Just breathe, Angel, breathe deep," he whispered. He felt her take a deep breath. He speared her slowly with his fingers. She took another breath and he moved his fingers rhythmically within her.

"That feels good," she sighed then moaned but held her body still. He felt the muscles of her body relax around his hand, then a warm wetness slicked his palm.

"Good girl," he said softly. He pulled his fingers from her and raised them to his lips. Sucking them into his mouth, he tasted the sweetness of her honey. Generously using his tongue, he wet his fingers then wiped the saliva on his hand over the crown of his cock then down his shaft.

He angled his serpent cock up, nosing himself closer to his fingers and her waiting pussy. With the blunt head of his red tattooed snake, he nudged her entrance. He rubbed against her, easing between her folds. Then he stopped and waited.

"Are you ready, Angel?" the Alchemist asked softly. She took a deep steadying breath then another. He felt her body relax around him. She nodded.

He shoved, burrowing into her damp heat. Oh, God, she's so damn tight, he thought.

She whimpered then moaned as he filled and stretched her slick, hot flesh. Her damp sheath gripped him tightly. She suddenly undulated, voluptuously rolling her spine with pleasure as she worked to get him deeper into her body.

He groaned. Unconsciously he pulled back then slid in deeper, pressing his hips against the soft fullness of her ass.

Control, damn it! Control! he reminded himself. He wanted nothing more than to take her hard and fast then spill into her. But that would defeat the purpose. The spell required restraint. To do this right, he had to hold his passion right on the edge of coming until he was done with the tattoo. Once the art was finished, he had to bring her to orgasm at the same moment as his climax to trigger and bind the spell.

"Close your legs, Angel," he panted. "I need you to hold me in while I work." She pulled her thighs together, clamping down even tighter on his lodged flesh. He hissed with the sensation then took a deep breath.

"Good girl." He took another deep steadying breath. His hardness throbbed in her hot grip. "Okay, I'm gonna coat the area where the tattoo's gonna be with some petroleum jelly to lube the needles." Dipping two fingers in the slick jelly, he slathered the base of her spine with a light coating. Replacing the jar, he readied his inkwells then reached for his tattoo gun.

"Okay, Angel, here we go." Buzzing from the gun hummed under the throbbing music pouring from the speakers.

The Alchemist began to chant. He spoke softly but clearly in an antique language. He placed the palm of his other hand on her back, over her heart. His voice rose and fell rhythmically, hypnotically in time with the instrumental music. He concentrated, forcing calm through his spell directly into her heart. She relaxed under his hand, taking deeper and deeper breaths until he felt her slip into a light trance.

Chanting over and over, he touched the needles to her naked and vulnerable skin. They pierced her fragile flesh and still he chanted.

Agonizingly slow, he pulled his heavy cock out of her moist sheath then slid back in.

His hands moved steadily and calmly as he vibrated the needles in elegant curves. A soft rag swiped excess ink and blood droplets from her skin as he worked. His mantra shifted in intent and purpose as he began carving and reshaping her soul through his enchantments.

He slid in and then out of her still body. Her honey drooled down his shaft to dribble down his balls.

She breathed steadily, right on the edge of true sleep. A light sweat formed on her skin as her semi-conscious body reacted to the droning pain of the needles and the slow fuck.

The music pulsed as his voice droned on. In and out he fucked. Sweat formed on his brow. The sigil on the small of her back took shape then colour as he changed needles and shifted inks. His heart pounded in his ears in time with the music and his chanting. He wove subtleties and variations into the spell he drew in permanent ink on the canvas of her skin.

His calves and ass muscles ached from pushing. His balls felt knotted and tight as he kept control as he thrust, fucking consistently enough to stay hard but not enough to come.

Focused and relentless, he worked, seeking to repair the damage and put her soul back together. The sigil took form in a riotous blaze of colour and purpose under his hands.

Then the drawing was complete. He snapped off the gun and placed it on the open book. Now, to finish it and set the spell, he thought. His chant shifted in tone and purpose.

The girl's breathing began to change as she rose up from her sleepy trance. She awakened fully with a breathless groan of rising passion. She pushed up from the bench and back onto his cock.

He slid his hands around her to cup her breasts. He squeezed gently, then tightened his grip. He tugged lightly on her hard nipples.

She undulated as she rocked her hips and fucked him back. Her body shuddered around him as waves of pleasure began to shove her toward climax.

He slid a hand down to cup her heat. His fingers delved to where their bodies joined and he touched her. Lightly he stroked and a moan escaped from her lips. She was very, very close. He pushed into her body harder and faster, increasing the tempo. His breath panted the words of the spell.

And still he chanted. He felt the tightening in his balls and the warm roll in his depths that warned of imminent climax. He wet his fingers in his mouth, tasting her passion, her excitement. Then he slid his hand back under her and delicately fluttered his wet fingers against her tender, swollen bud.

Magical power snaked up her body then roared to life as her orgasm consumed her. She moaned as her body hungrily clenched around his flesh lodged within her, pulling, sucking. He stiffened impossibly hard in her slick, pulsing sheath.

He finished the chant with a shout.

His soul alchemically and intimately locked with hers. He felt his body seized by her brutal pleasure and imprisoned as she forced him to share her ecstasy. Release ripped through him as wave after wave of frenzied rapture slammed back and forth between them and through them. Together they screamed.

"Angel, I want you to deliver this letter to a friend of mine. She'll give you a job and can probably find you a place to crash too." The Alchemist scribbled on a piece of fine parchment then folded it. Peeking below his lashes, he noticed that her aura was much brighter now.

Still naked and sweating from his labours, he sat on the rolling stool and leaned on the counter heavily. He heated the stick of violet sealing wax in the candle flame then let the melted wax spatter on the folds of the delicate paper. He picked up a silver stamp and pressed his shop logo, which just happened to be his Alchemical seal, into the soft wax. Scribbling some more, he addressed it.

"It's so beautiful," the delicate girl said as she gazed at her new tattoo with a hand mirror. Her smile was blinding. She glanced at him then took the folded parchment from his fingers. "This is the stripper joint down the block," she said frowning. "I'm getting a job as a stripper?"

"Hell, no," he said with a weary smile. "You're too damned skinny." He pulled a pack of cigarettes from a drawer in the counter and lit one on the scarlet candle. "You're getting a job as a cocktail waitress." He sucked in some smoke and examined her, while she slowly got dressed. "This way you get paid regularly and get to keep your tips too." He frowned as he realized that the T-shirt she was struggling into had more holes than fabric.

"That shirt's nasty," he commented. With a tired groan he dug into a lower drawer and yanked out one of the XL black T-shirts imprinted with his shop logo. "Put this on. It's clean."

"But . . ." she whispered as she tugged her dirty sneakers on. "OK." She tugged the dirty shirt back off then pulled the new one on. The Alchemist yanked her old shirt from her fingers and threw it over his shoulder. She looked over to the corner where her old shirt flopped half-in and half-out of the small trashcan in the corner.

"Oh? But?" he repeated with a tight grin. "The shirt's free, or you can pay me back after you get paid. As to the job, she's a friend of mine. She helped me once so I'm sending you to her, so she can help you too." He rose from the stool and wearily dragged on his jeans, zipping them but leaving them unbuttoned.

He led her by the hand to the front door. Night had fallen and the moon was up and full, sailing through a clear starry sky.

Angel gazed at the lights on the buildings across the street then up at the moon. "I guess I better be going."

"My friend should be there right now," said the Alchemist softly. "So why don't you go straight there?" He tapped the parchment letter in her hand. "She usually has food too; she likes her girls well fed. I'll call her and tell her you're coming." The bells on the door jingled as he opened it for her.

"I guess this is goodbye and I won't see you again," she said softly. Hurt crept into her eyes.

"Shit, no, Angel. I expect you to come back in a few weeks so I can check on that tattoo." He grinned then opened his arms, offering a hug. "Then you're going to tell me all about the new place you're staying in and how crappy your job is and . . ."

Leaping into his arms, she practically knocked him over. Laughing, he folded her into a firm hug. She squeezed back with surprising strength.

"Take it easy," he grunted, as she hugged him hard. "That's a brand new tattoo you've got there."

"Oh, I'll be careful," she said, pulling back with a sniff and damp eyes.

"Oh, yes, you will," the Alchemist said softly. "Whether you like it or not." Her new tattoo would forcibly keep her out of harm's way. It would also compulsively keep her from touching drugs or drinking.

"Huh?"

"Nothing," he said with a chuckle.

"Thank you," Angel said then practically ran from the parlour. At the corner, she suddenly turned to look back at him as he stood, framed in the light pouring from the open door. She waved.

He waved back then closed his door, locking it. Letting her go.

Hopefully the tattoo would encourage her to begin a new life. He wanted her to be able to keep a job then go back to school and use those incredible creative talents he had felt simmering in her soul. The artistic abilities that had burned brightly enough to draw the predators to her in the first place, such as her ex-boyfriend.

This time, with a little Alchemical help, she'd be able to protect herself from the soul-devouring animals of the street.

"Been there, done that," he sighed softly to the empty parlour. "I was living and starving on the streets myself, not all that long ago."

Making Woofie

Lilian Pizzichini

He was silky and smooth and brown as an otter. Furthermore, he was the best lover she had ever had. So Bella wasn't surprised when the puppies she bore him were the colours of chocolate and liver. They had been walking in the country-side. Timothy, her boyfriend, was wading through the thicket in waterproof trousers. He always made sure he had the right gear. This made Bella wonder what he saw in her because she had got it wrong again and was wearing shorts; purple satin, crotch-hugging, disco diva shorts. Practical yet comely, Bella had figured, with plenty of room for manoeuvre. Even so she could tell, from his glance at her bare, plump legs that they were hardly the thing for a hike through autumnal woods. Her vision of a verdant landscape – a glimpse of lush valley through leafy bowers – left no room for nettles, awkward stiles or clinging mud. But she was stomping down the lane bravely, splashing her legs with clomps of earth. She liked to think she was at one with nature; she liked even more to get down and dirty. Dirt made her feel alive, unlike pristine Timothy who was striding far ahead, walking stick in hand.

He looked as though he were about to take command of an army and invade the scene that splayed out before him. He stood atop a grassy mound, his binoculars at the ready for a rare sighting of some bird or other. Bruno – the faithful hound – romped backwards and forwards between them, appeasing his master and waiting for his mistress to catch up. Bruno, unlike Timothy, was always pleased to see Bella and didn't give a fig what she was wearing. He loves me for me, she told herself, and ran to him.

Her enthusiasm was contagious and Bruno knew exactly what to do to engender more. He rolled onto his back, legs akimbo, in a tacit plea for attention and tickles. His tongue lolled sideways and his eyes rolled into his skull. The delirium caused by her fingers as they roamed across his belly, combing through the thick mud clogging the hairs on his tender skin, was too much for him. She paused at the slick tassel that signalled his penis. It lurked deep in his hindquarters and Bella often wanted to give it a little tug. She really shouldn't go further. But she was feeling rebellious. Why shouldn't she give pleasure to one who gave pleasure to her? A green eye peeked at her from underneath a floppy brown ear; his torso was rigid with expectation. She passed the palm of her hand down the length of his hairy penis and cupped the purple plums at its base.

"Here, Bruno. Chase the stick," Timothy shouted. One long arc and Bruno was gone.

"Labradors are known for having a prolonged puppyhood," Timothy explained to Bella, searching her face for signs of eager attention. "Their attitude completely disregards their physical maturity. Take Bruno; at two years old he is still very much a puppy, and attendant with that, has a puppy's exuberance and energy. Labs don't start settling down until some time between two and four years of age."

You boring bastard, thought Bella.

Stick in mouth, Bruno yelped with joy as he threw himself at Timothy's feet awaiting further orders. But Bella noted that he turned his face towards her before their execution. The stripes of mud on his nose, ears and noble forehead were hardening as it dried.

"He looks like a Masai warrior," Bella mused, "daubed for war." She didn't share her aperçu with her boyfriend because she knew he would look at her strangely. He'd already said, with the air of a savant, that she was a psycho-traumatic unit in the hospital of the mind. He was always saying things like that. He was pretentious.

The indefatigable Bruno was true to his nature and retrieved the stick once again. Bella ran into a copse, beckoning him to follow her and disregard his master. Now that his blood was up, she knew what would ensue. Bruno galloped after her, barking and wagging his thick, stubby tail. His eyes were sparkling, the stick forgotten. His tongue was long and bubble-gum pink. She watched saliva cascade in bubbling streams over his serrated black lips. She loved his exuberance. It matched her own. Bruno and Bella, the perfect couple with their dark looks and sea-green eyes. They emerged in a vast, ploughed field where corn had been sown and the sky lay heavily above them. Husks were on the ground and Bruno rootled.

Bella needed a pee. She rolled her shorts down to her ankles and squatted underneath a bush. Her urine formed a puddle between her feet. Bruno smelt that something interesting was happening. He came up behind her and she felt a cold nose investigate her bottom. It was moist and left a damp trail between her buttocks. His whiskers tickled her cheeks, his nose probed her anus and his tongue swept the length of her welcoming slit. It felt good and right and Bella liked it.

Bruno was excited now. He could smell sex. As Bella rose to her full height, he saw his chance and grabbed hold of a leg. His forepaws were surprisingly muscular underneath that velvety pelt. He was no puppy now, Bella thought. He was bucking against his mistress's leg. A spurt of warm, sticky liquid shot up the inside of Bella's thigh. She wiped herself briskly and pulled up her shorts. She was just in time.

"I've spied a great spotted woodpecker," Timothy cried. "You know, *Dendrocopos major*. It must have been a male with that scarlet nape-patch. I must make a note in my book."

Bella held Timothy's binoculars while he pencilled in the details of the bird's undulating flight in the notebook he kept for such sightings. Bruno raised an eyebrow. Such an expressive face, marvelled Bella. Now it was betraying a quizzical air as he sat at her feet. He had paused from licking the mud from her boots to observe the self-absorption of his master.

Six weeks later and Bella was the proud mother of six Labradors crossed with Caucasian. She had left Timothy before the birth, giving no reason, and had taken a flat with a large garden for herself and her litter. But all was not well. You try raising four dogs and two bitches by yourself. Bimbo,

Bimba, Baby, Bubber, Biba and Boyo needed their father. So Bella stole him one day while Timothy was at work.

Bruno loved his new home, and what's more, he loved making love to the new mother. She had not been rent asunder by the birth. The little darlings had slithered out, wet and winsome.

She was ready for more sex with her beloved quadruped. All the more legs to wrap her thighs around, she reckoned. And this time it wouldn't be a rush-job, a crude knee-trembler in the woods. It would be slow and languorous and stretched out on Bella's king-size bed; the lighting low, the music moody. She wanted to feel the length of his big, rough tongue lapping the contours of her body. She wanted him to make her come with a few rapid strokes along her clit and vulva while she plunged her hands into his sinewy back. She grasped his shoulders and, as though it were a distant rumble of thunder, heard her blood coursing as she orgasmed. Now it was his turn so she took his sausage dick and guided it into her hole. Bruno howled with joy and relief.

The lovers enjoyed a post-coital dinner of steak tartare and pommes frites eaten from the same plate, their jaws mashing and munching side by side. Their bliss was complete.

The telephone interrupted their drowsy canoodling in the specially extended dog basket Bella had had made to order. It sat under the wooden table from whence Bella scattered spare scraps of meat to her doggy brood. A voice rang through the kitchen.

"Bella, I need to talk to you. Bruno's gone. He's missing. Someone's stolen him."

Bruno's ear cocked at the sound of his master's fretful voice. He emitted a small, sharp whine. Bella patted him and rolled over to sleep. When she awoke, her man was gone.

"Bella, it's okay. He's come back," Timothy's voice told the answer machine the following day. "He must have found his way home by himself. Good dog," he exulted, and Bella heard a bark of compliance.

Bloody men, she thought.

She wasn't a woman to take her troubles lying down. Her pups needed a father so she would supply one. The home check was a piece of cake; of course she met the requirements. All she had to do now was to choose her future partner.

A gallery of strays and waifs greeted her with sniffs and snufflings, yelps and eager tails. The white-coated attendant guided her down the aisle. She pointed out an angry-looking bull mastiff.

"Heathcliff came in as a stray two months ago. He is our grumpy old man," she laughed coyly. "He loves going for walks and spending as much time as he can patrolling his kennel yard."

Never mind that, what's his cock size? Bella wanted to ask.

"Next up is Alfie. He is a Boston Terrier mix. Unfortunately he is epileptic and has cardiac and respiratory problems. He needs medication twice a day."

Bella was beginning to despair when she spotted a young, blond Labrador smiling at her.

"Aah, Billy . . ." said the guide, following Bella's ardent gaze. "He has had two homes but didn't behave appropriately so he was returned. He is a very dominant boy who . . ."

"I'll take him," Bella barked.

"But he hasn't been neutered yet."

And indeed he hadn't. Bella could see the pink tip of Billy's member protruding above a mound of bristling hair. It was like a salmon leaping out of the water; untouched, virgin game, waiting to be plucked and plundered. Bella knew that Billy possessed the loving disposition and lust for life that only she could appreciate. She could tell it in a glance. His eyes met hers – they spoke of devotion. He was gagging for it – that wide, wide mouth promised licks and nibbles galore. She would let him bite her nipples and ferret in her undergrowth. They would go for walks and bring up her babies. They would eat from the same bowl. They were in love. She was sure he nodded and stamped a paw in approval of the short, thick chain she held in her hand. She couldn't wait to slip the halter around his ruffled neck. Once again, Bella was captivated, but this time, he wouldn't escape.

Six Before Nine

Michael Crawley

He – 6.

Her thighs were slender and pale. Even with the left laying on the right there was a triangular gap – well, not triangular, exactly. There were no straight lines. The two longer sides were subtly curved. The shorter one was bow-shaped, a cleft arc. All the lines were clean, no fuzz. She'd shaven, perhaps for me. I hoped it was special, for me.

I inhaled. There was a trace of talc, a hint of some perfume, Shalimar perhaps. Beneath the artificial odours I could just detect her own fragrance. Her musk was a blend of lemon and cognac, heady and slightly sharp.

My mouth was watering and she was likely growing impatient. I wanted her to be impatient. My lips pursed and puffed out a breath of air. It would have stirred fine hairs, if she'd left any, but she hadn't. There was just porcelain skin, fine pored, infinitely tempting.

My right arm stretched down the bed, to her knees. My hand flattened on them to hold them in place and together. It wasn't time to part them, yet. My left hand spread across the firm cushions of her buttocks and pulled. I wanted her taut but not parted. My pressure tightened the creases of her groin. There were tiny blue veins there, usually invisible, tucked into the creases between thighs and torso, but now exposed.

My head lifted. I extended my tongue. Its tip traced a vein. I think that perhaps she shivered. My tongue flattened and lapped, tasting her skin and the residue of her sweat. Tracing with tongue-tip is for her pleasure. Lapping is for mine. Tantalize, then taste.

I lowered my head and repeated the lick-lap in the other crease. She made a little muffled sound. The cheeks of her bottom twitched. I could feel that had I released her knees her upper thigh would have lifted in invitation.

Not yet, my love.

I increased my hands' pressure, bending her at her hips. My mouth opened wide, a short inch from her pursed sex. I didn't blow on it, but I breathed more heavily, warming her with my humid breath. Inhaling brought a taste of her to my mouth.

I pulled back to inspect her. The lips of her sex were still closed but they had thickened a little. My tongue crept out and touched, exactly between them but not penetrating. I held it there, letting her become aware of the immobile touch. Her hips tensed and tried to thrust but I was holding her too firmly to allow that.

My tongue retreated, made spit, and deposited a single droplet on the edge of one lip. When I puffed on it the drop trembled. Would she feel that? Likely not.

I released her knees. Her thighs sprang apart, the upper one at a sharp angle to her hips. When I took a sighting up along her leg it was stretched and perfectly straight, toes pointed at the ceiling. There was an angle of 90° between her thighs, giving me ample room to play in.

No half measures, my love.

My palms flattened on the insides of her thighs. She's limber. I didn't relent until her upper knee touched her ribcage.

The stretching raised the tendons inside her thighs. That left deep hollows. I grazed in them, lips and tongue and teeth. I nipped her skin. I pursed and sucked, and sucked, and sucked. It was not my intention to inflict pain, not then. I was leaving my mark. The bruise would be my brand. I was here. This is mine.

I hunched down the bed to get my face deeper between the straining division. It was our first time. She'd be expecting my mouth on her sex, and she would have that, but first she had a lesson to learn. I was taking ownership. She was to be mine, to use as I wished, when I wished. No modesty would be allowed.

My fingers parted the cheeks of her bottom. She didn't

object. With a ferocious lunge, I buried my face into her, tongue stretched and stiff, stabbing deep and wet, piercing the clench of her sphincter and worming beyond, into the dark dragging musk-laden tightness.

She sighed. Her buttocks clenched and relaxed.

For that, for being sweetly depraved, I love you, my love.

My tongue withdrew. Two fingers replaced it. Her bottom accepted the deeper penetration with the same grace as it had welcomed my tongue. I made a silent promise, "All you can take, my love, and just a little more."

The lips of her sex were thicker and darker. Their inner edges glistened. I tried the glistening with my tongue and found it delicious. My tongue wagged, not penetrating, just slithering between them no deeper than their parting allowed. As my tongue worked, her lips sighed apart, opening to me without my demanding entrance. For each fraction they parted, I penetrated. There was a pulse in one lip. I kissed it. It throbbed between my lips, a delicate, vulnerable flutter that connected me to her heart.

My lips sucked. The flat of my tongue smoothed. Like an orchid, my love opened up to me. An incredibly internal pinkness blossomed between chocolate-tinged petals. There were smooth, slick places and places that were corrugated and yet others that offered polyps of quivering flesh.

How tender, my love.

I sipped. I drew nectar into my mouth. My face burrowed, spreading the lips of her sex across my cheeks. It was six hours since I'd shaved. There would be tiny bristles. She'd feel that.

My lips made an "O" that fitted the dark opening beyond the external beauty of her florid, floral offering. This was the entrance to her secret places, the soft portal to her labyrinth. I blew and sucked, exchanging air with her womb, taking my breath from her inner recesses. My tongue scoured, running around a place that was *inside* her.

The root of my tongue began to ache. I withdrew, deliberately slurping. Making the noise intentionally obscene. My head lifted so that I could inspect her once more. The lips of her sex were engorged with blood, darkened until they were almost black. I nibbled one, then the other, toying. I let them feel my teeth. She was so malleable that I couldn't resist subjecting her most vulnerable parts to gentle abuse. My fingers, in her rectum, hooked and pressed. The floor of her sex was forced up and out. What had been inside her was everted. A wet pink plain invited my tongue to flatten, press and slither. I grazed on her skin, pressing the membranous division that separated her rectum from her soft vestibule between my tongue and my fingers.

You whispered, "Please?"

I could tell by her tone that she wasn't asking me to stop what I was doing. She yearned for more.

My thumb replaced my tongue. I had the muscular wall in a firm grip. I could manipulate her insides, tugging on her uterus and womb. I *owned* her.

I shifted back on the bed. Her clitoral ridge was thick with need. I hadn't touched her there but the glossy dome of her clit's head peeked from under its hood.

She asked, "My clit?"

"You want me to?"

A pause. "Yes." A longer pause. "Yes," again.

But my mouth had the smoothness of her mound to savour. It, and my teeth and my tongue, grazed. Each time I found the ridge, I lifted over it. My attention wandered, though not purposelessly. A nip at the delicate inside of a thigh, a tongue-slither in her groin, a chaste kiss on one pendulous wet and quivering lip, then back to the gentle swelling.

"My clit," she reminded me.

"Soon," I promised.

The tip of my tongue found the subtle place where the root of her shaft disappeared. It pressed. I tongue-stroked down the left side of her ridge, then down the right. She was leaking. My thumb was in a puddle of her essence. I removed it from the humid folds and sucked her from it before replacing it.

Her hood had half retracted, exposing a hemisphere of the tiny treasure it adorned. My tongue's tip prodded it back so that I could wonder at the miracle of its re-emergence. When it reappeared, it had overcome its shyness enough that it extended further, to the narrower part behind the head. How could I resist? My lips closed on its neck and held it firmly. My tongue touched it – just that – just a touch. Her sex spasmed on my thumb as if to draw it in.

I licked – one long slow hard lap. Touch, then lap, but harder and faster. Then no "touch", just a steady lapping until her rectum clenched on my fingers and she lifted towards me – when I stopped.

You sighed.

My tongue moved from side to side, punishing the core of your lust for being so desirable. I felt the urge to *bite*, but resisted. Instead, I let my teeth graze that vulnerable morsel for a few seconds before licking again.

There were noises coming from her throat. Her body was a drawn bow.

My tongue retreated to the back of my mouth. My lips pursed. I *sucked, and sucked, and sucked.*

Her clitoris was drawn out, elongated, a trembling shaft that my tongue whipped. It felt as if every muscle in her body was rigid and quaking. She inhaled and froze . . .

At the precise moment of her orgasm, I deserted her clitoris and fastened my mouth to her sex, a lascivious lamprey that drew her climax and the spring that it flowed on and *consumed* them.

When the incoherent noises stopped, I told her, "Your turn, my love."

Her – 9.

His cock lay heavy along the line of his groin. It wasn't erect, yet, nor was it flaccid. He was uncircumsized. His foreskin covered his glans and extended beyond it for perhaps an inch. Its mouth was a soft beak, like the tip of an elephant's trunk. There was a thick vein running up the underside of his cock and a network of tiny blue lines barely visible through the skin.

He'd used my anus. There was a nice obscenity in that. There is an unspoken protocol – a man services a woman, using his mouth on her sex, one night. The next night, or the one after the next, he explores her reaction to anal probing with some diffidence, testing, hoping.

He hadn't followed the rules. He was an arrogant bastard,

this one. I liked that, but . . . I wet my finger in my mouth. My arm circled his hip. My finger found the crease between his buttocks and explored. When I found the tight pucker I rimmed it twice, then plunged. My finger sank to its second joint. Although my finger had been wet he was dry and tight, hot and rubbery. When I moved my finger his skin moved with it.

His cock reacted. It grew longer and thicker and lifted a fraction. The skin over its head retracted far enough to expose a glistening pink. The side of my finger lifted it aside. My mouth made a line of tiny puckered kisses down the crease from his hip to where I had to nuzzle his sac aside and squirm my tongue in. There were a few drops of fresh man-sweat in there, brought out by what he'd been doing to me. I sucked each bitter-salt drop up.

My tongue and the tip of one fingernail found the place below and behind his scrotum. I scratched and licked, licked and scratched. Against my finger, his cock lifted and engorged. At the spot where his cock emerged from the wrinkled skin of his sac, I bit him. His cock twitched. My teeth nibbled up the ridge that ran up his cock's underside. By the time I reached the top his foreskin had rolled back, exposing his glans completely. I could see the little knot of twisted skin where his foreskin was attached to his shaft, just beneath his dome. His cock was straining hard, as if it wanted to grow even bigger but couldn't. I opened my mouth wide and closed it around his shaft. My head shook from side to side, sliding his foreskin, forcing it back further, masturbating his stem but not his head.

He groaned.

Did I hurt you, my love? Did I force you into an erection more powerful than any woman has before?

My finger worked in his rectum. I closed my lips on the knot and sucked it and licked it. His hips tried to move but I held him back with just a tiny crook of the finger that was hooked into his rectum. Wait.

It'd been a while since I'd had a foreskin to play with. My hand closed around his shaft, just beneath its head, and eased his skin up to cover the dome once more. As if the flaccid skin were a mouth, I planted a chaste kiss on its wrinkled lips. Still holding his foreskin forward, I inserted my tongue. It found a wet dimple and stabbed. He jerked. I rimmed his glans, running my tongue between it and his foreskin, round and round and round.

Men can whimper, you know.

My fist forced his foreskin back and released it. It stayed back. I spat into my hand and laid my palm on the head of his cock. I polished that bulbous knob, to and fro, then up and down. It drooled. The mixture of spit and precome was slicker than spit alone. My fist ran down his shaft, loosely, then up, tightening as it neared the top, smoothed over, then down again.

Was it torture, my love? Did the need to come tighten your balls?

My lips, soft and gentle, covered his glans. I let my mouth go slack and shook my head. As his cock wobbled between my lips, I made little noises. He grunted.

I took him deeper, still loose, still wet. My fist steered him into the pouch of my cheek. I rubbed him there, the tip of his cock on hot soft flesh. My tongue lifted his shaft and pushed it up, pressing his glans against the roof of my mouth.

I nodded. He went rigid.

I told you, "I want you to come in my mouth. I want it all." You didn't speak.

And I did want him to. I wanted to devour him, to drink him down. I wanted that which was *him* in me, to be digested by me, the cells of his body to feed cells of mine.

I pumped his shaft. My finger, in his rectum, found the walnut lump and massaged it. My mouth became ferocious. I slurped and mumbled and sucked and lapped and gobbled. I *willed* him to give me his essence.

You sobbed, I think, but my own noises drowned yours.

His legs stiffened. His balls retracted. It was time. I lifted my head and parted my lips. My tongue extended. My fist stroked and stroked.

Yes! Hot wet come flopped onto the flat of my tongue. I swallowed that first benison and swooped, engulfing his cock. My cheeks hollowed. I sucked hard and long. Manflesh was twitching and jerking in my mouth but I was adamant. I wanted it *all*. My mouth dragged every last drop from him, three spurts, less each time, and then just a trickle and finally there was nothing left to draw out.

I licked my lips and told him, "Your turn, my love."

Mothering

Jacqueline Lucas

It wasn't maternal.

It was very confusing.

I'm looking through a 21 mm lens and all his features are exaggerated. The red quiff. The black and white check three piece drape. The brothel creepers. Curling up towards me. The skin of a child. Fair. Milky. Soft as a cream bun. The injections are working. I can feel them. Soon I'll be ready to haul my fat arse down to the clinic for the egg collection. In the meantime. There's this little job. And I'm telling him he's gorgeous. It's just right. Could he lean into the lamp post. Incline his head just a touch. Show us your teeth. And I'm getting closer. I had no close-ups in mind but here I can feel his breath. He's sucking on a lolly. It's bulging out his cheek and I don't know if it fits the shot but I want to be the rhubarb and custard flavoured dome in his wee little gob being alternately sucked upon and layered in a good slather of saliva with a good tongueing all the way around. And he knows. And he likes it. And as far as everyone else is concerned. There's a weird mutton dressed as lamb taking photees in the Glasgow drisel of a summer's day of a boy. Not yet known. Not yet holding back, and self assured, and keeping a low profile, and covering his arse and cynical. A touch. Here's a young lad full of pleasure for his drape. His quiff. His hair wash at the end of the day. His ministering. The make up girls. The hairdos. The costume fiddling. And all those girls just waiting on him. All those girls just waiting on him. All those girls not ready to knock off till the last strand of his deep red hair is given a good rinse. And here. He's staring back into a lens that's closer and closer. And it's manned by a girl.

A woman rather. With long black wavy hair. Who's come specially for him. To look through one lens after another. One camera after another. Tell him he's just the fucking business. And she seems to understand he's got that extra bit. The look that means he's worth it. He's worth getting it bloody well right because he's heading off this Glasgow shoot and out of this drizzle for L fucking A. For London for sure.

FOR AN AGENT THAT COUNTS. AFTER THIS MOVIE. AFTER THIS BREAK. AND THIS GIRL'S A GOOD SIGN. AND SHE'S LOOKING INTO MY EYEBALLS AND I JUST MIGHT FIND MYSELF PULLING DOWN ON THAT DARK BLACK HAIR CAUSE SHE UNDERSTANDS. SHE CAN JUST SEE. I CAN TELL.

I'm on to group shots now. And I've got two of them waiting. But I can't stop. On these two. And I don't know who to look at. Cause now there's the naughty one with the dark curls and the side burns and he's so cute. You're just tremendous, boys. Will you look into the camera now. Will you lift your chin. What of a smile? Shall we go for a grin? Try a rollie again. Yes, give me the smoke. Let it out slow. No. Not you. Just that look you gave me there. You know the one. Try that again. You boys are just bloody amazing. D'you know that? And I've a mind to lay this fucking apparatus down on the damp ground and hold the poor wee boys' heads together in my palms and kiss them both. Licking the outline of their cupid bows. One, after the other. Taking my saliva to follow their teeth. Lap at their tongues. A messenger bringing saliva from number 1 to number 2. And I don't even know their names. Just their movie characters. And I know they know.

That they'd go along happily and excited cause it's all new and a lark and

HELL THIS FILM IS JUST THE BEGINNING FOR ME AND SHE'S GIVING ME THAT PIERCING LOOK AND I KNOW SHE CAN SEE IT'S ME THAT HAS

IT. THAT EXTRA WEE DOLLOP OF SEXUAL CHARISMA OR SUMMAT.

After the self congratulatories in the pub on Renfrew street I commandeer the lads. Like help us with the shopping, boys, my arms free, my steps jaunty with anticipation. They trundle my tripods, lenses and bodies past the chief cook and bottle washer of my tastefully decorated upmarket accommodation. This time she doesn't press her mushroom risotto, merely lets me feel her eyeballs on my back as she and her son watch from the empty dining room. Great shoot! I call to my friend of last night, strain for the plaque "visitors not allowed".

I lay them out like a box of Belgian chocolates fresh from their latest double whisky. I couldn't risk it. I need my clear head. I take it deadly serious and discourage any giggling. They're nervous. They can tell I mean business. The room is dead quiet. They are lying on twin beds in their clothes like two good soldiers ready for action. But with no guns or ammunition or nothing. Just waiting orders. And I've to keep the atmosphere silent and maybe a touch menacing or we all might lose it. It's like our minds are all in tune and know it. Know the danger of it. Know this need could disappear before we find a place to put it. They never take their eyes off me and they never look at each other. Not that I saw. One look and it'd all be over.

I'm lying here petrified and excited. I've never done anything like this before. Not with a woman. Not since I was fifteen and Cathy stuck her tongue in my mouth and pushed her bosoms round my chest. It was awful. And I was drunk. Now I'm pleasantly floating from the booze but I'm well in my body. And I'm scared. I don't know what will happen. Or even what I'd like to happen. And I can't even think of him. I know he's straight but what am I going to think when I see him starkers. I wonder if he'll turn me on. And what if she wants us to do things for her. She looks exotic and worldly enough. I bet she's got more up her sleeve than the lasses I've been around. But I don't know if I should be doing this. Not with a woman. Not in this family-run hotel with the pink chintz curtains and the cupboard with the kettle and the shortbread biscuits. I thought I'd pride myself in not having ever. And here it's a real older woman, for fuck's sake, not even one of those skinny types that looks like a boy. This is just the weirdest thing. Maybe I should just breathe deeply and relax.

She's got her clothes on. But I can see her belly under her short top. She looks like a belly dancer or something. She's curvy and soft. Strange. But I think I like it. Oh, God. She's taking off his things. I'm either pissed or she's doing it slow motion. I wonder if she knows about me.

Knows what I'll do if I lean my head in slow motion to watch them. My God.

I suppress the desire to pick up the body with the macro lens, hone in on the balls till they loom like the twin heads of an extra terrestrial, the pricks two species of cacti bursting with life-giving juice. The scene shifts to heightened colour and me so keen on black and white.

THIS WOMAN IS SO WILD. I COULD SCREAM I'M THAT READY. SHE'LL SEE JUST AS SOON AS MY KIT'S OFF. I'D LIKE TO HAVE HER ALL TO MY-SELF. BUT YOU CAN TELL SHE'S INTO WILD STUFF. AS LONG AS SHE'S NOT WANTING ME AND HIM TO DO STUFF. I DON'T THINK I'M UP FOR IT. IF I HAD SOME E, MEBBE. MEBBE NOT. OHMYGOD. THERE'S A VIDEO CAMERA STOOD ON A TRIPOD IN FRONT OF THE BATHROOM. IF I CLOSE MY EYES IT'S BETTER. I CAN FORGET HIM FOR THE MINUTE. AND THE CAMERA. SHE WOULDN'T, WOULD SHE?

THIS IS JUST AMAZING. I THINK SHE'S MY T-SHIRT IN HER MOUTH FOR FUCK'S SAKE. SHE'S LIFTING IT UP SO SLOWLY I CAN SCREAM AND I CAN FEEL HER TONGUE BRUSHING MY CHEST AS IF BY MISTAKE. I'M SWEATING. I HOPE MY ARM-PITS. SHIT. SHIT. SHIT. SHE'S LICKING AT MY ARMPITS. SHE'S LAPPING AT THEM. FIRST ONE AND THEN THE OTHER. I CAN FEEL HER SNIFF-

ING AT THEM LIKE A PUPPY. IT'S LIKE SHE'S
STILL WATCHING ME ONLY CLOSER THIS TIME.
OH, FOR GOD'S SAKE I'M GOING TO WET MYSELF.

I'm going to finish this chest routine with a good long suck of
his nipples and a nuzzle in his non-existent chest hairs. Gee.
They're as cute as a scatter of pubes on a very young boy. I can
feel him breathing quicker. And the silence. And I want to look
at the other one but I daren't break the spell. Just imagine a
freeze frame in close-up cutting back to a wide shot. It's
criminal not to get my gear out but I can't do both. Shoot
and perform, snap and choreograph. I'm not going to take the
top off. I'm going to leave him with his jeans round his ankles
not touching and just stroll over to number 2. Just as well it's
not a double. A twin at £55.00 per night for single occupancy.
It makes it easier to keep it dead serious.

My God. I can see his stiffy. It's not as big as I thought. But
thick and a fair size with red pubes, for fuck's sake. He looks a
beauty and the youngest I've seen like this. I go for older. He's
a beautiful pale skin and I'm hard just watching. I've no idea
how I'll look at him on set. I wonder if he's not as straight as I
thought. Can you imagine that. And I thought I was already a
bit of a streetwise. Jesus. She's at me now.
    She's not on my top. She's unzipping me with her teeth. And
it's nice. I can feel the tip of her nose on my Y fronts. God.
She's sniffing me! It's as well I'm clean as a whistle. She's
sniffing around my crotch and my trousers round my knees
and her hair's tickling my thigh. She's tickling me with her
tongue. And I'm so stiff I want her to take me and she's biting
me through my Y's and Jesus Christ. I'm in her mouth now.
She knows. She just knows. When to give me a slow lick
around the tip and when to give me a good sucking. And I'm
making these noises I make now. And I don't even care he can
hear me and I wish he'd leap up and ram his cock in but she
knows and she's teasing my arse with her fingers and tickling
inside me with her tongue.
    She's whispering now. I'm your mother. She tells me. You
need a good sucking my poor baby and you know I always look

after you and she tells me to stroke myself gently now while mummy goes to sort out my brother who's in agony she says and needs to wet himself.

I WATCH HER GIVE HIM AN INCREDIBLE TEASING BLOW JOB. AND THEY SAY HE'S INTO BOYS. I'M SCARED TO TOUCH MYSELF IN CASE I COME I'M SO WIRED UP AND SHE'S HERE. OHMYGOD HER HEAD'S DEEP BETWEEN MY LEGS AND SHE'S TURNING ME OVER AND LICKING MY BALLS AND NOW SHE'S WHISPERING. SHE WANTS ME TO PLAY GAMES NOW. SAYS I'M HER BROTHER. SHE'S MY OLDER SISTER AND SHE'S COME TO SHOW ME WHAT'S WHAT CAUSE I'VE BEEN EYEING HER UP FOR MONTHS AND SPYING ON HER IN THE BATH AND NOW SHE'S GOING TO GIVE IT TO ME. I BET THAT VIDEO'S GETTING ME AND SHE'S ROLLING ME OVER AND I FEEL SORT OF HELPLESS. THERE'S A ROLL OF FILM AND A CAMERA ON THE TABLE WITH THE PHONE BETWEEN ME AND HIM AND I CAN'T LOOK AT HIM BUT I CAN SEE HIM WANKING OUT THE CORNER OF MY EYE AND HE'S MAKING THESE SOUNDS AND I DON'T WANT TO HEAR THEM. BUT BEFORE I CAN THINK ABOUT WHAT THEY REMIND ME OF SHE'S TELLING ME TO BEG HER LIKE A BROTHER TO TAKE ME INSIDE HER. I'M THAT CONFUSED I FEEL SHE'S MY BROTHER AND I'M BEGGING HER TO FUCK ME. TAKE ME. I WANT YOU TO TAKE ME AND SHE'S RIDING ME. AND ONLY NOW I SEE HER BODY. CURVY. HER BREASTS ROUND AND FIRM AS THEY RIDE IN AND OUT MY LINE OF SIGHT. BEYOND HER THERE'S SOMETHING FAMILIAR ON THE TV. MY EYES ARE SHUT AND I FEEL LIKE A GIRL AND SHE'S MY BROTHER OR MAYBE HIM WITH HIS NOISES GIVING ME A GOOD BANGING AND I'M SCARED AND I CAN'T KEEP THIS UP MUCH LONGER IF SHE DOESN'T STOP.

This is speeded-up Super 8 like a home movie only it needs soundtrack like a trip to the beach or scary rides at Thorpe Park on the big screen shot in Steadicam, with cranes and 360 degree turns like Tarantino or de Palma. I'm taking them higher and higher riding the waves above the empty restaurant, available for private functions with her gourmet four-course dinner menu, including drink and coffee at £26.50 p.p.

She's making me keep up this long slow pull. She's her breast in my mouth and she tells me it's feeding time. Her baby's starving and she's my mother. And I don't know why. But when she tells me this she takes my cock in her mouth to clean me she says. And I know he's watching and I can hear my sounds as if they come from another room. From another place. Mother! I sob. Mother!

And the room turns quiet from all of our breaths. Nothing moves except for my shaking and the sound of this voice muffled as if from another time. Somewhere else.
   Mother!
   I cry.

Diver's Moon

E. M. Arthur

My oncologist squeezed my hand and pronounced me in full remission. "I'm sorry, Skyler," he said, "about Danni."

Danni had been my live-in nurse when I was too weak to get myself to the john. She was a youthful cliché of blonde, buxom beauty. My wife, Andrea, spent a lot of time with her. When my body betrayed my marriage, Andrea found comfort in Danni's arms.

"I couldn't have known when I recommended her," the doctor said. His narrow face went red with embarrassment. His hand sweated in mine.

He'd saved my life, but what did he know about my missing soul? What did he know about losing my body, a body that could grab the rings and rotate an iron cross into a dead still handstand? What did he know about watching your wife make love to another woman as a gift to you when the best you could manage was to hold your limp member in an emaciated hand?

"No," I said. "You couldn't have known she was a lesbian."

He pulled his hand back and hid it in the pocket of his smock. "I knew about that," he said. "It just never occurred to me that she and your wife would, well, leave you."

"Yeah," I said. "Took me by surprise too." We stared at each other for a long awkward moment.

I broke the silence. "Thank you, doctor," I said.

"Maybe you should get away for a while. Take a good long vacation. Go someplace new, someplace where there are no reminders you were sick."

"Maybe," I said.

"Someplace where you can enjoy being healthy."

I nodded, left his office and headed home to face my emptiness alone.

I pulled my Subaru wagon to a full stop at the intersection where Martin's Court crosses Black Diamond Way, the street that ends in my cul-de-sac.

Dark windows from across the paved circle stared at me. My grey, split-level ranch nestled in behind my weed-covered gardens and my brown, gone-to-seed lawn, accused me of failures. I sat in the August heat for a moment, white-knuckling the wheel. Hot beads of sweat rolled down my neck and under the collar of my shirt.

I couldn't pull across the street and drive up to that house of betrayals. When I was 34, I had a thriving business coaching gymnastics. My teams were winning. My body was my best asset.

At 35, I was old. I'd lost nearly a hundred pounds lying in a bed in that accusing house. I'd vomited in every room. My body had betrayed me, then the insurance company dumped me. I'd had to sell the gym. Finally, there was Andrea and the sponge bath that had gone too far.

Andrea only wanted to help me. My nurse had wanted to help us both.

I banged my head against the steering wheel. I wanted to drive the memory of that night from my head. It was too late. The images, the smells, the sounds rose up and filled me again. Danni had come to my room. She lit candles and burned incense. She put a card table beside the bed, draped it in a linen cloth, and set out a basin of warm water, some sponges, and scented massage oils. She pulled her blonde hair up and clasped it with a tortoise shell clip, then she took off her skirt and her white, button-down blouse. Beneath, she wore only her tan, cotton underwear, and a blue sport bra. "Don't want to get these wet," she said, dropping her blouse to the floor.

She'd given me sponge baths before, but she had never taken off any clothing. "Andrea?" I asked.

"She'll be along in a minute." Danni sat down on the bed. Long-fingered hands dipped a sponge in the basin of warm water. She squeezed the sponge until it stopped dripping. Then she pulled back my sheet.

Shame for my ruined body filled me. I felt like the sponge in her hand, like an empty, seeping, brownish lump.

Andrea came in from the bathroom. Andrea. Dark and succulent, my wife, my friend. She was half Mestizo, and her skin was molten bronze. Her dark eyes caught the flickering candlelight. She wore my green terrycloth robe.

"Danni's going to show me how to give you a special sponge bath," she said. She opened her robe and let it fall. White silk panties, stockings, garters, and bra made her skin all the more exotic. I wanted to lift a hand and touch her. I wanted to push Danni aside and pull my wife to me, to give her my love.

I tried to sit up. Danni's hand was firm. She used the sponge to press me back. She stroked my neck. "There, now," she said. "You relax and enjoy. Let us do the work here. We're taking care of you, not the other way around."

Andrea sat on the side of the bed beside pale Danni. Andrea leaned over and kissed me. Her breasts, cupped in white silk, pressed against me. Her breath was warm and sweet. The perfume I'd given her for our last anniversary promised me her love.

"Like this," Danni said. She handed Andrea a second sponge. She wrapped her pale hands around Andrea's dark fingers. Together, they squeezed the sponge. "Keep enough water to dampen the skin," Danni whispered. "You don't want the sponge to scratch."

I watched my wife do as she was told. I felt her sponge on my neck, on my face. Relax, I told myself. This may be the last time you experience anything like this. God, I tried to relax. But part of me wanted to rise, to give, to be more than a recipient.

Danni guided Andrea through my cleansing. It was warm, long and slow. Danni wrapped her arms around Andrea to better guide her hands. Danni's white arms embraced my wife from behind. "Can you feel the warmth?" she whispered to my wife. Andrea looked into my eyes. She seemed to be asking me if I was OK. I wanted her to be happy, to have what I couldn't give her. I forced a smile.

Andrea nodded.

Danni kissed her neck, nuzzled her beneath the ear, beneath

the dark, silken ringlets of hair. I saw the goose flesh rise on Andrea's arms.

I moaned. I reached for myself.

They laughed. Together, they moved me farther onto the bed.

Danni lifted a bottle of oil from the table. She opened it and poured it onto Andrea's open palms. The scent of patchouli and vanilla filled the room. Danni worked the oil into Andrea's hands and forearms. She placed Andrea's hands on my shrunken chest. Andrea slipped a leg over me. She sat above me like she had so many times. She looked down at me, her eyes both sad and filled with desire. Deep inside her dark eyes, I saw pity. God, that hurt more than anything else I saw that night.

Danni worked on my feet, slowly massaging, oiling, and working her up my calves and thighs.

I watched Andrea's face. I felt Danni's hands between my legs. I prayed I would respond. Then I realized Danni wasn't reaching for me.

Andrea gasped and arched her back.

Her bra fell away, released from behind. Her oiled hand went to one breast. A pale hand came around her from behind and took her other breast.

I felt Danni moving her fingers between my legs, beneath Andrea.

Andrea leaned forward, giving Danni more room to work.

"Andrea?" I asked.

"Oh, shit!" she said.

"Here," Danni said. She pulled Andrea off my hips. She helped her out of her panties and stockings. Andrea tugged at Danni's sports bra and panties.

I rolled on my side, trying to reach for my wife.

Danni pushed me back. She took my limp member in her oiled hand. "He wants to help," Danni said. She helped Andrea lift a leg and slip it over my oiled chest. She carefully settled my wife into position so my tongue could reach her rear. "Gently," Danni said. "You take it easy."

I nodded.

Danni put a pillow under my head. She slipped a finger into Andrea. When she pulled it out, she let me lick it. It tasted of oil and the familiar spice of my wife. I closed my eyes and savoured the taste.

Danni laughed. Then she disappeared toward the foot of the bed. I began to tongue Andrea's ass. I did what I could for her, but I knew her moans of pleasure were not from my feeble tongue.

I felt Danni's mouth on my cock. Oiled hands massaged my sac. A finger slipped between my cheeks. God, it should have been heaven. If my body had not betrayed me, it would have been.

My neck got sore. I had to let my head fall back, had to let Andrea go. Eventually, Danni gave up on making me hard.

Andrea turned herself around. "I'm sorry, honey," she said. "It's OK. It's not your fault." She kissed me then started to lift herself off me, but she stopped, straddling me, ass high, supported by one extended leg, kneeling on the other. Her eyes rolled upward and her back arched. "Shit," she said. "Danni. Oh shit."

Between Andrea's dark legs, I saw white hands pinching nipples on white breasts glistening with oil. Danni's blond hair had come loose from her clip. It brushed at those hands and breasts. Her face was in my wife's ass. The wrinkles on the bridge of Andrea's nose, the way her eyes rolled upward, the tension in her belly muscles. I could see my wife was about to come.

Poised above me like that, she screamed a woman's name. I wanted to be happy for her release. I wanted to be a man who loved his wife so much that he felt joy in her pleasure even when he couldn't be the source of it.

I wasn't the man I wanted to be.

Danni and Andrea rolled away from me. They made love on the bed beside me, oblivious to my pain.

It was the last time I saw Andrea nude, the last time I touched her, tasted her.

Andrea and Danni had stayed until I started gaining weight, until I was working for the gym part time. They had helped each other through until my hair came in enough to cut close for that Bruce Willis look Andrea said was sexy. The day I managed my first pull-up, I came home to an empty house.

Andrea and Danni took my dog, the living room furniture, and exactly half my remaining bank account.

I continued my recovery without them, at least physically. I fought until I could do 20 pull-ups. I cursed my wind and skinny legs until I could run for half-an-hour. I fought to improve, to live. Now, I was cured. The fight was over.

Without Andrea, the fight had been all I had.

I pressed my forehead against the steering wheel between my hands and started to shake. I was alive. I was coming home a cured man. It was supposed to be a wonderful moment, a celebration.

Instead, I had no idea who I was. My new life was empty. My body betrayed me. It left me with a wiry, stranger's body. My wife betrayed me. She left me a house full of ugly memories.

An impatient driver behind me laid on the horn.

I yanked the wheel left and headed for the interstate.

Three days later, I was in Glenwood Spring, Colorado, standing on top of the ladder of a three-metre diving board over an Olympic-sized pool. I hadn't stood on a board since diving in high school. My skin was oil slick from the minerals in the hot spring-fed pool. A ballet of steam danced across the surface of the water below. The sun was high. A fresh mountain breeze caressed my chest and arms.

The view could touch the soul, if a man had a soul to touch.

In front of me, three wings of chalet-style resort hotel wrapped around the steaming pool. Beyond and above the red-tiled roofs, snowy Rocky Mountain spires reached for the belly of a sky deeper and bluer than the pool below. Even I paused to stare.

"You afraid of heights?" the woman on the ladder behind me said.

I stepped forward onto the fibreglass diving board, then I turned to face her. "Sorry," I said. "The mountains are so . . ." I let it trail off, suddenly aware of how skinny I felt, of how explanations had become so complex, so tiring.

She smiled. "I know," she said. "It's a stunning view."

The dancing freckles on her smile-wrinkled nose held my

gaze the same way the view had. I hadn't seen a woman smile like that since my first few weeks with Andrea, since before . . .

She stepped up onto the board with me. Her dark hair was wet and smoothed to her shoulders. Her dun eyes flashed with humour under the high mountain sun. The lines near her eyes suggested maybe 30 years of well-lived life. Her dark-blue one-piece was a swimmer's suit, not a sunbather's advertisement for attention. She reminded me of a sleek, happy river otter in a Speedo.

Her smile faded. She cocked her head to the side, pulled her hair away from her neck, and twisted it until water dripped onto the board. "You don't want to stand up here too long," she said. "The breeze is cool, but that sun'll give you cancer."

I almost laughed. She wouldn't have understood. I wanted to say something else, to say something that would make her smile again. But I knew better. My blond hair was still close-cut. I knew I was still pale. I was getting stronger, but I looked more like a tofu-fed yoga instructor than the pommel horse, rings, and high-bar man I had been.

I wanted to run and jump from the board. I wanted to hide in the deep blue water.

"I've never seen anything –"

"New eyes on ancient beauty," she interrupted. The otter's smile returned.

I nodded.

"It reminds me to appreciate the things I see every day," she said.

"You live here?"

"Assistant manager," she said. "You going to dive?"

Dive? I was on a three-metre board for the first time in maybe 17 years. An otter woman was flirting with me. The sky was suddenly bluer and the air colder. A breeze swept in from the snowy peaks. Gooseflesh covered me.

"Breeze makes me a little cold up here," she said. Goose flesh rippled up her legs and under her suit. Nipples suddenly stood from the modest rounds of her breasts. She crossed her arms. Her breasts swelled.

My chest and legs were chilled, but my crotch moved,

stretched, and warmed for the first time since . . . I wanted to reach out and touch those hardening peaks.

She caught me staring. Her smile was gone.

I knew the flirt we had shared was gone, too. "You go ahead," I said. I stepped aside.

She strode to the end of the board, tugging at the bottom of her suit to seat it under the muscled curve of her ass.

At the end of the board, she turned around. The otter's grin came back. She nodded to me. Then her eyes changed. The spark left, replaced by a distant focus, by a look that turned inward, that found some quiet centre.

I knew that look. She was about to mount the beam. She was going to spike a new vault. She was fully in herself, and she was beautiful.

She lifted her arms in a ritual of balance I knew well. She set the toes of her right foot, then her left, on the very edge of the board. The mountains beyond her seemed to lean inward, anticipating her, preparing to spot her if needed. I wondered what it would be like to put my hands on those hips, to hold her aloft, to help her move through lithe, stretching tumbles.

She tested the bounce of the board.

Automatically, I stepped back onto the ladder so my weight wouldn't kill her spring.

I watched her breathe. Her breasts grew, stretched her suit, then relaxed. She lifted on toe tip. A muscled line appeared in her thigh, pointing upward to the hem of her suit. The blue fabric wrapped her flexing abs and curved under her, gripping her mons and cradling her sex in mineral dampness. She dropped her weight through her heels. The board flexed low, then rose. She lifted upward. Glossy thighs snapped up against perfect breasts; muscled arms embraced bent knees. She spun backward, hair spraying. She had more than a full rotation before she dropped below the level of the board. I saw her otter's eyes flash, and I swear she winked at me.

Two-and-a-half reverse. She stretched full out and her hard body slipped through mineral mists and disappeared without a splash.

She came up. The breeze shifted the mist. I saw her breasts

above the water, the flash of her smile. She teased me with a long, slow backstroke toward the shallow end of the pool.

She was challenging me.

I stepped up onto the board. It had been a long time. I wasn't in shape for it. I considered a simple jump. It might be less humiliating than a failed dive in front of her.

Forgotten pride rose and took hold of my mind.

When she dove, I'd felt the board rebound. I knew the bounce. I knew I could manage something simple, something that at least showed some control, some training.

I stepped out to my mark. I checked the water. She was there. Steam rose off the surface around her. She was watching, treading water, waiting.

I locked my eyes on the snow peaks. I took my breath. I let it go. The breeze was cool, the mountains silent. In the distance a hawk circled, sun glinting off its red tail.

One step. The board bent.

Two. The rhythm of the flex.

Three. Lift the knee and rise.

My body remembered. In the moment I touched down on the board to take my full bounce, I knew my new body would give me its full measure. I was, in that moment, fully in myself for the first time in over a year. I felt the grit of the board, the bend in fibreglass and knees, and I knew I had what I needed to make the otter woman laugh. Safe was no longer part of the dive. In my rise, I rolled my shoulder inward and crossed an arm over my belly. I had a full rotation with a full spin as I passed the level of the board. I carried the momentum into my second flip and spin. I nailed a double double and sliced the warm water toes-on.

I slipped deep through the silken water. My feet touched the bottom of the pool. I let myself fold downward through the caressing warmth. For a long, silent moment I hovered, fetal, near the bottom. Above me, liquid blue rippled and soothed. Tears cooled the warm water on my eyes.

The moment was forever, and it was less than the time it takes for breath to call for the next breath. I pulled my feet under me and pushed against the concrete floor. I broke the surface, took air, and looked for the otter woman.

At the shallow end of the pool, she climbed an aluminum ladder. I kicked into a breaststroke, not daring to dip my head into the water, not wanting to lose sight of her.

She stopped near a deck chair and picked up a hotel towel. She began drying her hair. She glanced my way. Her eyes flashed. Her smile played hide-and-seek behind the dabbing towel.

I kicked harder.

She turned away and padded across the concrete.

"Otter!" I called.

She disappeared into the shadows of the hotel.

I followed as far as the first shadowy intersection of corridors, but she was gone.

I returned to the pool and did several more dives. They were adequate, even skilled. My time in the gym had given me a new kind of flexibility and strength. Even so, without her watching, none of the dives held the magic of the first.

I fantasized that I might see her at dinner in the restaurant. I let myself linger there for hours, but she didn't appear. Later, in bed, I imagined us together in a tract house in Illinois, or in a cabin in Oregon, or in any of half-a-dozen fantasy homes where I thought her strength and smile might fit.

It was near 1 a.m. when moonlight slipped into my room and bathed my face. I decided it was ridiculous to stare at the ceiling wishing for the touch of a stranger with an otter's smile. I got out of bed, splashed cold water on my face, put on my suit and headed for the pool.

I ignored the hours signs and climbed over the damp wrought-iron railing. Thick mist blanketed the water, tendrils snaked upward, tickling the belly of the cool night. Moon-silvered ripples invited me to swim with them beneath the teasing mist.

I dropped my towel and climbed the tower to the board. I looked up to the moon and thanked it for the stranger's smile and the dive earlier in the day.

One.

Two.

Knee high.

Flex and stretch. Spin and tuck. Extend and reach for warm and wet. Penetrate, slip deep, smooth and slick. I slowed and smiled in the warm deeps. I snapped my hips to spin myself in the warm wetness. The silky mineral water kissed every inch of exposed skin. One long stroke. Another, and I was moving slow and weightless beneath the misty surface.

I broke surface and rolled onto my back. The board above me still shook from my dive.

She appeared there, tall and silvered in the moonlight.

One step.

Two.

Knee high, and she flew, stretched upward, arms out. Long, arched, sensual, and simple – she dove.

In the shallower end of the pool, my toes found the grit of the concrete bottom. She surfaced three feet from me. Through mist and moonlight, nose just above the surface, she pulled herself effortlessly toward me.

I backed away. She was too close. I was suddenly unsure, afraid. I was sick. No. I'd been sick.

She reached. One hand touched my chest.

I remembered Andrea and Danni. I remembered my failure.

Her other hand slid along the ridges of my belly. The root of my spine thrilled to her touch. My suit suddenly felt tight. I wanted her touch, knew she was what I had come to Glenwood to find. As certainly as my body had known how to dive in the afternoon sun, I knew I could reach out to her. I knew how to fold her into my arms, how to bring my lips to hers and how to slide thigh along thigh in the silken warmth of the pool.

We kissed. She tasted of the lime and sulphur of the pool. She tasted of heat and hunger. We parted to breathe. The mists surrounded us. She ran her hand up my thigh, across my bulging suit and up my belly to my neck. "Lean, sky dancer," she whispered.

"Otter smile," I said.

"I like that," she said. We kissed again, turning slowly in the water.

"I couldn't sleep," she said.

I slipped the strap of her suit from her shoulder and put my lips to the pulse at her neck. The mineral slickness, the warm water, her arching and her tiny moan all filled me. I bit lightly. I teased at her pearl earring with my tongue.

She laughed and twisted in my arms. Her hand slipped behind my thigh, slid upward, and gripped my ass. She pulled herself against me, and we fell back into the water, sinking slowly, kissing, rolling in the water and molding flesh to flesh.

She slid my suit off. I helped her with hers. Somehow, we knew when the other needed air. Like dolphins, we sank, surfaced, breathed, and let ourselves sink into the embrace of the healing waters again.

Slowly, we danced our wet dance. My mouth found her lips, her fingertips, her breasts, her belly. We touched bottom and rose again to breathe.

Sinking, her lips found my ear, the nape of my neck. Her fingers wrapped themselves in my hair. I dove deeper and bit at her thigh and traced my tongue along the mineral slickness of her outer lips, then the otter-musk sweetness within. I stayed there, tasting her, searching her for deeper mysteries, for watery pleasure. Her fingernails caught in my scalp. She writhed and shook. I plunged my tongue deeper, driving inward to taste her primal wetness fully.

She bucked against me and pulled at my head.

I broke away, and we rose to the surface to breathe.

In mist and moonlight, we kissed. Her hunger matched mine. Her soft hand pulled at my hardness. For a moment, I was surprised I was hard. It had been so long. Then she guided me to her, guided me from warm mineral water into her deep, healing wetness. She clasped her legs around mine and our hips found a rhythm that rotated us in the water, spun us one around the other, slowly sinking and rising and sinking again.

For minutes or for hours, we were one body, one soul writhing in primal waters, surging forward toward an epiphany of life. Our rhythms grew urgent. We sank deep into the silvery warmth. We pulled at one another, spinning faster, sharing what breath we had. We both knew we needed to rise for air. Instead, we pulled together tighter, harder, and we spun in liquid darkness one last time, separating our lips, screaming underwater, freeing joy and precious air in rising torrents of bubbles.

Gasping and laughing, we floundered to the surface. Together and silent in the moon-silvered water, we retrieved our suits then stroked to the edge of the pool. She climbed the ladder first, and I nipped her rear as it passed near my face. I followed her to her towel, and we slowly and gently dried one another.

My belly pressed to her back for warmth, I towelled her moonlit breasts. "What's your name, Otter Smile?" I asked.

"Cassey." She put her hands on mine and moved my towelling lower. "I like Otter Smile," she said.

"My name's Skyler," I told her.

"You're a hell of a diver," she said.

"You know how to move pretty well yourself," I said. She turned, and I dabbed her cheek with the towel. "Think you'll be able to sleep now?" I asked.

She took the towel, and we kissed. "I'm not planning to," she said. She took my hand, and we headed for the hotel.

Before we entered the hotel, I looked back at the mist-covered pool and thanked the moon, the mist, and the diving board. My body had never betrayed me. It fought. It brought me to Glenwood. I'd been reborn, given a diver's body. I was beginning my new life, a life that included laughter and love in the arms of a woman with an otter's smile.

The Little American

Sage Vivant

Their laughter began slowly; muted sporadic bubbles in his aching consciousness. The pulse in his brain, still erratic from last night's ouzo, knocked against his cranium, periodically drowning them out.

They had throaty, female laughs. Were they Greek? They spoke loudly, as most Greeks did, yet he did not hear that tone that sounded accusatory by English standards. Through the thin plaster wall, the voices also purred and growled. Sometimes it seemed they whispered but how would he hear that through a wall?

He swung his legs over the side of the bed. The door of the next villa opened and a woman called out *kalimera* to someone. A group of people (all women?) spilled out onto the shared veranda. The scraping of metal chairs along the rough cement made him wince.

He fumbled blindly around what he recalled was the nightstand, trying to locate his watch. After no success, he remembered it was still on his wrist. He squinted at its face, annoyed at the prolonged blur of it. Twelve fifteen. The morning was gone and he had no recollection of his return to the villa the night before.

Nothing was referred to as a "hotel" on Santorini, or at least, not in Oia, where he stayed. There were rooms, apartments and houses; all virtually the same, save for cooking spaces. At Strognopoulous, the units were a collection of apartments labelled "villas". As with all Greek accommodation, furnishings and space were modest but clean. The door of each villa was split down the middle, allowing half to be opened at a time and requiring most people to pass sideways through the portal. The doors led out to a semi-private veranda he shared with the villa next to him. Strognopoulous sat high enough to afford an expansive view of the Mediterranean, as well as the small, uninhabited islands of Palia Kameni and Nea Kameni.

He lay on his back with his legs still hanging off the side of the bed looking, he imagined, like one of those long, twisted slides that emptied into man-made rapids at an amusement park. His spinal discomfort was a welcome distraction from the bongo drums in his head. The ceiling spun whether his eyes were open or closed.

Their talking broke his inert concentration, yet he understood nothing of the human buzz that characterized their discussion. He rolled to his side, half hoping the movement would result in a landing on the floor. Instead, his face was smashed into the balled-up pillow and his legs flailed like a fish tail.

He could see one of the women on the veranda. When had he opened his shuttered window? Smooth, dark hair pulled back in a ponytail between her shoulder blades. If she turned to look, would she see him as clearly? The window had a screen, which he hoped darkened her vision of the interior. He lay naked, too numb to register the possibility of being seen.

Only her shoulders and head were visible to him. The subtle bronze highlights in her hair shone in the brilliant sunlight. She wore sunglasses and listened more than her companions. She occasionally raised a glass of dark liquid to her lips. The intensity of the sun on her skin and hair made him realize it was another unbearably hot day on the island.

He gratefully allowed the women to distract him from his head, which now felt as divided as his door. The woman he could see moved toward her friends, disappearing from the frame of his small window. There was much laughter and the sounds of struggle. He began to doze, comatose-style.

In minutes, a knock at his door jarred him. A giggle accompanied the second knock and a foreign feminine voice ventured, "Hello?"

If it had been a male voice, if he hadn't seen the fine features, the smooth, nearly black, lustrous hair, if he wasn't curious, even in post-inebriation, to see the rest of her, he would've ignored the knock. He would have chosen the spinning room over being neighbourly in virtually every circumstance.

Except this one.

With torpid speed, he stumbled toward the door, landing before it thanks to lucky projectory.

The cumbersome lock caused him some difficulty but he reasoned the noise would assure her of his impending response. He flung the half door open in victory, realizing simultaneously that his dick had not seen so much sunlight in years.

Smiling, she gasped both at his own realization and the sight of his unprotected genitalia. Suddenly more embarrassed than neighbourly, he closed the door in her face. She laughed aloud and called something in Greek to her friends, who squealed with delight.

Not that it mattered, but he imagined a variety of observations she might have conveyed to her friends:

"What a pathetic little man!"

"He must be crazy – he answered the door naked!"

"Oh, great! Hundreds of doors and we get the flasher!"

None of these observations was how he preferred to be remembered by a beautiful woman.

The pounding in his head did not diminish even slightly but he could ignore it now in the face of reparation to his reputation. He found his pants in the wrinkled heap near the dresser, grabbed them and practically jumped into them. He bounded out of his villa into the blinding sunlight, yanking up his zipper.

He stood briefly at his end of the patio, frozen by the four stunned expressions. The one who'd knocked was grinning. All of them waited to see what he might do next.

A slim patch of various succulents separated the two verandas. His momentary paralysis helped him notice this obstacle and he walked around it.

Establishing credibility under the circumstances was imperative but futile. He'd best settle for rendering competent assistance.

"Hi. I mean, *Kalimera*."

"*Kalimera*. Good morning. I am sorry to wake you," the

beauty replied slyly behind her sunglasses, not moving from her seat at the small table. She wore only a big, white, lacy overshirt. With a little stealthy dedication, he could probably make out nipples and pubic hair through it. But it was the long, shapely curves of her crossed thighs that jump-started his already beleaguered pulse. She was in her mid-thirties, soft but firm. Her tanned, curvaceous flesh riveted him and he tried not to stare, which was easy in the blinding sunlight.

The other three women stood near the table, with one holding a large canvas umbrella. One of them said something in Greek to the beauty, giggling under her breath. The beauty chuckled in assent and removed her sunglasses to reveal dark, exotic eyes.

"It's all right. It's time to get up, anyway," he said dismissively. Best not to mention the unsolicited birthday suit. "Did you need some help, ladies?"

"*Neh, efharisto.* Thank you, but I do not like to disturb you. I think you were out very late?" Her eyes ran up and down his body, and he grinned.

"Don't worry about that. I'd like to help if I can," he spoke slowly for her benefit but was grateful for the excuse to think slowly.

The three women hoisted the umbrella and aimed the bottom at the small hole in the centre of the iron table. The beauty held the table as they repeatedly missed their target. The bottle of Canaves wine wobbled slightly with the movement. All of them ignored him entirely.

The strong sun beat into his skull, causing both pain and clarity. He could not continue to stand there so effetely. With a confidence he didn't feel, he stepped toward them purposefully.

"I can help you with that," he said, grasping the umbrella and pushing into their sphere of cooperation. As he gradually wrested the apparatus away from them, he felt them surrender to his returning masculinity. He lifted the umbrella with both hands, filling his lungs with fresh Mediterranean sea air. Having failed to button his trousers, the zipper lost its tenuous anchor and opened with his exhalation. The beauty's hands grabbed the fabric just below his ass and tugged playfully as the umbrella slid into its slot in the table.

He stood immobile with surprise. He also stood undeniably naked.

The women erupted with laughter, including the beauty, who remained in her chair, delightedly smug about his predicament. One of the women, near forty and especially busty, pointed to his penis and exclaimed something he didn't understand. More laughter ensued.

He was not a large man. He'd never sauntered proudly through a locker room, bought a Speedo or found condoms too small. He knew there were men who, when flaccid, matched his size erect.

These were facts known to him for many years. But he loved women too much to allow an accident of birth to preclude his access to them. He'd made it his business to prove that size didn't matter.

That resolve, however, had never undergone this kind of test before. Being tittered at by four confident Mediterranean lovelies in broad daylight was unnervingly Fellinian. He stood frozen, the centre of their attention and stares, his mind a circuitous track of useless thoughts.

"They laugh because you are small," the beauty explained, stroking the fleshy curve of thigh crossed over her knee. "Maria says you look like her boy who has ten years'" the beauty said as if she dared him to grow before her eyes.

The presence of mind to retrieve his pants from the ground finally came to him. As he bent down, the beauty slid forward in her chair. From his stooped position, he watched her diaphanous shirt bunch into folds behind her bare ass as her meaty thighs moved toward his face. He forgot about his pants.

She shifted her hips to expose one luscious, tanned flank. Several dark pubic hairs strayed from the arc underlining the smooth slope of thigh. His face hovered only inches from her full, waiting ass.

The women were silent. The beauty's ass loomed so near his head, he could breathe in her subtle musk. He ran his eyes along her fleshy fullness and felt his face move closer, closer to that sweet spot hidden in the black line between her thighs.

He let his nose follow that line slowly from the curve of her flank to where it melded into voluptuous ass flesh. He licked at the little hairs that had tempted him, advancing deeper between her crack, burrowing to find her juicy centre.

Even her labia was abundant. As his tongue gingerly touched her thick lips, she moaned softly. He dropped to his knees at the sound.

She leaned to her right to better position her lovely ass into his hungry face, which he buried as deeply as he could between her round cheeks. His nose sunk into her plush, moist labia as he sought to taste her creaminess.

He slid his left hand along the underside of her smooth thighs while his tongue lapped away at her wet little flower. With his right hand, he lifted her uppermost cheek, wanting desperately to get as deeply inside her musky recesses as he could.

One of the women said something to the beauty who replied with distracted dismissal. He didn't care what they'd said as long as her luscious ass didn't move away from him. He darted his tongue in and out of the tip of her pussy; the angle did not allow full penetration. She squirmed with pleasure and emitted deep but tiny whimpers in response. He adored putting strong women into such helpless euphoria.

Fingers were suddenly running the length of his own ass cleavage. It was definitely a woman's touch; long, slow, soft caresses. But soon there were many fingers and more than two hands lavishing attention on his exposed rump. He felt his already hard cock tighten to an almost unbearably solid state. He sucked intently on the slippery pussy lips that smeared his nose and chin.

But the hands seemed to multiply. One grabbed his cock, another stroked his tight sac. A dainty finger rimmed his asshole, which he encouraged by spreading his legs and sticking his ass up in the air. The more they played, the more eagerly he feasted at the beauty's dripping snatch.

These Greek women continually confounded him, he mused amidst the probing tongues and digits. First, they giggle at him and now they fondle him.

A pair of strong but feminine hands grabbed his hips,

digging long, tapered nails into his skin. The hands gently but purposefully pulled him away from the beauty's succulent honey pot. He flowed with that motion, sensing the start of new pleasures.

The hands were assisted by another pair placed under his arms. They tugged until he was off his knees and squatting. They continued until he sat firmly on a folded blanket someone had thoughtfully placed on the rough cement.

The beauty rose from her chair and turned to face him. Her near-orgasmic daze was still evident but her natural composure quickly took hold as she looked down at him. She extended her hand in a gesture meant to help him up. He grasped it and got to his feet with her help.

"Please. Sit." She motioned to the chair she'd vacated.

He wanted to ask questions. Why were she and her friends playing with him? Why had they laughed at his size? Why did she offer her sweet, shapely ass to him? What was next? But he spoke no Greek and even the beauty's English was insufficient for conversation.

Four women stood before him, including the beauty, in various stages of undress. One, who looked to be in her mid-twenties, was completely naked and watched him with the haughtiness bred from confident sexuality. Her skin was smooth and very dark, with no tan lines whatsoever. Her breasts were neither small nor big. He noted that they were, in fact, perfect with their dark, pert nipples. As he admired them, she responded by grabbing one in each hand, as if reading his mind. She squeezed and kneaded, just like he wanted to do.

The next woman, probably close to forty, stood transfixed by his erect cock. Her zaftig presence felt motherly but richly erotic. She wore only a sarong tied loosely around her hips, emphasizing the contrast between her waist and her hips. But nothing could overshadow her impressive breasts. She stared at his rock-hard member as if it were a child's scraped knee. Seconds later, she caught his eye, penetrating him with rapacious intent. Her enormous tits gave credence to his initial reaction to her as motherly. Surely, hungry hordes could suckle at those mammaries and find sustenance! She lifted

one huge melon to her mouth and sucked at the hard pink
nipple.

The third woman, wearing only a bikini top, turned away
from him and bent over, swinging her long, loose sunstreaked
hair forward. She displayed an ass of superb proportions. She
spread her legs so he could see her deep pink pussy lips. Some
dark pubic hair obscured the sight, but it was clear that her
cunt was engorged and glistening with arousal. She reached
between her legs and frigged her own clit, wiggling her big,
luscious ass in syncopation.

He looked to the beauty for an explanation of this performance. She smiled with half her full mouth and stepped closer
to him, stopping by the side of his chair.

"They try to help you. To make you big." She took his rod
in her right hand and slowly massaged. She remained clothed
but as she coyly stared at him, the memory of her taste returned
to his tongue.

He watched the scene before him, reeling with conflicting
responses. He definitely wanted to fuck each and every one of
them, partially to prove he could. But their maternally inspired
intentions touched him and his curiosity took over. How far
would they go to make him grow? And how big was "big" to
them anyway?

He refrained from informing her that the five inches of
tumescent manhood she held was maximum size. Better to
wait and see what she planned to do with it.

The perfect-titted young woman spoke to the beauty and he
caught the word *Americano*. The beauty did not answer.
Instead, she continued the slow, sensual hand-job and whispered to him.

"She says all things in America are very big. She does not
believe you are American."

"Well, you can tell I'm American from my accent, can't you?
Anyway, how big do you think I should be?"

He knew he sounded manic and that she wouldn't reply. The
beauty straddled his lap. Little pink portions of her exposed
sex poked out from her thick bush, which he instinctively
reached out to stroke. He located her firm, slippery clit just as
she slid her hot cunt over his now throbbing dick.

She still wore her lacy overshirt but he could see her full titties bounce as she rode him. His fingers worked wildly at her clit, spreading juice all over his palm. With his free hand, he grabbed a handful of tit flesh and squeezed.

He lifted his hips to ram her with the same intensity she used to fuck herself with his love stick.

"*Neh, neh!*" she called out as he jammed himself into her. She threw her head back and held onto his shoulders, continuing to slide him in and out of her hot, wet hole. In and out, faster and faster, she slammed down onto him until she cried out, again with sounds and words unfamiliar to him.

Holding back his own eruption was excruciating, but he had to show these women he could please them. And he would fuck all of them if it were the last thing he did.

The beauty whimpered and collapsed, burying her head in his chest. He caressed her damp back through her shirt.

"Let me fuck your friends now," he whispered.

She grinned knowingly and dismounted. (He'd always found that "fuck" was a word internationally understood.) The three women, still playing with themselves, devoured him with their eyes.

He rose and staggered to the woman whose ass was spread so provocatively for him to sample. He grabbed both ass cheeks and leaned into her, sliding his cock along her creamy pussy lips. She moaned and wiggled, now frigging herself without any trace of inhibition.

He stuffed himself into her quickly and began to pump her hard. The other two women moved to stand on either side of him, both of them within arm's reach.

As he fucked the gorgeous ass, he reached for the pussy of the young woman while she continued to play with her own tits. The zaftig woman offered one of her monster melons to him. His mouth was drawn to her waiting nipple as if he needed her nourishment. She pushed her huge tit into his face as he suckled her.

The beauty stood in front of the faceless ass woman, holding her steady as he fucked her, sucked an enormous tit and fingered a slippery snatch.

The young woman burst into a powerful orgasm, her clit

twitching in his hand. Zaftig, who'd been beating her own meat as he sucked her tit, began to wail as her body shook in its surrender to pleasure.

His resolve gave way to the imminent explosion now brewing in his balls. The pussy he fucked suddenly gripped him urgently, spasming around his cock. The woman squealed and pushed her ass into him recklessly. He pumped back with the same abandon.

His come shot into her at warp speed. He couldn't stop fucking her! He pumped and pumped; she yelled louder. Her cheeks shook with every thrust. Finally, his dick twitched with unmistakable surrender and he knew he'd given his very last drop of jizz to this gorgeous ass.

The woman dropped to her knees and fell into the beauty's arms. He wobbled backwards into the chair.

His head spun with sublime exhaustion as he watched the beauty cuddle the woman he'd just reamed. The beauty's eyes penetrated past his psyche and into his soul. As she caressed the satisfied woman, he felt he caressed them both. Through her grounded but surreal presence, he touched both women, snuggling, nuzzling, and purring into them.

The young woman announced something in Greek after consulting her watch. The zaftig one stepped toward him, heavy breasts swinging freely. She ran her fingers through his hair and smiled at him as if he'd just won the spelling bee. Then, she bent down to kiss his cock.

"*Bravo, Americano!*" she whispered and floated away into the villa. The young woman grinned, winked and followed her. Beauty helped the woman to her feet.

Both of them appraised him fondly but the woman with his come inside her suddenly blushed and scampered into the villa.

The beauty approached, picking up his pants as she passed them. At his chair, she deposited the garment into his lap, grasped the arms of the chair and leaned forward to kiss his forehead.

"You are a special man," she cooed with that devastating half-smile. She ran the tips of her fingers along his cheek.

"Husbands are coming," she added.

He held her hand against his face and kissed those incredible lips, savouring their fullness in his memory before he returned to his own villa.

Fugu

Bianca James

Dedicated to the ghost of Itami Juzo

I came to Tokyo in the Year of the Snake, with the vague
intention of doing research for my doctoral dissertation.
When my informant fell through, I was left with an expired
student visa, and over a thousand dollars in debt. I took a
job waitressing at a seedy hostess bar in Kabukicho called
Papillon.

Kabukicho was a hot bed of sex clubs and mob activity, but
the bar where I worked paid well and let me drink for free,
and booze was about the only thing I cared about at that
point.

The thugs who frequented the bar were known as *chinpira*.
The *chinpira* wore cheap suits in hideous shades of purple, red,
and yellow, their hair teased into frizzy orange perms. They
were low-ranking *yakuza*, missing teeth and bits of fingers.
They were lecherous and rude, never tipped, sprayed me with
spittle when they insulted me in torrents of Osaka-tinged
Japanese. They never seemed to make it past the age of 30.
I didn't mourn when I found out that certain individuals had
been busted by the police. There would be a fresh wave of
over-eager 18-year-olds in less than a week's time.

Daisuke was 35, hovering somewhere towards the middle of
the *yakuza* hierarchy. It seemed improbable that a *yakuza* of
Daisuke's calibre would bother to penetrate the cramped
confines of Papillon, but it was also difficult to believe he
had ever been a *chinpira*. Perhaps the seven years he'd spent in
prison had refined him, his jail cell like the proverbial oyster
lovingly polishing the secret pearl tucked away inside.

Daisuke's fingers were long and slender, fully intact, though he was missing the small toe from his left foot. He wore a full body tattoo concealed beneath his cream-coloured linen suits, carp and dragons inked in lurid shades of red and blue. He was soft spoken and polite, and I had to repeatedly remind myself that this was an evil man whose money came from murder and extortion. I knew about his obsession with fucking white women. I knew he had come for me. I did not care. I graciously allowed him to pay my debts, wine me, dine me, and fuck my brains out. One does not mess around with the *yakuza*.

Daisuke was a gourmet when it came to both women and food, his tastes running towards expensive shellfish. Every night Daisuke took me to a different restaurant with a new speciality to try. During this time I developed a taste for hot sake, the culinary enabler. Mild drunkenness allowed me to bypass my gag reflex and enjoy the erotic intrigue of Japanese food. It all seemed vaguely perverse, yet prepared to obsessive standards of beauty and cleanliness. Certain foods reminded me distinctly of sex: a gummy fermented substance known as *natto* stunk like unclean genitals. Viscous *tororo* starch, served over noodles, was white and sticky like come. Powdery soft *mochi* cakes made from pounded rice had the silky weight of a testicle.

Eating these things made me feel as though I was a culinary whore, being mouth fucked by one strange flavour, odour, consistency after another.

Everything was eaten raw, served with horseradish, pickled ginger and strong liquor in order to combat the ill effects of any parasitic micro-organisms hiding in the muscular striations of fish meat. The danger of food poisoning or tapeworms loomed perilously near, yet never close enough to be perceived as a real threat. As long as Daisuke was picking up the bill, he ordered and I ate shamelessly.

At a family-owned *izakaya* in Asakusabashi, we ate slick pink pregnant female shrimp, belly bulging with shiny black caviar, spindly legs and antennae jutting out at random angles. I fought the urge to scrape off the gelatinous eggs and eat the otherwise innocuous shrimp on its own, but consumed the delicacy whole, enduring the chitinous crunch of the tail, savouring the creaminess of the flesh, the hundred

tiny eggs that popped in my mouth and got caught between
my teeth.

While we ate, Daisuke told me about the first woman he'd
made love to, a naïve peasant maid, "the most beautiful girl
he'd ever seen." They'd sneak off at night to fuck in barns and
fields. When she'd discovered she was pregnant, she'd killed
herself to protect the honour of her family. He'd fucked her
one last time as her body convulsed from the poison she'd
eaten, mixed into sweet bean cakes, her spasming body ripping
the orgasm from Daisuke's loins.

"I could have kissed her," he said. "The poison from her
mouth would have killed me, our sin would have been wiped
clean. But I didn't. Now you know why I am a criminal."

Daisuke related the tale with fond nostalgia. I took another
sip of bracing *shochu*, liquor made from the clean wheat in the
peasant fields where Daisuke had lost whatever semblance of
innocence he'd once had, and ate another.

A week later we had fresh spider crab, eaten cold with lemon
at a fancy restaurant in Ebisu. Daisuke told me what he'd done
that day – breaking all ten fingers of a man who'd defaulted on
his loans – as we snapped the spindly crab legs one by one,
teasing out the red and white flesh with picks and scissors.
When we had picked the crustacean clean of meat, there was an
elaborate ritual of sucking out the muddy brains, then sipping
hot sake from the bare shell.

At a bar managed by an Australian surfer in Hibiya, we
drank cold Sapporo beers and slurped fresh Uni, the slimy
orange innards of the sea urchin divested of its spiky purple
shell. Each glob was daintily served on an edible green leaf, to
be grasped by chopsticks quickly before it dripped to the
table like fluorescent snot. Daisuke told me about the special
sushi restaurant he went to, to celebrate his release from
prison five years previous. He called it "sushi in the raw",
sashimi served off the supine bodies of beautiful naked
women. The women shave their entire bodies and bathe in
ice water beforehand, in order to lower their blood tempera-
ture by a degree or two. Then the raw fish is arranged
artistically on the chilled body of the human serving tray.
He'd said he'd never been so aroused. His erection was so

hard it pained him. And they'd eaten his favourite, an exquisite tuna with fresh roe.

I asked him if he'd fucked the girl afterwards. He seemed appalled. She wasn't a whore, he said, just a serving tray. Her flesh was cold; it would have been like fucking a corpse. He preferred the warm-blooded women in Kabukicho, their wet mouths slicked the colour of fresh tuna *sashimi*. They call adult video stars *maguro*, he said, because of the way a lubricated vagina looks shiny red like slabs of raw tuna.

After our meals, we'd retire to the love hotels of Shibuya to indulge in the next round of carnal pleasures. We'd fucked on the whorehouse beds of a hundred different love hotels, heart-shaped beds, black leather beds, revolving beds, beds shaped like racecars. We'd fucked on shag carpeting, in bathtubs, in chairs, in every imaginable position until Daisuke would fall asleep, and I'd stay awake watching TV and smoking cigarettes, the terminal insomniac.

He made love as one would expect a criminal to, grasping my arms and legs with strong fingers, leaving bruises in the shape of fingerprints. Daisuke's sexual appeal was his violence: the fact that he was a gangster made me desire him more. I loved the shameless way he ripped off my panties and pulled my hair while he thrust his cock into me from behind. He rode the fine line between lover and predator that is socially unacceptable in the States, but it made me come like a hair-trigger every time.

His entire being fascinated me; he was so much different than a Western man. His body was hairless and smooth, lacking the musky animal smell that some men have. He was very lean and strong, the lines of his muscles outlined in golden skin and indigo ink. His hair was heavy, straight, and black like the feathers of the ominous crows that haunt the streets of Tokyo, getting fat on garbage, rumoured to occasionally attack dogs and small children. *Yakuza* were like crows in that way, despised, yet an unwavering necessary evil.

The love hotel we went to the night we ate *Uni* had red satin sheets and a black carpet. He'd removed his tie and his jacket, hung them carefully in the closet. Daisuke had placed his hands on my shoulders and gently pushed me back onto the bed. He unplugged the phone from the wall and used the plastic cord to bind my ankles to my wrists, leaving me splayed and open, an elaborate display of *shibari*. I felt like the sea urchin whose shell had been cracked open, oozing and vulnerable. Fully clothed in this absurd position, he unbuttoned my dress down the front, pushed my breasts up over the tops of my bra, worked his fingers in under the elastic of my panties, then cutting them off entirely using his knife, taking care not to nick my delicate skin.

Once my vulva was fully visible, he pushed the labia back with his thumb and index finger and squeezed lube into the crevice running from my pussy to my ass. He angled me against the mirrored headboard to display the *maguro*-pink of my cunt and ass. He worked his fingers into both holes, and licked my clit until I came, gasping. He grasped my hips to lift my glistening pink sex onto his, and entered me. Daisuke's cock was curved upward in long graceful lines. There were bumps along the underside – pearls, seven in all, one for each year he'd spent in prison. Each bump caught at the entrance before popping in, the smooth ridge working against my G-spot as he moved in me. He kept his fingers in my lubed ass and fucked me in both holes while telling me his fantasies – that he wanted to take me to the *Yakuza* headquarters for a gang bang, that he wanted to hire another *gaijin* girl and have us sixty-nine while he took turns fucking us from behind.

Then, once his dirty talk had reached its climax, his cock seemed to simultaneously tighten and expand, and pulled out wet and glistening to spray his foamy white ejaculate onto my swollen vulva, like liquid pearls. He licked my neck and nastily whispered, "*Maguro*." Sometimes I wondered if he viewed me as the great white tuna, chicken of the sea.

Daisuke called me at the bar one late afternoon in August. The day was unbearably hot and humid, my dress soaked in sweat. The air conditioning had broken and the heat was stifling. The bar was desolate, a few of us sitting drinking gin and tonics and fanning ourselves with the cheap paper fans the bar gave out to advertise drink specials.

I took a taxi to a hotel in the Ginza, the kind of place out-of-town dignitaries stayed when they visited Tokyo. Daisuke was holed up in a suite much classier than the love hotels where we held our nightly sex trysts. He opened the door wearing a white cotton *yukata*, a glass of whisky and crushed ice in one hand. The air in the room was so icy I felt as though I might faint from pleasure, my nipples visibly erect through my thin dress.

Everything in the room was cream coloured: the diaphanous curtains pulled against sealed French windows, the whipped-cream soft thick carpet, the huge bed covered in summer cotton sheets, the thin kimono that covered Daisuke's tattooed body. I wanted to pull the robe from his shoulders, touch his belly and his sex, taste the whiskey ice cube flavour of his mouth. He bolted the door behind me and led me into the white marble palace of a bathroom. He helped me strip from my sticky dress, and we bathed together. He washed every part of me carefully with a soapy cloth, and then we slipped into the vast tub of hot water together.

He dried me with a fluffy white towel and gave me a *yukata* like his own. He led me into a smaller, dim bedroom adjoining the bathroom. A man in a suit was lying supine on the bed, limbs sprawled. A wet, red hole gaped from the back of his head. I shrieked in surprise.

"There's nothing to be afraid of," said Daisuke grimly. "He's thoroughly dead."

"Who is he?"

"My assassin. It seems I have made myself unpopular in certain circles."

"He didn't do a very good job, did he?"

"If you want a job done right, you've got to do it yourself," Daisuke replied with little humour. He flicked on a bedside lamp and I jumped with a start. A white plastic bucket half-full of water was set on the floor beside the bed, and I was loath to look inside in case I might discover some disembodied organ quivering within. Instead, I found a grey, bulbous fish, swimming in circles, dazed by the light.

"Tonight, we celebrate," Daisuke proclaimed grandly.

"Do you want to go out?" I inquired feebly. I wasn't sure if I understood what we were celebrating.

"There isn't a restaurant in Tokyo that will satisfy my desire," he replied, lifting the plastic bucket. "The liver of the *fugu* is the most delicious of any fish. It is a delicacy a man gets to enjoy once in a lifetime. A mildly hallucinatory effect, followed by strong sexual arousal, and excruciating death. Even the finest restaurants in Tokyo refuse to serve the liver, it's too risky. Fortunately, my mother taught me the proper preparation. She herself died from overindulgence. I will be joining her tonight."

"Daisuke, you're fucking crazy."

Daisuke fixed me with a demented grin. "Am I? I have killed ninety-nine men in thirty-five years. Tonight, I will kill the hundredth, and then I will retire. I want you to help me celebrate. In fact, I plan to compensate you quite generously."

"Daisuke, I refuse to eat poisonous blowfish. That's where I draw the line."

"It's not for you, bitch!" Daisuke screamed. The door chimes sounded above his voice. He regained his calm, carried the bucket into the main room of the suite and placed it near the bed. He opened the door, and a bellhop pushed a golden cart laden with champagne, strawberries, and other delicacies into the room. The bellhop retreated with a bow.

Daisuke popped the champagne and poured it into two delicate glasses.

"There's a man who wants me dead. There's plenty more where he came from," he continued, blithely gesturing toward the other bedroom. "I guess you could say I'm something of a traditionalist. Death before dishonour. I'd rather kill myself than suffer a fool's death at the hands of some *chinpira* thug. I've had a good run. In fact, it's a miracle I'm still alive."

"What do you want me to do?"

"Don't worry, there's only enough *fugu* for one person. That's why I had room service bring the rest, so you could have a good meal as well. I will prepare the *fugu* and eat it within minutes. The poison can set in minutes, or it may take hours. The poison paralyzes the respiratory system, so I will become unable to move or breathe, but still fully conscious. I want you to fuck me to death. The orgasm achieved when completely deprived of oxygen is rumoured to be exquisite, and the exertion will most likely render me unconscious. Don't stop fucking me until you are absolutely sure I am dead. When you are finished, return home, but make sure no one sees you. Wait until my sister Minako arrives, she will bring you a parcel with the money in the morning, then leave the country. I don't want them going after you in my absence."

"You're completely serious, aren't you?"

"I am. There is one last thing. Under no circumstances should you kiss me once I have eaten the *fugu*, in case the poison is transferred from my lips to yours." Daisuke drew me close to his body. "So kiss me while it is still safe." He buried his hands in my thick hair and pulled my face to his, pressed his mouth to my lips and throat. My heart felt crushed, making it difficult to breathe and fight back tears. Daisuke ran his tongue along each eyelid.

"You needn't mourn me," he whispered. "I'm going straight to hell."

Daisuke prepared the tools of destruction – a sharp blade and the cutting tray. He removed the fish from the bucket and severed its head with a swift cut. He carefully cleaned and gutted the fish, and then he rinsed his hands and approached me.

"Don't do it." I tried not to get hysterical.

"It's too late."

"I love you."

"That doesn't matter. Maybe it's best if you didn't watch." Daisuke blindfolded me and had me lie back on the bed.

I felt cool sliminess on my belly. And then, I remembered – sushi in the raw. I laid still as I felt the fish being arranged on my stomach, breasts, and pubis, then sucked off without the formal assistance of chopsticks. He ate the fish from my body with pleasured moans, then licked my navel, my nipples, my groin. Then he entered me, slowly, one pearl at a time, and removed the blindfold. My heart was racing like a rabbit's.

"How soon until you die?" I asked.

"I don't know. But you may have to take over for me at some point."

"I wasn't kidding when I said I love you."

"I know."

He thrust his cock into me, harder now, slamming his hips against mine, grabbing my hair and biting my neck. I growled and buried my nails in his back. I felt my anger take over, and we wrestled with each other. He let me win, pushing him onto his back so I could ride him. I pushed his hands away when he reached to touch my breasts. "You bastard!" I shrieked. "I fucking hate you! How could you do this to me!" My screams made him push his cock deeper into my body. I slapped his face and yanked his hair, excited by the evil fire that glowed in his eyes. I pushed my cunt down to meet his upward thrusts, rubbed my clit with my left hand while making him suck the fingers of the other.

And then, his thrusts stopped, his body grown as rigid as his swollen penis.

The poison had set in. Daisuke's eyes were glazed with horror. I knew he was still conscious, though his body had frozen. I slowed my pace a bit, my pussy sucking sinuously around his thick shaft, gripping him tighter with my internal muscles as I slid up and down. That's when my orgasm set in, shaking my body with an unholy violence. My hair was tangled, my tits and back dripping with musky sweat. "I could kiss you right now, and you couldn't do a damn thing to stop me," I informed his dying body. I squeezed again, and felt his final jolt of life spurt into my cunt, and I fucked his come deeper into my body, savouring the extra lubrication.

Daisuke was dead. I was completely fucked up, exhilarated, probably in some sort of shock, my body stinking like sex and death. I pulled on my grimy dress and climbed out the hotel window and down the fire escape. I didn't want to be trapped in that room with the corpse of my lover, especially when there were men looking to kill him. Outside, the night air was warm and quiet. I ran away from the hotel, relying on my instincts to get as far away as quickly as possible. This must be how he felt when he killed those men, I thought, though I hadn't truly murdered him. Assisted suicide, the Dr Kevorkian of cocktail waitresses. Somehow I managed to find a cab to take me home to the relative safety and comfort of shower and bed.

I was awoken from troubled sleep by the doorbell. No dream could rival the nightmare I'd already been through. Minako, I thought. I answered the door haphazardly wrapped in the sheet from my futon. Minako was in her early forties, tall like her brother, and curvaceous, with beautiful long straight hair and full lips. She wore sunglasses to hide eyes that were red from crying. She was wearing a long black dress and was perspiring lightly, exuding a faint spicy odour. She entered and closed the door after herself.

Once inside, she reached for the hand that had been clutching the sheet to my body, leaving me standing nude in my shabby apartment. Minako eyed my body approvingly, traced the purple bruise that marred my throat with one long, red, fingernail.

"My brother loved you," was all she said. She handed me a package wrapped in red silk and tied with elaborately knotted gold cords. "I suggest you take the money and leave Tokyo as soon as possible," she advised. "Where you go is none of my business."

"Thank you."

"There is one last thing he asked me to do," she said hesitantly. She kissed me with her full red lips, probed me with her tongue. I felt electricity jolt from my mouth straight to my cunt.

"A last kiss from my brother," she finished. She turned away to leave.

"Wait," I called after her desperately. "Stay with me."

She smiled. "Tokyo is my home. I can't leave. And I am not Daisuke." She closed the door after herself.

I fumbled with the package she gave me, yanking on the complicated cords like an overeager child. A hefty stack of 10,000 yen bills spilled out. And then, seven identical silver pearls rolled from beneath the money and landed on the woven straw carpet of the room.

I went to Thailand and had them made into a necklace.

Deserving Ruth

Mike Kimera

"My wife says you like to come in her mouth, David."

We are only one drink into the evening and this isn't the conversational opener I'd expected. I nurse my bottle of Bud and say nothing.

Lars puts his arm around my shoulders, leans his head down towards mine and says, "Mei Mei does have a talented tongue, but I always wonder about a man who is able to resist her tight little cunt. There's something about the grip of a wet cunt on your cock that a mouth just can't match, don't you think?"

I am very aware of the heat of Lars' body next to mine. He is dressed in Levis and tight fitting black T-shirt and he looks like six foot four of pure muscle. For a moment it occurs to me that he could snap my neck without breaking sweat, but he is smiling and from the tone of his voice we could be talking about cars or sports.

I glance over at Mei Mei. She looks small next to my wife, Ruth. They both have the same long black hair and have conspired to wear matching outfits, black silk shirt-dresses that stop inches above the knee and tie with a simple belt at the waist. Their makeshift uniforms emphasise how different they are. Ruth has a strong Slavic look; her breasts and hips seem almost swollen and overripe compared to Mei Mei's compact Malaysian frame. The two of them are talking animatedly, leaning forward, their faces almost touching. Ruth's hand rests on Mei Mei's knee, her fingers pointing along the line of her thigh. Sexual intent seems to flash between them.

"Ruth has nice breasts, David," Lars says, "You must enjoy

pressing her tits together and pushing your cock between them.''

I feel the beginnings of an erection and I wish Lars would take his arm off my shoulders. I have never fucked Ruth's tits, she has never let me, but I have often wondered what it would be like.

I continue looking at the women to give myself time to decide how to get Lars to move his arm without causing offence. After all, this is his house; I was brought up not to insult my host.

Ruth's hand is now out of sight, underneath Mei Mei's dress. Mei Mei leans forward and pushes her tongue into Ruth's mouth. There is something staged about the kiss. The tongues are too visible. I know that, out of the sides of their eyes, they are looking at Lars and me, putting on a show for us.

Ruth is in charge, of course. Ruth is always in charge. She was the one who brought Mei Mei into our bed. She told me that they met at one of those Manchester sauna clubs that doubles as a swingers swap centre. Mei Mei was new and all the men had been trying to get her attention. Ruth pushed them aside, pulled Mei Mei's head back by the hair and then kissed her. Mei Mei kissed back and opened her legs slightly. Ruth said that Mei Mei was so wet she could have slid her whole fist into her cunt. As it was, pushing two fingers in was enough to cause general applause from the watching men.

Normally Ruth doesn't involve me in her promiscuous adventures, but she always tells me about them. She wants me to know the lengths that she goes to to find satisfaction.

Ruth has a set routine. Whenever she gets really horny she goes to the club and fucks. Then she comes back and tells me all about it. She makes me sit in the living room with the palms of my hands on the arm of the chair. If I move my hands she will walk out of the room and not tell me anything more. If I stay still, she will talk me through every detail, all the while coaxing my cock to get harder and harder. Then she'll let me be her last fuck of the day.

I was in the chair, being told about the Malaysian girl who had nipples like rivets and hair like silk and I was getting nicely stiff when Ruth said, "You'll love her mouth on your cock. She'll swallow you whole."

This was a departure from the routine. I was still trying to decide what to make of it when Ruth said, "You can come in now."

Mei Mei came out of our bedroom. She was naked. She didn't look at me, only at Ruth. Her look was full of longing.

"I told her she could only lick my cunt once her mouth was filled with your come," Ruth said, as if she was describing some everyday instruction.

I said nothing. Speech was beyond me. Mei Mei knelt and looked up at Ruth.

"Keep your mouth open and your tongue out," Ruth said.

Ruth began to work my cock with her fingers. Her grip was strong enough to hurt. She was interested in results, not finesse. She took care to rub my glans against the tip of Mei Mei's tongue from time to time. When she felt that I was ready to come she pushed Mei Mei's head forward so that I was in her mouth when the come pulsed out of me.

"Don't swallow that," Ruth said.

Mei Mei opened wide, letting my limp cock slip out, and showed Ruth the come she held in her mouth.

Ruth sat on my lap with her back to me, her legs spread on either side of my knees.

"Show me how deep you can push that come inside me," Ruth said.

As Mei Mei worked with her tongue, Ruth gave me a running commentary on her performance. She told me that Mei Mei was a much better cunt-licker than me and said that she must have had a lot of practice.

The narration became more and more breathless as Mei Mei buried her head between Ruth's legs. When Ruth came her whole body tensed against mine. I was hard again by now, my cock rolling around under Ruth and close to Mei Mei's mouth. I wanted to be inside one of them.

Ruth climbed off me. She pulled Mei Mei to her feet and hugged her.

"I'm taking Mei Mei to bed to reward her for her hard work," Ruth said. "I'll see you in the morning."

This was outrageous behaviour, even by Ruth's standards. I should have complained. I should have demanded to join them. I should have pushed Ruth to the floor and fucked her into submission. I just sat there looking stupid, my unwanted erection signalling my uselessness.

As they reached the bedroom door I heard myself say, "Please."

It sounded sad and pathetic even to me.

"Shall we let him watch, Mei Mei?" Ruth asked.

"I would like to see him inside you," Mei Mei said.

It was the first time I had heard her speak. Her voice was soft and gentle. It made me want to smile.

"Come along, David," Ruth said, "if you are still hard after I've rewarded Mei Mei I will let you be my last fuck of the day."

I went to her like a recently scolded puppy being offered a bone.

Ruth placed Mei Mei's hand around my cock.

"Hold on to that for me, Mei Mei. Don't let him come."

Mei Mei smiled encouragingly and then she closed her fingers around me as if she was grasping a luggage handle. We made an absurd chain of need as Ruth led Mei Mei into the room by the hand and I was pulled along behind them.

Ruth arranged us both on the bed, side by side. Mei Mei kept her finger and thumb around the base of my cock. Her arm was a line of heat across my belly.

"Watch and learn how to please a woman, David," Ruth said.

Ruth leant over Mei Mei, her knee between Mei Mei's legs, and tilted her long black hair until it stroked Mei Mei's breasts and belly. It was the only part of her touching Mei Mei. Slowly Ruth increased the speed at which her hair moved across Mei Mei's flesh until she was tossing her head from side to side and almost whipping Mei Mei with her mane.

I hadn't realised how hard Mei Mei had been gripping me until Ruth finally held her head still and Mei Mei sighed and relaxed her hand a little. Mei Mei's nipples were hard and her eyes were closed.

Looking at me, Ruth lowered her face towards Mei Mei and

kissed her on the forehead. She stroked Mei Mei's face with the tips of her fingers, brushing her lips with her thumb. Mei Mei suckled it slowly, gratefully.

Ruth withdrew her thumb and used it to trace a wet trail between Mei Mei's breasts and down over her belly. Mei Mei closed the rest of her fingers around my cock and seemed to hold her breath. Ruth let the moment of silent stillness grow until it was almost unbearable and then she finally took Mei Mei. Her tongue pushed its way into Mei Mei's mouth at the same time that two of her fingers entered her cunt. Mei Mei's back arched.

Ruth rested most of her weight on the hand that gripped Mei Mei's sex. I could see how she used her thumb to circle Mei Mei's clit as she worked two and then three fingers in and out, spreading Mei Mei wide and seeming to try and scoop the juices out of her.

I wanted to move but I didn't dare. I could smell Mei Mei's sex, see the sweat forming on her brow. Precome started to seep from my cock. I did my best to hold back.

Ruth was in rut mode now. She had trapped Mei Mei's thigh between her own and was working herself against it, all the time staring at Mei Mei and muttering, "Come for momma, baby, come for momma."

Then, like a bird of prey, she descended upon Mei Mei's right nipple and savaged it between her teeth. Mei Mei's grip on my cock was so tight it was painful. She was groaning and raising one shoulder off the bed like a wrestler resisting being pinned. Ruth's palm was slapping against Mei Mei's mound almost fast enough to be applause.

Mei Mei let out a long soft sigh, her body went limp and she lay there as still as the dead. Ruth stopped and looked at her, more with curiosity than fear. "Well, well, a come coma. I haven't seen one of those up close before," she said.

Mei Mei's eyes fluttered open. She let go of my cock for the first time since all this began and gently held Ruth's face.

"Thank you," she said, kissing Ruth on the lips. "Thank you."

Even Ruth showed some emotion at Mei Mei's gratitude; she smiled at her and ruffled her hair.

When Ruth made to get off the bed, Mei Mei said, "Wait! Please. I want to see him inside you. Please. I want to do something special."

Ruth looked as if she'd forgotten I was there.

"OK," Ruth said, "it looks like you've kept him harder than usual and I'd like to find out what 'special' means. Let's do it — or should I say him?"

Mei Mei kissed me quickly on the cheek and said, "Don't worry, you'll like this." Then she scrambled down the bed until she was facing my cock, her body pressed into my side.

"I'm going to help him fuck you," she said, sounding delighted with herself.

She pressed the index and second fingers of her left hand along the underside of my cock, so that the tips of the fingers were pushing up into the soft crown of the head and my balls were cupped in her palm.

"Please, lower yourself onto us," Mei Mei said.

"That's going to be a tight squeeze. I mean, I know he's only average size but will you both fit?"

"Please," Mei Mei said.

Very slowly, Ruth lowered herself onto me. Mei Mei's fingers were small but the extra width they generated made Ruth a very tight fit.

"Oh, fuck," Ruth said, "that's what a cock should feel like."

Mei Mei grinned, gave Ruth a quick kiss on the clit and said, "You'll like the next part."

Mei Mei used her fingers to roll the head of my cock against Ruth's G-spot. The sensation was intense and I wanted to come at once. I also wanted this to go on forever.

Ruth was biting her lip and pulling at her nipples, eyes closed in concentration. She looked magnificent.

I couldn't hold out any longer. Sperm started a rush from my balls and up my cock, a huge wave of energy battering through me.

Mei Mei took my release as the cue for her coup de grâce. She sucked Ruth's clit into her mouth and started to worry it like a dog with a rabbit. I'd never felt Ruth contract so much or so often. She was so far gone that she bit her lip. A narrow ribbon of scarlet traced its way over the edge of her chin.

Mei Mei withdrew her hand and Ruth's cunt suddenly felt cavernous around my shrinking cock. She positioned herself behind Ruth, her arms under Ruth's armpits, her hands on Ruth's breasts and kissed her wounded lip. She eased Ruth off me and laid her on the bed, stroking her head until Ruth slipped into sleep.

"I have to go now," Mei Mei said.

She reached for her clothes, which lay on the chair next to the bed. By the time she had slipped into her skirt and T-shirt, I was standing next to the bed, still a little dazed by the way I'd spent the afternoon.

Mei Mei stretched up and kissed me on the cheek. "Thanks, David. Tell Ruth I'll call her. You were both wonderful." She waved as she went out the door. Standing naked, spent and confused, I waved back, trying for a smile.

Ruth slept for 20 minutes. I covered her with a duvet. I knew I should have been angry with her, she'd treated me very badly, but I also knew that I deserved it.

We'd really loved one another once. Then, two years ago, I spoiled things. I had an affair, less than an affair, a one-night stand with an old friend I'd met by chance. I didn't think to use a condom. I never imagined that I might pass on a disease to Ruth that would rob her of the child she had always wanted and rob me of my wife's affection.

In Ruth's eyes I had rejected her as a lover and destroyed her as a mother with the one act of betrayal. Her promiscuity started as a means of punishing me. Now I'm not sure what drives her to it. We've made an accommodation of sorts, people always do, but there is an undercurrent of regret and anger and guilt that could sweep us away at any time.

"I don't know what you're looking so glum about." Ruth said, when she woke. "You just got your rocks off twice in one night. That must be some kind of record for you. I'm going to get a shower. Then I'm going to sleep."

I knew what that meant. I made my way to the guest bedroom. Laying there, replaying the sex in my head, I wondered what it was that Ruth really wanted and whether or not she'd found it.

Mei Mei didn't come back to the house again, but I knew

that Ruth had stayed at her house at least three times over the next two weeks. Ruth didn't share the details with me. She seemed a bit distracted. Her smile was brittle and she was drinking more than usual. I avoided asking questions. I'd long ago lost the right to hold Ruth to account.

Then this morning, the pattern changed. Ruth couldn't quite hide the tension in her voice when she said, "We're going to Mei Mei's house tonight. It will be a lot of fun."

Even staying quiet doesn't always keep me out of trouble. Ruth stepped close to me and said, "I'm sick of your wimpy silences, David. You should be glad I'm including you. I hope that, for once, I can depend on you to behave properly. Do you understand?"

I nodded my head and she pushed me up against the wall and kissed me. It was a wild kiss, almost a bite. When it was over she said, "Don't let me down, David. Not again."

So now I'm standing way too close to a large Swedish guy and watching my wife undo the buttons on Mei Mei's dress. I should be having a good time but I feel like an impostor in their company. I'm the sort of guy who reads CD titles in the kitchen at parties. I've never felt comfortable hanging out with the cool kids.

Lars lifts his arm off my shoulders, but things get worse when he taps my bum and says, "Let's get out of these clothes and show the girls why a woman needs a man like a fish needs water."

The "girls" stop fondling each other and watch Lars as he pulls off his T-shirt. His chest is completely smooth, he has a six-pack stomach and oh my God he has nipple rings. That's enough to make my balls retract. I hate the idea of being pierced.

I'm still unbuttoning my shirt when Lars climbs out of his jeans. I don't want to look at his cock but I can't help it. He's not erect yet but it's already clear that he's longer and thicker than I am. And the bloody man shaves his pubes. Even on his balls.

I stop getting undressed. I'm not at all sure I want to be here.

Lars pulls the foreskin back on his cock. His fist is wrapped around it below the head but there's plenty of meat still visible.

"OK, who'd like first lick?"

Something in the way he says that makes me certain that I'm included in the invitation. He grins at me. I look away. I'm relieved when he walks towards Ruth and Mei Mei, his cock bouncing ludicrously in front of him.

"Into position, girls. You know what I want."

The women have slipped out of their dresses. Mei Mei kneels on the sofa. In a move that looks practised, Ruth sits astride Mei Mei's thighs, facing her and then lays back with her head over the edge of the sofa. Mei Mei lifts Ruth's legs so that Ruth can hook her knees over Mei Mei's shoulders. With a smile, Mei Mei lowers her head and starts to lap gently at Ruth's sex.

"Don't they make a pretty picture, David?" Lars says. "Push your tits together, Ruth, and let's show David the new tricks you've learned."

I've already realised that they've fucked before. This is where Ruth has been spending her time.

Ruth's eyes are on me as Lars straddles her. He pushes his obscenely large cock between her breasts and she presses them tightly together for him. Then, slowly and deliberately, she lifts her head, extends her tongue and starts to lick his arsehole.

I can't read the expression in her eyes. It's not pleasure, or fear. It looks more like resignation.

"You know, David, it's impolite to fuck a man's wife without asking his permission." As he speaks, Lars is pushing backwards and forwards between Ruth's breasts. Ruth is doing her best to find his anus or his balls with her tongue.

"So I decided to show Ruth how a real man fucks. Seems like she hasn't been fucked properly in a long time. In fact, when we met, I don't think she'd ever had it up the arse at all."

I move closer to them, not sure what to do next. I'm trying to figure out what Ruth wants. I've been trying to figure out what Ruth wants ever since I betrayed her.

"Did you know that Ruth is good at deep throating? Well, I guess in your case it wouldn't really be that deep, would it?"

Lars steps back a little. Ruth lies with her throat in a straight line, her eyes on me, her mouth wide open. Lars grunts as he slides his cock into her throat. He does it four or five times.

Ruth really can take all of him. She doesn't gag but her eyes seem moist. I don't know if this is an involuntary reaction or an emotional one.

Mei Mei has stopped licking Ruth now. She is looking at me. She seems sad.

"Get ready for it, baby," Lars says. He is out of Ruth's throat now, fiercely stroking himself in front of her face. Ready to spray all over her, like a dog marking territory.

I am still holding my half empty bottle of Bud. It doesn't break when it hits Lars, but it is very effective at knocking him out.

Mei Mei scrambles to Lars' aid, pushing Ruth out of her way.

I reach down and help Ruth to her feet. I wrap her dress around her. She is shaking.

"You hit him."

"Yes, I suppose I did."

She is under my arm. We are heading for the door.

"You might have killed him."

"Yes."

We stop. She looks at me, searching for something in my face that she seems to find.

"Thank you," she says, and wraps her arms around me.

As I bundle her into the car I let myself hope that I may finally have become someone that Ruth wants.

Cat

Anya Wassenberg

The cell always rings when it's hardest to get at, not just driving, but turning some tight corner or in the middle of an intersection. Here I'm trying to get into this goddamn parking spot at the golf course and it shrieks from inside my bag.

"Hello?"

"Cat? It's Jimmy."

"Jimmy? So what's the good word?"

"Not just a word, Cat. I've got a special proposal for you today."

"Just hang on a sec." I steer with my left hand into an empty parking spot by the exit, setting the phone on the passenger seat while I manoeuvre the car into place. "OK, shoot."

"This one's video."

"Video?"

"Cat, honey, I know what you think, and you know I wouldn't ask if it wasn't something special." Jimmy hesitates. Fucking videos, it's no better than when I was working for the Agency, for Christ's sake – I told him I was sick of giving blow jobs to ugly jerks. "This one's a threesome, Cat, you and an older guy and some young chick. It's $750 US for about three hours' work, and the guy blows his load nowhere near you."

"OK, so I'm listening."

"You play the school principal, they wanted an attractive older woman and my first thought was you," he says.

"I'm touched," I reply with a short laugh, and Jimmy's encouraged.

"It starts out with you on the phone, the guy's supposed to be calling you about his daughter. Then he meets you at your place, it looks like you guys are going to get into it. There's some penetration, but only a couple of minutes. Then the young chick comes in, his 'daughter', and the two of you start doing her."

I laugh out loud.

"Great story. Somebody's getting paid to write this shit?" I ask between chuckles.

"Hell, I guess they are, honey. I sure didn't make it up. And like I said, he cums all over her face, nowhere near you. You're at the other end. She's a real sweetheart, this girl. Nineteen years old, very pretty."

"When's this supposed to happen?"

"Next month, either Buffalo or TO."

"Well, OK, do some more talking with these people. I'll call you when I get home and let you know what my schedule looks like."

"Great, Cat," Jimmy gushes. "I told you it was something special."

"OK, Jimmy. I guess you can call it special if you want," and I laugh again. "I'll get back to you later."

"Right. Talk soon." And he hangs up.

I set the phone down on the seat and finally get the car straightened out, looking around as I do. It's been a long time since I've been to Niagara-on-the-Lake. Niagara-on-the-*Take*, as some of the locals call it. Kind've an upscale party town, with some nice hotels and fine dining along with stores full of expensive clothes and curiosities. It's where I used to come to hide out, back in the days when I was working for the Agency over in Niagara Falls. Because where the Falls is neon and new hotels, Niagara-on-the-Lake is all small town Victorian quaintness, even with all the tourists. To get to the golf course you leave the main drag, the press of cars and humanity, turn off to a side street and follow the river to the club house. The oldest golf course in North America, so they say. So Randy used to tell me, at any rate. Randy the travelling salesman – lab equipment or something like that, he used to try and describe it to me sometimes. A regular from back in the days. Sold lab equipment all over the place but somehow he knew about every golf course from Niagara Falls to Windsor to Ottawa.

There's a foursome heading by me as I get out of the car and lock up, they pass me on their way to the club house.

"She still looks good," the youngest at mid forty or so says appreciatively.

He's looking at my car, a 97 Cutlass Supreme SL, fully loaded and still gleaming white. Flawless in the bright sunshine.

"She's holding up pretty well," I agree with a smile at all four of them.

This time, he's looking at me.

"I'll say!"

It elicits a laugh from me and his three compadres too. I hesitate, fiddling with keys while I let them get to the clubhouse before me, get settled at a table to order drinks and forget about me and my car. That's all I need when I'm trying to do a job, for Christ's sake, is a bunch of holidaying yuppies trying to get naughty while the wives are maxing out credit cards on imported linens and china. After a few minutes, I make my way in quietly, pulling up a seat at the end of the bar.

God, and it does take me back. Waiting for Randy at this very same bar, then a drink before heading to the hotel room. At least a dozen times over about a year and a half. He'd introduce me to local businessmen. They must have been used to Randy's ways, they never batted an eyelash as his arm snaked around my waist or a hand would drop nonchalantly on my thigh. Maybe they didn't even know he was married, though. Randy was like a lot of guys. He lived his life in little compartments and nobody really had a look at what was in all of them at once. The last while, just before I quit the biz, he used to hire me for whole weekends and we'd do it all – five star restaurants, plays at the Shaw Festival. I mean, if I was ever going to fall for a date, it would have been Randy, hands down. But, as always with these situations, it worked because we both knew the deal.

She clears her throat again, the bartender, and I finally let myself get pulled out of the memory.

"Sorry," and I smile, that one that you use on other women. "I guess I'm lost in space. I'll have a Caesar, please," and I smile again.

"No problem," and she smiles back.

I turn to look out the glass doors; from the lounge you can see the games starting and ending as the summer evening just begins to fade. She brings me my drink a few minutes later and I fiddle with the lime. My buddies from the parking lot are happily immersed in noisy conversation about the game they're about to play. There's no one here I recognize. It seems strange. Then again, the guys I used to see here were weekday regulars, leaving the manager or maybe the wife in charge of the store while they'd sneak out for a round. On a Thursday night in July it looks like a lot of out-of-towners.

"Can you tell me what time it is?" I ask my pleasant bartender.

She glances at her wrist.

"About twenty to nine," she says.

"Thanks."

He was supposed to start between seven and seven thirty, this guy, and it's only nine holes. So if he's not here now it should be any time. The minutes tick by as I sip on my Caesar and sit quietly, unobtrusively for now. I order a second drink somewhat reluctantly after half an hour. It's not recommended, getting drunk when you're trying to outsmart somebody, and that's all this really is. But, on the other hand, they won't just let me sit here.

"Waiting for someone?" she asks while handing me the glass.

"No," I answer. "I used to come here, some years ago. Maybe four of five. I was in town on some business, and I just thought I'd drop by and reminisce."

This time my smile is a little more irregular, more genuine, and it's accompanied by a rueful little sigh. It's what happens when you're silly enough to tell the truth. She answers something and turns to the next customer, but my eye has already caught them on the last green. It's gotta be my boy Edward. Medium height, dark, wavy, extravagant hair. Same sunglasses as the picture. And the blond giant there has got to be the friend she mentioned. The wife, that is, she said to look out for the blond giant in Edward's foursome.

I watch as they finish the round. I can't tell by their faces who won, they're all laughing.

"Could you watch my drink for a few minutes?" I ask the bartender.

"Sure."

It's timed just perfectly. I slide off my jacket as they're entering the clubhouse, turn elegantly on my heels to take a slow, tight walk across the floor to the ladies' room. The theatrics are necessary in this case. The guy's here with his buddies, they just finished a round of golf and they want to drink and tell stories. Just sitting there at the bar and batting my eyelashes won't work. But if he's as much of a dog as the wife says, this should get his attention. And I do need to check the exterior at this point.

I stare back at myself from the mirror for a moment after I wash my hands, rubbing a smudge of mascara out from under my eyes. The make-up's good still, it's flawless. And the pink dress, well, I never liked it much, but other people seem to. Men always like it. Eye make-up and a tried and true outfit. A formula that's never failed me yet. I walk back to my stool, stopping just for a second to open and look into my tiny purse as if I just thought of something. Push my hair back over my shoulder seductively. Look under my eyelashes for a reaction. Bingo. He's looking right at me. And I smile back, this time the one that's reserved for men.

I climb back on the stool, conscious of every move. Crossing my legs, leaning over to pick up my drink. The neckline of this dress hangs loosely, it's a little too big upstairs to tell the truth, but it does afford flashes of titty for those in the right line of view. A few sips later, I look over at his table again. He's the best-looking of the four. They usually are. His forearms are muscled, tanned, and he's wearing probably the least geekiest outfit you can get away with on a golf course – a basic polo shirt and khakis. Nice watch, and a couple of sparkly rings, but not overdone. The blond guy, the friend he's here with, he notices me looking and turns away quickly. Edward, he glances over to see why and we exchange looks again.

It's hard not to smile at this point. This guy's just way too easy. I mean, you marry the rich bitch and get a corner office in

Daddy's company – you'd think he'd be a little smarter. Three years, too. At least, she says it took her that long to figure it all out. I linger in his direction just a couple of seconds more, then turn back to the bar to take a drink. It doesn't take him long.

"Four draught," and the voice is right beside me. "Two Rickard's and two Upper Canada." I turn on cue to smile at him as she goes to get the drinks. "You live in town?" he asks me.

"No, just here on business today," I answer with another smile.

"Oh, yeah? What kind of business would that be," and he pauses with a little smile of his own, "if you don't mind my asking?"

"Modelling," I explain. "I do a lot of work as a model."

"Really?" Now he's really interested. They always are, it impresses them. It's the greatest hook for all these married guys looking for a quick hit, especially when they find out what kind of modelling. And it's true, as a point of fact, I do model part-time – more and more if Jimmy has his way. It's important. You either have to tell the truth about this kind of stuff, or rehearse it until it sounds real. That way you have the details, the stories to tell when they want to know more.

"Yessir," and I take a drink because it's not much in the way of conversation.

The bartender brings the beers.

"Listen," he says, "I'm opening my own restaurant soon. We might need models for some promos and things. You do hostessing? At private parties and functions?"

"Sure. I do . . ." and I wave my hand in the air ". . . lots of things."

He laughs.

"Got a business card?"

"Yes, I do."

I dig in my purse and draw out one of my cards. He takes it and smiles.

"Cat – figure and erotic modelling? Now I'm really interested."

"That's me," I agree, skipping over the invitation in his last

remark. *Erotic modelling*. Let him just think about that one for
a while. "You got a card?"

"Oh, sure," and he hands me one from his back pocket.
Edward Deliotto.

"Edward," and I reach to shake his hand.

"Ed," and we shake, fingertips lingering just a second too
long. "Actually, most people call me Eddie."

"OK, Eddie, that's great. But I think your friends are
getting thirsty."

He looks at his table, where the three of them are pointing
and snickering.

"Yeah, right," he laughs and heads back.

I watch him show the guys my card, they start a round of
laughing and joking with each other. I drink up in ten minutes
or so and slip back out to my car, pulling my cell phone from
my purse.

"Santos Investigations."

"Yeah, Davey? It's Cat."

"Hey, Cat. What's the news?"

"Piece of cake, man, that Deliotto guy. Hook, line and
sinker. I mean, I've only got a phone number so far, and he's
saying it's business. But I'm sure business is the last thing on
his mind. I should have it wrapped up in no time."

"Good work. You're the pro, man."

"Not really, Davey, not any more," and David chuckles as I
hang up.

"Hello?"

"Oh. Hi. I was looking for Cat."

"Yeah, this is Cat."

"It's Eddie. Remember? From the golf course. In Niagara-
on-the-Lake."

"Right. Eddie," and now my mind's racing to put all the
pieces back into place. "So how are you?"

"Great, I'm just great," he says, his voice more confident
now. "I checked out your website, by the way. Nice, really
nice."

"Thanks," and I'm never quite sure what to say.

"Are you busy Saturday?" he asks.

"No, why?"

"Do you sail at all? Do you like to? I have a boat at Niagara-on-the-Lake, the marina near Queen's Landing, do you know it? Would you like to go? I can tell you about the restaurant, what I had in mind for work," he says.

"Sure Eddie," and I laugh a little, "we can talk about whatever you want." He laughs too, after a slight hesitation.

I wake up early and leave with enough time to take the old route down highway 8. The day is splashed with a hard glitter from the sun as it makes its way across a mottled sky, all of it balanced by the cooler and quieter green of trees and fields. This way into the Niagara Peninsula is still beautiful, still retains much of its farmland charm. But ugly development is creeping in everywhere, and more and more of the orchards are giving way to acres of new housing and soul deadening sameness. I lived in the Falls during the lean years, before the Casino, and I have to say I liked it better. But I'm not such a hypocrite I don't recognize that I'm just a tourist here too. Just part of the problem.

The wind lifting the hair from my face is warm, and it's too impossibly gorgeous out here to be brooding about anything. After St Catharines and over the bridge, I slip off the highway again to wind down country roads, past houses with huge porches and gingerbread trim and estate wineries set in the fields. I can't help the feeling I get – I still get – taking the drive into town. Like I was far away from the rest of the world and its problems, somewhere that, in spite of the prevailing tourist trade, always had an atmosphere all its own.

The marina is down on the river, behind Queen's Landing, a five star hotel in the guise of a Georgian mansion. I have to park a few blocks away on a side street. A couple of minutes wandering around and I see Eddie down at the end of the pier. He waves as he spots me. I walk quicker to meet him. His smile is real, he reaches for my hand and kisses me on the cheek like an old friend. I hate it now when these guys are nice. I used to be able to keep my distance a lot better.

"Come on!" and he takes me by the hand.

It's a lovely boat, 30ft or more if I'm not mistaken, a dark navy blue with white trim, and the name – Ariadne's Thread.

"How literate," I joke.

"Not my boat really. Belongs to the family." Eddie jumps in, helping me and my bag. I fall against him and he takes his time steadying me, looks down at me with approval.

"You like the sailing outfit?" I ask. It's white shorts and a bikini top, a pale yellow blouse knotted at the waist.

"I do." He smiles wider. "I know I saw smoked oysters in the fridge when I was here on Wednesday. Champagne too."

"Is that all we're here to do?" and I'm kittenish. "Eat sex food? I thought this was business."

"Oh, sure," and Eddie's sudden efficiency as he unties the boat and takes over the controls. I follow him into the cabin. "I thought we'd make it out to Burlington this afternoon. I can moor it at La Salle, and drive you back to your car." He glances over at me quickly. "But I want to eat sex food too."

I'm laughing and I really mean it. I've heard lots of lines over the years, men have told me lots of stories. But it doesn't prevent me from responding now and then. Eddie seems like he'd be a lot of fun. The thing I have to keep in mind about decoy work, this guy isn't the client. He's supposed to think all of this is for real. After a while we're both silent, making good time down the river to Lake Ontario. The land rises in rocky cliffs on either side. This is the nicest part of it here along this stretch, unspoiled by tourist helicopters or the Maid of the Mist, just blue water under the sun and the trees that cling to the cliffs. Time seems to have stopped, I have no idea how long we've been going. Just ahead the river widens into the lake, it stretches far to the horizon. Eddie's doing something with the boat, it stops. He's dropping the anchor.

We head for the deck, and he sits back in the sunshine with obvious pleasure.

"What a day," he exults.

"I'm with you," and I sit down near him, closing my eyes. I slip out of my blouse, and we're quiet again for a few minutes. He moves closer to me, till his thigh is touching mine, casual like.

"Hungry?" he asks.

"Starving," I tell him.

"Good. You do like smoked oysters?"

"Love them."

"OK," and he springs up again. "Be right back."

There are strategies for moving things along quicker. Like sometimes when the date hesitates, or maybe you're just getting tired of the small talk. In public places, natch, there are alternatives, maybe a little whisper in the ear, like "let's go back to your room and fuck, honey," or "God, I would love to wrap my lips around your cock, right now!" But nothing beats a visual for dramatic effect. A look around and there seems to be no other boats in the vicinity, no houses directly in view. I slip out of the rest of my clothes, and when Eddie comes up the stairs to the deck again I'm lying on my stomach wearing nothing but my sunglasses. I see him start, almost dropping the champagne bucket.

"I hope you don't mind." My voice is soft. "I hate tan lines."

He laughs, then sets down the champagne bucket and a plate of goodies to open the bottle and pour us a glass. I take a sip, and a quick bite of the oysters. Eddie brings his glass to sit next to me again, and I finish my bubbly while he strokes my shoulder, down my back to my ass. Soft skin has always been one of my trademarks, and it's been worth the time and money spent on it. He pets me just like you'd pet a cat, but I like this. I half close my eyes, rest my chin on my hands, and I could fall asleep in the sun. But Eddie's not getting sleepy. He pours another round of champagne, and his petting turns to kisses. It goes on from there, down the steps and back inside on the plush carpeting of the cabin.

Most of the time, with these decoy jobs, I don't end up in bed. Not unless I really like them. I mean, I'm not supposed to. Like, my God, that would be prostitution!! We just need a compromising enough position, whatever the wife needs to be sure the guy is really the dog she thinks he is. But here, I mean, I can't exactly walk off the boat. And I'm liking this Eddie, he's uncomplicated. Or at least he is with me.

Anyway, the whole day is spent naked, eating and boozing and fucking Eddie all over the boat. Fucking and sucking and licking every orifice of his, and of mine. Not such a bad job to have, on a Saturday afternoon in July. He's like a child, he just wants to have a playmate. And he tells me all kinds of things about his life, about growing up in a small town up north, coming south to Hamilton.

"Supposed to be on my way to Toronto," he says with a laugh, "but somehow I never left."

I smile and laugh back, and listen wondering for about the millionth time what exactly it is about naked women that makes men want to spill their guts.

It's early evening by the time we get back to the marina in Niagara-on-the-Lake.

"Hey, you promised me Burlington," I protest as we jump off the boat. "And wasn't this supposed to be about working at your restaurant?"

Eddie secures the boat, giggling like a school boy.

"You want Burlington that much, we can go next week. How about Monday? And don't worry about the restaurant, there'll be enough work there to keep you around for as long as you want."

He's charming, too charming. Too guileless.

"Sure Eddie. That would be great."

He kisses me good-bye and we're both still wrapped in that warm glow of physical closeness, giddy and faces creased into an unbreakable smile.

"Call me," he says, and I promise to.

I walk back to my car slowly, get in and pull out of town. Fuck David anyway, and fuck the wife. They'll get their report, sooner or later. But there's no need to hang the man yet. The strangest thing, I've found, is the way some of these guys – like Eddie – actually give a shit about whether I'm having a good time or not. Whether I come, even. And I have to wonder how bad it could be to have a husband like that.

Admittedly, though, this is not my area of expertise.

If It Makes You Happy

Cole Riley

"You're not so damn tough and probably not so bright either, big man."

The woman looked directly at him when she said it. Her voice. It was the voice of a colour: deep, dark red. Fiery, suggestive, and full of passionate promises. Her voice, rich-toned and throaty, was the first thing he noticed about her and the thing he would always remember about her. Her voice of sexy, crimson hymns.

He knew the moment his eyes saw the woman that trouble would soon be on his doorstep. She was handcuffed, metal confining her wrists behind her back, silhouetted against a high white wall. The guys from Hopewell Corrections Centre were trying to figure out how she had managed to escape from her cell for three days before a traffic cop spotted her coming out of a fast-food joint. She never told how she did it. Now she was being admitted to Newton psychiatric facility for observation. Her behaviour was deemed erratic at the time of her capture. He couldn't see it. She seemed calm and serene as she stood in custody. But it was what happened in the elevator going up to Processing that twisted his mind out of joint and started his obsession with her. With guards flanking her, she stood in front of him, her hands behind her, touching and caressing his genitals. Stroking him until his legs were almost buckling by the time the ancient elevator reached the seventh floor. She was something else, not your usual brand of woman.

"Don't forget me," she whispered to him as they led her away down the dimly lit corridor to the front desk.

And he didn't forget her. He was totally fixated on her.

Being a guard at the facility meant he often saw her on the grounds, in the hall, or in the cafeteria. There were always people around her, usually men, laughing and talking loudly, so he had no access to this woman who was slowly driving him mad. He watched her eat, how her mouth with its large soft lips worked, how her long tongue flicked at its corners. He watched her walk, the smooth rolling of her wide hips, the inviting space between her thighs as she moved seductively among the other inmates. Once, going up the stairs before him, she stopped, backed into him, and did a quick bending twist of her ass into his crotch. Oh, he was hooked. Totally and completely. Yet another black man bamboozled by lust and a hard dick.

"Don't forget me, sweetheart," she whispered to him again. An orderly, carrying a tray of meds, interrupted their chance meeting, standing watch until the couple exited the stairwell and went their separate ways. No fraternizing between staff and patients.

He never asked anyone her name. He wanted to hear it first spoken from her very own lips. In that dark red voice. The day before he tossed his life away because of lust, a vivid imagination, and a stiff libido was the first time they really talked. They squeezed into a supply room among shelves laden with towels, gowns, rubber gloves, and canisters of liquid soap. The woman was pressed close to him, too close for comfort, and notions of taking her right there flooded his mind. With her young, gorgeous, Lena Horne–looking self. The post–Cotton Club Lena, in full bloom. But everything had to be right. Exactly like he pictured it over and over every night as he lay in bed and touched himself. Her and her dark red voice.

"I see you watching me, every day, all day," she said, her eyes locked on his. "You don't have to say what you want. I know what you want because I want it too. But everything comes with a price. Nothing is for free, not in this world."

"I hear that," he replied, thrusting one hand into a pocket to subdue his growing excitement. "What is your name?"

"You know it. Don't play dumb. I hate an ignorant man." She stepped back some.

"I really don't know it. I didn't ask. I wanted to hear it from you." That made her smile, the full soft lips parting like lush rose petals.

"Amina. What's yours, Mister Man?"

"Terrance Stokes. My friends call me Terry. What is it you want? What is the price?"

He moved back within kissing range, so close to her that she could feel the heat of his flesh through his cheap uniform.

"I want out," she hissed at him, the coloured heat sparking in her words. "You get me out and you can have me any way you want. Nothing is too kinky, too freaky. Anything you want but you must get me out first. Once I'm back in the world, baby, I'm yours to do with as you please. How does that sound?"

"Hey, I'm no fool," he said, afraid to admit to himself that he was even weighing such an offer. "How do I know you'll keep your end of the bargain? How? I'm risking everything here. My life will be fucked as soon as I break you out. It'll be over."

Amina laughed softly, the sound of it much like the tinkling of piano keys. She reached down, unzipped her hospital-issue pants, and inserted her fingers into herself. That got her squirming a bit and she coated her digits with her juice, laughed again, and brought them to his lips. Tart yet sweet, like the taste of an exotic fruit from a tropical island untamed.

She knew how to close a deal, playing on his dissatisfaction with his job and life, putting a spotlight on the collection of failures and disappointments that had hounded him from the very day he graduated from high school. He was a loser. But this would change things. It was a chance to tell the whole world to kiss his black ass. The entire planet, all the doubters and badmouthers. Now he was calling the shots in his life for once.

Everybody would know his name, if only for a hot moment. His fifteen minutes of fame, coming right up.

Busting her out was not that hard. All it took was a few Benjamins for the guys at the main gate, some more for the crew on the supply truck, several lies and even more for the cat with the small plane to take them to the Texas border. The pilot, with his tiny Cessna eggbeater that shook and fluttered with every breeze, was spooky with his endless talk of the ancient Aztecs and their knack for human sacrifices. Terry didn't want to hear that mess.

Just get them to the border. When it was all done, he was tapped out, very little green in his reserves. Spent some more bucks on a little cheap Tex-Mex grub and a run-down 1949 black Mercury Club Coupe. Slipped the Mexican guards a fistful of Yankee dollars, ensuring that they were not stopped at the border nor were their suitcases opened and searched.

"When do I get a chance to collect?" he asked while they walked in an open market among the stalls, buying sombreros and sandals in a Godforsaken, unnamed Mexican village. "When do I get my night? I've done my part."

"Be patient." She laughed, showing very few teeth. "I gave you my word."

They crossed the street to where the car was parked, in this area where gringos were rarely seen, especially black ones. He concluded that Amina was a beautiful pit bull with a mouth-watering body and vacant eyes, more Hustler than Penthouse and Playboy. The town was essentially dead, except for the burst of activity at the market. Walking together, they entered the battered hotel, its awning hanging by a couple of bolts, and went up to the desk where the sombre man took their money and gave them a key.

"I'm beat, wore out," Amina mumbled. "I need some sleep. A few winks and I'll be as good as new. Then you'll get your surprise, big man."

She shed her clothes quickly and quietly, allowing him his first real look at her shapely brown body. It didn't seem to matter to her that he watched her so intently. The heat was stifling. He wondered if this was normal, if it was because of the diminished ozone layer or the abundance of satellites in the atmosphere. What was he doing with this crazy woman? He knew some things about her, much of her troubled history, her dark fugue states, her loose grasp of reality. Her criminal file was sealed, so much of the information he really needed to know was lost to him. Getting off the plane, she'd hinted she was a murderer, but didn't elaborate on that bombshell. Before she went to sleep, she told him she'd forgotten to bring her

Thorazine when he broke her out of the state hospital back in St Louis.

He lay on the bed beside her as she slept, their bodies clinging together with a sensual dampness, close in spoon fashion. Through the window, he could see an old man wearing a frayed sombrero leading a swaybacked mule packed with baskets of fruit slowly across the square. His red-lidded eyes followed the man's wobbly steps, one by one, until he disappeared from view. Amina stirred in slumber, mumbled under her breath, then flopped her curvy brown leg over his.

Gently, he took her tiny hand in his big one and kissed it, noticing the diagonal lacerations along both wrists, deep and multiple. Tributes to her madness. He felt a strange compulsion to lick her wounds, softly and lovingly, but he moved closer instead to kiss her full on the lips. Suddenly she opened her hypnotic eyes, the stare in them still vacant and unforgiving, and did nothing while he tenderly planted kisses on her heart-shaped face.

"I think you're frightened of me," she said. "You know I killed somebody."

"But you explained that. You said it was an accident. You said he came at you wrong and you had to cap him. Shoot him before he raped you."

She worried her eyes with the heels of her hands. "Yeah, right, forced vaginal entry. He wanted to pop the coochie. I told you that, but I left out some things."

"What did you leave out, Amina?" He couldn't afford to let her off the hook.

"Nothing I want to get into right now," she replied flatly.

Quietly, they lay on their sides, naked and sweating from the unnatural heat, pressing their fronts against one another full length. A total body hug. This was driving him over the edge, the nearness of her and her deep red voice, the touch of her soft bronze skin. Occasionally she kissed him, near the ear and on the neck, swift and popping kisses much like a boxer's jab. He couldn't stand it. But then nothing had gone exactly as he'd planned it. The thought that he couldn't go back to his old stale life lurked in the back of his mind, and then there was what she'd said: *But I left some things out*. What the hell did that mean?

To be honest, he didn't want to think about whatever she had not told him. But that was not cool either. What you didn't know could kill you. This was their third day together.

Finally, with some coaxing, she started talking, first about her family, about herself and her hospitalizations, and once she began, there was no stopping her. Her past suicide attempts. Both wrists, pills, overdoses. A dive off a four-story balcony, a fall broken by a landing on some bushes. Her walking in front of a car on the turnpike. The things she heard and saw in her head. Paranoid, schizophrenic, slightly delusional, with psychotic thoughts. But none of that mattered. She was a beautiful black woman who had survived, was still standing despite everything, and maybe all she needed was some guy who loved her. Really loved her.

"What are we going to do if you get sick again?" he asked after the reality of her condition hit home. "We're on the run and there ain't a doctor or hospital for miles. Who knows what kind of care you can get down here?"

"What are you saying?" she asked, gazing up at the ceiling.

He watched her hungrily, naked, stretched out on the dingy white sheets. Her breasts and nipples seemed swollen, ripe for seduction, her long neck, her slightly rounded stomach, the triangle of short black curly hair between her damp thighs. While she chatted away, he scooted down so he could put his lips on the dark areolae of her breasts. Even from there, he could smell the exotic scent of her sex. One of his big hands could barely conceal what this delicious vision of her was doing to him, his flesh hardening and throbbing, wanting to be inside her, if just for a moment.

"You know . . . with all this pressure and shit . . . anything can happen," he sputtered. "Hey, you haven't been out of lock-down that long and you're not back to your real self yet. And we don't have any pills to cool you out if something happens. I don't know what other junk you got in your bag."

She glared at him, her face morphing from a mask of concern to one of growing indifference. He'd touched a nerve, fingered an old emotional wound, and she was pissed off. She got up in his face and jabbed a finger into his chest.

"Don't come at me like that," she snarled. "I thought you

were on my side. That's why I left with you. Don't disappoint me. I've been through really bad shit. I'm due for some good times and real happiness. And if I can't find it with you, then I'll go elsewhere."

Then I'll go elsewhere. That's what his wife had done years ago. He'd been here before. Like that time when this honey, a coworker from the facility, drunk at an office party, called his house and left a jive message on his answering machine. *It's yours if you want it, Terry*. And his wife intercepted it, almost cost him his marriage then and there. She made him pay dearly for that one, went elsewhere, and for a time they both ventured outside their marriage with other lovers. New carnal thrills. She only came back to him when one of her Romeos went berserk and whipped her ass. He took her back for a time, until the whole mess started up all over again. Now he was here, waiting to collect, waiting to get the reward of a very special night. It'd better be worth it.

"Are we still cool?" she asked. "I need to know."

He was still somewhere in his head, mulling over old terrain. He'd heard her question but didn't answer right away.

"Hey, Terry, are we still tight or what?" she asked with teeth in her words. "You're taking too long to answer. Don't scare me, man. Don't get shaky on me now, not when I need you most."

"No problem, sweetheart," he replied halfheartedly. "It's all good. I'm in this to the limit, to the end. You and me."

Close to tears, she leaned back on the bed. "Don't fuck this up. I'm counting on you."

That short explosion of talk had certainly altered the mood in the room, settled something between them, and now he looked at her, really looked at her. Amina. Without the fog and haze of their situation blocking his view, he saw she was possibly one of the finest women he'd ever met, a real fox. Bronze, curly black hair, classic looks, a puffed mouth that guys would love to kiss, and the leggy body of a model with full, natural breasts. No silicone, not like his insecure ex-wife.

It was time to collect. Through the window, he could see the full golden moon rising in the dark blue of the Mexican sky, an Aztec night with infinite possibilities. Her hand on his rod broke him out of his thoughts and it sprang back to life, lengthening. He scooted back to her again, landing quick feather kisses at the soft base of her neck, up on her eyelids, and then down around her nipples. Slipping one nipple at a time into his mouth, he worked on them with consummate skill, all the while stroking her between the legs, teasing her clit with his thumb. She seemed to relax, submitting to her body's urges, her eyes rolling back in her head, ecstatic, as he trailed his tongue along the smooth flesh of her inner thigh, sending a long surge of heat up into her stomach. When he traced his tongue in soft motion along the soft, meaty folds of her sex, she wiggled underneath him, her hips lifting off the bed. He parted her restless legs even more with his rough hands, his nose pressed against that precious slit, his mouth relentless against it. Her moans increased in volume as he slipped expertly deeper down into the wet, fragrant cleft between her legs, the pink snake in his mouth exploring the sensitive nerves just inside her box, rotating and caressing her into new levels of desire, until she grabbed his head and held him hard and fast there. After her moist body trembled a second and third time, she broke off his oral assault on her and told him it was her turn to please.

Slowly, she moved over him on all fours, her butt high in the air, stopping only when her face was mere inches from his dick. She gripped it at the base, squeezing the engorged flesh until it became this monstrous thing of a deep violet hue with thick veins crisscrossing its shaft. Giggling to herself, she took him into her mouth, sucking and humming, head bobbing, bathing it with hot breath on her tantalizing downstroke. His legs quivered and bounced on the bed from the waves of pleasure rushing through his entire body. Her hands cupping his ass, she drove him deep into her throat, as if she was determined to swallow him whole.

"Easy, baby, easy," he mumbled, feeling himself close to the brink. "Stand up, follow me. I don't want to get my knees scraped up."

She followed his lead and got up, with him watching her every sultry move. It was as if they were young lovers, unable to keep their hands off each other: their first night of passion together. He cleared off the top of a wobbly wooden table against the far wall, knocking everything in haste onto the floor. Neither of them spoke. He motioned for her to come, kneel over the chair onto the table, with her smooth, unblemished brown ass turned toward him. When he rasped for her to show it to him before he entered her softness, she did as he asked. Ravishing thugass thoughts. Of taking her long and strong.

Passively, she showed it to him longer, her glistening pinkness. He moved in behind her, breathing in short bursts, entering her gently, grinding against her with purpose, each hand gripping a finely formed butt cheek. Each plunge was rapture. He accelerated his rhythm, picked up the pace as she arched up to meet his thrusts, her hands powerfully grasping the table.

"Tell me you love me," she said in that deep red voice. "Tell me, Terry."

He didn't want to appear soft, a wimp, so he said nothing. He kept busy, rolling his hips, feeling himself pulse inside her. She reared back, opened her legs wider, letting him slip even farther into her, into her sweetness, making a hissing sound much as an agitated cat would do. She wanted him.

He gasped, gripped her shoulders now as he urgently pumped into the back of her womb. At the same time, he felt her change her tempo, rocking her plump ass against him in faster, wilder circles. They banged harder into one another, lunges, and this was crazy love. Maddening, animal passion like he'd never experienced before. He felt her dripping, wet on him to the base, tightening around him. She vibrated again and again like an unruly tuning fork, as though she sensed every throbbing inch of him inside her, her fingers moving slow and intense on the swollen nub where the centre of her pleasure lived.

"Say it, please," she pleaded. "Tell me you love me."

He finally conceded and said the magic words while she rode him as if she couldn't get enough. It had been a long time for the both of them and never like this. His dick filled her again and again, to the hilt, withdrew and then went back inside to the point of her muffled shout. His thrusts became faster and harder still as they rushed toward climax, their moans in harmony as they soared together, their sexes matching thrust for thrust.

Soon she was peaking once more in an intense burst of pleasure, overcome so strongly with the power of a clitoral explosion coupled with his continued pounding, coming so hard that she lost her senses for a moment. Her eyes went wild, crazed. When the raging storm of desire finally subsided, she stared at him like she wanted to kill him. Her eyes burned into him, dark and brooding. Eventually, her mood passed and she eased into his arms, lying still, mouth to mouth. It was evident that something had snapped inside her. But I left some things out. That was the last thought he had before sleep seduced him.

A few hours later, they got a bite to eat, beef tacos, beans and yellow rice, chased with three chilled bottles of Corona beer. She wanted to walk around town after the meal, although the sun was still strong and very few people were out. He relented and let her have her way. On the outskirts of town, they rented horses from a wizened old man who thought they were gringos, albeit "Los Negroes Americanos", brought in to repair the roof of the ancient cathedral there. They rode out into the flatlands several miles away, following a dusty trail that ran south along the river. She laughed when his horse, a brown stallion, whinnied loudly from thirst and stopped to drink the grimy water. He stayed atop the animal, clutching the reins tightly, feeling its warmth and bulk beneath him. She dismounted and walked in front of her horse, near the ragged sagebrush and cactus. For him, it was good hearing her laugh.

Eventually, they tied up the horses, took off their clothes and waded out into the river. The water went up to their necks, briefly cooling them. She swam closer to him, smiling, and put her arms around his neck. Her weight made him slip and he went under, the water going into his nose and mouth before he could resurface. They laughed and kissed after he got his breath back. He watched her swim out into the middle of the river with short, powerful strokes, the water shimmering as it rolled off her back and neck. Twice she dived under the surface of the water, with her exposed sex pointed up toward the heavens. He swam out to meet her and they played like kids, swimming side by side, floating on their backs and splashing water on each other.

When the frolicking was over they swam back to shore, where she took a blanket from her animal and brought it out to the riverbank. They sprawled on the blanket, ate the last of the dry tacos, shared the remaining warm beer, and cleaned sand from their toes. She kissed him and closed her eyes, holding an arm over her face to shield it from the blazing sun. He lay there silent beside her, enjoying her company.

After a time she moved close to him, touching his face. "Baby, I left some things out."

"Huh? What?"

She said nothing else. Her full, soft mouth covered his own and her tongue slid easily between his lips. Maybe his leaving everything behind was not so bad. His ex-wife was never this hot or spontaneous. Everything was planned, thought out to dullness, according to schedule.

"The man I killed was my husband." Her voice was drab, lifeless. "He deserved to die. He wouldn't give me a divorce. I was in love with another man and he knew it. He made my life hell. I only turned to someone else because he was such a mean bastard. My young lover left me too, walked out, after I killed my husband for him. Something went haywire in my head. The doctors said I had a complete psychotic break, totally nuts. Lost my mind completely. Do you hate me now? Do you still love me?"

"Yes, I still love you," he stammered. But he had some doubts and fears.

"Does this change anything with us?"

"Not really." He examined her face carefully for obvious signs of madness and found none.

"I really am nuts, you know," she said, taking his hand to suck on his fingers until he pulled away. He could feel his sap rise along with his dread of her.

Later, they made love all night, going at it in every variation possible, until they collapsed exhausted in the juice-soaked sheets, totally sated. He slept the sleep of the dead, as the saying goes. When he awoke, Amina was gone, all of her belongings as well. Most of his remaining money was gone from his wallet. She had left him chump change, a few dollars. Panicked, he raced down to the street to see if everything was gone, and yes, his precious black 1949 Mercury Club Coupe had been stolen too. His woman with the deep red voice. Damn her!

While he stood bare-chested in his shorts in the spot where his car had been parked, a very pretty Mexican woman with dark features carrying a basket of white plastic skulls approached him, holding something. An envelope. She stood and watched him open it.

The letter consisted of four sentences, hurriedly scribbled in childish handwriting. His hand trembled with anger as he read its painful black-widow message:

> I still left some things out. *I am crazy and you could get hurt. I really like you. There have been others, before you, like you. This is the best way, for both of us.*

He stood there dumbfounded, completely confused, like he had been slapped three or four times in the face with a blackjack. Or knifed in the heart. A real fool. Threw everything away for one night of pleasure, his entire life. Across the square, he saw three people in skeleton outfits marching in a group toward the empty market. A truck full of mariachi musicians, fully dressed in their stage costumes with guitars, pulled up and the men jumped off and walked into the hotel. One of them held a large skull in his hand.

Tomorrow was the start of the two-day Mexican Day of the Dead festival, the celebration of Death and its many wonders – how appropriate for him right now.

And maybe he was crying a bit because the cute Mexican woman patted him softly on the shoulder and said: "*Mujeres, ellas dan mucha lata.*" Which loosely means: "Women can sometimes be a pain in the neck." Possibly true, if you don't know where and how to pick them. But not in this case. Amina knew who she was and what she was about. He was the one who didn't know anything about himself. She did him a favour, walking away before she took his life too, and added his scalp to the others. A real blessing, her gift of his life after that night of miracles. In his hands was this new start, this fresh possibility, Amina's gift. All he would do now was wash up, eat, and take another accounting of his few assets, and then there was time to think about tomorrow and the day after that.

Going Out With Angela

David Surface

He met her in a writing workshop in the basement of an old church. The other women seemed either angry, fearful, contemptuous, or unapproachable in some way. She alone moved and spoke like what in some other place and time might be called a lady – settling herself into the ridiculously small school chair with a calm, deliberate grace, measuring out her words the same way.

When she read a story about the house she'd grown up in, it was clear to him that this was someone who cherished things. It was generally not permitted, he was noticing, to cherish things. People here wrote the same way they drove their cars, to establish dominance, to force their personalities on the world and mow each other down with their big, angry voices. Like the skinny woman with the spiky black hair who turned on her one night, calling the story she'd just read "sentimental".

"Thank you," Angela smiled. Untouched.

"Thank me all you want." The dark woman wouldn't let up. "Crap is still crap."

Despite the evidence of his eyes and ears, he'd still thought she might need some comforting after that, so he spoke to her for the first time after class.

"Don't worry about her," he'd said. "She's just mad because she can't write like you."

"Oh, her." Angela smiled sweetly. "She's just mad because I wouldn't fuck her."

Her laugh, a throaty giggle, made him feel like something was coming untied inside him. Her skin was soft white, her features, small and delicate like a Victorian doll, did not go with the black leather biker jacket with its unfriendly arsenal of zippers and the single earring that dangled over her soft cheek like a little scimitar. He knew that if the point pressed too hard there would be a single drop of blood that would look almost black against that white cheek.

They began going out for drinks after every workshop, to the dark little bars she knew on the scrambled downtown streets he still had trouble figuring out. Walking past all the lighted windows with people eating and drinking and talking inside, he used to imagine he was being shown a series of beautifully lighted tableaux he could make his own if he wanted to. Now he was part of one of those couples in one of those lighted windows, and he thought of the young man or woman outside, newly arrived in the city, walking by and looking in – what would they see? A man, still young, leaning across a booth toward an ageless-looking woman in flowered silks and black leather, hanging onto her every word, struggling to make his own equal to hers.

When she talked about fucking it confused him. Women fucking women. He did not understand how that was supposed to work. Did they use something? Angela laughed. "I thought that's what all men liked to see – two women together."

He had seen it, of course, in magazines and videos, but most of it did not move him and he'd fast-forward through those scenes to get to something he could recognize.

"I don't know," he said. "It's kind of like watching a woman make love to a mirror."

"So," she said. "One woman is just like any other woman?"

"No," he said, quickly, "I mean – I'm talking about that stuff in magazines and films. You know."

"So," she said. "You need to see a man."

"Sure." Then, quickly, "With a woman."

"Not by himself?"

He realized he'd never seen that, and he said so. "I don't think I've ever seen that."

"Of course you haven't," she said, "You see plenty of women by themselves, but never men, because the men who make those films think straight men don't want to see that. They don't even care if a woman might want to see it."

"What about you?" he said. "Would you like to see it?" He was drunk now, by God.

"Honey, please." She smiled, reaching into her purse. "I've seen it."

While she talked he was aware of her digging around in her purse. Cigarettes, he thought, until he saw smoke from the one she already had burning in the ashtray. He glanced back down in time to see her withdraw the hypodermic needle from her soft white forearm and slip it discreetly inside the slim, cream-coloured plastic case and close it with a pop.

"So," she said, quietly. "Does this bother you?"

"No. I mean – why should it?" He didn't think his face showed any alarm but when he looked into her eyes he knew he was caught.

"I don't know," she said. "Why should it?" He couldn't tell if she was angry with him, then she smiled her sweet smile again and he wondered if what she'd just put in her arm was already working on her. "It does bother you."

"No." He couldn't get rid of the lie – he'd been raised to lie where other people's feelings were concerned. "It's just – I guess I'm just not used to seeing that."

"You will be," she said, taking a sip of her martini. He felt a conspiratorial energy surge across the space between them.

"I don't think I could ever do that. Not with a needle, anyway." More than anything, he didn't want her to think that he was afraid of it – or of her. He leaned across the table and half-whispered, "Can you toot it?"

She stared at him over the rim of her glass, eyes wide and unbelieving. "Toot it?"

"Yeah, you know." He put a finger over one nostril and sniffed. She stared for a moment longer, then laughed a wild, undignified laugh he'd never heard from her before and covered her mouth with the back of her hand.

"Sure, John, we're all junkies here in New York." Then she told him. "It's insulin."

The shame hit him so hard that he went blind for a moment – wasn't that what happened to diabetics? "I'm sorry . . ." he said.

"Don't be," she said, still laughing a little. "Maybe I should try it that way."

If he could have made himself disappear into the ground he would have done it. Instead, he sat with his eyes shut tight, unable to look at her.

"John," he heard her say, "Open your eyes."

He heard something low and musical like a challenge in her voice, and thought, Kiss me. Then he felt cold liquid running in all directions down his scalp, through his hair and into his collar. He opened his eyes and saw her smiling at him, his empty gimlet glass still in her hand, then the big manager who was suddenly standing over them, frowning.

"It's all right." Angela smiled graciously up at the big man. "We were just going."

For the rest of the evening, whenever he heard her rattling around in her purse he kept his eyes trained on her face and would not look down until he heard the pop of the syringe going back into its plastic case.

"I'm sorry, you can't do that here."

John looked up and saw their waitress looking down at the space on the floor between their table and her feet.

"What do you mean?" Angela said – quietly, but with an unmistakable edge.

"That," the woman said, thrusting her chin toward the hypodermic needle in Angela's hand.

"This is insulin. I'm a diabetic."

"I know what it is," the young woman said, "But you can't do that here. You'll have to go somewhere else."

"Like where? Where do you think I should go?" Angela's smile, her voice stayed calm. "Would you like me to go into the restroom? In the toilet stall? Maybe out back in the alley?"

John saw the waitress stiffen. She was getting more than she'd probably bargained for – John almost felt sorry for her. She made one last attempt. "My boss says you can't do that here."

"Listen," Angela said, "you tell your boss to show me the law that says I can't do this here."

John watched the young woman walk away and huddle by the bar with a big man in a stretch green sport shirt. "You were pretty tough," John said, admiringly.

"She's just doing what that asshole is telling her to do." John saw the man point his finger at them, talking faster, the young woman looking down and shaking her head.

"Is there a law?" John asked.

"They don't want me to stop because it's illegal. They want me to stop because they don't like seeing needles." Angela lit a cigarette and frowned against the smoke that curled around her eyes. "If I have to see it every day, they can see it once in a while."

They had many things in common, he was finding. They had both suffered at the hands of men. She in a different way than him, but also not different, he thought, not so different at all. Neither of them had been raped, exactly, but both had got caught in something that had gone too far. He thought of the common phrase he'd heard in discussions of rape, that when sex becomes violent it's no longer sex, and he wondered if the inverse was true, that when violence becomes sexual, is it no longer violence?

They had held him down. In the bathroom of the high school, on the cold tile floor with the smell of piss and disinfectant in his face. While they were hurting him he'd wished that he could no longer have what he had between his legs so they would have nothing to grab onto, nothing to hit and hurt. If he'd been a girl, he imagined, they could not hurt him, at least not in that way. How could you hurt what wasn't there?

He wondered if she had been held down too. She did not seem to be the type that could be held down. He pictured her dissolving under someone's grunting, blind weight, turning to white smoke in their hands, leaving only her black leathers behind, and one glittering earring.

Outside, he was surprised to see it was still light. He wanted to walk on the hoods of all the cars like stepping stones, walk all the way to the river like that. With her. They came to a park, a sort of triangular brick island where the avenue split in two with giant sculptures of twisted metal painted fire-engine red, sharp and dangerous-looking. He was looking up at them when he realized she wasn't walking beside him any more. He turned and saw her sitting on one of the benches several yards behind him, head bowed like she was praying.

"Are you OK?" he asked.

"Yes. I'll be fine in a minute." Her voice sounded flat and strange to him, and her face looked more pale than usual. She was holding herself perfectly still like she was listening for something. He felt panic start its slow, cold rise inside his stomach.

"Do you want me to go get you something to eat?"

"No." He waited to hear *I'll be all right in a minute*, but she didn't say it. He stood over her, feeling clumsy and useless, knowing there was nothing he could say but unable to keep from saying it. "What can I do?"

"Nothing." He understood and was prepared to do nothing since that was what she wanted, then she spoke again. "Just don't look at me!" Anger flashing out at him through whatever she was fighting. It was the first time she'd ever spoken in anger to him and he felt tears jump into his eyes.

He went to a bench several yards away, sat with his back to her and waited, completely held there by what she'd asked him to do. He could no more have moved than if he was bolted to the ground like one of these sculptures.

He knew she was up before he looked. "OK." He heard her voice, still a little strange but better, "Let's go." He turned and saw her on her feet, adjusting her skirt and blouse. Smiling and walking toward him.

It was over the third martini that the idea came to him, sitting in the corner bar with the huge red vinyl booths with a hard rain peppering the plate glass windows that flared up with taxi light and faded.

She was angel thin with lovely breasts that were not large but seemed too large for her slender boy's body. "I love the smell of gin," she told him.

"Smells like Christmas trees," he grinned and she grinned back, both of them meeting in the gin and the pictures that the word Christmas caused to flash inside.

The rain had stopped making noise and for a moment he thought it might be snowing, even though it was only October.

He wished it was Christmas so he could give her something, though it was probably too early for that too. He wished she was not gay so he could kiss her. More than once it had felt like they were going to kiss but even drunk he could not bring his mind around to a place where that would be possible. Still, he wondered how she would kiss, whether the kiss would taste like the gin or the cigarettes she smoked or some third flavour that would be her.

He thought of a conversation he'd once had with two friends of his, a man and a woman, about when sex begins. When does sex begin? With a kiss? With the removal of clothing? Which article? The shirt? Pants? What has to be touched? Finally his friend brought it all to an end with his quote: *Sex begins when you know you're going to have sex.* He knew that feeling, that undertow that could take hold in any room. He thought he felt it now.

It was when he tried to picture it happening that it all fell apart. Any picture he could call up felt ridiculous. The trouble was his cock. The choices – her being "won over" by what he had, or, instead, her coolly humouring him, humouring it – both stopped him cold. Also, any pretence that he was different, that he was not just the same as all other men, would disappear the moment that came out into the open.

"I wish I was a lesbian," he said sometime after their fourth drink. He'd waited until then so she'd believe it was the gin talking and forgive him the way she always did. What she said surprised him.

"You'd make a terrible lesbian."

He felt hot blood rush to his face and knew this had actually hurt him. "Why?"

"Because," she smiled, "you're such a man." She said the word man like what she meant should be perfectly obvious to him but it wasn't. He had no idea what she meant.

"That's a shitty thing to say."

She laughed. He saw she didn't understand he was serious, but he laughed with her anyway because that still felt better than anything.

All his life he had been most comfortable around women. There was a softness in him that wanted to come forward to meet theirs; when it did, boundaries fell, but never the one he wanted. For that he still had to act, remind himself to remind them that he was a man, which felt like acting by that time, so soft had he become, and it occurred to him on this night sitting in the red vinyl bar with the rain lashing the windows that he could just keep going, let himself go softer and warmer until every man-part of him had sunk out of sight and there would be two women sitting at this table, not one woman and this in-between thing he became sometimes.

If he could make it happen, he knew he would want it to happen with her. She would know what to do with him, and he would let her.

There would be some slow unbuttoning in the hallway. Both of them in their big coats, his back against the row of mailboxes, her long white hands would part his coat like stage curtains and go to work slowly but surely, cupping his new soft women's breasts that would be there under his shirt. Under his bra. Would there be a bra? If she would like it, he thought, and that made him like it too, the thought of her eyes shining at the lavender or dark brown material, surprising against his skin. For her. His nipples tenting the material in the centre of each cup, scratching the palms of her hands, moving in slow circles. In the dream he was having wide awake, he felt his nipples graze the palms of her hands, felt it in his own hands and realized he was now her, showing himself to himself, but this was wrong, was not what he wanted, to crowd her out like this, and he looked for a way to bring her back in.

He tried to feel what it would be like to have what she had between her legs between his. But he could not. He could only feel it as an absence, a hole. It was when he thought of her putting her fingers inside him that the jolt went through him like an electric shock.

She would do it to him standing up, both of them standing in the dark hallway with the radiator ticking and pinging, making its little music for them. He thought of her fingers sunk deep into the hot cave between his legs, her knuckles pressed hard against the crisp hair he would still have down there, hair that would be the same and not the same. She would whisper things into his ear, things he'd never realized he wanted to hear until now.

As the vision frayed and dissolved, he realized what he'd known from the beginning, that this woman's body was a ruse, a Trojan horse, a costume he wanted to wear to trick her, to let her let him enjoy her. Not for her to enjoy him. He could get close to that thought but not close enough. In the end he would shut her out that way. He would always shut her out that way.

"What's wrong?" she said. "Are you crying?"

"You know," he said, looking out the window at the cars, "sometimes I'd just like to cut my dick off. Just cut it off and throw it down the fucking toilet like a piece of fucking shit."

In the long silence he thought he could hear snow falling. Soon he would be covered up by the cold. Then he heard her say, quietly, "Don't do that. You may want it back some day."

Diving Into Oceans of Air

Renée M. Charles

Just as I sliced open the packing tape which sealed the large, flat box of Gunter Blum posters I'd special-ordered directly from the photographer's native Germany, I heard a metallic *whump!* from the old-fashioned horizontal flap inset in my shop's front door. (The slot was occasionally useful for my infrequent snail-mail, like my *Empaths Unlimited* newsletter). The *whump!* was followed by the muffled *whuff!* of something thick being wedged tightly into the narrow opening. After ripping open the top of the greyish box and confirming that they'd sent the right set of art-quality blow-ups (that almost take-off of Lewis Hine's "Steamfitter" with the beautifully lean and slick-haired model posed against a grittily rendered piece of machinery, the hair on her pubis wiry and fierce against her taut thighs), I hurried over to the door. A tightly wound roll of sticky dots sealed paper jutted through the tight labial opening like a crude dildo.

The Blum posters could wait. The *Empaths Unlimited* news-letter only came out once a month, snail-mail thanks to it being too massive for an e-mailing. I'd been a long time between mind-seductions. Not that I didn't get my fill of illicitly-obtained fuck-fantasies gleaned from the fuzzy little brains of my customers, the men and women who either boldly or timidly entered my establishment, to fulfil whatever moist fancies their minds and bodies craved. But after a while, their craven wants grew tiresome and even easily anticipated – the stately, perfectly coiffed matrons who selected the largest, thickest dildos to use on their college-age lovers, both male and female; the "I'm buying this for my collection" types who were already yearning to shoot a steaming wad at the model in the sexcapades CD ROM they'd just shoved into their initial-adorned briefcase; or the eyes-cast-at-the-floor meek ones who tried to rip the edible panties they'd just bought off their own bodies once they got them home and wiggled into them in their lonely, steamy bathrooms.

I could picture and feel each one of their memories, their wildest (or tamest) conceits, as they drifted about my store like windborne dandelion seeds, aimlessly letting their eyes drift over items they had no intention of using, would never want to own, lest I discern their true desires should they hone in too quickly on the object of their longing. Perhaps I should have written WARNING: TELEPATH/EMPATHIC ON DUTY! under the heading under the existing lettering on my store's front window. But as it was, I thought that HOMME-DONNA was already a bit artsy-classy, surely enough to keep away the truly vile and the hopelessly tacky away from my establishment.

Glancing quickly at the clock above my counter, I noticed that it was close enough to closing time for me to turn around the OPEN/CLOSED – PLEASE COME AGAIN sign resting at the bottom of my discreetly mauve-curtained window and turn my full, pussy-throbbing attention to my torn-open newsletter. Once I'd seated myself in plain view of the Richard Avedon framed, non-glare-glassed posters opposite my counter-stool (several actresses and models whose names I only vaguely recalled caught in nude, but dignified glory), I flipped through the "Women Seeking Men", "Men Seeking Women", "Men Seeking Men" sections. Each bore that alphabetical string of abbreviations along the bottoms of the pages: M = Male, F = Female, E = Empathic, T = Telepathic, PC = PreCognitive, G = Gay, Bi = Bisexual, FT = Fetishist, N/D = No Drugs, N/S = Nonsmoking, and so on. The list purposely omitted the more typical Singles Paper designations, B = Black, W = White and H = Hispanic because *that* particular point was a moot one when it came to espers like me, and the other readers of this newsletter. I finally chose "Women Seeking Women".

Three pages' worth in this issue, both sides of each sheet. But I'd scanned the first page and a half of listings ("BiFT seeks open-minded/open-hearted G/BiFT/E for discreet but intense shared visions of –''), and come across nothing but the same-old, same-old, variations of "Let's blend feelings and fantasies" with no inherent bite, no suggestion of something fresh in their advertisements – let alone the one or two word "MindBytes" which followed each listing. Those teasers, when concentrated upon by the reader, gave off a faint, residual echo of that person's thought-waves, their fingerprint-like unique signal which could be momentarily savoured like a whiff of encapsulated perfume molecules trapped between the folded strip of paper in a magazine insert.

By the time I was halfway through this month's crop of psi-potentials my mind was gummy with after-images of romance novel-cover tepid embraces under the ubiquitous full moon and wisps of cloud, and cloyingly cuddly mental snuggles under postcard perfect sunny skies. Weren't there any hot-minded lesbian or bi empaths *left* any more?

The offerings in last month's issue had been little better. I'd received a long-*long*-distance virtual finger fuck from a woman in England who was expert in transmitting her bodily sensations to me via a phone line (her voice was even sexier than her mind), and the telepath over in Queens who'd been too timid to phone me was marvellous at pseudo-cunnilingus while we both literally pictured ourselves in a Grecian temple, but neither woman was seeking anything more than a one-mind stand, as it were. Once the last of the orgasm died down, I felt their minds gently but firmly close to me, leaving me sated but hardly satisfied.

Things were getting so bad for me, I'd recently been trying to tune in on the thoughts of some of my customers after they'd left my shop, discreetly bagged purchases in hand, but tracking them amid a clamouring, seething ocean of mental voices and bodily sensations was often much too difficult – aside from one store-to-apartment track on a rainy, not too bustling evening, when I'd seen/felt an outwardly confident-looking young executive type receive a deliciously thorough whipping/humiliation from her surprisingly femme-looking Mistress, my efforts at connecting with Unawares were close to futile.

The best Mindfuck occurred between two espers, period.

Which is why the *Unlimited* was created. The only trouble was, most of the truly hot and gifted espers already had partners, and didn't need to advertise for a mind-mate.

I morosely flipped through the remaining listings, letting my gaze wander over to that opened cache of Blum posters (what was in that model's mind, I wondered). I was sorely temped to run my own advertisement: "GFE/T wants to know – are there *any* hot G/Bi/E/T/PC's out there? With imagination and libidos to match?" . . . until my eyes drifted back down to the tight columns of newsprint, and saw:

> TIRED OF MIND-F – KS THAT LACK IMAGINA-
> TION? Try me. I'm G/T/E, N/D, N/S and a water F/T;
> seeking G/Bi-? to swim the steaming waters of my mind.
> Shed those clothes along with your hangups/inhibitions!
> Think: *OCEANOFAIR

If the Unlimited's listings weren't so blasted PC (and I'm not thinking PreCog here), she could've come out and said "Mind-Fucks" in print, but knowing that she was thinking it, and not wallowing in pseudo-Romanticism only, was a most bracing revelation.

Squirming in place on the already-smoldering vinyl cushion of my stool, I closed my eyes. I let my mind go placid, numb, figuratively limp, then clearly imagined the huge, cerulean word OCEANOFAIR across the forced-clear backdrop of my mind's eye.

So suddenly I felt almost literally cold, actually drenched, my body was diving into a horizon-to-horizon ocean of wave-lapped slightly frigid waters. Once I was submerged, I wiggled forward with almost no effort, toward a waiting, legs-scissor-ing figure, whose dark hair was clipped professional-swimmer short. Only a gently waving thatch of sea-grass-shifting hair was on the top of her head, and a matching close-trimmed wedge of sharply angular pubic hair covered the rising mound of Venus. The straps of her diving gear crisscrossed between her small, nipples-jutting breasts, and the clear diving mask over her nose and eyes revealed a light dusting of pale freckles over her nostrils and lower bridge, and a pair of orbs whose dark-brownness was intensified by the light-diffused blue-green waters around her.

With each kick of her flippers-encased feet, she moved closer to me . . . me, who wore no diving gear at all and who just then realized that I didn't need it. My own legs and lower body now sported overlapping, glistening scales, which culminated in a fin-leg tipped with delicately feathery fins which undulated and writhed in the rippling waters which surrounded me.

Glancing down at my own breasts, I saw that they were coyly cupped with purple-and-white mottled shells, strapped with thin ropes of sea-kelp. My hair – now suddenly long, waist-touchingly long, was floating about me like a nimbus of green-tinged gold. As she moved nearer, her left hand reached out to caress what would've been my own mound of Venus, but now, as I glanced down at it, was a small, tight vertical-lipped orifice resting parallel to my former hip and pelvis area. As her fingertips, cool yet subtly ridged along the fingerpads, made contact with my rippling, scaled flesh, I quivered. The touch of her skin on my own transformed fish-skin was exquisitely sensual, like being finger fucked with a leather-gloved digit.

As the first pulsing wave of pre-orgasm rippled through me, moving in ever-smaller concentric rings toward the narrow base of my tail, my body began arcing backwards in the cushioning waters, until I completed a full circle in that ocean. She maintained contact with my transformed mermaid's cunt, keeping that one pressing, gently probing finger in contact with me as she matched my gyrations in that soothing liquidity, now using one of my breasts to better hang onto my whirling body.

Remembering that I, too, was free to touch her, I mashed my hands – now greenish-tipped, with pearlescent nails – over her taut breasts, feeling the tender, puckering nipples dig into my palms. As her ribcage heaved toward me, pressing her manna tighter into my kneading hands, she shoved her finger all the way into that hermetic glory-hole, until the tip brushed against what had to be my deeply buried clit.

As we cart wheeled in aquatic free-fall, the depthless blue of the waters now frothy with bubbles, I heard her clear, chime-like thought-question: Your name . . . what is it?

Not missing a rotation in those buoyant waters, I thought back, Sima Rozyczka . . . that's Scottish for "listener" and Polish for "rose".

No sooner had the thought burst from my mind than she and I were out of the water, out under the low-hanging brassy sun, resting on a beach covered not with sand, but with millions upon billions of tightly curled, dried white rose petals. Their scent was an overpowering contrast to the salty brine of the sea, whose waves lapped at our now bare feet and outstretched legs. Both of us were nude, our shining skin covered with dewy beads of some exotic scented oil. I was once more shorter-haired, the artfully braided and beaded coils only reaching down to my shoulders, and a glance at my pelvis revealed my usual thatch of golden-brown curls. Beside me, her sheared-short black thatch was dried to a lacy covering over her swelling labia and high-rising upper mound. But both our breasts were tipped by raisin-shrivelled nipples, the darker brown flesh around them dimpled and pulled taut above the smoother pale mounds below.

As she lay on her side next to me in that shifting shore of petals, she fluttered her thickly-lashed dark eyes and thought: Mine is Claudia Muirfinn . . . the latter is also Scottish. For "dwells near the beautiful sea". My sea is beautiful, is it not?

An encircling expanse of calm azure waters surrounded our isle of convoluted, deeply curled petals, the sunlight shining off the surface like a wide-flung scattering of golden coins.

Very beautiful, I thought back: then, as I rolled on my back, letting the sun press down on my waiting body, I asked: And Claudia stands for . . . ?

I felt a swath of shadow cool my midsection when she stood up abruptly before padding out to the edge of the sea with long, loping strides. Turning her head sideways toward me, so that I could see one dark winking eye, she flashed back: Something you'll find out all too soon . . . I'll swim back to you soon. What is *your* MindByte?

She was already diving into the waters as I concentrated: Listener! As her left arm rose up above the waters, followed by the strong kick of her legs and feet, I almost slid off the counter stool, and broke my almost-fall by slamming both hands hard against the inside edge of the counter.

That had been the most intense MindByte sample I'd ever experienced. Usually the newletter's customers only expended a minimum of intense imagination when leaving their Mind-Byte, just enough for a brief taste of their mind. But Claudia Muirfinn's Byte was more like a feast, a gushing forth of long-stifled images and experiences, concentrated in – I glanced up at the clock, and was astonished by what I read there – a mere three minutes of actual thinking time.

But, as I massaged my sore palms after getting to my feet, I realized that Claudia's MindByte *was* merely that. Her ad had clearly stated that she was an Empath, too, yet I hadn't felt one thing *she* was experiencing during the Byte.

For Claudia, "soon" meant a mere hour later, when I was back in my west-side apartment, soaking in a tub filled with a sprinkling of fragrant herbs and a few drops of lavender oil. As I went to gently massage a huge sea-sponge between my slightly parted-at-the-knees legs, I instead felt her fingers wrapping around mine. We lolled in a circular tub whose surfaces were composed not of porcelain, but of close-set slightly domed individual small tiles, in a mosaic of ombre blues, violets, indigoes and deepest black, a swirl of grout-divided colour that extended up onto the deep ledge which also surrounded the tub, extending out three feet or more. Beyond the tub and the ledge was a room mirrored in black-veined smoked mirrors and dividing panels of oiled ebony wood. Only one of the wooden panels was knobbed, a smooth black-enamelled irregularity in all that linear shining perfection.

The waters which lapped and splashed around us were lit from a frosted greenish bulb set into a fixture located at least twelve feet above us in the domed ceiling. The bathwater itself felt sensuously silky, almost oily; its warmth brought the scent of sea salt and some bright, *green* odour to mind, something living, something tangy to the nostrils, yet sweet, too, as if concealing a flowering centre.

The inside of the tub gently sloped, so that we could recline side by side without slipping to the bottom. My hair – now pinned up to the top of my head, only ringlets hanging down to my wet shoulders on each side of my face – rested slightly damp on my head, as if Claudia had imagined me being in the tub so long that the surrounding moisture would wick into my tresses. Claudia's hair, while still short, still sleekly wet, had been coaxed into one coy, tight curl along the left side of her forehead. Letting my hands glide down along her lithe, limber body, I rubbed my fingers over her Mound of Venus, the short hair down there now silky smooth and soft over her fleshy cleft. As I eased one finger into her slick, tight quim, she reached over and began fingering my nipples under the water, massaging each of them in a counter-clockwise motion, while she thought: This is better than your tub, isn't it? Would you like to body-feel it? Actually . . . see it?

So this is real?

A mental pause, as the fingers spread out over my breasts to tenderly cup them, then: Doesn't it feel real? Doesn't it sound real? She bent one of her legs at the knee, so that it broke surface with a liquid *splash*. Working my fingers deeper into her, gently rubbing her clit with my middle finger, I returned: Yes, and yes, but . . . I feel the tub, I feel your flesh, but . . . how do I feel within you? You're an empath, so –

The hands on my breasts stiffened, then slid down off them, to the slightly convex roll of my belly, then down, down, to my waiting watery-drift of loose curls, and the slightly gaping ache between them. I had to lean back hard against those tiny, knob-like tiles. First she fingered me, then, after shifting around so that she was facing me, ducked her head under the surface and began tonguing me under the rippling waters until my pelvis began thrusting upward in short, hard pulses. I started to reach my arms outward, hugging the surrounding curve of the tub, while she thought: Just relax, *feel* it . . . never mind about me. Just let it flow –

And as the shivering jerks of the orgasm made my leg muscles writhe under the damp flesh, I felt her tongue narrow and burrow deep within me like a bee tunneling into a half-opened rose. When the tip of her nose brushed against my clit, I lifted my pelvis free of the water, feeling the air touch it warmly, yet with a strange completeness. When I opened my eyes and took in my own familiar bathroom, in all its familiar pink-and-whiteness, it was like being exposed to a flashing bulb, for my eyes had grown so familiar to that soothing blue-violet blackness.

But as I slid deep into my bath, letting the water rise up to my chin, my lower lip, I heard Claudia's parting thought, slightly distant and muffled, as if shouted underwater, but nonetheless clear:

I'll tell you the meaning of my name when you visit me . . .

I moved to an upright position with a noisy splash, asking: Visit . . . as in see-see you? In . . . *person?*

This was something almost unheard of in esper circles. The whole purpose of the newsletter, of all the esper singles newsletters all over the world, was to facilitate meaningful *mental* relationships. Not the petty body-dates which were based solely on looks and other uninspired, mundane aspects of our bodily trappings. Phone calls were only used as a tool to better solidify an esper transfer. For most of us, making voice contact intensified the images, made the emphatic bonds all the more tactile and real.

Since Claudia's bond was already so strong (if lacking in my being able to read *her* physical responses, something I'd chalked up to some sort of shyness on her part), I already thought we had something special, something even a phone line couldn't really improve upon. But her answer was unmistakable, if faint:

Of course . . . how else do people visit? Phones are for wussies. Dive in, the water's fine here.

Before I lost all contact with her, I leaned forward in the tub, my forehead almost touching the spout, and shouted:

How do I find you??

Her reply was as faint as the distant drip-drip of a faucet left barely turned on in a far away room:

I'm in the *book*, Sima . . .

Although she wasn't in the Manhattan directory, there were plenty of view-phone books for surrounding cities in my shop. The next morning (after a night spent wallowing in moist, blue-tinged dreams) I shoved aside the still unpacked box of Blum posters and looked under my counter, through every view-phone book on the shelf, until I finally found the name

Muirfinn, C. A., in the Lake Placid directory. Hers was the only address listed for that particular street (Blue Fin Drive, appropriately enough), so I suspected that hers was either one of those spreading country-style estates, or a private cul-de-sac.

The Blum posters – and my meagre-visioned customers – would have to wait a few days . . . until I'd rented an old-style gas-powered car (thanks to her place being too far away for an electric car's reserves) and personally checked out C.A. Muir-finn.

And, as if to acknowledge the rightness of my decision, Claudia whispered in my mind: You were right the first time . . . it is an estate. Right near the lake, in fact, before closing off the contact, leaving only a subtle whiff of briny sweetness in my nostrils . . .

It was a long drive up to Lake Placid, and another five miles beyond the city to Blue Fin Drive, which was within less than one hundred yards of the twin islet-dotted lake itself. As I made the turn onto her winding, sinuous driveway, which led in lazy loops and twists toward a massive, deep blue-sided, grey-roofed deluxe ranch-style mansion, I couldn't help but notice that the driveway looked incredibly *new*, as if few cars used it. There was a two-car garage near the house, but the gravel before it looked virtually pristine, as if this was the bottom of a fish tank, and not someone's private driveway.

When I exited the car in front of the garage door closest to the house, I noticed that there was no actual landing before her front door, just a slightly sloping-concrete walkway which slanted subtly upwards, plus a metal hand-rail next to it, decorated with stylized verdigris-coated brass dolphins. The house seemed to grow larger as I walked up that slight incline; it had to be over one hundred and twenty feet long, and almost half that wide, not counting the garage. That the place was only one-storey didn't detract from its sheer size: in many ways, it reminded me of an ocean of air, capped by a pale, glittering island of silvery sand.

While Claudia had remained strangely silent, even when I'd tried to use her MindByte while trying to figure out how to gas up the unfamiliar car I'd rented at the automated garage a few miles back, during my trip up here, she did choose to speak to me just as I was about to place my finger on her door-bell:

You came . . . you actually did come to see me.

There was an unexpected pause in her mind-voice, followed by something akin to awe in those silvery tones. Before touching the bell, I thought back: But didn't you invite me? Tell me to look you up?

Her answer was as soft as the *plash* of raindrops on new grass:

Of course, of course . . . but I didn't think that you wanted to so badly.

Pressing my forefinger against the bell, I was about to think her a retort when I felt a twinge of queasiness ripple through me, the first empathic touch I'd felt from her. Not a physical sensation, but a deep feeling of – what? Could it actually be fear, of *me?*

Bold Claudia fearing more reticent Sima? On the second ring, the door swung open on its own, revealing a cathedral-like expanse of blue-green-violet lit hallway carpeted in what had to be a soothing low-pile sandy broadloom, its surface delicately pebbled in the diffuse light. No furniture adorned that long hall, but the walls were dotted with wall-mounted fishing nets from which hung sand dollars, flat shells, and rigid starfish and dried sea horses . . . and as I entered that passage-way, and lightly touched the various remainders of the ocean, I felt the deepness of Claudia's affections for each object, and knew/felt that she'd gathered them all herself.

The hallway stretched out for about fifteen feet before it opened onto an extraordinary room – that same sandy-nubby flat carpeting ringed the outer parameters of the huge room (fifty by fifty, or twice that much?) whose centre was dominated by an amorphous blue-green-black tiled pool whose waters gave the room a faint but not unpleasant chlorine smell. This scent was almost masked by the hanging rattan baskets of pungent dried herbs and flowers which dangled from various hook-suspended chains all around the pool area. The area around the pool was brightly tiled, with hand-painted sea creatures fired upon their surfaces. The overhead lights cast bright, rippling ribbons of light upon the pale aquamarine waters: almost blinding in their intensity, they made me partially shield my eyes against the glare, so that I missed Claudia's initial entrance on the opposite side of the room. But when that queasiness gave way to a sense of heart-lopping panic, I looked across those waters and saw –

– the woman of my mind-fucks, only she was wearing this oddly strapped and buckled and reinforced-from-without blackish-blue bodysuit, which covered her entire body, fingers and all. For a second, I was reminded of some of Gunter Blum's more personal-looking shots from the mid-1990s, the studies of that bald-pussied woman trussed up in those leather and vinyl corsets and lace-up bustiers, her legs encased in semi-opaque black stockings, but Claudia's outfit didn't look so much erotic as . . . *functional*. Like every strap and supporting rod had a very specific purpose.

When she took a step toward me, I recalled another image, also from the last century – that film about the robot-man with no hands, only flicking, twitching scissors, the man whose body *was* his strange leather suit. Each movement she made was twitching, seemingly isolated from the next, and her legs didn't so much as scissor but jerk forward, forward, as if the strings guiding her were welded by a palsied hand. Her arms didn't quite move in synch with her legs, but randomly pulsed out, to the sides, and back again, as if yet another set of hands were guiding *those* strings . . .

But when I saw her pinched, deeply concentrated expression, I realized just who those guiding hands belonged to . . . or rather, to *what*. I'd heard of suits like hers, read about the late-twentieth-century limbs-only prototypes which plugged directly into the limbs themselves. But I'd never before seen a full-body "walking" suit in action.

As Claudia reached the outer edge of the carpeting on the other side of the pool and paused to make the transition between the nubby surface and the slicker tile (I saw something move on her "booted" feet, and suspected that some sort of grippers were now positioned on her soles), I actually spoke to her . . . aloud:

"How did it happen to you? Was it . . . a diving accident?"

Stopping, but only as if she'd planned to, she awkwardly

brushed at the sides of her tight-shorn head, and replied, using her own voice (which was quite similar to her mind-one), "Yes . . . I was at a diving contest . . . the board had a flaw in it. It broke and I fell straight . . . down, hit the edge of the pool. All this around you is part of their insurance settlement, and most of the lawsuit. Paid for this suit, too. Luckily, I still could breathe, after being weaned off the respirator. Had good muscle tone, so the suit was my best option . . . but, it isn't everything –"

As in, it couldn't give her back physical sensation, couldn't feel for her . . . not in the way another empath could. Making my way closer to the edge of the pool so that I was stepping on the colourful marine-inspired tiles, I asked, "Was that why you . . . so I could be your skin, your . . ."

" 'Pussy'? Not actually . . . I can mind-fuck with the best of them, even *before* this happened . . . but, there's something else –"

Unable to speak what she so deeply felt, Claudia felt it to me:

The fast-moving rush of flat water coming close, closer to my forward-pointed fingers, then the enveloping, sensual closeness of the water churning over and around me, seeping into my private parts, rushing across my close-cropped head, like being buried in the juiciest quim, flowing with musky oils.

Despite the exactness of all the sensations she felt toward me, I realized by their fuzziness in duration that I was actually feeling only a memory of sensation, not her current state of being.

As realization crept over me, I thought to her: You . . . you can't get into that pool any more, can you? Not while wearing that suit –

And when it's off of me, I'm helpless. Can't get in or out of the pool alone. My attendants, they come by twice a day, to wash me, but . . . they're mundanes. Not even gay or bi. To them, I'm just a limp body studded with receptor plugs. I can't even get *into* water, not all the way. The plugs by my neck are water-sensitive. Have to be sealed shut just to wash my hair. Can't even . . . can't even dip my feet into the pool. But I like to see it –

Coming closer to her, to the pool, I began to unbutton my

blouse, then dropped it onto the decorated tiles at my feet, while slipping off my clogs one foot at a time. Freeing up all my senses, leaving myself as wide open as mentally/physically possible, I stepped lightly across the cool tiles, my feet splapping with each forward, clothes-shedding motion, until I was standing slightly shivering and naked at the edge of the pool, directly across its shimmering surface from Claudia. She'd been watching my every move, feeling each sensation, and her eyes were half-closed in something far greater than ecstasy – something almost serene in its blissful intensity.

When I slid feet-first into that warm pool, feeling my skin goosebump lightly as it entered that swirling moistness, Claudia slowly, laboriously, got down to her knees, then stretched out alongside the pool, to better watch me swim across toward her. With each stroke, I was myself and Claudia, so that the waters around me were now an ocean kissed by a ruby setting sun, then the waters of the lake beyond the house itself, then a bubbling jacuzzi filled with champagne froth . . .

Each of her water-memories were so vivid, so detailed, I realized how hard it had been for her to give up her beloved seas in favour of an almost independent, if totally arid, life. When I reached the opposite side of the pool and was close enough to Claudia to reach out and touch her smooth cheeks, her firm chin, I whispered, "You promised to tell me what *your* name meant." I was rewarded with a burble of only slightly ironic laughter, as she said, "It actually means 'lame' of all the crazy things . . . one of my nurses told me, in the hospital. Showed me the name in a book, just to prove it. Isn't that delicious? As if my mother was a PC instead of a mere empathic . . ."

Her laughter was a brittle thing that echoed off the waters and distant walls around us, until I clambered out of the pool and sat down spread-legged and dripping beside her, and asked, "Do the fingers . . . work? If you'll do me, I'll share it with you . . . I love the feel of leather on my pussy," while pulling up the top of my mound with my fingers, so that my slit was a taut, vertical smile before her. And when those band-reinforced leatherette fingertips caressed my labia, my clit, both of our eyelids became suffused with blood, as we peered at each other through the capri-shells of our lowered lashes, and everything in the room grew crimson-bright . . .

And when she creakily bent down her head (the neck encased up to the bottom of her hairline in a collar-like device) to tongue me, I stretched out with one hand lazily dipping into the pool, the other caressing cool, slick tiles, so as to give her the most sensation possible, until I was so blown away by my climax that my entire universe was that wiggling, supple tongue poking deep in my most sensitive fissures and folds . . .

Later, much later that evening, I watched as her attendant undressed and bathed her in that same blue-green-black tiled room she'd shown to me during the mind-fuck . . . only she'd left off the special plastic contour chair upon which she had to sit while being bathed from that sloping tub. She'd merely told the woman doing the bathing that I was a visiting friend from her college days, to which the woman (older, coarser, and totally disinterested) merely grunted.

Claudia had told me to watch very carefully, which hadn't been necessary. Rather than being saddened, or repulsed by the sight of her pale, pluglike studded limbs and torso, I was fascinated by the soft texture of her skin under the greenish light, which made her resemble an exotic sea creature cast up on a shining marble shore. As the woman mindlessly moved the soapy washcloth over and around Claudia's inert, statue-like limbs, I tried to tune into what she was feeling, but there was simply nothingness. No cold, no wet, no . . . anything. Not from the face down. Just memories of touch, and the eagerness to feel *through* me . . .

Before the woman had a chance to dress her, Claudia asked, "Could my friend help you?" Another noncommittal grunt, then she began showing me where each male end of the inner suit fitted into Claudia's artificial "female" parts, until we'd suited her from foot to neck in the metal and plastic armoured suit, and she was able to place an arm around my waist as the woman trundled out of the little sea-coloured room, leaving us alone.

Without a need for words, I slipped off my clothes again, and slid into those still soapy waters, and began massaging my body with that same cloth, while Claudia shared each swipe

and caress of my terrycloth covered fingers. Once she'd felt
what had been happening to her for too many physically
unconscious years, I drained the tub, then refilled it with
clear, pure water, in anticipation of a mind-fuck like no other
I'd ever experienced.

Once Claudia entered my mind, it was like there were two of
her in the room with me: an inert insect-like being who sat
rigidly on a corner chair, almost out of our sight, and the live,
pliant Claudia who sloshed in the tub with me and fingered and
tongued me until I was gasping too much to see or hear . . .

Only when the orgasm died down did I wrap my mental/
physical arms around her/the surrounding waters and whisper:
Now that I know what to do for you, do we really need her
around?

Not after the end of the month . . . I only hire them by the
month, just in case . . . But Sima, tell me, do *you* really need
that shop of yours? The job of . . . personal attendant pays
quite well –

Resting my head against her watery shoulder, I thought it
over, then said: Have you ever seen the photographs of a
German called Gunter Blum? I have a feeling they'd go well
with your decor . . .

The Water Hole

Michèle Larue

Raymond's place was a little one-storey affair in the shadow of
Saint Eustache; twisted and grey, it stuck out like a wart on the
front of an apartment building. The man had approached me at
an opening in Saint-Germain-des-Prés. I'd been instantly
taken with the intensity of his gaze. Dark eyes set wide apart,
with a fire burning in them that fascinated me. The long white
eyebrows curling up towards his temples made him look like a
poet from the Midi. The owner of the gallery introduced him
as a leading conceptual artist. I had only the vaguest idea what
lay behind that label, something transient, fleeting. Raymond
was old enough to be my father. He was from Toulouse, went
back there now and then to visit a younger brother interned in
a mental hospital. There were a few friends of mine at the
opening, but seeing me deep in conversation they refrained
from butting in for the ritual kiss: I had only eyes for Raymond. Whenever I tore my gaze away from his, I found him
dumpy-looking. But that only endeared him to me all the more.
I felt an abstract tenderness for his efforts to be gracious and
charming, he belonged to that anxious species, the conquis-
tador in jeopardy, the ageing Casanova. As I stepped out of the
bubble he'd blown around me, I agreed to a date for the
following week. And now, on my way to keep it, my heart
was in my mouth.

The huge bulk of Saint Eustache loomed through a heavy
mist. At 2 p.m., it was almost dark. The trysting place was so
run-down it seemed to belong to another era. Raymond opened
the door and whistled at the sight of my black miniskirt. I
wiped my shoes with a torn floor-cloth lying on the parquet.

He returned to the chessboard on a table and resumed his seat. His partner, an elderly Asian, looked up. I shook the limp hand and began inspecting the room. I peered at yellowed volumes piled up on sagging bookshelves, old mirrors, tarnished candelabra, my new idol's home surroundings. At 22, I was looking for male figures to admire. The old-fashioned setting conflicted with what Raymond had told me of his occupation. I saw him wreathed in the glory of the crazy artworks he'd told me about at the opening, such as covering a city with a huge mantle of parachute silk, stretched between a dozen helicopters. I toured his house. The toilets were located in a makeshift bathroom with flower-patterned walls. An ashtray kitchen, all the surfaces spattered with coffee-grounds. Perhaps my admirer was just a noisome hippie.

Back in the sitting room, I couldn't find a folding bed and concluded that no one actually lived there. I sat down in the only armchair and crossed my legs. My skirt rode up around my thighs but neither of the men so much as glanced at my knees. I took the opportunity to examine my host, noticed his baggy grey trousers needed shortening. Finally he did see me. His gaze slid over my legs and back to the chessboard. His stone-coloured beard clashed with those eyes which darted at me from time to time, two tiny black and silver pools, fluttering in the gale of emotions stirred by the sight of my body, prepared to give me the world. The divine love he seemed to feel for the insignificant little puppy I was, made me melt like sugar in a cup of scalding coffee. He thought I was bored, but he was wrong. I was getting a kick out of the waiting, the furtive glances he gave me, his opponent's annoyance. He apologized for the game dragging on, and said: "Look round the room, darling, and help yourself to anything you like, a knick-knack, a book, whatever." I walked to the table, picked up his queen and put it in my pocket.

An hour later, our feet were treading the sandy soil of the Fontainebleau forest. The rain had stopped. Over the tops of the pine-trees, the cirrus clouds were breaking up. As we walked and talked, I wanted to put my hand in his, or rather wanted him to take it. He was doing the talking. About Nietzsche. About Bourdieu. When my hand had brushed against his pocket a few times, he caught hold of it. Nestling in his dry palm, my fingers quite naturally began to stroke it.

Only a few minutes had gone by when I had a violent urge to pee. I pulled my hand away and skipped off, shouting, "I'll catch up with you!", then turned and ran to hide behind a tree. I could still see him. He had his back to me. I squatted down, keeping an eye on him. I peed sparingly at first, then with a gush of relief as my bladder emptied. The earth began to steam. The sickly odour rose between my thighs. When I put my hand back into Raymond's – he had tactfully walked on – there was a long silence. Then he told me what had happened.

It was just before my sally into the bushes. When we'd left the car on the parking lot at the Gorges de Franchard, he'd needed to pee himself. The sexual urge that prompted him to take my hand conflicted with that other, more bodily urge. When our hands joined, the bodily became excruciating. Though usually helpful in such cases, a Zen technique of abdominal respiration had failed to ease the pressure – breathing quickly and as far as possible from the prostate, which was partly responsible, he confessed, for his discomfort. Never again would our relationship be as intense as at this moment, he'd said to himself. Never would we be so close. And he held it back. Our hands fondled each other, my flesh gave off vibrations that went straight to his heart. He was right about the intimacy. I wouldn't have let him touch my breasts, not even through my sweater. And since Raymond had wanted to keep that little moment of happiness alive, he'd decided to pee as he walked. Drop by drop at first, then in little spurts, letting the urine dribble down his pants-leg. And I hadn't suspected a thing.

A few months later, in August, I saw Raymond again. He was just back from Japan and made a date with me at the bar of a trendy restaurant near Montparnasse, *la Closerie des Lilas*. Avoiding the crowded dining room, we took supper by the terrace hedge. Elbows on the big white tablecloth, chin in hands, I listened to his account of Tokyo "love hotels". A prostitute who spoke no French had agreed to be his escort. Raymond was talking to me like an old cohort: I felt flattered and thrilled by a natural intimacy, a simplicity I'd never known with anyone else. Making extravagant gesticulations, he described to me those suggestive Japanese decors, revolving beds in the shape of a car or a woman's shoe and painted a bright Chinese red, sulphurous water cascading down over the young woman (a devout Catholic) who laughed making the sign of the cross in an attempt to communicate. They'd watched a porn movie where the women wore white triangles between their thighs instead of pubic hair.

He brought up what had happened in the Fontainebleau Forest the previous spring. If only he'd been able to catch a glimpse of me squatting . . . Or at least heard me doing it! He'd have closed his eyes, knowing I was behind the branches. But from that distance, it was inaudible.

"Did it excite you to know I could have turned around at any time and seen you?"

"A little. I was afraid . . ."

"Of being seen?"

"Yes. Ashamed."

"Would you have rather peed standing up?"

"Like a man?"

"That's right."

"Like you in your trousers!"

We burst out laughing. The waiter brought the desserts. Raymond glanced at his plate and looked me in the eye: "I would even have drunk from you . . ."

We'd had a full bottle of white wine. I looked around. Two tablefuls of Americans were talking at the top of their lungs, like stock-market traders on the floor. I slipped my wineglass under the table and sat on the edge of my chair. With one fingernail, I pulled aside the elastic on my panties and peed into the glass. I regulated the flow with the tip of my index finger, aiming the jet by obstructing the orifice. My middle-finger gauged the level. I didn't let it brim over, but I had trouble stopping. The glass reappeared and I handed it to him over the immaculate tablecloth. "Here . . . fresh from the spring."

He sniffed the warm wine, wet his lips and began to sip.

Raymond dropped out of sight for years, staging musical comedies in New York. From time to time, we spoke on the phone.

In the meantime, there was Joseph: tall, crewcut, he became my closest friend, my collaborator and, by dint of spending all that time together, my lover. After two years of a beautiful friendship, he whined for sex. A human being, he argued, could not be regarded as pure intelligence. Especially not him. Not the bosom pal who lived inside that big carcass quivering before me. I had to love the whole animal. Thinking back, I wonder if he didn't lift those lines from some Rohmer movie.

I'm still fond of Joseph, but I have a terrible time loving him physically, even the least little bit. However, we work together, we live under the same roof, and I don't meet any other men. So I let Joseph fuck me. His tongue is coarse and clumsy. Sucking and lapping away without a break. Personally, I love the occasional time-out. Anticipation. Kisses inside my thighs. The mouth pulling away, breathing on the fluffy hairs, coming back to work. Sad for me, Joseph just loves to lick.

When he fucks me, I come, but only then. A battering ram he's got there, a long, thick sledge-hammer, a very efficient tool. But his skin repels me, and so does the obscene way he throws out his chest when he poses for me, kneeling on the bed with his thighs apart. He has the exhibitionism of a she-puppy. Besides, he's too tall. When I lie on him, my mouth is nipple-high. Which makes kissing on the mouth a contortionist's exercise. And Joseph is not very flexible. So I nibble. My fits of contained rage suit him to a T: he has sensitive breasts. Anyhow, I said to myself after our first screw, it's just as well: he has halitosis.

As soon as we became friends, Joseph had asked me to tell him about my sexual adventures. From the day we became lovers, every fantasy he had was based on some experience of mine I'd told him about. He'd do somersaults on the bed trying to suck his own cock because I'd had a West Indian lover who could do it. When he heard about what happened in the forest and at the *Closerie des Lilas*, he insisted on following me into the WC there he begged to be my receptacle, my chalice, my loving cup. He offered himself as toilet paper to wipe my lips.

Today, Joseph and I have over a thousand subscribers to our Internet site, "The Water Hole". Recently we've put live images on line, with credit card payment in advance (Visa and American Express only) but, aside from that, we provide all sorts of advice for golden shower enthusiasts, everything from diuretic herbs to tricks for overcoming inhibitions.

While I sell my holy brew in chats with net-surfers who dream of the virtual creature going into action right over their faces, Joseph creates new graphics for the site. When it's his turn to run the chat-room, he pretends he's me on the Web while he gets an eyeful of the trickling video screens.

Last month we installed a Webcam in our bathroom. Whenever Joseph goes to the toilet, he turns it off. Understandably: it's the only time he's ever really alone. When I'm not emceeing the chat-room, I'm peeing in front of the camera in real time. Our customers jack off watching me. I thrust out my pelvis with my weight resting on one hip like the dancers with silver wigs at the Crazy Horse Saloon. Except that my act is motionless. Only the stream trembles a bit. For viewers with classical tastes, I squat in the bathtub and pull down my white panties, an athletic model by Calvin Klein. Perched on the edge of the wash-basin with the camera behind me, I spread my buttocks with my hands so lips and anus are both in the shot. Standing in front of the bowl, I pee into it like a man. Naked under a wasp-waist corset, or wearing a gold chain around the waist and a black g-string which I pull aside with one fingernail, I do it into a wine carafe. I gauge the trickle. I concentrate on letting my belly fluids gush. Online wet-nurse. "*L'Origine du monde*." I soon learned to take sensual satisfaction from a pee. I came to enjoy it. But I miss the touch of other flesh: skin contact, violent caresses have become my most cherished fantasy. I envy prostitutes the warmth of the customer's body.

As for you Web-surfers out there, I know only your name, your age, the alleged size of your penis and sometimes the colour of your eyes. Not one pubic hair in sight. No odours except for Joseph's, and he smells of piss. I suspect him of collecting drops from the enamelled bowl when I've finished my stint. I'm afraid of smelling that way, too. Sometimes, dear water sports lovers, I hate your guts.

What about me in all this? I feel brutalized by my work. But the money has tamed my "me". The Water Hole, on the other hand, has long since ceased to be a source of pleasure. At the gym, I meet young men working out. They're vain and shy. I go straight up to them, propose we go to their place right then, that afternoon: "I've got this husband, you see . . ." And I'll come like a bomb in some athlete's mouth. Instinctively, mechanically. As if I were starving for sex. Light-years from those laborious orgasms with Joseph. Practical, acrobatic sex. I like to sit on top. Releasing an orgasm, I dribble a few drops out of habit, and sometimes one of them will pull a face. Not aficionados, just ordinary boys.

And yet when Raymond, now seriously ill, invited me to dinner in his new apartment, I was delighted at the prospect of seeing him again. I didn't hold him responsible for what had happened, but I wasn't going to ask him to endorse "The Water Hole", either. Nor did I plan to mention Joseph. Raymond is my secret garden.

I got there around 8. He was heating a frozen meal in the micro-wave. A confirmed bachelor who'd never learned to cook. Here too, the sink was an ashtray: against doctor's orders, he still smoked. We drank white wine, a *Bourgogne aligoté*. The moment I rose from the table, glass in hand, Raymond followed me down the dim corridor. Our ritual took place in the passageway leading to the WC. Six feet away from the closed door he stood with his back turned, listening intently. When I came out, he groped about till his hand closed around my potion.

"Here, my friend . . . drink!"

And at that moment, I actually felt a little something again.

Translation by Noel Burch.

The Adventure of Thomas the Rock Star in the Court of the Queen of Faery

John Grant

Because of his name, they called him Mad Tom and they called him Tom o' Bedlam and they called him Thomas the Rhymer, but really he was Thomas the Rock Star, and he played lead guitar for Critical Assembly, ignoring the screams and yells of the fans and focusing entirely on his fingers and the frets as behind him the banked speakers sang and wailed as they slid from something that was a bit like Mozart to something that was a bit like Bo Diddley to something that was a bit like Led Zep. He was the quiet one of Critical Assembly, the one who always wasn't there when the groupies penetrated the carefully lax security and gatecrashed the band's hotel suite. He was the one whose long, pale, smooth, almost girlish face, framed in hair the colour of polished oak, the unloved imagined as they gave themselves comfort to keep away the loneliness of the dark.

He was the one who once, after a gig, when the great auditorium was empty except for the echoes of that night's excitements, found a backstage corridor that he'd never noticed before, and out of curiosity followed it to see where it would lead him, and discovered himself abruptly in a place of forest and insects from which there was no easy road back.

The only thing that startled him about this sudden transition was how little startled by it he was. Although somewhere inside him a little voice was protesting that passageways backstage in a Chicago concert hall don't lead to daylit leafy glades, that the whole thing was an outrage, most of him simply accepted the overwhelming sensation of *naturalness* coursing through him. He was not to know at the time that this feeling came about because he had been ensnared by enchantment, although later of course he would recognize what had happened.

Thomas stood by the edge of a small, clear, slow-moving stream, watching the reflection of his face with behind it tiny white puffy clouds in the blue sky, and rapid, unexpected, polychromatic darts of motion that he knew must be king-fishers flying overhead. He let his mind float like a dead twig on the current; he breathed deeply of air that sparkled like cold water and had not been breathed before him by automobiles.

A sound that was no sound, coming from behind, made him turn.

She was standing just inside the shadows at the edge of the trees, watching him through eyes that were the green of jade yet flecked with occlusions of copper. She was wearing a gauzy gown upon which his eyes refused to focus, and she had hair spun of midnight that hung to her thighs. Her skin was as dark as the shadows that framed her.

"Who are you?" he said quietly, afraid his voice might burst the world.

She said nothing, just continued to stare at him. A light breeze made the folds of her gown move like smoke. A sharp tongue-tip peeped from between her lips and flicked sideways, then was gone again.

"Who are you?" he said again. "My name is Thomas. I've not long arrived –" he spread his hands "– here."

She nodded slowly and beckoned to him that he should follow her. Without pausing to see that he was following, she turned and walked slowly into the woods, the twigs and the grasses turning aside so that they wouldn't catch in the light cloth of her gown. After a moment's hesitation, he hurried to catch up to her, but always she remained the same distance ahead of him even though the pace of her walking never changed.

At length they arrived at another glade, a cuplike space among the trees into which the sunlight fell to fill it. Here she halted, waiting with her back towards him, still silent. The sounds of his feet through the undergrowth seemed clumsy and intrusive to him as he moved to join her.

She was taller than he had thought, only slightly shorter than he was himself.

Thomas reached out to touch her shoulder, but before his fingers came close she spread her arms high to either side, so that the soft folds of the misty cloth unfurled and he saw that it was not cloth or a gown at all, that these were her wings – wings the colour of a young birch-tree's bark – and that she was naked aside from them.

Slowly she turned again, this time to face him, and she gazed deep into his eyes. As for Thomas, he found himself lost within her gaze, seeing there a ruthless sensuality, a cold exploration of all the myriad varieties of passion, a cynical wisdom of carnality.

He shuddered in the chill of her stare, terrified by its inhumanity, wanting to flee, flee, flee from her through the forest and somehow back to the grimy familiarity of the deserted concert hall and beyond that into the safety of a cab and finally the impersonal sanctuary of an anonymous luxury hotel room, but at the same time a flame kindled in his loins so that he could not move.

At last she dropped her eyes from his, slowly lowering also her arms. Freed from the grip of her gaze, he too looked downward, seeing the curves of her dark body, her small breasts, the flatness of her belly – unmarked for, as he suddenly knew, she had not been born – and the woven triangle of grasses that, in place of hair, hid her sex from him.

She put the tips of her long dark fingers on his chest, then ran them down towards his waist, beneath which his treacherous excitement loomed. Thomas knew what she wanted him to do. Taking a pace backwards, he shrugged off his black T-shirt, eased his feet out of his shoes, unfastened fumblingly his black jeans and shoved them down so that his shaft sprang free, then further down until he could stumble and kick his way out of them, all the time aware of his own ungainliness beside her silent grace.

He stood, finally, before her. She washed her gaze slowly

down over his body, and he felt its soft caress exploring him. When she reached the place where his manhood jutted it was as if she had taken it gently into her mouth, and he felt the heat of his groin build even higher. He shut his own eyes, then, leaning his head back, feeling his lips tight against his teeth as all of his awareness fled toward the focus of her attention. And then, just as he feared he was hurtling irrevocably towards the precipice, her gaze fell to his thighs and his calves and finally his feet, where it lingered, stirring the small hairs there.

She spoke for the first time, her voice like the hushing of the trees as the sun fades.

"Open your eyes, Thomas. You have no choice but to see me."

He obeyed. She was only inches from him, staring earnestly once more at him. She put a finger to his lips, sealing them, while with the other hand she took his pulsing shaft, fondling its ripe end with her small palm, draping her fingers down its sides.

Still he was filled with fear; still he was filled with desire. He had never dared to venture so far into this forest of the senses before.

"I am the Gate," she whispered between sharp white teeth. "Only through me may you enter the court."

She put both her hands behind his neck, then raised one of her long, long legs and wrapped it around his waist. The woven grasses of her pubis rubbed scratchily against him, stirring new sensations into life. After a moment that seemed like a day to him, she lifted herself, putting her other leg around him, her little breasts flat against his chest, and lowered her hips so that he was gradually engulfed in her warm, mossy dampness until he was entirely inside her.

She weighed almost nothing. Gently, knowing she had far greater strength than humanity could encompass yet afraid for her fragility nonetheless, he held the rounded smoothness of her small hard buttocks, pushing his fingers into the crack between them, then scampering his touch up the cleft to the hollow of her spine's base. In response she let one of her own hands fall from his shoulders and behind and under her, taking the bag of his balls into a clasp so slight that, because he could hardly feel its touch, he felt through every last shred of his body.

She made no attempt to ride up and down upon him, and he obediently kept his own hips still. But then he felt slow ripples deep inside her, flickering regularly along the length of him, squeezing him knowingly like hands in velvet gloves, each time moving on just before he'd fully sensed their presence. Sensing that at the coaxing of these unseen hands his time was approaching, he shifted his mouth to hers, wanting to kiss her, to put his tongue into her in imitation of his rigid shaft; but she pulled her face away almost waspishly and instead he watched over her shoulder as a deer trod into the clearing and paused there, ready at any instant to bolt, sombrely regarding their two entwined bodies motionless in the near-invisible sheath of her wings.

The pulses inside her were growing stronger and more urgent now, increasing in frequency and intensity and heat. He knew his hands on her back and her buttocks were losing their coordination, jerking from one place to another, all smoothness gone from their strokings; he was powerless to control them as his consciousness shrank until all there was in the world was the forceful moist waves of pressure on him.

Urgency built up around the base of his shaft – an urgency that could not long be resisted. Her grip firmed on his balls, which rolled in her hand, the sack tautening.

Now his hips did begin to move. A dam broke inside him. He threw back his head and yelled a bestial shout at the canopy of leaves as the surges forced their way ponderously up the length of him and broke free of him, great rolling waves breaking against the shore of her depths. Forever it lasted – pleasure, yes, delight, the joy of attainment, but there was pain there as well, the pain of so much being drawn out of him, as if what he was losing were not just his seed but all the juices of his body, sucked from him, stolen.

And, astonishingly, she screamed too, arching her back, throwing her hair behind her to carpet the turf, her loins at last beginning to jerk against him, her tightness pulling on him as if trying to draw still more out of him. As his awareness leached back into him he felt as if the swollen end of his penis were raw and bleeding and being rubbed bloodier. And still a further pulse forced its way up his rigid, unyielding shaft, oozing rather than flooding into her, its energy drained.

His body juddered one last time, and then his shoulders slumped. Drawing hoarse rasps of breath, Thomas stared despondently down the length of her dark, wing-draped back and her torrent of hair at the short grass of the glade, feeling the sting of tears at the rear of his eyes. She rested her shadow-light head in the crook of his shoulder, her nose and lips against the side of his neck, her eyelashes brushing his skin.

"What is your name?" he muttered hoarsely.

"You may not know that," she hissed in his ear. "All you may know is that I am the Gate."

At long, long last she peeled herself from him, removing herself with a surprising delicacy. Cloaking herself in her wings, she dropped to her knees in front of him to lick and suck the final remnants of their mixed juices from him.

Standing, she spoke once more in that strange sibilant voice of hers, that voice like an echo heard after it's gone.

"Close your eyes," she said. "The Gate to Her court is open, but you are not permitted to see anything of your entrance there."

Thomas made to grab for his clothes, but she halted him with a fingertip. She did the same when he moved to cover his unflagging erection with his hands. "You may not shield your maleness from Her sight," she sighed.

He gaped at her, but her face offered no explanation. Then he shut his eyes as she had told him to do, and she whirled her wings about them both like mist creeping close to a hillside, and when she said for him to open his eyes once more they were in the court of the Queen of Faery.

The throne upon which She sat was a great black bear, its jaws agape and its pink tongue lolling amid yellow teeth; around its neck was a ruffle of crimson. To either side of her stood or knelt half a score of winged men, their skins a spectrum; all were naked, some vastly priapic, others flaccid; all wore crowns of flowers knotted about their brows, while hair of many colours tumbled and looped to their shoulders; none had

navels, for like all here except Thomas they had not been born.
Other flowers grew in purples, blues, vermilions and veridians
all over the floor of this great forest clearing, and swarmed up
the boles and along the branches of the trees beside it, so that it
was to Thomas as if he were standing in a huge womb of
flowers. In front of the Queen and her frond-bearing male
retinue stood a dozen winged women, their skins as diverse in
colour as those of the men, their hair all waist-length or longer
and varying from the blue-black of a cave's deepest depths to
the yellow of a bird's beak, and each as strangely lovely to look
upon as the woman who had been the Gate, who was now gone
from Thomas's side. The women, like the men, were naked,
but some had vines growing out of and over them, so that it was
as if they wore knotted serpents and bright flint arrowheads.

Yet Thomas saw little of Her retinue except for glances at
the fringes of his vision. The Queen herself seized his gaze and
fixed it upon her form.

She seemed both tall and tiny at the same time. Her hair was
the colour of sunlight, and covered the ground around the
throne upon which she held herself. Her eyes were the pink of
coral, smouldering briefly to a deeper, more passionate yet
somehow colder red when her interest was caught – as it was,
just now and then, while she studied Thomas. Her skin was the
silver-yellow of a young birch's bark, like the wings of the
Gate; her own wings shimmered in the gleaming cacophony of
the inside of an oyster's shell. Her eyebrows were cusped
arches; her lips were like the curled succulent leaves of a
rainforest plant. Under her wings she wore nothing, and
Thomas could see enough through them to know that she
was slender-waisted and smooth-bellied. Her breasts were full
and yet not over-large, pale apples with the coral of her eyes at
their tips. Between her legs was an intricate, tightly woven,
perfectly symmetrical garland of daisies and cornflowers. The
fingers of her hands were twice as long as mortal fingers, and
twice as supple.

One of those hands was now outstretched toward Thomas.

"Come here to me, lost stranger," she said in a voice
shrouded in distance yet full of power, like an unseen waterfall.

Thomas's legs moved without his command, so that in a

moment he stood directly before her. He was acutely conscious of his manhood still prodding in front of his belly, its full tip licked shiny clean by the one who was the Gate.

She ran her hand around the curve of his cleanshaven cheek, and tucked his hair on one side behind his ear. He felt her sweetly peaty breath on his face. "You could almost be one of us, mortal," she said. "Almost one of us."

And then she slapped him across the mouth, hard, so that the world spun, blurred, bled brine.

"But *not* one of us!" she shouted as he dropped to his knees, clutching his head between his hands. "He is a mortal trespasser here in the world of Faery, and as such he has offended your Queen! Take him! Take him and stake him to my wheel, while I devise his torments!"

Two of her handmaidens moved swiftly to Thomas's side, and not ungently forced him to his feet. His vision still numb from the Queen's blow, he followed their tuggings near blindly, obedient as they pressed his back against an upright four-spoked wheel and spread his arms and his legs, tying his limbs each one to a spoke with a rope stranded of springy vines. His head hung so that his chin brushed his chest. Yet, though he slouched, his shaft still stood firm, unabashed by his pain.

"Raise your head," commanded the Queen's voice. "Raise it, and look at me, mortal." Her hands were on his shoulders, her fingernails knife-like against the flesh there.

He did as he was told, and saw the full, splendid, beautiful cruelty of her silvery face with its flaring pink eyes.

"I could do with you anything I wished, mortal," she said, "and my courtiers here would call it fair justice for your intrusion into my realm. But tell me, first, what punishment is it that you think yourself you deserve?"

"I strayed," he mumbled. "I was brought here. I stepped through a portal that I did not know was there. I have not despoiled your land with my presence by intention, your majesty, but only stumbled into it."

"That does not lessen your crime," said the Queen. To urge her point she traced her fingernails down over his chest and belly, stopping just short of his groin, drawing rivulets of bright blood from beneath the skin, the heel of one palm touching the plum-like end of his shaft. "There is no such thing as chance; all things have their causes; I permit no talk of accident in my court."

Thomas thought quickly. "But I am a mere mortal," he said, his voice feeling clumsy in his mouth now that his lip was beginning to swell. "How could I even aspire to have knowledge of the ways of your court, great Queen?"

She turned away with a flounce and a flow of her great iridescent wings and her cascade of hair.

"You two –" she designated a pair of her women with a beckon of her hand "– you two torment him as you will."

Thomas steeled himself to bear savage, brutal pain, and sure enough the pain did come. The handmaids opened their mouths and smiled to show the predatory shine of their needle-sharp teeth, then moved around behind him, one to either side. At first all they did was stroke him, their small but long hands flitting down his back and buttocks. One inquisitive finger twitched briefly in through the ring of his anus; another tracked a line from there to the folds where the bag of his scrotum hung from the base of his branch. Blood dripped between his legs. If such a thing were possible his shaft grew even harder as he surrendered himself to the ecstasy of the pains they were inflicting on him.

And then, as the Queen and the rest of her court watched him unconcerned, one of the handmaids bit him in the side, just above the waist. The blissful agony rushed through him like the crescendo he had shared with the Gate only minutes ago, and he let out a shout that was in part protest, in part triumph.

Another bite, and another. His blood was flowing freely now. The handmaids raked their fingernails down his back and buttocks, carving out channels of erotic anguish, sending him into a frenzy that was distanced from the world by redly pulsing banks of fog. A hand snaked around him and clutched his maleness tightly, moving the skin back and forth over the wood within; yet he hardly noticed this, so sensitive had the rest of his body become to the delicious lances of pain that the paired courtiers were inflicting upon him. Already, though he had been drained by the Gate so lately, another flood was building up inside him . . .

"Halt!" cried the Queen.

The handmaids' fingers and mouths froze in place.

"Let him alone."

They stood aside from him, and walked demurely away from him to join the others by the Queen. There was blood staining their wings and mouths and bodies; his blood.

"Attend to me," the Queen commanded Thomas, and all at once his vision was crystal clear, so that the colours and the lights in the clearing were brighter than they could possibly be, as if he were seeing them through a shattered prism.

"You are mine," she said, "to do with as I will. Do you understand me?"

Although his blood was puddling at his feet, although his mind was still staggering from the pounding it had received, Thomas summoned up some last shred of resolution. "You may torture me until I am dead before you, but I will never be yours," he said.

Her eyes flamed.

She said nothing, but gestured to two of her priapic courtiers. Without needing a word of instruction, they hurried forward until they were standing one to either side of Thomas, their mighty phalluses brushing his blood-slicked sides. Then, still without a word being spoken, they abruptly pushed against the wheel so that it fell backwards to lie flat with a crash against the ground, and Thomas spreadeagled on top of it. His wrists and ankles feeling torn, he stared at the sky through the lacing of the twigs and leaves.

The Queen came into view above him, her wings draped like glittering cobwebs around her, in one hand a bunch of stinging nettles. She stared down at him, her lips skewed into a grimace of scorn.

"The ladies of my court were too gentle with you, it seems," she said, her voice now almost thoughtful.

The Queen knelt down beside him, as a lover might kneel, and the act tricked his mind into anticipating an exquisite kiss or a soft caress. Instead, she placed the stinging nettles to his chest and then slowly, deliberately guided the constellation of erupting agony down across the plain of his stomach to wrap the plants around his maleness.

His scream as countless points of sharp pain shot through his raw skin caused birds to flee jabbering in fear from the trees. And yet still more powerful than the anguish he felt was the delight, the sinister eroticism of the pricking plants. The Queen kneaded the nettles into and around the bulb of his penis, so that the sublime agony grew greater and ever greater; and yet his mind was not flinching and cringing away from the pain but was instead embracing it and dancing with it in a slow ballet of sensation.

Thought departed Thomas; sight departed him too, as did pride and selfhood, until all that was left of him were the splinters of pain he felt.

And then the Queen threw the nettles aside.

"Attend to me, Thomas!" she commanded once more, and his rationality and vision returned. She was leaning over him again, her face and her gaze no less merciless than before. "Are you mine yet?" she whispered.

"I am *mine*!" he whispered in return.

The Queen gave a shout of fury. The small white clouds seemed to pause their scuttling across the blue, aghast. She spread her shimmering wings outspread until they seemed broader than the sky to him. From where he lay on the wheel he could see that, between her legs, in place of the adroitly pleated garland which had once dangled there, there was now a knotted fist of rose-thorns.

She lowered her face to smile at him a truly dreadful smile. He felt his shaft jerk amid its cloud of pain in anticipatory response. The Queen picked her way fastidiously over the rim of the wheel until she was standing astride his chest, then she cast her long, long hair forward and her wings back to create a cavern that contained only the two of them. Still looking upward, he could discern through the gloom the lips of her sex spying at him from among the thorns, with a nubbin like an infant's thumb just above.

The Queen frowned down at him. "Must I torment you further?" she said.

"You have not yet tormented me at all," Thomas replied. "You and your lackeys have not done anything to me that I have not welcomed, have not devoutly desired. I believed I had come to this place by mischance, but now I see that I brought myself here of my own yearning, that I guided my own destiny until my footsteps brought me to the portal that led me from the mortal world."

"But you are not mine?" she said, her frown deepening. "You are in my power to destroy."

"That is where I *wish* to be," said Thomas.

She slowly went to her knees, her legs across his strained shoulders, so that her sex was only inches from his face. "You are not terrified by the cruelty of La Belle Dame Sans Merci?"

"I adore your cruelty."

The Faery Queen lowered herself still further, so that the thorns at her pubis ground into Thomas's face. His tongue darted forward through the thicket of points to dash its cut tip against the moist acorn he had earlier seen. Blood sprang from his cheeks and his lips and his nose as his tongue made its frantic foray again and again. Moaning her own delight, the Queen pressed ever more firmly against him, so that now his tongue could caress all the folds of her sex, tracing them around and around, lapping her saltiness, then returning ever and again to tease the hard little nub once more.

The Queen was moaning her pleasure as she rode his face. "You are my captive," she grunted softly, each word isolated from the next.

"And you are my captor," agreed Thomas, the words likewise seeming to be pulled individually from him. His back was arching against the ties that held him to the wheel, his hips in free air, the spasms of his excitement coming ever more frequently, ever more strongly, so that a new dull ache of his shaft came to replace the lingering pain of the nettle-stings.

And then the Queen's thighs suddenly locked around him and she growled like a wolf – growled once, growled twice, paused, howled as if to a cold and distant moon. From her sex poured sweetly salty nectar, golden in the twilight of the cavern she had made for them, glistening as it trickled through the knitted thorns.

"I am your captive," said Thomas softly to the heat of her sex, smelling her elixir, then drinking of it all that his bleeding tongue and lips could seize.

For a long time the Queen quivered, her cool smooth thighs flat against him, and for a long time did Thomas drink of her essence, absorbing it into him so that gradually, gradually some of her became a part of him and he, Thomas, became partly her, his eternally powerful captor. There was no world at all outside the curtains of her hair and wings; only those two, each possessing the other, sharing her soul.

And then there was a cool breeze on Thomas's face. He opened his eyes, which he had closed some while before in order more fully to savour the taste of her, and saw that she had swept her hair back over her silvery-yellow shoulder, letting the world in once more.

She was smiling at him, her coral eyes gentle at last, and now he saw that her cruelty had been only a mask donned for him; or perhaps this lover's guise was just another mask that she was wearing, for he knew from having drunk from her that the Queen of Faery was not just a single person, as mortals must be, but many.

The Queen stood and stepped away from him. She swirled her wings once, and where there had been courtiers there were now only tall sunflowers, bobbing their heads as the light wind played with them. She swirled her wings twice, and the vines that held Thomas's wrists and ankles to the wheel sprang apart, wriggling away from him to tunnel themselves into the ground like blindworms. She swirled her wings a third and final time, and the blood on Thomas's body dried into flakes that became red butterflies which rose in a cloud above him and fluttered away on the air; and where there had been wounds on him there was now unmarked smooth skin; and where there had been pain all through him there was now only warmth.

She reached down to take his mortal hand in her long-fingered faery one, and pulled him to his feet. When he was standing directly in front of her she threw one winged arm around him as a cloak of light; her other wing she draped across his manhood, which, hard as ever, felt the weightless touch of her gossamer. He put his own hands to her breasts, so that her firm little nipples pried between his fingers, then dropped one hand to her sex, garlanded as it was in flowers once more.

"I am entirely your captive," he said.

"We are *both* the captive, *both* the captor," she corrected. "We are both now merely the one, Thomas."

Then she led him to another patch of grass, and laid him down on his back, and straddled him, guiding his eager ship into her warm wet harbour where, time after time as the day rolled into evening and the bright birds watched, he gave her in return the essence of himself.

Thomas remained with the Queen of Faery for a week and a day, but when he returned to our world through the portal, guided there by the Gate, he found that all the others of his band Critical Assembly were now fat and fifty except one, who was fat but dead this past year. Without him, and without his guitar that could sing of the spaceways where the stars are a blaze of cold and distant light, they had turned from music to paint their world instead with children and three-car garages.

But Thomas, still youthful though his mind was now aeons old, took to playing lead guitar with Look at the Evidence, where he stands on the stage as if apart from them, ignoring the screams and yells of the fans and focusing entirely on his fingers and the frets while behind him the banked speakers sing and wail as they slide from something that is a bit like Mozart to something that is a bit like Bo Diddley to something that is a bit like Led Zep. He is the quiet one of Look at the Evidence, the one who always isn't there when the groupies penetrate the carefully lax security and gatecrash the band's hotel suite. He is the one whose long, pale, smooth, almost girlish face, framed in hair the colour of polished oak, the unloved imagine as they give themselves comfort to keep away the loneliness of the dark.

And what they see set in his face above them in their solitude are eyes that are deeper than the ocean of time himself, and wiser than the night. And the hands of his that they feel upon them are the sensitive hands that caress the neck of his guitar – hands that seem to have fingers twice as long as mortal fingers, and twice as supple.

San Sebastian

Justine Dubois

It is half past five in the morning. The sky is a haze of half grey, curiously illuminated. Under a canopy of wrought iron the fish market is setting up. The street shutters are painted blue and orange. He is tall and she only a little less so. His dark hair is slicked back cruelly from his forehead, above eyes that are cool and grey. His wide mouth, whose smile spells sensuality, is downturned in disappointment. She dances at his heels. They pass another couple quarreling.

There is something familiar in the shape of the argumentative man's head, distracting him momentarily. "It seems as though the whole world is quarrelling today," he sighs. "Not just us."

"Can't you understand that I am too tired to climb some damned mountain at five in the morning," she says shrilly, "just in the hope of seeing an exceptional sunrise?"

He looks at her with a frown, shocked, as always, by the philistine in her. But she doesn't notice.

"You always were impossible, and selfish," she continues. "Yesterday, we walked all round Madrid in the midday heat, which was your idea; we stood up all night on the train without a seat, and now you want to go for a walk, rather than find our hotel?" The look in her eyes is close to hatred.

"But it is almost dawn and still cool enough to climb," he pleads gently. "The view of the town and the bay will be spectacular, breathtaking. God knows, we only have one night here. And you can rest as much as you want later on. By this time tomorrow morning we will be back on the train. And it could be years before we return." He scans the lines of her face for some sign of relenting good humour. "Couldn't you just make the effort?" But she is closed off.

The Spanish fishermen and traders watch them knowingly, warily, their impassive features hinting part sympathy, part contempt. The fish pass through their flat, bronzed hands in flashes of colour, the turquoise of a fin, the rose pink underside of an octopus. Bouffant heads of carnation form mini hedgerows, dividing the stalls and their produce. This is a different aesthetic, he thinks to himself, this is Lorca country. The land where hatred and beauty and love form an eternal triangle. "Perhaps it is fitting for us to quarrel against such a backdrop of emotion and colour?" he says.

"How pretentious," she replies.

He glances down at his wife's tight features. She is almost unrecognizable. He abandons the argument. "I'll go on my own," he states baldly, trying to conceal his disappointment; he feels that touristic pleasures ought to be shared. "Which would you prefer," he asks, resorting to chivalry, "to go and find the hotel now on your own? It is too early to check in. Our room won't be vacant until midday, but we could leave the luggage there. Or shall we find a café where you can wait for me, have some breakfast, a *tortilla jamon*?"

She looks up at his handsome head, all its normal charm dissipated in strain. His eyes are pale, too pale, no feeling animates them. His formality and politeness are a bad sign. "How long will you be?"

He glances away. He can just make out the distant silhouette of the statue of Christ on Monte Urgull, one arm outstretched in benediction. "Difficult to say exactly." The early morning heat is still burning off the cool moisture from the night before. There is a haze in the air. Distances are deceptive. "One hour, two at the most," he hazards.

"You always were a bore," she says.

He looks at her coolly, assessing her in terms of distances too. "Maybe," he replies uncertainly. He is hurt by her insult and attempts to explain. "This something I have always dreamed of doing."

She shrugs. "Very well. Let's find a café. I'll wait for you there and then go to the hotel if I get fed up."

"Won't you change your mind and come with me?" he pleads, his mood softening.

"No chance," she replies. "I don't know how you even dare ask after the night we've spent."

He tries to smile. Perhaps she is right? Maybe his demands are too many? His stamina is greater than hers. He frowns, but guilt does not sit easily with him.

They choose a café on a street corner midway between the fish market and the near end of the bay. Its chairs are glossy wicker structures, interwoven with strands of bright red and green, the tables fat, menthol-green circles of glass. She sits down, fussily trying to arrange her luggage neatly around her. The waiter appears, his body as flexible as a toreador's, his features immune to charm.

"Are you going to stay and have a coffee with me first?" she asks hopefully.

"No, I want to catch the dawn light over the bay." He glances impatiently at his watch and looks towards the statue, just visible now in the distance above the mist. "No time to lose."

"Very well." She orders herself coffee and croissants, a *tortilla jamon* and a small glass of Spanish brandy. He raises his eyebrows. "You had better go." she says.

He turns on his heels. It occurs to him to plant a kiss on her face, but her expression forbids it.

As he turns to leave, he again half registers the back view of the man sitting alone at another table, something familiar. Was it he and his girlfriend who had also been quarrelling in the fish market? Perhaps they were on the same train? He glances back once more at his wife and then moves on swiftly. He feels guilty, like a recalcitrant schoolboy who has insisted on his own way. But, as he turns from sight of the café, his mood begins to improve. He begins to breathe freely again. Two more turnings and he is on the Paseo Nuevo, the wide promenade that almost encircles Monte Urgull and opens on to the Atlantic and La Concha, a superb long curve of bay, whose elegant Edwardian hotels exist in the dreams of aristocratic Spain and France. His destination is the sculpture of Christ, which stands high above one end of the bay.

He walks at an even pace. The sea is still grey with the remnants of night. The path ahead of him begins to climb, imperceptibly at first. Then suddenly, he is above the bay, higher up than he anticipated. The walk is part woodland, part shrubbery. He climbs further. The path zig-zags from shelf to shelf of terrace, disguised by shrubbery. The land has the luxuriant quality of green, uncultivated gardens. Halfway up, he pauses to catch his breath and look back at the view. Now that he is alone, he begins to feel exhilarated. The quarrel that had flattened his mood now raises and heightens it. He feels intoxicatingly free, as though only this minute and this view and this exquisite feeling count. He senses all the possibilities of freedom, of hope; also the senselessness of shackled love. He begins to feel at one with nature.

He stops briefly to light a Gitanes, its heady perfume mixing with the bougainvillea and the salt from the Atlantic. As he smokes the cigarette, he takes a battered book from his pocket and reads a scrap of poetry by Lorca. By now he has lost all sense of time and regained every sense of himself. His wife, her coffee and her discomfort have disappeared.

Within the dark eyes of the Nun
Two horsemen gallop . . .

He shuts the book and starts to climb the final stage. Suddenly, towering above his head, one arm outheld in beatitude, is the statue of Christ, welcoming him.

The girl is sitting at the base of the sculpture, as if waiting for him. Her smooth dark hair moves in a single, well-cut shape about the delicate features of her face. She is dressed simply in white skirt and blouse. She looks out greedily over the bay, anxious not to miss the first bright slivers of sunshine. He guesses she is American. She turns her head towards him and smiles. "I have been watching you climb, saw you stop to read. I thought you might get here too late."

He half apologises. "I expected to be alone." He laughs thoughtfully. "So, I expect, did you." He sits down next to her.

"I have seen you before," she says.

He scans her features. She is beautiful, delicate, with a body as agile as a cat's. A distant glow in the sky; it is getting lighter. "I am ashamed to say that I don't remember."

"You are reading Lorca" she says, surprise in her blue eyes.

Under the blaze of twenty suns
How steep a level plain inclines.

She takes the book from his hand. The first piercing rays of sunshine, pink and gold, appear over the bay. They both fall still, spellbound. As he turns towards her, her features are suffused with the pink light of the sun. They glance at one another, with a cold hard light of recognition, and then look deliberately away. They refocus on their conversation. The book falls from her lap and they both scrabble to retrieve it. In the dust at their feet their hands meet; a quicksilver animal electricity runs between them. They look at one another in surprise. "I was quarrelling too," she says. They sit back, seeking equilibrium. They both feel sharpened by their respective quarrels, both racked with emotion. The sun is warm on their faces. Around them the light begins to dapple the trees.

The sunshine plays a game of chess
Over her lattice with the trees.

It travels the cold stone of the statue. They look outwards, tension in their buttressed arms. They turn towards one another at the same moment. He does not remember thinking of kissing her. Yet her lips beneath his are soft and sweet. Her body folds and ricochets within its frame, yielding and urgent within the circle of his. As his arms engulf her, he feels the narrow, bird-like cage of her diaphragm, feels her rapid heart-beat. Her skin has the dry, burnt musk perfume of sea and sun. They exchange one last glance of recognition before closing their eyes against the fierce, piercing sun.

His hands slip over her, laying her bare on the stone, teasing and spreading her body in reply to his. His caresses are a torrent of regret and discovery. She picks shyly at the buttons of his shirt, at the buckle of his trousers. It is her last positive act before he invades and devours her. As he enters her, her legs curl around him in welcome. His muffled kisses travel her breasts, her neck, her mouth. He tastes her skin. She judders in his arms; sweet abandon. He still does not ask her name. Beneath the impact of his caresses, she becomes malleable like plasticine. He pulls her upright in his arms to sit on his lap. Her legs tighten enthusiastically around his waist. The figure of Christ looks down on them in blessing. They move in unison, excitement building. Almost. Almost . . . And then he leaves her, momentarily bereft, to stand her leaning in front of the statue, her back naked to the cool stone. She is now rag doll, propelled only by his passion. His whole body roars at her; a threshold of pain, and then twin cries. A brief moment of recollection shifts and collides in his mind. He falls in love with her. He feels his old life fall from him, like a useless garment. He rocks her in his arms, stroking her hair, kissing her lips and neck, teaching her true ownership. She is pliant, exhausted and joyous. She smiles up at him, a strange familiarity mixed with the unknown.

Hand in hand they walk back to the bay and go, fully dressed, straight into the sea to swim together. By now the sun is hot. As they emerge, their light cotton clothes dry on them. They walk back towards the café. They have both decided to be brave, to explain.

His wife is no longer sitting alone. The man at her table rises to greet him. "Hello, my friend, I thought I recognized you earlier. It must be years since we last met, not since I left for America." He turns to the dark-haired girl at his friend's side. "Oh, good, I see you have already met my fiancée. How was the view, darling?"

His wife also smiles up at him, no longer ill-tempered. "Was it wonderful . . .?" she begins enthusiastically. But the question dies in her throat.

Wanting that Man

Karen Taylor

From almost the first moment I spotted him, I wanted to suck his dick. I know, not appropriate behaviour from a lesbian. But then, he wasn't an ordinary man, either. I knew that when I saw him that first time at the dyke bar, surrounded by women. And what women! I mean, I go to the dyke bar for company and to get laid, but a lot of these other women go there to get away from men. Years of anarchist politics, progressive city governments, and low-cost lands made the I–5 corridor a haven for lesbian separatists in the 70s and 80s. Although not many of the wimmin I hung with had been part of those early years, Seattle's lesbian social system was still influenced by decades of separatist politics. While I didn't mind men, most of the women in here would be steering away from anything with a whiff of testosterone. But there he was, surrounded by babes, laughing and drinking a beer just as naturally as if, well, as if he wasn't the only man in a dyke bar.

I watched him carefully. He was handsome, in a boyish way. Lanky body, dark curled hair cut short in the back and on the sides, a moustache resting gently across his upper lip. The contrast between the dark hair and the flash of his white teeth when he smiled or laughed was a delight. His hands were delicate, with long fingers that caressed his beer when it was resting on the bar counter. He didn't preen, the way I see straight men preen when they're surrounded by women. His crotch didn't thrust out aggressively, the way gay men sometimes do when they're in unfamiliar territory. His hip remained cocked against the bar, one boot kicked on the railing. I watched, long enough to enjoy the lazy shift of his weight from one side to the other, turning away from me, giving me a lovely view of a tight, hard ass. One of the women spanked it jokingly, and he laughed, twitching his butt back and forth a few times in rhythm to the music.

I think that's what did it. The flirtatious move of that ass had me transfixed. I wanted to spank him, too! I wanted to touch that ass, caress it, and move my hand slowly around to the front . . . and realized, in a flush of embarrassment, that I was in the midst of daydreaming about sucking a man's cock while I was standing in the middle of a lesbian bar.

Well, I've never been afraid of my psyche. I decided I had to know this guy – and soon, whispered my hungry cunt. So I asked one of my friends, when she stepped away from the group.

"I knew him back in San Francisco, when he was still a butch dyke," she said, and I had a sudden sense of dizziness.

"You're telling me –" I started, and she laughed.

"Yeah, that's right, he used to be a she," my friend explained. I turned again and stared openly at the man at the end of the bar. Was he lanky, or slender? That smile pleasant, or sweet? Something about the face seemed feminine. Or was it? The body language was definitely male. Or was it? Lucky for me, I'm not shy. I introduced myself when it was convenient. I bought him a beer.

"I'm Kate."

"I'm Larry," he answered, smiling. I wondered what his name used to be. But when I shook his hand, I stopped wondering. His palm was smooth, his hands strong. Those fingers . . . I was sure those fingers would feel wonderful in my cunt. And with sex so strongly on my mind, I dropped my eyes briefly to his crotch.

Bad move. Because when I looked back into his smiling, inquisitive eyes, I felt something I hadn't felt in years about any guy. I wanted him. I wanted to take him home and fuck him. I wanted to suck his dick, feel him come in my mouth. I wanted that man.

You have to understand. I haven't wanted a man, not for years. When I get the urge for penetration, I use dildos or fists, just like any other healthy, horny dyke. I had separated my desire for getting my cunt filled from my desire for a penis. But Larry's presence made me remember the joys of cock-sucking. Remember the way a living dick pulses in a wet, hungry mouth. The hot, sucking sounds as my lips would tighten or loosen around a cock shaft, tugging on the head while my tongue would tickle a wet piss-hole. And especially remembering the tension in the flesh just before my mouth would fill with hot, salty come. I wanted that again. And the urge was so strong I could barely keep up my end of the conversation.

Lucky for me I can sometimes keep my cunt and my brain separated – or at least act like it.

"It's strange to see a guy so comfortable in a dyke bar, Larry," I said. "Most of these wimmin would rather spit at a man than invite him in. You've got balls walking in here." I winced internally. Maybe I should have used a better term. But Larry just smiled back, ignoring my possible *faux pas*.

"I've got a lot of friends here," he said. "Some of whom have known me for a long time – back when I was still living in California. I'm up visiting for a few weeks."

"Good," I said recklessly. "I mean, good that you'll be here for a while."

"Is it?" he asked, still smiling. I noticed this close that his eyes were green, with gold flecks dancing in the irises.

"Yup," I answered. "Because, Larry, my new friend, I think you're very attractive." Larry chuckled, pretending great shock.

"How un-lesbian of you!" he said in mock horror. "Attraction to a man! Unless," he said, "you're thinking I'm not really a man." I saw that under his joking demeanour there was something else.

"Look," I said, "Seattle's grapevine is notorious the country over for its speed and viciousness. I got word about you within two minutes of walking into this bar."

He nodded, his eyes clouded. "Yeah, well, despite rumours to the contrary, I'm *not* the butchest dyke you'll ever meet, Kate. I've spent a lot of time and money to be something – someone – else."

The silence between us was growing, and I didn't want it to. But it was clear that this was not the place to continue.

"Larry," I finally said. "I didn't think you were a butch dyke. I still don't. And I would really like to see you. Would you be interested in having dinner with me tomorrow night?" He was surprised, but pleased. I gave him my address and phone number, he gave me his. By the time we parted, the clouds had left his eyes, and he was smiling again. And my level of horniness was back on the rise. Our date was at 7. Less than 20 hours away. Already I couldn't wait. I nearly rushed over to a group of friends to announce, "I've got a hot date with Larry tomorrow." But suddenly, I didn't want anyone to know. I didn't want them to treat my date with Larry like it was just another trek into Kate's adventures with the odd and unusual. My date with Larry wasn't just another unconventional experience, another feather in my proverbial cap. Was it?

Yeah, well, maybe it was. After all, I was the one who giggled with the drag queens and flirted the most outrageously with the butchest diesel dykes in the city. Those gender edges always attracted me. But this was more complicated. After all, Larry was a man in a dyke bar. There just isn't a place in our world for people like him. On the other hand, no amount of drugs or surgery could change the fact that he had been part of the dyke culture for several years before making this decision. I wonder how it felt, to make a decision that would always keep you on the fringe of an already fringe community. I wonder if he ever talked about it with anyone.

I lay awake that night thinking about Larry. Whether the skin on his face was rougher than mine. Whether his nipples were responsive to a light touch, or to a quick, sharp twist. Whether he clenched his toes when he came. And especially, whether he liked his cock sucked. I wondered if he had a cock. Or if he used anything in its place. I fell asleep dreaming of those freshly masculine hands caressing my body, that low voice murmuring in my ear. Spreading my legs. Larry fucking me slow.

The next day he came to my place right at 7, and I was waiting for him. I wanted to be as femme as I could be against his masculinity, so I wore a light summer rayon dress with a floral pattern, sheer stockings and a lace garter belt that matched my bra and panties. Larry was handsome in his creased slacks, crisp white cotton shirt, bright tie. We went out for Mexican, drinking margaritas and eating spicy food. I waited until we were near the end of the meal before I told him about my dreams the night before.

He smiled, but there was something else with it.

"You flatter me," he answered, his dark eyes bright and smiling at me. I smiled back, but pressed on in my usual, subtle-as-a-tractor way.

"This isn't about flattery, Larry. This is about attraction. I'm attracted to you. I noticed you as soon as I walked into the bar last night. OK, OK," I said, laughing as he grinned. "It wasn't hard to notice the only man in the place. But what I mean is, I saw you and I thought you were hot! Who knows why? Because I'm attracted to 'female' energy in men and 'male' energy in women? Or is it simply because you have a cute ass?" By this time Larry was laughing with me. I grabbed his hand (oh! getting fisted by a man! My cunt clenched so hard I almost lost my train of thought), took a deep breath, and continued.

"Larry, you are so fine, I can't stop thinking about you. I don't know all the reasons why, either, but I do know you're the first *man* that's interested me in years. The more important question for the moment is whether you want me." He stared at me, a good long time. I refused to drop my eyes, challenging him back. When he smiled, I knew I had him. I was floating on air all the way back to my apartment.

I waited until we were inside before I kissed him. I had a feeling that his moustache would make my knees weak, and it did. I nibbled at it, testing the sensation against my tongue and lips, hoping Larry would taste my hunger for him. I let him undress me, wanting to feel his hands on my body, and I unbuttoned his shirt. He hesitated as I touched his collarbone, then sank back on the bed with me. I traced the scars that followed the line of his muscles on his chest, memories of his old life. When I asked, he told me the feeling in his nipples was duller, and then he rolled my nipples in his fingers lightly. I moaned as they grew under his touch. Larry licked and sucked them into hardness, my back arching as I clawed at his hair, pulling his face into my breasts. I begged him to fuck me and he answered, "Not yet," his mouth working its way down my belly. I shivered when his tongue opened me, flicking against my clit, then howled as he nibbled and worried the sweet inner flesh. His delicate fingers pushed gently into my cunt, then curved, rubbing the back of my clit. I felt the wave carry me into an orgasm, his mouth staying on me, fingers buried deep inside as I bucked and jerked. I discovered my fingers tangled in his hair when I finally stopped shaking.

Larry pulled himself up next to me, caressing my belly, my breasts, my collarbone, and I let my body respond wholly to his touch. I felt my arousal grow again, and I rested my hand against his crotch, feeling his bulge through the fabric of his slacks. I rolled against him, unbuckled his belt. His hand stopped me.

"I want to suck you," I said. He shook his head.

"It's not – they haven't perfected the surgery for a good penis, yet," he said.

"I don't care," I answered. "I only care whether you'll get off if I suck your cock. Will you? Can you get off like that?"

"I don't know," he answered. I sat up, surprised.

"Hasn't anyone ever sucked your cock before?" I asked.

"No. Not since the change."

"I'm willing to try if you are," I said, grinning at him. He hesitated, giving me time to open his fly and breathe lightly on the bush of hair I discovered hidden beneath. He moaned, and sighed. To me, it sounded like, "All right, I give up."

So I pressed ahead, letting my fingers do the talking. There was a dildo, half-soft, resting in the bush of hair. Carefully I rested my hand over it. I wrapped my fingers around it through his pants, and squeezed gently, bearing down at the same time so he could feel the pressure against his crotch. His eyes closed and he let out a long sigh. I continued to rock my fist against his package until I could see all the muscles in his neck and shoulders relax. Then I made my next move.

I kissed his neck, gently, brushing my lips against his skin. "Larry, I'll suck this, I've sucked plenty of dyke dicks, but I'd really like to taste you, if you'll let me," I whispered, letting my breath tickle his ear. There was a slight tightening in his shoulders, but Larry didn't open his eyes. I kept my hand rocking against his groin as I increased the intensity of my kisses. He moaned a little, and I took his earlobe into my mouth, tugging on it gently with my teeth. That seemed to do it. Larry groaned and arched up against the bed, tugging his slacks off, and removing his packing dick. His eyes were still closed. Was he scared?

Of course he was, I admonished myself. If no one has sucked this man's cock before, he's probably nervous as hell. And while I wasn't exactly subtle about what I wanted – did I really know what I was getting into?

Without rushing too much, I started to move down his body, leaving a trail of hot kisses from Larry's neck across his chest (with some time focused on his nipples to get an idea of what he liked there), and down his stomach to his thick bush of hair.

He smelled different than I remembered men smelling. But at the same time, he didn't smell like a woman. There was a tang that was definitely not female. I used my hand to part the hair, and immediately discovered his dick, pushing up from between the two folds of skin. I pulled the lips slightly away from his cock, freeing it.

What can I say? It was a lot like a big clit, but not really. More fully developed, thick as my thumb, and there was even a head. My own clit was pretty small, and I'd never looked at it that closely, so I don't know whether Larry's cock was just a bigger version of what his clit had looked like. And frankly, I don't care. Because it looked like a great cock to me. A dream cock. The kind of cock I could suck and tug and tickle and never have to worry about whether he would choke me.

I breathed on it first, warming the skin. Larry shivered, and one hand opened and closed. I flicked my tongue quickly across the tip of his cock, and as he moaned, I covered his cock with my mouth.

Oh, the ride that followed! When I closed my lips and began to suck the length of Larry's cock, it was like all of his fears melted away. I felt a hand drop heavily onto the back of my head, and when I looked up, I could see him playing with his nipples with his other hand. I found that a little nibbling around the base drove him to thrust hard into my mouth. When I tugged hard at the root, he arched his back, and I got my hands under him, cupping his ass and spreading his ass cheeks slightly. The hand on my head gripped my hair as I tongued the length of his shaft, and tickled the head of his cock. He was pulling and twisting his nipples, which sent hot rushes to my cunt and made me suck harder.

We finally got into a rhythm that I knew would lead to his orgasm, and I let him take the lead, his hand tugging and pushing at my head. Cupping his ass cheeks, I pulled him toward me in the same rhythm, deepening his thrusts into my mouth. His moans had changed into animal grunts, and I could feel Larry's cock flexing, the way cocks do just before they come.

And indeed, he did come, shooting a hot, bitter fluid into my mouth that definitely wasn't semen, but tasted too tangy to be women's juices. It didn't fill my mouth to bursting, which I appreciated – I hate coughing out come as the ending to a good sex scene – and I savoured its unique texture and flavour. I resisted the temptation to start sucking again, and instead disentangled myself so I could slide back up Larry's body and rest my head on his chest, listening for his heartbeat to slow down.

Larry finally sighed heavily, putting one arm around me. "Kate, that was – I mean, I never thought –"

"I'm giving you fair warning," I told him. "I'm lousy at making breakfast, but I grind fresh coffee every morning *if* I get fucked first."

He laughed. "Lucky for you I'd do anything for a good cup of coffee," he replied, and then kissed me, long and slow, the kind of kiss you know you're going to want every night and every morning right after you fuck your brains out. Yes, indeed, I wanted that man.

La Déesse Terre

Madeleine Oh

Why on earth was she doing this?

Other women, when their husbands walked out on them, got drunk with their best friends or gorged on Swiss chocolate until they saw double. Dea Sullivant ran away from the US and fled to France.

It seemed a good idea at the time but, as she peered though the twilight and the driving rain, Dea began to realise why they offered cheap flights in March. Her decision to leave the autoroute because of blinding rain had been a mistake. As the country road stretched through the night, the dark seemed filled with echoes of Rob muttering about her uselessness, her stupidity, her abysmal map-reading skills, and her general inadequacy.

"Fuck you, Rob Sullivant!" she yelled. "Your idea of a big trip is driving to Blackburgh for a ball game. I'm in Europe!" And lost. But what the hell. No one here knew she'd been declared obsolete, and replaced by a skinny speech therapist with acrylic fingernails.

No one cared. She wouldn't either.

The road forked. Dea took the wider one into a deserted village square. A few chinks of light showed from shuttered windows, but the only other sign of life was a stray dog lurking by the darkened church. So much for her dream of a charming country inn with soft beds, quaint rooms and fabulous food.

As the windshield wipers dragged back and forth, the prospect of a soft bed grew from want to lust. Dea turned down a narrow lane between shuttered houses and a row of darkened shops. Surely, somewhere – yes! There was an inn, on the right, beyond the last cottage. Dea turned into the parking lot and almost crashed her rental car into an immense standing stone. After swerving around it, she parked and killed the engine. The rain had eased to a steady and miserable drizzle but the lights of the inn spread a welcoming warmth. On her way to the front door, Dea paused by the menhir. There was just enough light from the inn to see it was a rudely carved, female stone figure. She looked ancient and weather-worn, much the way Dea felt, but Dea had the advantage of not having to sit out in the rain. Hefting her bag on her shoulder, Dea glanced at the painted sign over the door and entered La Déesse Terre.

She stepped straight into a large room with a beamed ceiling and a wide stone fireplace with a crackling fire. Three men clustered round the warmth turned to stare. Across the room, a woman sorted knives and forks at a side table. She gave Dea a cautious nod.

Dea walked up to her. "I'm looking for a room for the night."

"Of course." The woman put down the pile of gleaming forks and gestured Dea to follow. She led her up the side oak stairs to a large room with an immense, carved bed. The air smelled of lavender and old dust but the sheets looked crisp and clean. There was no bathroom adjoining but Dea decided not to get picky. She had antique furniture, a stone fireplace and shutters painted with the moon and stars. The room overlooked the parking lot and the stone woman, which seemed larger than ever in the moonlight.

"What is that statue?" Dea asked.

The woman crossed herself. "*La Déesse Terre*." The Goddess Earth? No, Earth Goddess, the Earth Mother. Made sense, given the name of the inn. Dea reached to open the window.

The woman stopped her, and swept into a long torrent of French. Dea caught something about the evening and some sort of presence outside.

A sudden squall threw rain hard against the glass, slashing into the window panes and drumming on the roof overhead. Thank heavens she was out of the weather. All Dea wanted now was a hot shower and something to eat, preferably with a couple of glasses of good wine. The woman apologized, saying that the restaurant was closed but offered ham and cheese and the possibility of soup.

The bathroom was across the landing. Dea gathered up towels and soap and took herself off. The water was hot, the towels large, and the soap deliciously scented with herbs. She stood under the warm water and washed away the worries of the last few weeks. Relaxed by the warm spray, she lathered up her hands, spread the soft bubbles over her breasts and belly and turned full face to the shower jet. Her breasts tingled under the fine points of water. She shifted to let it flow over her belly and her pussy and turned to let the soap run off her back and flow down her thighs to pool at her feet. The vast towels smelled of sunshine and fresh air and Dea slathered her body with scented lotion. This might be the back of beyond but they understood comforts for travellers.

Pulling on jeans and a sweatshirt over her still-damp skin, Dea made a turban of one of the smaller towels and padded barefoot back to her room. From downstairs came the sound of singing – not exactly singing, more a melding of plainsong and humming. Male voices blended together in a strange, almost sensual cadence. The sound enticed and fascinated. Dea was halfway decided to descend and listen closer, when she realized she was barely dressed.

No way was she bopping into that bunch of yokels barefoot and wet-headed. Better get back to her room, dry her hair and wait for Madame to bring the promised sandwich.

Dea's door was ajar and she'd darn well closed it. Squaring her shoulders, Dea pushed it open wide and stepped in. "Hello!"

"Madame." The woman was on her knees, laying a fire in the grate. As Dea watched, she arranged the last couple of logs from a stack in the hearth and struck three or four matches, dropping each one in the bed of pine cones and crumpled paper. Satisfied the fire had caught, she stood up and launched into fast French.

Dea understood about a tenth of it.

She did catch her apologies, that they were honoured to have her stop by, and her arrival had caught them by surprise. As she spoke, rain slashed against the panes. The woman looked over her shoulder at the open shutters and turned to cross the room and close them.

"No," Dea said, "leave them open."

That seemed to bother her, but Dea wasn't budging. Rob had always insisted on sleeping with drapes tight shut. She'd celebrate her singleness by leaving the shutters open to the night and, OK, the torrential rain.

Accepting Dea's wish, the woman nodded and asked if there was anything Dea required.

"A bottle of good wine."

Having assured her she'd pick one out herself, she closed the door, shutting off the chanting. The only sounds now were the logs crackling as the fire caught and the intermittent slash of rain against the window. She was utterly alone in a foreign land and she'd left all worries and heartache an ocean away.

Minutes later, Madame reappeared with a laden tray.

For a last-minute, unexpected, scratch supper, she hadn't done too shabbily. A small tureen held a thick meaty soup that wafted herbs and garlic as Dea lifted the lid. The promised ham came with thick slices of crusty bread, and, for good measure, Madame had added a dish of poached pears and a wedge of crumbly blue cheese. Best of all was the freshly opened bottle of wine, neatly wrapped in a linen napkin.

Dea had a crackling fire, hot soup and wine. She had no complaints, even if the chanting was getting louder. Or did she hear it more now the wind had dropped? No matter, it wasn't an unpleasant noise, just monotonous, and they could hardly keep it up all night.

Two glasses of wine and a good supper later, Dea stretched out by the fire, wineglass in hand, and watched the flames play over the sweet-smelling logs. Were they fruit trees of some sort that they gave off such an aroma? Magical, mythical trees that scented the air and her dreams? Slowly Dea sipped on her wine and contemplated her flight.

She'd run away. Plain and simple, she'd retreated. Why not? She'd been supplanted by a younger woman with skinny hips and a flat chest. Dea glanced down at her ample breasts. OK, they weren't up to the endowment of _La Déesse_ outside in the parking lot, but boyish she'd never be. Seemed Rob wanted young and androgynous these days. "Tough shit, Rob," Dea muttered to the twisting flames. "See if I care." Surprisingly, she didn't any more. Was it distance easing the rejection and the hurt? Or plain common sense coming to the fore? Common sense hadn't sent her buying the first cheap ticket to Europe. More like craziness or primal urge. Here, in the warmth of the fire, she did did feel primal. Why not? Hadn't she found her way to the abode of the Earth Goddess?

Dea watched until the fire died down. Then she pulled on flannel pyjamas, fished her book out of her bag and took herself and the rest of the wine to bed. She'd just drained the last glass when the storm strengthened with renewed force, smashing rain hard against the windows as great gusts of wind tore at the outside walls. A clap of thunder vibrated off the windows, followed fast by a flash of lightning, and the lights went out.

Great! She'd hold her breath and her wineglass and count to ten for the lights to come on again. They didn't. Not even for fifty. There was just enough light from the fire to see and she had a flashlight. Damn, it was in the car. That wasn't stopping her. The house had gone quiet. With no one about, she'd slip out and back without any trouble. Dea stepped into her shoes, and pulled on her raincoat over her pyjamas.

She made it almost to the bottom of the stairs when Madame stepped forward carrying a lamp. Over the woman's shoulder, Dea saw the group still seated round the fire. So much for slipping out unobserved. Dea jabbered about looking for something, pulled open the heavy door and stepped out.

Big mistake. Water bucketed down from the sky. The path from the inn resembled a small stream and she could barely see her car. Dea splashed down the path and squelched over the gravel. As she opened the passenger door, the rain came down even heavier, beating a wild tattoo on the roof.

She shoved the flashlight in her pocket and stepped back out. The rain came horizontally now, slashing into her face, running down her neck and stinging her legs. She should have stayed dry and warm and lumped the dark. She pulled her raincoat over her head and ran. Losing a shoe, she turned back trying to find it, but gave up and raced the rest of the way, half blinded and totally drenched. A misstep on loose gravel pitched her forward. Reaching out to save herself, Dea fell slap into the granite bulk of *La Déesse*.

Wrong direction entirely.

Or was it?

The bulk of the Goddess protected Dea from the wind and the worst of the rain. Nice to find a woman broader and even better endowed than she was. Dea raised her hands to cup the splendid stone breasts, the weather-worn stone smooth and cool under her fingers. Another loud clap of thunder and almost simultaneous lightning had Dea pressing closer for the shelter the Goddess offered. Dea stayed, breasts flattened against the Goddess's granite torso, unwilling to step away and face the relentless storm.

She had no idea how long she clung to the Goddess. Dea's hands began to tingle as if drawing power from the stone – rekindling life and passion not yet dead. Dea moved her hands. Her fingers itched. Her body throbbed with the cadence of the storm. She cupped her own breasts. Her nipples were hard with cold and her flesh was soaking with desire. Desire to feel the power once again. She closed her eyes, reached out her arms and stepped into the Goddess's embrace.

Dea's entire body shot with sweet darts of fire, meeting the cold and damp with an inner warmth that swelled like a spring tide. A small, far part of Dea's mind insisted she was nuts, plastering her body to a standing stone in the middle of a parking lot in rural France. That part was soon silenced by the peace and warmth that flowed though every pore and pulsed with each heartbeat.

The rain stopped. The wind calmed. Dea looked up at the weather-worn face of *La Déesse Terre* and smiled. In the moonlight the Goddess smiled back.

Gathering her useless raincoat around her, Dea paddled back to the inn. She was minus both shoes now but scarcely noticed. The life force of the goddess afforded more warmth than a pair of sneakers. A wild heat flowed in Dea's veins, her hands still tingled, her nipples throbbed hard under the damp flannel, and wetness ran between her legs. She looked back at the Goddess, half expecting the stone to turn and nod encouragingly. The Goddess never moved. She couldn't. She'd handed over her power to Dea.

The door stood half open. The inn waited. Dea slipped inside and let her clothes drip for a few seconds. A row of small lamps and night lights lit a path up the wide staircase. She'd better sneak back up to her room and take her aroused body with her.

"Ah, *Madame Déesse!*" The woman stepped forward, clasped Dea's hand and led her towards the fireplace.

The men waiting stood and bowed, the firelight casting shadows on the ceiling and their faces. The same sweet wood burned in this fireplace, and an ancient oil lamp glowed on the low table.

Dea was doubly, triply, aware of the wet flannel plastered against her breasts and legs and the sodden raincoat flapping round her ankles. They didn't notice, or rather they saw but regarded her with admiration.

"*Déesse,*" the oldest man began. As if unsure of her response, he spoke slowly. She followed each word, understanding without needing to translate. He was asking her to choose. One of them.

Her body rippled in reply.

The dim light flattered them all but the flickering illumination showed beyond their exteriors. In the old man, Dea saw wisdom, a mind shaped by long years fighting the elements but never conceding failure. The youth possessed a vigour and an energy Dea envied, but he lacked the substance and depth of the older man. It was the third she looked at longest, the one nearest her own age. He stood tall and broad-shouldered. His dark eyes glimmered in the firelight, and in their depths burned a raging desire – for her.

Without a word, Dea smiled and held out her hand.

The other two stepped back, as if ceding the field to the victor, as he took her hand and knelt at her feet. His dark hair fell forward, exposing the tanned nape of his neck.

"*Madame, la Déesse,*" he said, his voice thick with promise, "Lucien Valpert, *à votre service.*"

Was it the close warmth of the room, or the heat from his

bowed body that spiked her own need? "OK, Lucien," Dea said, squeezing his hand and raising him to standing. He was so close, a half-step would bring their bodies into close contact. "Let's go."

Dea turned and climbed the candlelit staircase, Lucien's footsteps heavy on the broad steps behind her. Her bedroom door stood open. Someone had built the fire up to a roaring blaze. A row of candles burned on the mantelpiece and four more flickered, one on each post of the bed. And Lucien waited just inside her open doorway.

"Come in, shut the door." Had she spoken English? French? It hardly mattered as he closed the door with a soft thud and crossed the floor and prepared to kneel. "No." She stopped him with her hand. His eyes met hers, questioning. "I want you upright for now. You can get on your knees later." She rested the flat of her hand on his chest. Feeling warm muscle under the soft-washed shirt, Dea looked him in the eye and parted her lips.

He lowered his mouth.

Slowly.

His lips were warm and male and opened hers with a promise of sweet fire. Wet heat roared between her legs as his tongue swept hers. His arms closed round her shoulders in a fierce grasp. Her breasts flattened against his chest, his thigh eased between hers, his erection pressing against her belly. He was more than ready. She wasn't. Not yet.

"Wait," she said, pulling back. He obeyed. The twitch in his jaw showed his effort to serve no matter how she willed. "Soon," Dea promised, relishing the wild light in his eyes as she slowly opened his shirt. Each button gave at her touch until she parted the faded cotton and ran her hands over warm flesh and soft hair, his heart racing under her hand. His breath caught as her fingers rubbed his nipples to stiff points. She ran her tongue over his left nipple, sensing his need and relishing her power. She moved back as he gave a little gasp.

He was watching her with glinting eyes, his broad chest rising and falling with each slow breath. "Strip," Dea said. He stared, not understanding. She brushed his shirt off his shoulders and watched it settle on the floor by his feet. "You take off the rest."

Lucien got her meaning. With controlled but efficient movements, he unbuckled his belt and stepped out of his pants and underwear. Dea walked behind him as he bent to undo his shoes. Nice butt. Nice back. Splendid body. Firm muscles shaped by years of physical labour, not workouts on chrome-plated gym machines. She walked back in front as he stood up, and she smiled. Lucien might have been surprised at being chosen, but he was more than ready for the office. His cock was magnificent, jutting at her from its nest of dark hair and hers for the having.

She skimmed her fingertips over the erect flesh and circled him with her hand. He gasped as she moved it up and down, easing back his foreskin to reveal the dark head of his cock. She squeezed.

"Madame!" Lucien gasped. A glistening bead of moisture gathered on his cock. He'd have stepped back, she was certain, but she had him hard in her hand. She stroked the head of his cock with her thumb, spreading his moisture, fascinated by the tender end of his erect cock and how his foreskin moved at her touch.

"OK," she said, letting go of him. "Now you undress me."

He stepped behind her and removed her raincoat, crossing the room to hang it on the wall. Her pyjama top he unbuttoned and tossed on the chair. His eyes widened with admiration at her breasts. He reached out but paused, looking at her for consent. Unable to hold back a smile, Dea nodded. "You may."

His fingers were rough but gentle and certainly not untutored. He caressed the full undersides of her breasts with cupped hands, slowly eased his thumbs over the swell of her breasts until he caught her nipples between thumbs and index fingers and tugged. He rubbed her areolae until little nubs around them stiffened and she shuddered with desire.

His hands eased down her belly and he paused, waiting for her approval. She smiled. Heck, she grinned, and with a nod of understanding Lucien eased his hands into the elastic at her waist and lowered the last of her clothes. He knelt at her feet as she stepped away from the damp cotton. Dea looked down at his dark head and tanned shoulders and the hand around her ankle, his eyes gazing at her pussy as if she were the wonder of creation. He looked up, his eyes dark with need. "Madame, *vous permettez?*"

Aware of her awesome power, Dea watched him for a few seconds. "Oh, yes."

Warm air brushed across her pussy, ruffling her curls like a quickening breeze. His fingers opened her. Wide. His breath came closer as the flat of his tongue lapped her. She whimpered as his arms closed around her thighs and a gust of rain hit the windowpanes. If the glass had caved in, she'd never have noticed. Lucien was devouring her with slow perfection. He covered her with his lips as his tongue narrowed and played her clit, flicking and teasing until she moaned with need. He paused and she grabbed his head to hold it to her. He could not stop. Not now. She would not permit it.

But he'd paused only to slide one hand from her thigh. The other held her as firmly as ever. His mouth continued its slow caress as he pressed one finger, then two, inside her cunt. He played her, his fingers pulsing a beat that matched the thrust of his tongue.

She was lost. She was found. She was all and everything she'd ever longed for as a lover knelt in homage at her pussy. His fingers, slick with her arousal, smoothed her ass as his tongue drew her towards climax. Need blazed deep in her belly. She cried aloud as his fingers curved deep and his mouth worked her faster. He was merciless. He was magnificent. He was all. She clutched his head, thrusting her hips into his face, reaching for her coming climax. Her shouts increased as her need climbed. Until she came in a wild crescendo of joy and release that had her screaming aloud as her legs buckled.

Lucien held her firm. Steadying her as his mouth fluttered little kisses up her belly. It was almost too much. She would never have enough.

He gathered her up in his arms as easily as if she were a lightweight. His mouth, wet and warm with her juices, met hers. A slow kiss, gentle as a whisper, that sent her body wild. Nothing could satisfy her but his magnificent cock deep inside.

He grinned with knowing pride and male arrogance as he sat her on the bed and turned her on to all fours.

He stroked her ass, smoothing up her back as he dropped soft kisses up her spine to her neck. The mattress shifted under his weight as the power of his erection pushed between her legs. He grasped her shoulders. He was hard against her, pressing to meet her need. His hips rocked. His cock slid though her wetness. Dea cried out as he thrust. She was tighter than she'd expected and Lucien filled her, stretched her, and possessed her. Driving with grunts and animal need, pressing into her soul with his male heat. Pumping her, taking her, possessing her, giving all a man could. He was Primal Man, potent and firm. She was Goddess, power and life. They melded in one life rhythm that took them both higher and harder through his grunts and her cries until, with a relentless thrust, he drove deep as she screamed aloud her triumph and he poured his jism into her heat.

She collapsed, his weight pressing her into the mattress, his cock embedded in her cunt, her mind drunk with joy and life, and her heart racing at one with the storm outside.

Through a haze of grogginess, Dea felt his weight ease off her. Lucien shifted her so her head rested on the pillow. Lips pressed on her forehead, arms held her close and she passed from frenzy to satiated rest.

She woke to electric light blazing overhead. Damn! The power outage. She'd left the lights on. Padding across the room to flick out the switch, she realized she was naked. Her night clothes lay in a crumpled heap in front of the last dying embers and she was wet halfway down her thighs.

She had just fucked a total stranger!

So what? It had been stupendous and her body still vibrated with the memory of Lucien's tongue on her skin and his cock planted deep.

But fucking a completely unknown man! She made herself stop. No longer was she thinking like Rob Sullivant's wife. She was Dea. Goddess. She curled up between sheets that smelled of sex and life.

Bright morning sunshine woke her later. Time to be on her

way. She may have to face Lucien over coffee, but so what? He'd fucked a total stranger too. Her shoes waited, cleaned and polished outside her door, and breakfast was set at a lone table by a window.

As Dea sat down, Madame appeared with croissants and fresh bread, and a slab of firm cheese and little curls of butter. "Did you sleep well?"

Was she being facetious? A look at the woman's face and Dea decided it was a routine enquiry asked of any guest. "Yes, very well. Apart from the storm." No need to specify which storm.

Madame nodded. Fierce storms were to be expected. It was the time of year, the *point vernal*.

The vernal equinox: the season of wild tides and gales that marked the beginning of spring. A time of new life and renewal. Of course. Dea was alive, well satisfied, and drinking aromatic coffee several thousand miles from her humiliation. She cut off a corner of cheese, chewed it slowly and decided to stop and pay homage to the Goddess in the parking lot, on her way forward.

To Remember You By

Sacchi Green

"A movie!" she exulted from three thousand miles away. "They're making a movie of our book!"

"Our book" was *Healing Their Wings*, a bittersweet, sometimes funny novel about American nurses in England during World War II. My grandson's wife had based it on oral histories recorded from several of us who had kept in contact over the past half-century.

I rejoiced with her at the news, but then came a warning she was clearly embarrassed to have to make. "The screenwriters are bound to change some things, though. There's a good chance they'll want it to be quite a bit, well, racier."

"Racier?" I said. "Honey, all you had to do was ask the right questions!" How had she missed the passionate undertones to my story? When I spoke, all too briefly, of Cleo, had she thought the catch in my voice was old age taking its toll at last? The young assume that they alone have explored the wilder shores of sex; or, if not, that the flesh must inevitably forget.

I had to admit that I was being unfair. Knowing what she did of my long, happy life with Jack, how could she even have guessed the right questions to ask? But it hardly matters now. The time is right. I'm going to share those memories, whether the movie people are ready for the truth or not. Because my flesh has never forgotten – will never forget – Cleo Remington.

In the summer of 1943, the air was sometimes so thick with sex you could have spread it like butter, and it would have melted, even on cold English toast.

The intensity of youth, the urgency of wartime, drove us.

Nurses, WACs and young men hurled into the deadly air war against Germany gathered between one crisis and another in improvised dance halls. Anything from barns to airfield hangars to tents rigged from parachute silk would do. To the syncopated jive of trumpets and clarinets, to "Boogie Woogie Bugle Boy" and "Ac-cen-tuate the Positive", we swayed and jitterbugged and twitched our butts defiantly at past and future. To the muted throb of drums and the yearning moan of saxophones, to "As Time Goes By" and "I'll Be Seeing You", our bodies clung and throbbed and yearned together.

I danced with men facing their mortality, and with brash young kids in denial. Either way, life pounded through their veins and bulged in their trousers, and sometimes my body responded with such force I felt as though my own skirt should have bulged with it.

But I wasn't careless. And I wasn't in love. As a nurse, I'd tried to mend too many broken boys, known too many who never made it back at all, to let my mind be clouded by love. Sometimes, though, in dark hallways or tangles of shrubbery or the shadow of a bomber's wings, I would comfort some nice young flier with my body and drive him on until his hot release geysered over my hand. Practical Application of Anatomical Theory, we nurses called it, "PAT" for short. Humour is a frail defence against the chaos of war, but you take what you can get.

Superstition was the other universal defence. Mine, I suppose, was a sort of vestal virgin complex, an unexamined conviction that opening my flesh to men would destroy my ability to heal theirs.

These very defences – and repressions – might have opened me to Cleo. Would my senses have snapped so suddenly to attention in peacetime? They say war brings out things you didn't know were in you. But I think back to my first sight of her – the intense grey eyes, the thick, dark hair too short and straight for fashion, the forthright movements of her lean body – and a shiver of delight ripples through me, even now. No matter where or when we met, she would have stirred me.

The uniform sure didn't hurt, though, dark blue, tailored, with slacks instead of skirt. I couldn't identify the service, but

"USA" stood out clearly on each shoulder, so it made sense for her to be at the Red Cross club on Charles Street in London, set up by the United States Ambassador's wife for American servicewomen.

There was a real dance floor, and a good band was playing that night, but Cleo lingered near the entrance as though undecided whether to continue down the wide, curving staircase. I don't know how long I stared at her. When I looked up from puzzling over the silver pin on her breast she was watching me quizzically. My date, a former patient whose half-healed wounds made sitting out the dances advisable, gripped my shoulder to get my attention.

"A friend of yours?" he asked. He'd been getting a bit maudlin as they played "You'd Be So Nice To Come Home To", and I'd already decided he wasn't going to get the kind of comfort he'd been angling for. I shook off his hand.

"No," I said, "I was just trying to place the uniform. Are those really wings on her tunic?" I felt a thrill of something between envy and admiration. The high, compact breasts under the tunic had caught my attention, too, but that was more than I was ready to admit to myself. I watched her movements with more than casual interest as she descended the stairs and took a table in a dim corner.

"Yeah," he said with some bitterness, "can you believe it? They brought in women for the Air Transport Auxiliary. They get to fly everything, even the newest Spitfires, ferrying them from factories or wherever the hell else they happen to be to wherever they're needed."

His tone annoyed me, even though I knew he was anxious about whether he'd ever fly again himself. But then he pushed it too far. "I hear women are ferrying planes back in the States now, too. Thousands of 'em. Next thing you know there won't be any jobs left for men after the war. I ask you, what kind of woman would want to fly warplanes, anyway?" His smouldering glance toward the corner table told me just what kind of woman he had in mind. "Give me a cozy red-headed armful with her feet on the ground any day," he said, with a look of insistent intimacy.

"With her back on the ground, too, I suppose," I snapped,

and stood up. "I'm sorry, Frank, I really do wish you the best, but I don't think there's anything more I can do for you. Maybe you should catch the early train back to the base." I evaded his grasp and retreated to the powder room; and, when I came out at last, he had gone. The corner table, however, was still occupied.

"Mind if I sit here?" I asked. "I'm Kay Barnes."

"Cleo Remington," she said, offering a firm handshake. "It's fine by me. Afraid the boyfriend will try again?"

So she'd noticed our little drama. "Not boyfriend," I said, "just a patient who's had all the nursing he's going to get." I signalled a waitress. "Can I get you a drink to apologize for staring when you came in? I'd never seen wings on a woman before, and . . . well, to be honest, I had a flash of insane jealousy. I've always wanted to fly, but things just never worked out that way."

"Well," Cleo said, "I can't say I've ever been jealous of a nurse's life, but I'm sure glad you're on the job."

"Tell me what being a pilot is like," I said, "so I can at least fantasize."

So she told me, over a cup of the best (and possibly only) coffee in London, about persuading her rancher father that air surveillance was the best way to keep track of cattle spread out over a large chunk of Montana. When her brother was old enough to take over the flying cowboy duty, she'd moved on to courier service out of Billings, and then to a job as instructor at a Civilian Pilot Training Program in Colorado, where everyone knew that her young male students were potential military pilots, but that Cleo, in spite of all her flight hours, wasn't.

Then came all-out war and the chance to come to England. Women aviators were being welcomed to ferry aircraft for the decimated RAF. I watched her expressive face and hands and beautifully shaped mouth as she talked of Hurricanes and Spitfires and distant glimpses of German Messerschmitts.

As she talked I did, in fact, fantasize like crazy. But visions of moonlight over a foaming sea of clouds kept resolving into lamplight on naked skin, and the rush of wind and roar of engines gave way to pounding blood and low, urgent cries. Her shifting expressions fascinated me; her rare, flashing smile was so beautiful I wanted to feel its movement under my own lips.

I didn't know what had come over me. Or, rather, I knew just enough to sense what I wanted, without having the least idea how to tell whether she could possibly want it too. I'd admired women before, but only aesthetically, I'd rationalized, or with mild envy; and, after all, I liked men just fine. But this flush of heightened sensitivity, this feeling of rushing toward some cataclysm that might tear me apart . . . This was unexplored territory.

"So," Cleo said at last, looking a bit embarrassed, "that's more about me than anybody should have to sit through. What about you? How did you end up here?"

"I'm not sure I can even remember who I was before the war," I said, scarcely knowing who I'd been just half an hour ago. "It seems as though nothing interesting or exciting ever happened to me back then. Not that 'interesting' will be a fair description of life now until I'm at a safe distance from it."

She nodded. We were silent for a while, sharing the unspoken question of whether the world would ever know such a thing as safety again. Then I told her a little about growing up in New Hampshire, and climbing mountains, only to feel that even there the sky wasn't high and wide enough to hold me. "That's when I dreamed about flying," I said.

"Yes!" she said. "I get that feeling here, once in a while, even in the air. Somehow this European sky seems smaller, and the land below is so crowded with cities, sometimes the only way to tell where you are is by the pattern of the railroads. The Iron Compass, we call it. I guess that's one reason I'm transferring back to the States instead of renewing my contract here.

"The main reason, though, is that I've heard women in the WASPs at home are getting to test-pilot even Flying Fortresses and Marauders. And that's only the beginning. Pretty soon they'll be commissioned in the regular Army Air Force. In Russia women are even flying combat missions; 'Night Witches' the Germans call them. If the war goes on long enough . . ." She stopped short of saying, "If enough of our men are killed I'll get to fight," and I was grateful.

"History is being made," she went on, "and I've got to be in on it!"

In her excitement she had stretched out her legs under the table until they brushed against mine. I wanted so badly to rub against the wool of her slacks that I could scarcely pay attention to what she was saying, but I caught one vital point.

"Transferring?" I leaned far forward, and felt, as well as saw, her glance drop to my breasts. The starchy wartime diet in England had added some flesh, but at that moment I didn't mind, because all of it was tingling. "When do you go?"

"In two weeks," she said. "I'm taking a week in London to get a look at some of the sights I haven't had time to see in the whole eighteen months I've been over here. Then there'll be one more week of ferrying out of Hamble on the south coast. And then I'm leaving."

Two weeks. One, really. "I've got a few days here, too," I said. "Maybe we could see the sights together." I tried to look meaningfully into her eyes, but she looked down at her own hands on the table and then out at the dance floor where a few couples, some of them pairs of girls, were dancing.

"Sure," she said. "That would be fun." Her casual tone seemed a bit forced.

"I don't suppose you'd like to dance, would you?" I asked, with a sort of manic desperation. "Girls do it all the time here when there aren't enough men. Nobody thinks anything of it."

"They sure as hell would," Cleo said bluntly, "if they were doing it right." She met my eyes, and in the hot grey glow of her defiant gaze, I learned all I needed to know.

Then she looked away. "Not," she said carefully, "that any of Flight Captain Jackie Cochran's handpicked cream-of-American-womanhood pilots would know anything about that."

"Of course not," I agreed. "Or any girl-next-door nurses, either." I could feel a flush rising from my neck to my face, but I ploughed ahead. "Some of us might be interested in learning, though."

She looked at me with an arched eyebrow, then pushed back her chair and stood up. Before my heart could do more than lurch into my throat, she said lightly, "How about breakfast here tomorrow, and then we'll see what the big deal is about London."

It turned out we were both staying in the club dormitory upstairs. We went up two flights together; then I opened the door on the third floor landing. Cleo's room was on the fourth floor. I paused, and she said, without too much subtlety, "One step at a time, Kay, one step at a time!" Then she bolted upward, her long legs taking the stairs two, sometimes three, steps at a time.

Night brought, instead of a return to common sense, a series of dreams wilder than anything my imagination or clinical knowledge of anatomy had ever provided before. When I met Cleo for breakfast it was hard to look at her without envisioning her dark, springy hair brushing my thighs, while her mouth . . . but all my dreams had dissolved in frustration, and I had woken tangled in hot, damp sheets with my hand clamped between my legs.

Cleo didn't look all that rested, either, but for all I knew she was always like that before her second cup of coffee. When food and caffeine began to take effect, I got a map of bus routes from the porter and we planned our day.

London Bridge, Westminster Abbey, Harrods department store; whether I knew how to do it right or not, every moment was a dance of sorts. Cleo got considerable amusement out of my not-so-subtle attempts at seduction. She even egged me on to try on filmy things in Harrod's that I could never afford, or have occasion to wear (what on earth, we speculated, did Harrod's stock when it *wasn't* wartime?) and let me see how much she enjoyed the view. I didn't think she was just humouring me.

In the afternoon, after lunch at a quaint tearoom, we went to the British Museum and admired the cool marble flesh of nymphs and goddesses. Cleo circled a few statues, observing that the Greeks sure had a fine hand when it came to posteriors; I managed to press oh-so-casually back against her, and she didn't miss the chance to demonstrate her own fine hand, or seem to mind that my posterior was not quite classical.

Then we decided life was too short to waste on Egyptian mummies and wandered a bit until, in a corner of an upper floor, we found a little gallery where paintings from the Pre-Raphaelite movement and other Victorian artists were displayed. There was no one else there but an elderly female guard whose stern face softened just a trace at Cleo's smile.

Idealized women gazed out of mythological worlds aglow with colour. The grim reality of war retreated under the spell of flowing robes, rippling clouds of hair, impossibly perfect skin.

Cleo stood in the centre of the room, slowly rotating. "Sure had a thing for redheads, didn't they?" she said. "You'd have fit right in, Kay."

I could only hope she herself had a thing for redheads. Standing there, feeling drab in my khaki uniform, I watched Cleo appreciating the paintings of beautiful women. When she moved closer to the sleeping figure of "Flaming June" by Lord Leighton, I gazed with her at the seductive flesh gleaming through transparent orange draperies and allowed myself, experimentally, to imagine stroking the curve of thigh and hip, the round, tender breasts.

"I don't know how this rates as art," Cleo said, "but oh, my!"

A hot flush rose across my skin: desire, yes, but also fierce jealousy. I wanted to be in that bright, serene world, inside that pampered, carefree body, with smooth arms and hands not roughened by scrubbing with hospital soap. I wanted to be the one seducing Cleo's eyes. "She could have a million freckles under that gown," I blurted out childishly. "The colour would filter them out!"

A tiny grin quirked the corner of Cleo's mouth. As always, I wanted to feel that movement of her lips. "Freckles are just fine," she said, "so long as I get to count them." She turned and leaned close, as shivers of anticipation rippled through me. "With my tongue," she added, and very gently laid a trail of tiny wet dots across the bridge of my nose. I forgot entirely where we were.

Then she bent her dark head to my throat, and undid my top buttons, and gently cupped my breasts through my tunic as her warm tongue probed down into the valley between. I couldn't bear to stop her, even when I remembered the guard. My breasts felt heavy, my nipples swollen, but not nearly as heavy and swollen as I needed them to be.

Cleo's grey eyes had darkened when she raised her head. "Where," she murmured huskily, "is a bomb shelter when you need one?"

But we knew that even now, with the Luftwaffe so busy in Hitler's Russian campaign that there hadn't been a really major attack on London in over a year, every bomb shelter had its fiercely protective attendants.

The guard's voice, harsh but muted, startled us. "There's a service lift just down the corridor. It's slow. But not necessarily slow enough."

She gazed impersonally into space, her weathered face expressionless, until, as we passed, she glanced down at Cleo's silver wings. "Good work," she said curtly. "I drove an ambulance in France in the last war. But for God's sake be careful!"

In the elevator Cleo pressed me against a wood-panelled wall and kissed me so hard it hurt. I slid my fingers through her thick dark hair and held her back just enough for my lips to explore the shape of her lips and my tongue to invite hers to come inside.

By the time we jolted to a stop on the ground floor my crotch felt wetter than my mouth, and even more in need of her probing tongue.

There was no one waiting when the gate slid open. Cleo pulled me along until we found a deserted ladies' room, but once inside, she braced her shoulders against the tiled wall and didn't touch me. "You do realize," she said grimly, "what you're risking?"

"Never mind what *I'm* risking," I said. "One nurse blotting her copy book isn't going to bring everything since Florence Nightingale crashing down. But you . . ." I remembered Frank's bitter voice asking, "What kind of woman?" Tears stung my eyes, but it had to be said. "You're holding history in your hands, Cleo." I reached out to clasp her fingers. "Right where I want to be."

"Are you sure you know what you want?"

"I may not know exactly *what*," I admitted, drawing her hands to my hips, "but I sure as hell know I want it!" I reached down and yanked my skirt up as far as I could. Cleo stroked my inner thigh, and I caught my breath; then she slid cool fingers inside my cotton underpants and gently cupped my hot, wet flesh. I moaned and thrust against her touch and tried to kiss her, but her mouth moved under mine into a wide grin.

"Pretty convincing," she murmured against my lips.

I whimpered as she withdrew her hand, but she just smoothed down my skirt and gave me a pat on my butt. "Not here," she said, and propelled me out the door.

On the long series of bus rides back to Charles Street we tried not to look at each other, but I felt Cleo's dark gaze on me from time to time. I kept my eyes downcast, the better to glance sidelong at her as she alternated between folding her arms across her chest and clenching and unclenching her hands on her blue wool slacks.

Dinner was being served at the Red Cross club, probably the best meal for the price in England. Cleo muttered that she wasn't hungry, not for dinner, anyway, but I had my own motive for insisting. The band would be setting up in half an hour or so, and with the window open, you could hear the music from my room. Well enough for dancing.

So we ate, although I couldn't say what, and Cleo teased me by running her tongue sensuously around the lip of a coke bottle and into its narrow throat. Her mercurial shifts from intensity to playfulness fascinated me, but the time came when intensity was all I craved.

"I don't suppose you'd like to dance, would you?" I repeated last night's invitation in a barely steady voice. "If I tried my best to do it right?" I stood abruptly and started for the stairs. Behind me Cleo's chair fell over with a clatter as she jumped up to follow.

I reached my tiny room ahead of her – nursing builds strong legs. I crossed to the window to heave it open, and then the door slammed shut and she was behind me, pressing her crotch against my ass, wrapping her arms around me to undo my buttons and cradle my breasts through my sensible cotton slip. I longed to be wearing sheer flame-coloured silk for her.

When she slid her hands under the fabric and over my skin, though, I found I didn't want to be wearing anything at all.

"So soft," she whispered, "so tender . . ." and then, as my nipples jerk taut under her strokes, "and getting so hard . . ."

A melody drifted from below, "Something To Remember You By". I turned in her arms. "Teach me to dance," I whispered.

We swayed gently together, feet scarcely moving in the cramped space, thighs pressing into each other's heat. Cleo kneaded my ass, while I held her so tightly against my breast that her silver wings dented my flesh.

"Please," I murmured against her cheek, "closer . . ." I fumbled at the buttons of her tunic. When she tensed, I drew back. "I'm sorry . . . I don't know the rules . . ."

"The only rule," Cleo said, after a long pause, "is that you get what you need."

"I need to feel you," I said.

She drew her hands over my hips and up my sides until she held my breasts again; then she stepped back and began to shed her clothes. Mine, with a head start, came off even faster.

The heady musk of arousal rose around us. A clarinet crooned, "I'll Get By". I cupped my full breasts and raised them so that my nipples could flick against Cleo's high, tightening peaks, over and over. The sensation was exquisite, tantalizing. I gave a little whimper, needing more, and she bent to take me into her mouth.

I thought I would burst with wanting. My swollen nipples felt as big as her demanding tongue. Then she worked her hand between my legs, and spread the juices from my cunt up over my straining clit, and my whimpers turned to full-throated moans.

Cleo raised her head. Her kiss muted my cries as she reached past me to shut the window. "Hope nobody's home next door," she muttered, and suddenly we were dancing horizontally on the narrow bed. I arched my hips, rubbing against her thigh, until her mouth moved down over throat and breasts and belly, slowly, too slowly; I wanted to savour each moment, but my need was too desperate. I wriggled, and thrashed, and her head sank at last between my thighs, just as in my dreams. Her mobile lips drove me into a frenzy of pleading, incoherent cries, until, with her tongue thrusting rhythmically into my cunt, my ache exploded into glorious release.

In the first faint light of morning I woke to feel Cleo's fingers tousling my hair. "If I were an artist I'd paint you just like this," she whispered. "You look like a marmalade cat chock full of cream."

I stretched, and then gasped as her fingers roused last night's ache into full, throbbing resurgence. "Sure enough," she said with a wicked grin, "plenty of cream. Let's see if I can make you yowl again."

This time I found out what her long, strong fingers could do deep inside me, one at first, then two; by the end of the week I could clench spasmodically around her whole pumping hand.

Sometimes I think I remember every moment of those days; sometimes everything blurs except the feel of Cleo's hands and mouth and body against mine and the way her eyes would shift suddenly from laughing silver to the dark steel of storm clouds.

We did more sightseeing: the Tower of London, Madame Tussaud's Wax Museum, St Paul's Cathedral scarred by German bombs. We took boat trips up the Thames to Richmond Park, where we dared to kiss in secluded bits of woodland, and down river where we held hands across the Greenwich Meridian. One night, in anonymous clothes bought at a flea-market barrow, we even managed to get into a club Cleo had heard of where women did dance openly with women. We couldn't risk staying long, but a dark intoxication followed us back to her room, where I entirely suppressed the nurse in me and demanded things of Cleo that left both of us sore, drained, and without regrets.

On our last night in London we went anonymously again into shabby backstreets near the docks. I brought disinfectant, and we chose what seemed the cleanest of a sorry lot of tattoo parlours. There, welcoming the pain of the needle as distraction from deeper pain, we had tiny pairs of wings etched over our left breasts.

We parted with promises to meet one more time before Cleo's last flight. I mortgaged a week of sleep to get my nursing shifts covered, and at Hamble Air Field, by moonlight, she introduced me to the planes she loved.

"This is the last Spitfire I'll ever fly," she said, stroking the sleek fuselage. "Seafire III, Merlin 55 engine, twenty-four-thousand-foot ceiling, although I won't go up that far just on a hop to Scotland."

From Scotland she'd catch an empty cargo plane back to the States. I had just got my orders to report to Hawaii for assignment somewhere in the South Pacific. War is hell, and so are goodbyes.

"Could I look into the cockpit?" I asked, wanting to be able to envision her there, high in the sky.

"Sure. You can even sit in it and play pilot, if you like." She helped me climb onto the wing, with more pressing of my ass than was absolutely necessary, and showed me how to lower myself into the narrow space. Standing on the wing, she leaned in and kissed me, hard at first, then with aching tenderness, then hard again.

"Pull up your skirt," she ordered, and I did it without question. She already knew I wasn't wearing underpants. "Let's see how wet you can get the seat, so I can breathe you all the way to Scotland." She unbuttoned my shirt and played with my breasts until I begged her to lean in far enough to suck my aching nipples; then, with her lips and tongue and teeth driving me so crazy that my breath came in a storm of desperate gasps, she reached down into my slippery heat and made me arch and buck so hard the plane's dials and levers were in danger. I needed more than I could get sitting in the cramped cockpit.

We clung together finally in the grass under the sheltering wing. I got my hands into Cleo's trousers and made her groan, but she wouldn't relax into sobbing release until she had her whole hand at last inside me and I was riding it on pounding waves of pleasure as keen as pain.

I thought, when I could think anything again, that she had fallen asleep, she was so still. Gently, gently I touched my lips to the nearly-healed tattoo above her breast. Tiny wings matching mine. Something to remember her by.

Without opening her eyes she said, in a lost, small voice, "What are we going to do, Kay?"

I knew what she was going to do. "You're going to claim the sky, to make history. And anyway," I said, falling back on dark humour since I had no comfort to offer, "a cozy ménage in Paris seems out of the question with the Nazis in control."

Then, because I knew if I touched her again we would both cry, and hate ourselves for it, I stood, put my clothes in as much order as I could, and walked away.

I looked back once, from the edge of the field. Cleo leaned, head bowed, against the plane. Some trick of the moonlight transmuted her dark hair into silver; I had a vision of how breathtaking she would be in 30 or 40 years. The pain of knowing I couldn't share those years made me stumble, and nearly fall. But I kept on walking.

And she let me go.

In June of 1944, against all justice and reason, the bill to make the Women Airforce Service Pilots officially part of the Army Air Forces was defeated in Congress by 19 votes. In December, the WASPs were disbanded. By then, though, after going through hell in the Pacific Theatre, I had met Jack, who truly loved and needed me, whose son was growing below my heart. His kisses tasted of home, and peace, and more unborn children demanding their chance at life.

Thirty-three years later, in 1977, when women were at last being admitted into the Air Force, the WASPs were retroactively given military status. It was then, through a reunion group, that I found out what had become of Cleo Remington; she had found a sky high and wide enough to hold her fierce spirit, and freedom as a bush pilot in Alaska.

And she was, as I discovered, even more breathtaking at sixty than she'd been at twenty-six.

But that's another chapter of the story.

Death on Denial

O'Neil De Noux

The Mississippi. The Father of Waters.
The Nile of North America.
And *I* found it.

— Hernando de Soto, 1541

The oily smell of diesel fumes wafts through the open window, filling the small room above the Algiers Wharf. Gordon Urquhart, sitting in the only chair in the room, a grey metal folding chair, takes a long drag on his cigarette and looks out the window at a listless tugboat chugging up the dark Mississippi. The river water, like a huge black snake, glitters with the reflection of the New Orleans skyline on the far bank.

Gordon's cigarette provides the room's only illumination. It's so dark he can barely see his hand. He likes it, sitting in the quiet, waiting for the room's occupant to show up. Not quite six feet tall, Gordon is a rock-solid 200 pounds. His hair turning silver, Gordon still sees himself as the good-looking heartbreaker he was in his twenties.

He wasn't born Gordon Urquhart those 40 years ago. When he saw the name in a movie, he liked it so much he became Gordon Urquhart. He made a good Gordon Urquhart. Since the name change, he'd gone up in life.

He yawns, then takes off his leather gloves and places them on his leg. He wipes his sweaty hands on his other pants leg.

The room, a ten-by-ten-foot hole-in-the-wall, has a single bed against one wall, a small chest of drawers on the other wall, and a sink in the far corner. Gordon sits facing the only door.

He closes his eyes and daydreams of Stella Dauphine. He'd

caught a glimpse of her last night on Bourbon Street. She walked past in that short red dress without even noticing him. As she moved away, bouncing on those spiked high heels, he saw a flash of her white panties when her dress rose in the breeze. He wanted to follow, but had business to take care of.

Sitting in the rancid room, Gordon daydreams of Stella, of those full lips and long brown hair. She's in the same red dress, only she's climbing stairs. He moves below and watches her fine ass as she moves up the stairs. Her white panties are sheer enough for him to see the crack of her round ass.

They're on his ship from his tour in the US Navy. Indian Ocean. Stella stops above him and spreads her legs slightly. He can see her dark pubic hair through her panties. She looks down and asks him directions.

Gordon goes up and shows her to a ladder, which she goes up, her ass swaying above him as he goes up after her, his face inches from her silky panties. Arriving at the landing above, she waits for him atop the ladder. He reaches up and pulls her panties down to her knees, runs his fingers back up her thighs to her bush and works them inside her wet pussy. She gasps in pleasure.

A sound brings Gordon back to the present. He hears footsteps coming up the narrow stairs up to the hall and moving to the doorway. Gordon pulls on his gloves and lifts the 22-calibre Bersa semiautomatic pistol from his lap. He grips the nylon stock, slips his finger into the trigger guard, and flips off the safety as the door opens. He points the gun at the midsection of the heavyset figure standing in the doorway.

Faintly illuminated by the dull, yellowed hall light, Lex Smutt reaches for the light switch. Gordon closes one eye. The light flashes on and Smutt freezes, his wide-set hazel eyes staring at the Bersa.

"Don't move, fat boy!" Gordon opens his other eye and points his chin at the bed. "Take a seat."

Smutt moves slowly to his bed and sits. At five-seven and nearly 300 pounds, Smutt knows better than to think of himself as anything but a toad. He runs his hands across his bald head and bites his lower lip. Wearing a tired, powder-blue seersucker suit, white shirt, and mud-brown tie, loosened around his thick neck, Smutt is as rumpled as a crushed paper bag.

"Keep your hands where I can see them." Gordon rises, his knees creaking, and closes the door. In his black suit, Gordon wears a black shirt and charcoal-grey tie.

Yawning again, Gordon says, "Long time, no see."

Smutt lets out a nervous laugh.

Gordon's mouth curls into a cold grin. "Lex Smutt. That's your real name, ain't it? It's a stupid name. You stupid?"

Smutt shakes his head slowly, his gaze fixed on the Bersa.

"You know why I'm here."

Smutt's eyes widen as if he hasn't a clue.

"Give me the 15,000. Or die."

A shaky smile comes to Smutt's thin lips. "I don't have it."

"Then die." Gordon cocks the hammer – for effect – and points the Bersa between Smutt's eyes.

Raising his hands, Smutt stammers, "Come on, now. Gimme a minute."

"You'll have the money in a minute?" Gordon's hand remains steady as he closes his left eye and aims careful at the small, dark mole between Smutt's eyebrows. The loud blast of a ship's horn causes Smutt to jump. Gordon is unmoved.

As long seconds tick by, Gordon takes the slack up in the trigger and starts to pull it slowly. Staring eye-to-eye, Smutt blinks.

"I got six grand," Smutt says.

Gordon's trigger finger stops moving, but his hand remains steady. He blinks and nods.

"Where?"

"On me."

"Where?"

Smutt wipes away the sweat rolling down the sides of his face and exhales loudly. "For a minute there I thought –"

"Where?" Gordon interrupts.

Leaning back on his hands, Smutt looks around the room.

Gordon raises his size-eleven shoe and kicks him in the left shin. Smutt shrieks and grabs his leg. He rocks back and forth twice before Gordon presses the muzzle of the Bersa against the man's forehead.

"Where?" Gordon growls.

"Under the bed." Smutt rubs his shin with both hands. "Under the floorboard."

Gordon grabs the seersucker suit collar with his left hand and yanks Smutt off the bed, shoving the man to the floor. Kicking the bed aside, Gordon orders Smutt to pull up the floorboard.

"Come up with anything except money and you're dead."

On his hands and knees now, Smutt crawls over to where his bed used to stand. Reaching for the loose board, he looks up at Gordon and says, "We have to come to an understanding."

Gordon points the Bersa at the floor next to Smutt's hand and squeezes off a round. A pop is followed by the sound of the shell casing bouncing on the wood floor.

Smutt looks at the neat hole next to his hand, looks back at Gordon, then yanks up the loose board. He reaches inside and pulls out a brown paper bag. He hands it to Gordon without looking up.

Snatching the bag, Gordon takes a couple of steps back. He opens the bag and quickly counts the money. Six grand exactly.

"You're 9,000 short."

Smutt rolls over on his butt and sits like a Buddha, hands on his knees. He wipes the sweat away from his face again and says, "Mr Happer will just have to understand. You just came into this but it's been goin' on awhile. I need time. Most of the 15 is vig . . . interest. You know."

Gordon points the Bersa at the mole again. "You're certain this is all you have?"

Smutt nods slowly, looking at the floor now. He waves a hand around. "Does it look like I got more?"

"Try *yes* or *no!*"

"No!" Smutt's voice falters and he clears his throat.

"I heard you won more than this at the Fairgrounds."

"Well, you heard wrong."

Gordon waits.

Smutt won't look up.

So Gordon asks, "Why deny it? You cleared over 20,000."

"I had other bills to pay."

"Before Mr Happer?" Gordon's voice is deep and icy.

"I told you this has been going on awhile. I need time."

"You shoulda thought of that before. Now look at me."
Gordon closes his left eye again.

Smutt looks up and Gordon squeezes off a round that strikes just to the left of the mole. Smutt shudders and bats his eyes. Gordon squeezes off another shot, this one just to the right of the mole. Smutt's mouth opens and he falls slowly forward, face first, in his lap.

Gordon steps forward and puts two more in the back of the man's head.

Then he carefully picks up the spent casings, all five of them, and puts them in his coat pocket. The air smells of gunpowder now and faintly of blood. He searches the body and finds another 400 in Smutt's coat pocket. Still on his haunches, Gordon looks inside the hole in the floor, but there's nothing else there.

He ransacks the room before leaving.

The night air feels damp on his face as he walks around the corner to where he'd squirrelled away his low-riding Cadillac.

Gordon checks his watch as he ascends the exterior stairs outside the Governor Nicholls Street Wharf. It's 9.00 a.m., sharp. He looks across the river at the unpainted Algiers Wharf. Shielding his eyes from the morning sun glittering off the river, he can almost make out the window of Smutt's room.

At the top of the stairs, he enters a narrow hall and moves to the first door. He knocks twice and waits, looking up at the surveillance camera. He straightens his ice-blue tie. This morning Gordon wears his tan suit with a dark blue shirt. Before leaving home, he told himself in his bathroom mirror that he looked "spiffy".

The door buzzes and he pulls it open.

Mr Happer sits behind his wide desk. Facing the TV at the far edge of his desk, next to the black videocassette recorder, the old man doesn't look up as Gordon crosses the long office. Happer looks small, hunkered down in the large captain's chair behind the desk.

The office smells of cigar smoke and old beer. The carpet is so old it's worn in spots. Gordon takes a chair in front of Mr Happer's desk and pulls out an envelope, which he places on the desk.

Raising a hand like a traffic cop, Mr Happer leans forward to pay close attention to the scene on his TV. Gordon doesn't have to look to know what's on the screen. It's Peter Ustinov again and that damn movie Mr Happer watches over and over. By the sound of it, Ustinov and David Niven are slowly working their way through the murder on the riverboat. What was the name of that French detective Ustinov plays? Hercules something-or-another.

Mr Happer suddenly turns his deep-set black eyes to Gordon.

Pushing 70, Mr Happer is a skeleton of a man with razor-sharp cheekbones, sunken cheeks, and arms that always remind Gordon of the films of those refugees from Dachau. Mr Happer reaches with his left hand for the envelope on his desk, picks it up with his spider's fingers, and opens it.

"That's all Smutt had on him," Gordon volunteers.

Mr Happer nods and says, "400?" He focuses those black eyes on Gordon and says, "What about the twenty grand from the Fairgrounds."

Gordon is careful as he looks back into the man's eyes. He shrugs. "He said he had other bills to pay."

"Before me?"

"That's what I said to him."

"So?"

"So I took care of him. Tossed the room and that's it."

Mr Happer shakes his head. Gordon watches him and remembers the man's name isn't Happer either. The old bastard was born Sam Gallizzio and tried for most of his life to become a made man, working at the periphery of La Cosa Nostra. Trying to be a goomba, Happer failed. He did, however, manage to remain alive, which isn't easy for an Italian gangster who's not LCN, even if he's only a semi-gangster.

Shoving the envelope into a drawer, Mr Happer pulls out another envelope, which he slides across the desk to Gordon. Gordon picks it up and slips it into his coat pocket. He doesn't have to count it. He knows there's a thousand in there – the old bastard's cut-rate hit fee.

Mr Happer picks up a stogie from an overflowing ashtray and sticks it in his mouth. He sucks on it and its tip glows red. He shakes his head again.

"It's worth it," Mr Happer says, as if he needs convincing. "The word'll get out. Make it easier later on. That's what the big boys do."

Gordon nods.

"He woulda never come up with the fifteen," Mr Happer says, and Gordon wonders if the old man is baiting him. "He woulda never paid me."

Fanning away the smoke from between them Mr Happer says, "You sure you tossed the place right, huh? You weren't in no hurry."

"No hurry at all." Gordon feels the old man squeezing him.

Mr Happer raises a hand suddenly, leans to the side to catch something Ustinov says. He nods, as if he's approving, then props his elbows on the desk. He looks at Gordon.

"You sure?" And there it is. *The* question.

"I'm sure, Mr Happer." Gordon likes the way his voice is deep and smooth.

"I gotta ask you straight up, you know that, don't you?" The old coot's face is expressionless.

Deny. Deny. Deny. Gordon doesn't even blink. He feels good.

Finally, the old man blinks and Gordon says, "Mr Happer. I've always been straight with you. You know that."

Mr Happer waves his hand again as he falls back in his chair.

"Son-of-a-bitch dumped the money awfully fast." Mr Happer looks again at the TV.

Gordon stops himself from reminding the old bastard that their agreement was simple. Find Smutt, get as much as you can from him, then whack him and leave him where he'll be found. He did his job. A contract is a contract.

Gordon waits. He wants to say, "Well, if that's all –" but knows better. He waits for Mr Happer to dismiss him.

The old man turns around and looks at the windows that face the river. He takes another puff of his cigar, lets out a long trail of smoke, and then says, "That's what I get for dealing with bums like Smutt. At least he got his."

Turning to Gordon, the old man smiles, and it sends a chill up Gordon's back.

"I was thinking of asking you if you happen to know where Smutt used to hang out. Maybe he had another place. But the money's long gone."

When the old man looks back at his TV, Gordon casually looks at the windows. A gunshot rings out and excited voices, including Ustinov's, rise on the TV. Gordon waits.

Finally, after the commotion on the riverboat calms down, Mr Happer looks at Gordon and says, "I know where to get you."

Gordon stands and nods at the old man and leaves, Mr Happer's dismissal echoing in his mind. He knows where to get me. Goodbye and hello at the same time.

Stepping out into the sunlight again, Gordon squints and stretches, then walks down the stairs. He looks at the brown, swirling river water and laughs to himself. Ustinov is still on the riverboat, floating on his own brown water, trying to solve the murder with Mr Happer watching intently. It strikes Gordon as very, very funny.

Before pulling away in his Caddy, he slips on his sunglasses and looks around. He spots the tail two minutes later, a black Chevy.

Gordon Urquhart's bedroom smells of cheap aftershave and faintly of mildew. Waiting in the darkness, Stella Dauphine sits on Gordon's double bed, her .22 Beretta next to her hand.

She wears a lightweight, tan trench coat and matching tan high heels, a pair of skin-tight gloves on her hands. A young-looking 30, Stella has curly hair that touches her shoulders. For a thin woman, she's buxom, which made her popular in high school but proved a hindrance in the mundane office jobs she held throughout her twenties.

Beneath the trench coat, she wears nothing except a pair of "barely there" sheer thigh-high stockings. She runs a hand over her knee and up to the top of her left thigh-high, pulling it up a little as she waits.

Closing her eyes she listens intently.

She didn't used to be Stella Dauphine. Born Carla Stellos, she changed her name after a year in New Orleans. After seeing a late-night movie on TV – A *Streetcar Named Desire* – and after parking her car on Dauphine Street, she decided on the change. She felt more like a Stella Dauphine every day.

Her eyes snap open a heartbeat after she hears a distinct metallic click at the back door. The door creaks open. Standing at the foot of the bed, Stella picks up her Beretta, unfastens the trench coat, her gun hidden in the folds of the coat as she waits.

She feels a slight breath of summer air flow into the room and hears a voice sigh and then light footsteps moving toward the bedroom. A figure steps into the doorway.

The light flashes on.

Gordon Urquhart's there, a neat .22 Bersa in his hand.

Stella opens the trench coat and lets it fall off her shoulders.

As Gordon looks down at her naked body, Stella squeezes off a round, which strikes Gordon on the right side of his chest. He's stunned, so stunned he drops his gun. Gordon's mouth opens as he stumbles into the room, falling against the chest of drawers. Blood seeps through the fingers of his right hand, which he's pressed against his wound.

"You shot me!"

"Kick your gun over here."

Gordon's face is ashen. He blinks at her, looks at his chest and stammers, "You *shot* me!"

"If you don't shut up, I'll shoot you again." Stella's mouth is set in a grim, determined slit. "Now kick the gun."

Gordon swings his foot and the gun slides across the hardwood floor. Stella steps forward and kicks it back under Gordon's bed.

The big man is breathing hard now. Blood has saturated his shirt.

"I think you hit an artery," he says weakly.

"Then we don't have much time, do we?"

"For what?"

Stella points her chin at the bed. "Sit, before you collapse."

Gordon moves to the bed and sits.

Stella moves to the doorway between the bedroom and kitchen, the Beretta still trained on Gordon.

"So," she says. "Where is it?"

He looks at her as if he hasn't the foggiest idea.

"Mr Happer told me to give you ten seconds to come up with the money you took off Smutt." Stella narrows her eyes. "One. Two. Three –"

"I gave him the 400."

"Four. Five. Six –"

Gordon raises his head and says, "Go ahead and shoot me. There's no money."

"Seven. Eight. Nine –"

"If I had it, you think I'd be dumb enough to have it on me? I spotted your Chevy as soon as I left the Governor Nicholls Wharf."

Stella squeezes off another round, which knocks the lamp off the end table next to the bed.

"Dammit!" Gordon groans in pain. "I don't have any more money. Smutt blew it all."

Stella brushes her hair away from her face with her right hand and tells him, "Mr Happer doesn't believe you and I don't believe you."

Gordon clears his throat and says, "Mr Happer and me go back a long way, lady. He knows better."

A cold smile crosses Stella's thin lips. "I'll just whack you and toss the place. I'll still get my fee."

"This is crazy. I tell you, there's no more money."

Stella aims the Beretta with both hands again, this time at Gordon's face. She says, "So you and the old man go back a ways, huh? Well, I'm the one he calls when things go badly. And you're as bad as they come."

Gordon nods at her. "I seen you around. I know all about you. And you got me all wrong, lady."

Stella watches his eyes closely as she says, "When Smutt left the Fairgrounds, he went straight to his parole-officer's house and paid the man off. Three grand. Stiff payoff, but Smutt figured it was worth it. Then he went to two restaurants, gorged himself. Then dropped some cash at the betting parlour on Rampart."

She watches Gordon's pupils. A pinprick of recognition comes to them as soon as she says the words, "Six grand. He had about six grand left. You took it off him."

"No way."

Stella fires again, into Gordon's belly, and he howls.

"That's it." Stella's smile broadens. "Keep denying it."

"I don't have it!" Gordon slumps backward.

Stella levels her weapon, aiming at Gordon's forehead. She pauses, giving him one last chance.

"I don't!" He screams.

She squeezes off a round that strikes Gordon in the forehead. Stepping forward, she puts two more in his head before he falls back on his bed. For good measure she empties the Beretta's magazine, putting two more in the side of the man's head.

She picks up all eight casings and slips them into the pocket of her coat. She leaves his Bersa under the bed. Let the police match it to the Smutt murder. Then, slowly and methodically, she tosses the place.

An hour later, she finds the 6,000 in the flour container on Gordon's kitchen counter. The giveaway – what man has fresh flour in a container?

Mr Happer, sitting back in his captain's chair, bats his eyes at the TV as Peter Ustinov taps out an S-O-S on his bathroom wall, a large cobra poised and ready to strike the rotund detective. Stella, standing at the desk's edge in the trench coat outfit from last night, recognizes the scene and waits for David Niven to rush in with his sword to impale the snake.

When the scene's tension dies, Mr Happer turns his deep-set eyes to Stella and says, "OK. You got the money?"

Stella shakes her head.

Mr Happer's eyes grow wide. "It wasn't there?"

"I tore the place apart. If he had it, he stashed it."

"Dammit!" Mr Happer slaps a skeletonic hand on his desk. He picks up the remote control and pauses his movie. His black eyes leer at Stella's eyes as if he can get the truth just by staring. She bites her lower lip, reaches down, and unfastens her coat. She opens it slowly as Happer's gaze moves down her body.

Stella lets the coat fall to the floor and stands there naked except for the thigh-high stockings, which give her long legs the silky look. Rolling her hips, Stella sits on the edge of the desk. Mr Happer stares at her body as if mesmerized. It takes a long minute for his gaze to rise to her eyes.

"You sure you tossed the place right?"

Stella nods.

Mr Happer picks up the remote and looks back at the TV. The riverboat is moored now, against the bank of the wide Nile River.

"Well, the word'll get out. Make it easier later on," Happer says. "That's what the big boys do."

Stella climbs off the desk and picks up her coat. As she closes it, she looks at the old man. Mr Happer turns those black eyes to her and says, "You *sure* you tossed the place right?"

She's ready, her face perfectly posed. "I'm sure."

"OK." Mr Happer looks back at the TV and mouths the words as Peter Ustinov speaks. Without looking, he opens his centre desk drawer and withdraws an envelope. He slides it over to Stella, who picks it up and puts it in her purse.

"Good work," Mr Happer says.

"Thanks." Stella turns and leaves him with his Ustinov and David Niven and riverboat floating down the Nile.

On her way down the stairs she looks at the dark Mississippi water and whispers a message to the dead Gordon, "So you and Mr Happer go back a long way. Well, we go back a longer way."

And I have tools, plenty of tools to work against this man, against all these men.

Three minutes later she spots the tail, a dark blue Olds.

The Sweater

Tara Alton

I had a sexy dream about her – my crush – a writer from a cool local magazine, but I wasn't sure because it was a girl on girl type thing. I'd only had one experience with a woman so far, and I was left wavering, not sure which way to go. And yet I hadn't been able to stop thinking about her all week, especially since I'd seen her at the Laundromat.

In my dreams, I was at my favourite coffee shop with a cappuccino and a molasses cookie. I was reading her most recent article when she came over and sat beside me. She spotted my sample case where I keep the jewellery I made, and she opened it.

Inside, she found a pair of my dangle earrings and held them up to my ears. Because of my thick tousled hair, she couldn't see them so she brushed my hair off my shoulders. Her fingers lightly touched my skin. An electric sizzle passed between us.

Next came a choker. She leaned in close to fasten it around my neck, her breath on my ear. I felt like I was melting inside from the warmth of her mouth.

To go with the choker, she selected a pendant on a long chain. It joined the choker, but she couldn't get the pendant to lie right on my shirt so she slid it inside my cleavage. The chain slithered down my skin. My breath caught short. The pendant nestled between my breasts. Slowly, she hooked a finger inside my shirt and peered inside to see her work. Her breathing changed. My bra felt tight. I was getting flushed all over.

I looked around us. No one was watching. She completely unbuttoned me. My bra was exposed for the world to see.

Gently, she unbuttoned my cuffs and with her hands under my shirt, she pushed my blouse off me.

More necklaces joined the pendant. She paused. A whole cluster of pendants were in my cleavage. She dipped a finger inside them, swirled them around. Then she unhooked my bra. It fell away. I was bare-breasted. She cupped my breasts in her hands, rolling my nipples between her thumbs and forefingers. They got painfully hard.

She took a sip of coffee and placed her steaming mouth on my nipple. I nearly fell off the chair with the pleasure of it. Coming up for air, I saw a twinkle in her eye as she took another sip of coffee and took a big bite of my molasses cookie. Crumbs fell into my lap. Like a lap dancer she slid in between my legs and started biting off the crumbs near my special place.

I awoke with a jolt. My body was sweated through and the sheets were in an awkward ball between my legs. There was a deep, troubling throbbing down there. I had to do something. I freed myself, went into the bathroom and put a cold washcloth on it. The shock made me cry out.

"Are you OK?" my roommate called out.

"I stubbed my toe," I lied.

In the morning, Paula was having a cup of Chai Tea and a whole wheat bagel when I found her in the kitchen. She gave me a knowing look.

"I know that girls have needs," Paula said, in her best friend voice that sounded very similar to a mother's voice sometimes.

"It was nothing like that," I lied again.

I paused.

"But since we're talking about it," I said, "sometimes I'm afraid of it. What's inside me. Really letting go. I was with this guy once. He got me really excited. I said things."

"What things?" she asked.

"I can't say," I said.

"Come on. You can tell me."

I shook my head.

"Hey, I told you about the time I had sex with that guy and we couldn't find the dildo after. It turned out it was still up my butt," she said. "So you can tell me."

"Fuck me like a dog," I said.

She laughed.

"He said I was a freak and never called me again," I said.

"Then he's the freak," she said.

I smiled. I liked Paula. She was the neatest girl I'd ever met, although she was a dead head, a Grateful Dead fan, and she loved hippy stuff. When we first met, she asked me to go with her to pick out some stickers for her car. I thought since she was a vegetarian like me, she wanted animal stickers, but she wanted Grateful Dead-type stuff. She asked my opinion between a skull with roses or a skull with dice for eyes. I told her I liked the roses. At least they were flowers.

We met when she was working upstairs at the tattoo parlour as a receptionist. She came downstairs to the bead shop, where I worked, asking for a ride home, because she had ridden her bicycle to work and it was raining. I always thought she was riding a bike because she was healthy, but it turned out her licence had been suspended for drunk driving.

Now we were roommates. With the tattoo parlour behind her, she worked at the Safe Sex Store, selling condoms.

I decided to tell her about my crush. I knew I had to do something about it. My career and my love life depended on it. By meeting the woman of my dreams, I could maybe get a mention in her art column. One year after graduating my jewellery career wasn't going anywhere fast, but I needed a kick in the pants from Paula to do this. She was the best motivator I knew.

"Guess who I saw at the Laundromat?" I asked.

Paula raised an eyebrow at me.

"Melanie," I said.

"Who's that?" she asked.

"She is a staff writer for the Metro Weekly."

"Isn't she the one whose column you read every week?"

"Yeah."

I'd also read almost everything else she'd written from her first movie reviews to her restaurant reviews when she first came out. Now she wrote about gallery openings, art shows and artist profiles. I loved the personal tidbits interspersed throughout her articles. I would love for her to come racing

into the bead shop to interview me, out of breath, holding a
falafel sandwich and a diet coke, a little hole in her red canvas
tennis shoes.

"What about it?" she asked.

"A write-up from her could do me a lot of good," I said.

"So meet her."

"There is a catch. I think she's hot."

"No, you don't. You're being trendy again."

"I'm not."

"Look what happened with Kit," Paula said, getting up to
make some more honey butter.

I squeezed my right arm, where my tattoo was. Kit was the
tattoo artist from upstairs. She did the brown-eyed Susans on
my arm. They were my favourite flowers in the fields behind
our house when I was growing up, and I was tired of seeing the
parade of roses and lilies coming out of Kit's studio. I wanted
something different.

She was the woman I had the experience with. It happened
after hours. During the tattoo she kept telling me to breathe
because I kept holding my breath. "You've got fantastic skin,"
she said. "Yellow just loves you."

When she was done with the tattoo I felt a little dizzy, but I
was happy with what she'd done. She took me into her office
and got me a soda.

"I feel high," I said.

"That's your endorphins," she said.

She patted the sofa next to her. I joined her.

"You know what would be lovely on you?" she asked, and
motioned me to stand. "Take off your pants."

"I'm a little shy."

"I see everything all the time. I'm like a doctor."

I took them off. She started sketching more flowers on my
thighs. In the quickest of moments, she pulled aside my panties
and gave me a quick kiss on the clit.

"Did you mind that?"

I thought hard. It felt good, really, really good.

"No."

Without any decorum she pulled me back onto the sofa,
climbed on top and ate me out.

No kissing. No foreplay. She was at an all-you-can-eat buffet. And she was good.

I came so fast it almost hurt.

"Wow," I cried.

She looked startled for a second, but then a sly triumphant look came over her face. "I need a diet cola."

I got up and pulled my pants on.

"Your arm," she said, all business now. "Use Noxzema."

I let myself out and told Paula the next morning.

"You what? When?" she asked.

"After you left."

"Where?"

"On the sofa."

She screwed up her face. "I can never sit there again. You only did it to be trendy."

"I did not."

I waited for Kit to come and see me the next day. She didn't. The whole incident sort of went away. The next time I saw her, she acted as if nothing had happened.

Paula quit the tattoo shop a week later. I wasn't sure if it was because of me or not. I looked at her now, spreading her freshly made honey butter on her bagel. She seemed much happier at the condom store.

"Are you really interested in Melanie?" Paula asked.

I nodded. "I don't know why I find her attractive. Or why I'm intrigued by her."

"Maybe it's her self-confidence. What she projects, you sorely lack. What would you do with her if you got her?"

I paused. "Hang out."

"Then go to the Laundromat. Wear something sexy and meet her. Hopefully she'll like girls too."

I went to the Laundromat the same time I had seen her the previous week. My heart leapt at the sight of her, but she was with a guy. She had a boyfriend, I decided. I wanted to turn around and leave, but it would look strange if I left with my laundry after just walking in. Still, I could get her to notice the jewellery I'm wearing and maybe spark some interest for a mention in her column.

Melanie was already at the dryers. I chose a washing machine close by, but not too close. As I stuffed in my clothes, I glanced over at her a few times. She had a sexy bratty look about her that I loved, like she used to be a quasi-popular cheerleader who loved to shock her friends with her exploits and frank language, while all the adults thought her so sweet and innocent. Her body was amazing, like she was a little girl and a nymph all rolled into one.

I checked out the clothes she already had on hangers. They were all very trendy and expensive. All her towels matched. Compared to her stuff, my stuff looked mangy.

"God, how I miss the fluff and fold," she said. "Whoever said being on a budget was fun?"

"Being a responsible adult is never fun," the guy said. "But the key word in that last sentence is adult."

Wishing my washer wasn't so loud on wash, I tried to hear what she was telling him now.

I caught bits and pieces about her frightful crush on a girl. I smiled. So she liked girls. I had a chance. But she wouldn't even look my way. I took off my shirt to reveal the tank top beneath. Maybe my brown-eyed Susans might get her to look my way.

The guy looked my way, but not Melanie. He was nice looking, but he didn't match with her at all. He looked like the type of guy who would work in a used record store. Maybe if you had one too many beers at the Half Moon Bar you might do him.

She said she had to go to the bathroom. Impulsively, I followed her, thinking I might bump into her in the hallway and start a conversation. At the bathroom door, I found it ajar. I heard her going. It sounded like a gentle rain. She flushed. I saw a flash of her ass. I gulped. Pulling up her jeans, she zipped them.

Before I knew it, the door swung open. I startled. She was in front of me, looking alarmed.

"I thought no one was in here," I said.

"Well, knocking would be the polite thing to do," she said abruptly and left.

I wanted to follow her, but how could I? She thought I needed to use the bathroom. I stepped inside and shut the door. Facing the mirror, I looked at the embarrassment on my cheeks. I had been almost caught spying on another girl in the bathroom. What a freak.

I glanced at the toilet seat. This was a weird thought, but her warm, heart-shaped butt had just been there.

When I came out, I found they had left. I put my clothes in the dryer she had just used, knowing this took me to another level of stalking, when I found a sweater. It was obviously hers – pink, with long sleeves and ribbon embroidery. The label was like something you would buy at Jacobson's. Surprisingly, it looked like it had shrunk.

I debated on what to do. I could give it to the attendant, or she might come back for it and I could hand it to her. Unsure, I laid it on the counter as I finished drying and folding my clothes. I can't say I did the right thing. My judgment was a little cloudy with lust. I took it home.

By the time I got there, Paula had already gone to bed. I went to my room and put away my clothes. Like a fifteen-year-old boy craving his first crush, I smelled her sweater. A summer afternoon filled my senses. It was her softener sheet, I realized.

I smoothed the sweater on the bed, imagining she was on her back. She caressed my face and slid her little finger inside my mouth. Her fingertip explored the tip of my tongue. She pulled it out. I ran my tongue alongside her finger and licked the inside of her finger cleavage. Aroused, she squirmed. Having me hold the cuff of her sweater, she pulled her arm free.

With my face pressed to the sweater, I played with my clit, lost in my fantasy, but reality started to interrupt. My finger was cramping, and I realized how silly I looked from my teddy bear's point of view. I was practically humping this sweater. Fantasy Melanie dissolved. I liberated my finger and sighed, everything down there left wet, loose and lonely. I threw the sweater over my teddy bear's head.

By the next week, I was so sexually frustrated that I knew I had to do something drastic. I decided to go to the Laundromat and wear the sweater. It was a small, while I was a medium, and it had shrunk, so it ended up being a midriff with three-quarter length sleeves, but my breasts did look good in it. My plan was that she would notice the sweater on me, question me about it, and I could casually say I found it. Thus starting a conversation that could only bring good things.

There was a major catch in my plans though. Melanie wasn't there. Her guy friend was though, washing what looked like dozens of worn-out jeans. Disappointed, I slunk to a washer and stuffed in my clothes.

Bored, I looked around. He was the only other customer. I hadn't thought to bring anything to read, and the ancient baby magazines by the soda machine didn't look the least bit interesting.

I glanced at him. He was wearing the same worn-out coffee house T-shirt from last time. Was he looking in my direction as well?

"Isn't that the place that fired staff for having piercings and tattoos?" I asked.

"Yup," he said.

"Are you supporting them?"

He walked over to me.

"No. It's a soft T-shirt. It feels good. Feel it."

I did. It was soft.

"It takes months to get a T-shirt like this," he said. "Now, it's in that worn-in time frame."

"Come again?"

"You know. Like you've got a blue jean jacket. You've worn it for years. It's worn in some spots, maybe a couple of well placed holes. It looks real cool for a month or two like that, and then suddenly it looks like garbage."

He paused and looked me over.

"Speaking about clothes. Isn't that Melanie's sweater?" he asked, an eyebrow raised.

"This?" I asked, feigning surprise. "I found it. Who's Melanie?"

"The girl you were checking out last time. I don't blame you. She's hot."

"I don't know what you're talking about."

"You weren't looking at me. That chick boner you had was all for her. Admit it."

I blushed. A *chick boner*. I had never thought about it like that. A dryer light came on inside my head amongst the lint lust. Talking to him might be a good opportunity to pump him for some information about her.

"With you being her friend, what's she like?"

"Pretentious. Spoiled. You're not her type. Neither am I," he said.

"Who is her type?"

"Tomboys. No make up. Slender bodies. Baseball shirts. Short hair. Nothing like you."

"Hey, I'm not a miss priss," I said.

"But every inch of you is a girl. From behind there is no mistaking what you are."

I glanced at my ass. It didn't look so great to me. And what was he doing looking at it?

"If she's so spoiled, why are you friends?" I asked.

"Habit. Entertainment. Nothing better to do."

"That's awful."

He shrugged.

"I was her neighbour back when she had braces," he said. "Before the nose job. And the dye job. And way before the 'I'm a journalist' stuff. Sometimes, I think she likes me because I liked her when she was just Melanie. Other times, I don't think she likes me because I remind her of her past."

"Really."

"The only reason she got the Metro Weekly gig is because her aunt is the publisher. Don't tell anyone. She doesn't even write them per se."

"What do you mean?"

"She gathers some and adds some opinions. I whip them into shape. Add some humour. Things about my daily life."

"Those are your personal tidbits?" I asked, panicking.

It was his sense of humour I liked. Not hers.

There was a pause.

"She even told me what she likes to do to other girls, but it's far too explicit to say out here," he said.

How I wanted the details. "Where can we go?" I pressed.

"The store room."

The attendant wasn't watching. I followed him into the store-room. I felt like I was in high school, stealing off for a cigarette.

Inside, there was a metal desk, boxes of mini soap powders and an ancient gumball dispenser. He locked the door behind us.

"What does she like to do?" I asked.

"I know she likes to sit on their laps like lap dancers and squirm around."

My breath caught short. Images of her lap dancing me filled my head.

"One time at a party," he continued, "she had her top off with some chick and they got caught by the hostess."

"No way," I said.

"That gave me a boner for weeks thinking about it," he confessed.

"What else?"

He paused, thinking. "She likes to eat out girls in weird places. Backs of cars, dressing rooms, restaurants."

I sighed. Maybe this wasn't such a good idea hearing all this. Now I was horny and, judging by the way he tugged at the front of his jeans, so was he. He stood by me.

"You smell like her," he said.

"It's her dryer sheet."

"Could you strap on a dozen of them and pretend you're her?" he asked.

I hesitated. I couldn't believe what had popped into my head. "I could pretend to be her in this sweater."

He looked at me slowly, his eyes dilated, and it was very obvious what was happening in his pants. I swallowed. I had that butterfly feeling I used to get in third grade when I played horses in the playground with my friends. Only this wasn't grammar school.

"What would you do first?" I asked.

"Kiss her and fondle her sweater," he said.

"OK," I said.

He kissed me. It left me a little breathless. "Wait a sec," I said.

I slipped my bra off from beneath the sweater. He resumed the kiss, but he was putting way too much emphasis on my mouth. I backed up and sat on the old metal desk. He stood between my open legs. He pinched my nipple too hard. I smacked his hand away and pinched him back.

"Ouch," he said. "I think I liked that."

"You're sick."

He cupped my breasts. "We have a problem. Yours are a lot bigger than hers," he said.

"Pretend they are small."

"I can't," he said, kneading them. "Yours are magnificent. I can't deny what I'm feeling."

"You're getting off track," I said.

"Have you ever been titty fucked?"

I shook my head.

"A girl can't do that," he said, smugly.

Undoing my pants, he kissed my belly. "This isn't in the vicinity of the sweater," I said.

"But it's something I would do."

"You would eat her snatch?"

He nodded. I helped him get my jeans off. "I saw her bare butt," I said.

"Where?"

"In the bathroom," I said. "I was standing outside the door when she went."

"You peeping Tom."

"It was an accident." My jeans were on the floor. We both looked at my underwear. "What type of panties does she wear?" I finally asked.

"How would I know?"

"If you are into her as much as I am, and you are that close to her laundry, you would know."

He continued to concentrate on my panties. "Now that I think about it they are very similar to yours," he said.

He kissed me down there. It felt good. Suddenly, I panicked. By the look in his eyes, I knew what was coming next. A good round of pussy eating, but I was afraid he wouldn't compare to Kit. Her tongue was like a contortionist at a big top circus.

His manoeuvres were so different they took my breath away. It was French kissing my pussy, really kissing it, like he would my mouth. It wasn't something to attack. It was something to savour. It was like slow, sweet dreamy jazz. My whole body felt it. Every muscle relaxed and moved with the flow. It felt so good I wanted to laugh out loud, but I bit it back.

He stopped. I was left panting and throbbing.

"I have to fuck you," he said. "You. Not pretend her. I have to be inside you."

"You would screw her in a laundry room?"

"Not her. You. She is mean and insipid. And I don't think she would taste half as sweet as you."

Me, I thought. He wanted me. I nodded, peeled off the sweater and tossed it aside. He slid inside me. I wrapped my arms and legs around him. He took it slow with shallow strokes, just the tip inside. I revelled in the sensation and the scent of his skin on his shoulder. For a second, my thoughts returned to Melanie. He's fucking her. No. He's fucking me.

He was fucking my crush right out of my head. I felt that worked-up feeling coming over me, where I wanted to say things, scream and groan. It was a fight to keep back all those dark, carried away things. Brimming over the edge. On the tip of my tongue. Spilling out of my head.

"Fuck me like a . . ." I said and choked down the last word.

"Like what?" he breathed.

I shook my head.

"Say it," he demanded.

"A duck. Fuck me like a duck," I cried. I giggled, groaned and arched my back.

"Oh, yeah," he said. "I'm going to fuck you like a duck. Quack for me."

"What?"

"Quack for me now."

Sick fuck that I was, I quacked. Over and over, I quacked as we both came, until my voice was hoarse.

My legs were completely jelly when we pulled apart.

"You're awesome," he said.

"Yeah?"

He nodded and handed me his T-shirt, worn in just right. I had no idea where the sweater was nor did I care.

"I think the Melanie fan club has had its first and last meeting," he said.

"And so much for my write-up with my jewellery," I added, lightly. Not that I really cared anymore.

"I'll fix that," he said and paused, looking at me. "You look really good in my T-shirt."

Trying it on

Jennifer Footman

Smith and Logan, The Theatrical Outfitters of the Professional, are located in the older industrial part of Edinburgh. Their new building, once the hallowed space of the Niddrie Presbyterian Church, now has a bright red and black sign saying that it's a theatrical costumier and that they have been in business since 1870.

Mary and Barbara walked into the hazy gloom from the brilliant sunshine of the mid-morning. For a moment or two they stood, uncertain, in the white-tiled lobby. Cracked brown linoleum covered the floor.

"Interesting," Barbara said, a half smirk on her face.

"Wait and see. Appearances can be deceptive. Alison had a fantastic Mary Queen of Scots outfit from them. Amazing. It was wicked. So sexy she could hardly get any peace."

"I can't imagine Alison would want peace. I can't imagine Alison wearing anything if she felt it would come between her and her piece."

"Ho. Ho. You're so funny. You know your trouble, Miss Misery Guts?"

She shook her head. "No, but I'm sure you'll tell me."

"You need a good shag. A large juicy shag. A young man. A large well-hung young man."

"Thank you for those kind words, Miss Know-All. Perhaps you should buy me a giant vibrator? King size. Amazon size."

A young man came to the oak counter. He stood tall and his skin was tanned gold, bronze, silver. Fair as a Viking, his curls haloed his face. His body rippled under his thin cotton shirt.

"Morning, ladies, can I help you?" His voice lilted with a strong Welsh accent.

"Ceruti and Smith. We have an appointment for a fitting . . . for a party."

"Follow me." They did as they were told and obediently trotted behind the young man's tight bum into a narrow corridor.

Mary whispered aside, "You wait and see. Brass and black leather. I've seen through you. Behind that soft, cuddly exterior is an animal. You need to maim. A tiger. Or a leopard."

"More like a tired lizard. You should have been a psychiatrist instead of being a dentist. Or a writer of horror stories. Fantasy, Madam."

For over a month Mary had known what she wanted for the costume party. She had to have the full, black leather look. Executioner. Cruel. What was the point of getting dressed up if the dress-up personality was more or less the same as oneself?

They were in a hall where pulleys and racks hung from the ceiling. It seemed as if the ceiling was totally covered by robes and costumes lined up, in row upon row between the rafters like soldiers waiting for an order to charge. Men's clothes on one side and women's on the other. Under white dust-sheets draped over railings, Ancient Rome faced modern ballroom.

They both stood with their heads tilted up, fascinated by the array of clothes. In the thick air, dust motes shone in the coloured light from the stained glass windows.

"And what were you ladies thinking of?"

Barbara glanced at Mary as if looking for some kind of approval before speaking. Mary made a face and said, "Well, I know what I want. Something in black leather. Executioner, perhaps. Tight. Hard yet silky. Fitting like a second skin."

"Right. Just the thing for you. And what about the other young lady?" He faced Barbara.

"I don't know. Haven't really thought about it. Not black leather I don't think. For sure, not black leather. Never leather. Something soft, something white, perhaps an angel? Why did I say that? Angels on my mind. Yes, that's it." She pointed to an old print of an angel leaning on a windowsill. "The angel. And this being a church. That's it."

"Angel it is, then. Beauty and the Beast. Right. No diffi-culty, none at all." He rubbed his hands together. "We have a lovely line in angels. The best in the whole of Europe. Our angels go everywhere. You will be the most angelic angel they have ever seen. The most angelic.

"Now, if you could come into the fitting room. I think we can fit you from stock. Both of you are . . . so slim and . . . well formed, so well formed. Lovely."

They were in a large fitting room lined by mirrors. A chaise in dark brown leather was the only furniture. Hooks were set into the walls above the mirrors and a thick tartan carpet covered the floor from wall to wall. It was like a crypt, Mary thought, or a womb perhaps, yes, more like a womb.

The young man reappeared and asked if it was all right for him to take measurements as their fitting lady was off sick. Or would they rather take each other's measurements? They both shook their heads and mumbled something along the lines that no, it was fine if he took the measurements. Barbara slipped off her skirt and blouse and stood in bra and pants. The fine black briefs accentuated the line and rise of her pubis. Mary exam-ined her in the mirrors and yes, she did look . . . edible. The cheeks of her bum rose as if held in by elastic and her breasts were just covered by the tip of the heavy black lace bra. Mary sat in evident admiration, a half smile on her face. She shrugged. "Not bad, not bad at all."

Barbara pirouetted as if to show herself off even more. The young man laughed and took her breast measurement, then her waist and then her hips. After each measurement he jotted numbers into a little notebook. He had an aroma of spice and all things nice, a rich smell. Barbara rolled her eyes at Mary over his head while he was down measuring the length of her legs, his fingers in her crotch. Mary winked. He seemed to make quite a meal of measuring.

"Lovely, it is. We have just the right thing for you. Pale, pale pink it is, quite like a baby's christening dress. Angelic. Pure. Butter wouldn't melt in your mouth in it. No one would be purer than our angel. No one."

"Nice.

"Now for the other lady."

Mary stripped down to her bra and panties. A large bruise glistened on her hips – Alex had bitten her there last night. She noticed the young man glance at it and half shut his eyes and get on with the measurement.

"We have the thing. A man's it is, but I think it will be lovely on you. You have those fine hips, almost like a boy's. Yes, I know it will do just fine."

He rolled up his measure and tucked it into his shirt pocket. He studied his notebook for a few seconds and then put it away.

"Ladies, make yourselves comfortable. Someone will bring in coffee and our stock girl will find your costumes. Relax and make yourselves at home, it'll be about ten minutes."

A pimply boy of about 16 came in with a jug of coffee. For all he seemed to care they could have been wearing shrouds.

Mary slid along the chaise and sat beside Barbara so they could both look at themselves in the mirror. She curled one finger round Barbara's lacy panties and touched her clit. "Aren't we a pair of pretty ladies, don't you think?"

Barbara smiled and lightly stroked her own breast. "Something about a man running a tape round you. It's sort of . . . you know? Kind of . . ."

"Yes, I know. Sexy. Lovely. Makes me all tingly. All over sensuous."

They sipped coffee and looked at each other.

Mary said, "So what now?"

Barbara shrugged. "We wait."

"We could do something while we wait."

"Like?"

"Use your imagination, girl."

They weren't given a chance to find something to amuse themselves. They had just finished coffee when the young man came in with two bags over his arm. He hung them up on the hooks and opened them. One bag held a creation in pale pink froth, the other a cloak of fine white velvet.

"Try the angel on and I'll be right back. In a jiff. Just have to check on something. Not quite happy with the pants. See what's happening."

Mary helped Barbara into the dress and pulled up the zip. Her fingers smelt of Barbara's musk. Lovely, rich and warm.

Goodness, Barbara was transformed into an angel. Mary sat licking her lips. "You look gorgeous. It's amazing. The pink of the dress makes your skin even finer, fine and tight. Good God, look what it does to your breasts. It . . . it makes them bloom. Yes, like a pair of bulbs. And your legs . . ."

"You're getting all too poetic about this."

"Well, you do look lovely. Perfect."

The skirt wafted long and transparent, hanging loose from a velvet tie under her breast. "I think this will do."

"Do indeed. Too damned right. It's gorgeous. Just gorgeous. Now, wasn't it worth coming, Miss Misery?"

There was a knock at the door. "Come in," Mary said.

"It's just me." He entered and stood admiring Barbara. "Lovely, she looks. So she does." As if remembering the reason for him coming into the room he said, "The leather will be a little time. Perhaps Miss Ceruti would want to leave and you wait? We need to do a bit of a patch-up. Some of the stitching has come undone. About a half-hour. Sorry about that but I wasn't happy about the pants. They had done a bad job before cleaning them and it wasn't right. Needs to be re-stitched. Our seamstress is working on it right now." He left.

"I'll wait' " Mary said. "You go on. I know you have an appointment. No need for us both to hang about here, is there?"

"I have to get to the bank before it closes and do some bills."

Barbara removed the angel costume and dressed in her street clothes. "You sure you don't mind me going?"

"No, of course not. Get on with it."

"I'll just take this back to the front. I suppose . . . they want it in the office." She lifted her costume and left the room.

Mary was quite happy to be left alone for a half-hour or so. She settled with a book. She was trying to get through *The Brothers Karamazov* and carried a paperback in her bag all the time. It was a challenge and what else was there to do in waiting rooms or on train trips? She should have read it. It's important. It's necessary for all good women to have read it. If only it wasn't so long and so . . . so boring. No, she would never admit to anyone she found it boring. Never.

The brass door handle turned and she looked up. Good, that didn't take long. No, it wasn't the man with a costume for her. A man stood at the door. About six foot, thin and rangy. He had bushy hair and hot black eyes and was wearing a riding habit. Tight jodhpurs and black boots up to his knees. A fitted beige riding jacket. He carried a whip. The jodhpurs were like a second skin but for the crotch area where a surplus of materials accentuated the bulge. His skin was that shot silk purple black which just begs to be stroked.

"You're in the wrong room," she said sharply.

"I don't think so. In fact I'm sure I'm in the very right room."

"What do you want?" The room boiled as if someone had turned on a sauna. Even in her bra and pants she felt as if she was melting. She wished she was dressed but was not prepared to let this man see that she was uncomfortable in her underwear.

"Wondered . . . who was in here. What you were like. I hear you're getting a similar outfit. We're both going to be in black leather." Leather and flesh and skin. His lips were full and glistening and soft. "I have to wait for something and it seemed a good idea to wait with someone."

"Oh, yes?"

"Well . . . Isn't it?"

"I don't know. It depends who that someone is." Just a little she resented this intrusion. Having made up her mind to read the stupid book she thought she should be left in peace to read it. Well . . . the book wasn't stupid. Not stupid. She was stupid not appreciating it and being quite relieved that she was stopped from reading. She decided that the relief outweighed the resentment. She studied him. His thighs were all rock. Solid. His legs went on forever and forever. The room filled with the smell of his body.

"Your angel was sweet. Sexy."

"How do you know? And how do you know about my black leather?"

"I know everything."

The heat in that outfit had to kill him. So hot. So very hot. He had to be suffocating. Sweat stuck her thighs together.

"Well . . . do you want me to wait with you?"

She shrugged. "It's up to you." No, she can't read this now. She turned over a page and placed the book in her bag. She smiled. What the hell.

He shut the door and slid a bolt. He knelt before her and kissed her knees, stroking the inside of her thighs. He followed the knee kisses with tiny feathery kisses right up, up, up to her panties. He spread her knees and folded her panties to one side. The narrow crotch of her French panties was soaking wet. He slid a finger along the wet silk and sniffed it. "Lovely. Lovely. And soaking wet. You seem to have been a busy lady."

He gazed at her sex. She had never had a fully kitted-out horsy stranger before. In fact, she had never had a stranger before or even a man in riding gear. Time to let go and be free. He had the kind of thin face where she couldn't tell if he was smiling or not. He spread her lips and slid a finger up until he touched her clit and then down and then up and down. He circled it and licked his fingers so that he had them glistening and silver.

He looked into her eyes. His eyes glittered dark and crinkled. It was unreal to be sitting there; she semi-naked and he dressed from head to toe. He danced slow and delicately round her sex as if wishing to find out about every inch of it. He rolled her panties down and off. He circled and stroked and rolled and investigated. Now his tongue was right on the spot and he expertly rolled, licked, circled and sucked, so much a master she was nearly climbing the walls.

As if he knew she was nearly coming he stopped and stood with his crotch in her face. "Yes," he said. She unbuttoned the six buttons and exposed his hard, thick cock which sprang out to meet her. She pressed her nose against it. The only sound in the room the sigh of her breath.

She looked up. "You smell of leather and sweat and musk."

"Been riding before coming here. Friends in Biggar have a farm and stables."

She ran her tongue along the tip of his cock. Gently. Gently until she felt him move, oh, he was almost touching his edge, but he withdrew from her, stood still as a statue. So he thought he could drive her mad and leave himself in control, did he?

No, she was the boss this time and this dance would be at her pace. She was so ready she could come and come. Come and come. Yes, that's how she saw it. No, she would not let him come this way. She took a cognac-flavoured condom out of her bag and opened it and slid it onto his cock. It crackled and crinkled as she unrolled it. He moaned gently.

She debated sucking him or shagging him and decided that she needed that beautiful, now golden, cock inside her. She bent down and took him in her mouth and gave him a couple of large long slow sucks, holding his balls in both hands. The taste of brandy tickling her palate. She turned and knelt on the floor, supported by the chair. Gently he slid it into her, at the same time stroking her clit. Tender at first and then harsher, harder, firmer, longer, slow and deeper and deeper until she couldn't stand it any more. With thundering final thrusts he came. She had just missed him but the polite man made sure he stayed in and stroked her to an equally fine climax.

"Goodness," he said as he drew away and draped the full condom off his cock, tied a knot in it and deposited it in the waste basket. "That was something. Amazing."

He pulled a large ironed handkerchief from his pocket and wiped her with it then carefully slid her panties up her legs. He placed the buttons of his jodhpurs into the holes. Just as he did this there was a knock at the door.

"Good timing." She could hear the smile in his voice.

"Yes," she said. He opened the door and left the room.

A young woman entered with a black leather outfit on a hanger.

Tomatoes:
A Love Story in Three Parts

Claire Tristram

I

What made me leave my husband Boris? Tomatoes. There is no other explanation.

When I think of those days just before I took flight my teeth begin to hurt. My husband Boris had for six years done little more than squeeze my hand and get a melancholy look whenever I asked him to make love to me.

I persevered. I invited him to drink wine from my navel. I lost weight. I gained weight. I invested in latex and paraphernalia. Nothing. I still loved him in some ways, like one might love a puppy or a tree. I suggested counselling and he yawned.

In Year Six I resolved to try adultery. You may wonder what took so long. Well, I am an extremely hopeful person. I hoped one day I'd come home to find Boris, bottom bared, waiting for me to spank him. Something would happen. How could it not? Also we lived in Manhattan, where making personal connections is not easy.

Woman proposes – the universe complies.

I was in the laundry room, there in the basement of our co-op building, musing about who to approach with my delicate need for more sex. I considered options. They all seemed very complicated. As I was leaning against the washing machine, feeling how good the spin cycle felt against my centre, I noticed the video camera in the corner of the room. Ah. Dan the

Doorman. Who had nothing to do except sit quietly all day watching various black-and-white television screens for signs of unusual behaviour. Of course. So I began to behave unusually, at least for me. I rubbed my breasts through my clothes and looked into that camera lens. A few minutes later Dan himself stood at the door of the laundry room. It was that simple.

I thought sex with Dan would free me from Boris. But the simple pleasure of getting banged against a washing machine every afternoon wasn't, after all, what got me to leave. It was Marge, a woman who lived in our building's garden apartment. She was old, in her eighties at least. Maybe she felt guilty about being the only tenant with a yard, because she brought us fresh vegetables from her garden all summer long. One Sunday morning she came bearing tomatoes the size of my fist. Boris was out. I asked her in. I put the tomatoes on the sill over the kitchen sink. Before I could thank her she seized my hands in hers.

"Oh, no, you better eat those right up, honey," she said. Her grip was amazingly strong. "Nothing gets better with age!"

So the two of us sat right down at my table and ate those tomatoes. I let the juice drip down my chin. She licked her fingers. A few weeks later Marge died of a heart attack, wearing her gardening gloves. Three weeks after that I was watching Boris sit in his favourite leather armchair, his jaw set, his temple pulsing, drinking a bottle of Evian and watching Sixty Minutes. My neighbour was dead. I thought of her poor fragile life. I thought of how old Mike Wallace looked. Boris drank his water. I thought of leaving him. I thought of killing him.

It is at such times that all things become possible.

II

My mother always told me that I was begotten on Haight Street during the Summer of Love, in a room full of mattresses just four doors down from where Jerry Garcia hung out with his pals. She says my father was either Jack Nicholson or a dead ringer for Jack Nicholson. She is hazy on the details.

I have no proof that any of her stories are true. And despite these infrequent hints of bacchanalia in her past, Mom grew more subdued over the years, until I can hardly imagine her other than as a pearl-wearing Republican. By the time I remember, she and I were living in White Plains, and she was married to Bob, a real estate broker.

In those days there was no talk of sex. There was no sex. I buried my own urges by learning how to play tennis. Thwack, thwack, thwack. Lots of grunting. Not until I was 14 did I finally become cock-sure. It was because of the tennis. There was a local tennis player, Dick Hawkes, who was ranked in the state in mixed doubles. His partner broke her ankle and he read about me in the local sports pages so he called my parents to see if I would play tournaments with him.

"A great opportunity, honey," my stepfather said in his heartiest voice.

Never mind that Dick Hawkes was twice my age. The alarm that would usually have gone off in my stepfather's head was strangely silent. This was sport, damn it. Mr Hawkes wanted to coach me. There could even be a four-year scholarship at the end of it. So Bob and Dick shook hands, right there in our living room. A few minutes later Mr Hawkes and I were off for our first practice session together.

"Call me Hawkso," he said just after we pulled out of the drive. A wave of pity overtook me. We actually did play some tennis that day. By the third game he'd taken his shirt off and draped it on a bench. He had a little belly, some sparse hairs on his chest. He did not look particularly good. But the way he touched me when we changed sides – shoulder, elbow, breast, for God's sake, this was broad daylight, people were on the court next to us – was getting to me. I double-faulted many times. He won the set. "Good play," he said, and shook my hand across the net, sweat dripping from his temples.

On the way home we climbed into the back seat of his Porsche where we made love over a prescient crate of beefsteak tomatoes. What were those tomatoes doing there? Making a mess, I tell you. By the time we were done no amount of bleach would take out the stain on those tennis whites. But I firmly believe those tomatoes had a purpose. Tomatoes are my totem.

For the next four years Hawkso and I played tournaments

together across the state. On the way home we would scramble into his tiny back seat where he would rip my frilly tennis bloomers off and rub them over his face while he ploughed me. Then he would swoop down between my legs and suck and drink and hum on me until I came myself senseless. Or he would nestle his cock between my breasts, which even back then were absurdly huge for my frame, and rock back and forth until he sprayed all over my chin and lips with his come.

I did not win a tennis scholarship. I have lost track of Hawkso since. But Richard, if you are perchance reading these words, thank you for those happy juicy times.

III

"Goodbye, Boris," I said.

"You're on a quest to find your father," my mother shrieked, when I called her from the Newark airport and told her I had left my husband and was about to board a 14 hour flight to Caracas. My mother has always approved of Boris. She calls him "a keeper". But she is wrong. Oh, I was on a quest, maybe. But not to find my father. I wanted Truth. Enlightenment. Perfect Joy. I wanted it over and over again. Is it too much to ask?

When I was younger I used to have great faith in my life working out the way it was supposed to. Whenever I was at a crossroads, something would appear out of the mist to guide me. While I was with Boris I'd forgotten. Now suddenly the world was once more filled with giddy scents and possibilities, signs of what was to come. I found myself having a difficult time refraining from touching everyone in the airport, they all looked so good to me.

At the gate I found myself in line with a group of Japanese businessmen. One gestured grandly to my chest, his hands held before him as if he were supplicating himself before two cantaloupes. I found myself wondering how I might sit next to him on the plane. Alas, I was seated instead next to a ruddy-faced woman in her fifties wearing a navy business suit, on her way to South America to buy antiques. Never mind. We talked. She seemed a safe enough audience, nodding and mm-hmming at just the right intervals. Just as we crossed the border I even let spill a little about Dan, my laundry-room man.

"Oh, honey, you're doing it all wrong!" she said, and looked at me, horrified, over the rims of her demi-glasses. "You just can't have sex like that! The diseases! The consequences!"

At that moment our dinner arrived, complete with precision-wedge tomatoes atop a salad wrapped tightly in yards of plastic wrap.

Ah, I thought. Now I understand. My triptych message was complete. My quest was doomed. But these signs must work in mysterious ways, I argued with myself. Anyway, was I going to let a measly tomato wedge tell me what to think? So I took control right then. I unwrapped that salad. I put a wedge in my mouth and chewed and chewed until it finally spit back its measly juice on my tongue. I tried to hope.

Nevertheless, by the time we landed I was sure I was either dying or pregnant. I must have looked stricken with fear and guilt, because as my companion said goodbye she leaned toward me and kissed me, the slightest edge of her tongue raking over my lips. Then she disappeared into the crowd, trailed by the wheels of her carry-on luggage. But her taste remains, warm, a little salty, as I stand here waiting for my bags. At times like these I understand the natural, beefy roundness of things and I want to weep from the joy of it. But I'm in a foreign country, where the customs are unknown to me, so I'll refrain.

The Whore Gene

Lisa Montanarelli

I love money. No, that's not quite right. I lust after it. As far back as I can remember, I was trading kisses for pennies and nickels on the school playground. My father was a gambler and my mother a whore. One morning when I was about five I walked into their bedroom. They'd been in Monte Carlo for a month, and I'd missed them terribly. I knew they'd gotten back late the night before – long after my bedtime – and I wanted to see them. I heard the squeaking of the bed and heavy breathing. I pushed open the door. My parents were lying naked on a huge pile of money. My father was on top of my mother, who was digging her nails into his back and groaning. I thought he was hurting her and started to cry. They stopped what they were doing immediately and my mother got out of bed naked, money sliding off her body to the floor. She picked me up, carried me over to the bed, and placed a wad of cash in my hand.

"Look," she said. "Your daddy won this money. We're having a good time." Years later, I finally understood what she meant.

Memories like these have been flooding over me lately. Three years ago my mother was charged with pimping and pandering. Rather than go to jail she fled the country, and I haven't heard from her since.

As a kid, I thought about money every night in bed, rubbing the spot on my body that felt so good. When my cunt began aching for something inside it, I slipped coins in. I was a human piggy bank. When I went to the bathroom at school, I'd find coins in my panties – coins I'd put in the night before,

warmed from being inside me. They slipped out of me in class.
When I stood up, they'd slide down my pants leg, as if I had a
hole in my pocket. But no one guessed my secret, and I put
more coins in. They jiggled, clinked, and slipped out onto the
floor when I jumped up and down. I liked the weight of the
cold metal. By the time I was in high school, I was a human
pocket-book, walking around with rolls of dollar bills in my
cunt.

It's not that I can't have sex with people. I can. But there has
to be money involved. Otherwise my body won't do it. I won't
even get wet unless money's nearby. I have to be counting it,
rolling around in a pile of it, or getting paid for sex. I'm the
perfect whore.

Some of the other girls don't think so. I work at the Coochie
Ranch, a legal brothel in Washoe County, Nevada. As far as I
know, I'm the only girl here who actually enjoys having sex for
money. Oh, I'm sure the others do too; they just won't admit it.
They think it's sleazy, degrading. As long as they don't get
turned on with clients, they can pretend they aren't really
whores. It's as if they're saving their virginity: if they don't
have orgasms with customers, they're somehow pure. Gail says
she'd be cheating on her boyfriend if she enjoyed sex with
clients. Lanna says the pimp who turned her out taught her
how to have sex without getting aroused. He got all his friends
to fuck her, while he sat right beside her on the bed, coaching:
"Just think about anything else – beaches, your kids – anything
that doesn't get you hot," he said.

I think it's sad that these girls don't enjoy their work the way
I do, but I keep my secret to myself. Not that I'm ashamed of
it: it makes me one of the top earners at the ranch. Once a guy
comes to my room to talk prices, he rarely ever leaves. Just
talking about money turns me on. As I lead him to the cashier,
I feel his come dripping down my thighs. I rarely ever put
money in the bank. I keep the cash locked in my closet, so that I
can take it out and roll around in it. And when payday comes, I
get a rush as the cashier hands me the money I've been waiting
for all week.

I've been having little orgasms with clients and with the cash
in my closet all week long, but this is the big one I've been

waiting for, tension building in my body. I take the envelope to my room, let the cash spill out on the bed, and run my fingers through it. I start counting and soon lose track of the numbers – lying on the bed, smoothing the loose bills over my chest, stroking my wet pussy lips. Since we can't lock the doors to our rooms, I hide the money under my covers in case anyone walks in. I don't want them to catch me masturbating in a pile of money. Sometimes I go on like this for hours, rolling over the greenbacks, soaking them in my sweat and come.

One day Suzanne, our Madame, calls all the girls into the parlour and announces that a scientist named Dr Maude Baine is coming to live at the brothel to study us. We groan; we've heard all the media hype about her study. She's trying to find the so-called "whore gene" – a gene that determines whether or not someone will become a prostitute. A lot of people think she's a total quack, but she's still getting tons of publicity and government funding. She's been on *Oprah* with a pair of identical twins who were separated at birth. The twins, Vanna and Lanna, wear the same skimpy white dresses and have identical blond perms. Reunited 25 years later, they are shocked to discover that they're both prostitutes. Even more remarkably, they both charge $300 an hour for full service, and their specialities include Greek, golden showers, and strap-on play. All these weird coincidences are supposed to convince us that Vanna and Lanna are genetically predisposed to whoredom.

After the show, prostitutes'-rights activists and geneticists criticize her work, claiming that identical twin whores simply aren't common enough to be statistically significant. Several whores come forward and claim that Vanna and Lanna met several years earlier and only became working girls after meeting Dr Baine. But despite widespread criticism and accusations of fraud, Dr Baine wins more grant money to study whore twins, and Vanna and Lanna quit prostitution and start a business making T-shirts and bumper stickers that say "Genes 'R' Pimps". They donate 30 per cent of their proceeds to Dr Baine's research.

Suzanne says we all have to participate in the study and consent to being interviewed by Dr Baine.

"Why?" asks Sheila, as we groan in unison.

"Because her project is funded by the federal government, and the brothel is making a lot of money off her," says Suzanne.

"But what do we get out of it?" Justine asks.

"You might get some money for your participation."

"She should pay us as much as our customers," says Justine, "since she's taking up our time."

"We'll see about that," says Suzanne.

When Dr Baine arrives Suzanne calls all the girls into the parlour again. Dr Baine looks prim and schoolmarmish in her tailored gray business suit and pince-nez. She explains her study in the simplest terms, as though we're children. She's trying to find the gene that determines whether or not you become a prostitute. This gene, she says, accounts for the occurrence of prostitution throughout history and in all cultures.

"I am not a prostitute!" shouts Marla. "I'm only here for another week to make some money to support my kids. Then I'm outta here!"

"Yeah!" says Victoria. "What are you calling 'whore' anyway? Do we have the same gene as streetwalkers and gay hustlers and geishas? Do wives have the 'whore gene' because they get money from one man instead of hundreds? Are you looking for a 'wife gene' too?"

The other girls laugh and nod.

Dr Baine pauses. She wasn't expecting these questions from girls who worked in a brothel. She didn't think we'd been following the controversy, but we'd all been watching the TV interviews and her appearance on *Oprah*.

Finally she continues: "I'm surprised and delighted that some of you are familiar with the issues surrounding my study. I hope that this study will benefit you and prostitutes all over the world. People may show more tolerance when they discover that prostitution is not necessarily something we can change about ourselves. It is a genetic predisposition, occurring naturally throughout the animal kingdom. Even female penguins trade sex in exchange for stones to build their nests."

"So if you think those penguins are prostitutes, why don't

women who marry for money and security count as prostitutes?" asks Victoria.

"I *chose* to be a sex worker!" yells Clara. "And I can change my mind if I want. I wasn't forced into it by anyone or anything!"

Lauren raises her hand and asks, "What if they start testing everyone for the 'whore gene' and aborting foetuses that have it? The 'whore gene' could be used as evidence to convict people of solicitation and lock them in prison or in psychiatric wards and deny them insurance coverage, or give them pharmaceutical drugs."

"Yeah," shouts a chorus of whores.

"I understand your concerns," Dr Baine says confidently. "And I'm going to patent the results, so I'll have some control over how they're used."

Does she think we're stupid?

For the next few days, Dr Baine hangs around the parlour of the Coochie Ranch, wearing business suits and jotting things down in her notebook. She interviews the girls who want to talk to her first. I notice her looking at me. I think it's my imagination, but after a few more days I see she's staring at me every time I come into the parlour. I wish I could just stay out of that room. I avoid her gaze. She tries to stop me in the hall, but I pretend I don't hear. Why is she singling me out?

The next day I'm sitting in the parlour waiting for customers to ring the bell. Clara stomps out of her interview and flops down next to me on the couch, pouting.

"So, what did that crazy bitch want from you?" I ask her.

"She wanted to meet my family!" says Clara. "She wants to test them for the whore gene too! She said she'd pay me $1,000 for each parent or sibling and two-fifty apiece for cousins. I told her no way! None of those people know I work in a brothel!"

Later on I'm walking down the hall, and I see Dr Baine coming the other way. I quickly duck into my room. She knocks on my door.

"Who is it?" I ask, gritting my teeth.

"It's Dr Baine. Please open the door."

I swing the door open. She jumps back, startled by the look on my face.

"What do you want?" I ask.

"I'd like to interview you, Wanda."

"No chance. I want my privacy." I slam the door.

A few minutes later, there's another knock.

"Wanda. It's Suzanne."

"Hi, Suzanne. Come on in."

She sits down on my bed.

"Dr Baine said you won't let her interview you."

"Why should I?"

Suzanne sighs and shakes her head.

"Bill wants that woman here, and he owns the ranch. You're one of our best girls, but if you don't talk to her, you might lose your job."

Grudgingly, I knock on Dr Baine's door.

"Come in."

She's sitting stiffly behind her desk with her pince-nez and her hair up in a bun. I feel like I've been sent to the school principal's office for misbehaviour.

"Have a seat," she says, eyeing me up and down.

Silently I sit down in front of her desk.

"Wanda," she says. "I realize you've been avoiding me, so let me get right to the point: you're exactly the kind of person I need in my study."

"What do you mean?"

She looks me directly in the eye. "Excuse me for being blunt, but one of the other girls told me your mother was also a prostitute."

So that was it. I figured as much.

"So," she says, still staring at me. "Is that true?"

"Yes."

"Well, is your mother still alive?"

"Yes."

"I want you to introduce me to her."

"I'm afraid I can't do that." I have a gut feeling that if I tell this woman my mother is a fugitive, she might try to track her down.

"Before you give me a definite no, I think you should hear the whole offer." Dr Baine stands up and sets a black briefcase on her desk. She turns the key in the lock and lifts the top. My jaw drops. Stacks of money – freshly minted $100 bills. This briefcase contains tens of thousands of dollars – more money than I've ever seen. I can't take my eyes off it. I'm going to come just from looking at it. My pants are getting wet.

Dr Baine walks slowly around her desk, sits down beside me, and puts her hand on my thigh.

"Wanda," she says, "all this is yours on two conditions – if you introduce me to your mother, and if you have sex with me."

I swallow hard. She leans forward, trying to look me in the eye, but I can't. I'm losing it.

"Wanda," she continues, stroking my thigh, "I want you and your mother to be on *Oprah* with me, and I'm going to pay you $30,000 under the table."

That's it. My cunt contracts, and I come hard and long. As little as I trust this woman, it's all I can do not to fall into her arms.

After I come, all I want is to get out of there. I steady myself on my feet.

"You've got a deal," I say, shutting the door behind me.

I stumble down the hall to my room and lie down in my bed. I can hardly believe what just happened and all I have to do.

First I have to find someone to play the part of my mother. This isn't so hard. I take the next morning off and visit Madame LeAnn at the brothel down the road. I've known her for ten years, and she's glad to help. I tell her everything and promise that she'll get some money out of it too.

"I know someone who can make me a fake ID in 48 hours," she says.

"That should work, unless Dr Baine checks with the police and finds out my real mom's a fugitive."

"I doubt she'll do that," says LeAnn.

"But when she checks the DNA samples, she'll be able to tell you're not my mom."

"My advice to you," says LeAnn, "is to get the money up front, fuck this woman, and run."

When I get back to the Coochie Ranch, Dr Baine's standing in the parlour with her notebook and her gray business suit, eyeing me up and down. I stop and glance at her awkwardly.

"My mother can see you in two days," I say.

She smiles approvingly. "Thank you, Wanda."

Two days later, LeAnn and I knock on Dr Baine's door. I'm carrying my toy bag – full of stuff I can use on Dr Baine when we have sex. LeAnn has a fake driver's licence. Dr Baine sets the briefcase on the top of her desk and opens it. We don't have time to count all the bills, but she invites us to leaf through them and check the watermarks. I take out my counterfeit bill detector and check some random greenbacks. My pants are moist, my cunt lips trembling. It feels so incestuous, since I'm supposedly here with my mom.

When I'm satisfied, Dr Baine asks for our IDs. She copies them on a Xerox machine and gets us to sign contracts agreeing to participate in the study and exempting her from all liability. We start the interview. She asks LeAnn about her experiences as a whore. LeAnn speaks from personal experience. Then Dr Baine asks how she feels about her daughter being a whore. LeAnn smiles at me with pride and squeezes my hand. I squirm, trying not to stare at the money. Finally the doctor takes our DNA samples. I admire her professionalism throughout this process. Nothing in her manner would lead me to believe that, in less than an hour, she and I will be rolling naked in $30,000 cash.

After taking the samples, she excuses my "mother", who kisses me on the cheek and leaves me and Dr Baine sitting across the desk from each other, the briefcase in between us.

"So, Wanda," she begins, "you've finished the first half. Now tell me what really turns you on."

"All I want to do," I say, "is roll in that money."

"In that case, follow me into the bedroom." She picks up the briefcase. I follow her into the other room, where she lies down on the king-sized bed. She opens the briefcase and dumps the money on her chest. The loose bills spill onto the bed around her.

"Now come and get me," she says.

Shaking, I touch the money – freshly minted bills. They slip between my fingers and stick to each other like thick paper. I spread them over her grey business suit and watch them curve over her breasts. She moans, moving slowly under me, like a well-tuned instrument. For the first time, I notice what a babe she is. She takes off her glasses and spreads her long, light-brown hair over the pillow. I reach through the bills, unbutton her jacket, and open it like a shell. The bills slide off onto the bed. I gather them up and smooth them across her grey silk shirt. They slide more easily, and her eyes go wild.

Now we're sitting up on the bed, taking off our clothes, picking up wads of bills and smoothing them over each other's skin.

"Show me what you can do," she says. "Show me how good you are."

I empty my toy bag at the foot of the bed. I fasten cuffs around her wrists and ankles, chain her to the bed, and blindfold her. I need to make her be still, because everything's moving too fast. Trembling, I can hardly believe what's happening to me. It's like finding a lost dream – one that I lost so long ago that I'd forgotten I missed it.

"Fuck me! Please fuck me!" she pleads. I strap on my harness with a thick black dildo. Spreading greenbacks between us, like lettuce in a sandwich, I lie down on top of her and start fucking her slowly, feeling the bills crumple between us.

"Harder!" she begs, and I pump hard into her, pounding her. We're sweating, and the money is sticking to our stomachs and chests. She squirts all over my thighs. I pull out. The air is thick with cunt juice, and the money underneath her is sopping wet. I pick up the dripping bills and stick them to her breasts like papier-mâché.

"I'm making a plaster cast – of your whole body."

She laughs. But I'm not lying. I cover the entire front of her torso in wet bills – then her neck and face. I replace the blindfold with wet money, so that she still can't see. But the money on her face keeps moving and falling off as she smiles and laughs.

"Be still," I say.

"I can't help it." She breaks out laughing. "It smells like pee!"

"Don't move. I'm serious!" I wrap a $100 bill around her shoulder. This woman made of money is so perfect. I worship her, kiss her all over – my money goddess, who drinks up our juices with her skin. Slowly I move my hands over her whole body – wishing this could last forever.

Five hours later we kiss goodbye.

"See you tomorrow," she says. I walk out with a briefcase full of money soaked in cunt juice. It's heavy, but almost all the bills are still in one piece. I smile, thinking about how I'm going to travel across the country, cashing $100 bills that smell like come and piss. I stop by my room just to pick up the cash I have stowed in my closet and a few things I'll need on the road. Leaving the rest of my belongings, I sneak out of the brothel and spend the night in LeAnn's trailer. We stay up late, laughing about the wet money, counting and talking. I fall asleep that night thinking of Maude Baine wrapped in wet money.

I wake up thinking about her and run my hand along the soft, wet groove of my pussy. Over breakfast, I tell LeAnn I'm going to call Dr Baine's office. She looks at me funny over the scrambled eggs. I dial the number. Her secretary answers.

"Dr Baine left this morning for a conference in Mexico. She'll be back in a week."

I hang up and turn to Dolores. "She's gone for a week. Maybe we don't have to leave town right away."

"You crazy girl," she says. "I say we go, before she finds out I'm not your mom." After breakfast, we take off across the desert in her RV. We drive all that day and the next. We're making great time, but I'm still thinking about Maude Baine. I want to see her again, and I can't shake it. She's the woman of my dreams and of all that crap I haven't believed since I was a teenager. I picture myself going back to the brothel and telling her that LeAnn isn't my real mother – apologizing, begging her to forgive me. Just let me be near you. We can share the money.

It's all only fantasy, but LeAnn looks at me and shakes her

head. "I swear, Wanda. In the ten years I've known you, I've never seen you like this."

That second day we pull into a gas station at dusk. LeAnn gets out to fill the tank. She comes back with a newspaper.

"Hey, Wanda. Take a look at this!"

I read the headline: "Renowned Geneticist Embezzles $50,000 in Federal Funds."

Investigators were searching for Maude Baine, who allegedly fled the country on a plane to Mexico the day before.

I look at LeAnn in shock.

"Looks like we better keep moving," she says.

Show Time

Julia Peters

I'm in the middle of being a dutiful girlfriend when I finally tell Paul we've just got to break up. He nearly drops the figurine he's holding, a ceramic superhero. I'm helping him pick out presents for his twin cousins in Maine at a movie theme store we'd never go to otherwise.

"I can't do this any more," I say. I mean us and the store, but I mostly mean us. All this boyfriend-girlfriend crap we do isn't any fun. A Midwestern family of eight pushes past us to stand right in front of the escalators and begins a loud, confused debate about whether to go up or down.

"Ann," he says. "This is a really bad time to start this discussion." He looks exhausted, his auburn hair and dark eyes both rumpled after a long day. He looks down sadly at the floor and notices a pair of yellow cartoon canary slippers with stupid plush eyes. He squats down next to them and looks up at me. "Are these appropriate for a twelve-year-old?"

"Very. So's this whole damn store." I glance around and just see a blur. They've rigged up fake vines and cardboard cut-outs swinging on mechanized ropes to push merchandise for a kids' movie about the jungle. It's six o'clock and I have to head to my waitressing job in two hours. Twenty-four hour French food. What a mess.

"Hey, I told you it was OK if you didn't come. I knew you'd get all New Yorker-than-thou. I just, I trust your opinion."

"I'm sorry. I hate those slippers."

The mother of the Midwesterners, who has a winged haircut and several plastic shopping bags, directs the rest of them upstairs. I hear her say, "How often do you get to see original animation art?" Her husband and the kids, some of them, I realize, friends of the daughter, happily step on the escalator and glide up to the top floor.

"Fuck the slippers," Paul says. "You're saying you want to break up."

"You're right," I say. "We shouldn't talk about this here."

"Well, it's too late for that. I want to talk about it now."

"I have to head to work soon."

"OK. We'll go for a walk. Could we get this out of the way first, though? If you do dump me, I'm not coming back here by myself."

We leave with bags full of backpacks and stickers and emerge into Times Square. The sun sets like a long good-bye and the billboard glow is just starting to take effect. Everyone is in a line or in the push. Either way, it's wall-to-wall bodies, looking ahead, looking up. We circle the same few blocks again and again. I steal glances at Paul as we talk. His carefully shined boots, something he does so they'll let him wear them at work. The side of his strong jaw. The faintest touch of his stomach beneath a green sweater. I watch his parts as he listens to me drone on. He drones on in response, stuff we've been over before, long lists that boil down to shared unhappiness.

Times Square is dying out of its decay, being reborn into safe, fake glory. Used to be you couldn't walk across Forty-second without getting your pocket picked or worse. Not that I miss that. But it's like the whole city got a boob job. It used to be less than perfect, but definitely suckable. Now it's this bigger-than-life, aerodynamic knockout, but without any feeling in its nipples. Paul's less than perfect, but suckable. I'm nuts about Paul. I'm bored as Paul's girlfriend.

We end up standing in front of the wonderful, ugly Port Authority, lingering there since my train stop is deep inside it. All kinds of young men prowl along the edges of the terminal.

"OK, we're back where we started," I say. "I like you but I don't like us as a couple."

"I can't keep having this conversation, Ann," he says.

"Do you want a break?"

"I don't want to have this conversation any more. I want

more time in the day. I want to do all the stuff we keep saying we'll do."

"Like?" A car hesitates in the taxi lane and everyone attacks it with honks and curses. The licence plate is New York. Go figure.

"I don't know," he continues over the cacophony. "Teach you chess. Go to the beach. Our jobs are just so fucked up . . ."

"Well, Show World's right over there. That takes ten minutes." I'm mostly kidding when I say this, watching the marquee wink at me from around the corner in red plastic letters. But I've always been curious and Paul knows it. Paul knows something else too. He's staring at me like his grandmother just walked in on him having sex. Oh. "When's the last time you went there?"

He looks around at the sidewalk, at the buses creaking out of Port Authority. "Three weeks ago."

"Really?"

"Yeah. You know I do that."

"Not lately," I reply, sounding a little angrier than I want. "You could have told me."

"Yeah," he says. It's a weird *yeah*, both *yeah, I'm sorry*, and *yeah, right*.

"No, It's OK. I mean, you know I'd be into it. But I understand it's like, your thing."

The crowd continues to brush by us. We're just a detour in their collective path. Paul stands with my hand in his. There are so many ways he could go. He looks past me at the marquee, at the many possibilities of taking his girlfriend with him into the small rooms he doesn't discuss.

"I'll go with you," he says. Before I know what I'm doing, I say OK. If we're going to break up, at least I'll have been to Show World before it gets zoned out of existence.

We're in a dark, empty hall on the third floor. Steps lead up to a large, bright room full of pool tables, but there aren't any balls or cues. Not much left since the new laws took effect, re-zoning the sex clubs in favour of the citizens, or at least the tourists. Paul plays tour guide for what used to be the centre of Times Square sleaze. Now to stay open it has to shut down most of its operations and add in a dime store downstairs.

We've already toured the fanciful circus sculptures, the long moaning hallway where the video booths still run, and a whole floor that is just empty and silent.

"What used to be up here?"

"A main stage with live performances, and a larger theatre with dancing."

"Live performances?" I ask.

"Sex shows."

"Oh. Really?"

"Well, yeah, but not that real. Pretty real, sometimes, people just going at it, a guy and a girl, two girls. But I was never into that so much. The booths are a whole different thing, but the shows were a real spectacle."

"What are the booths like?" I ask.

"Hmm. They're whatever you want with someone who's only there for you, but you can't connect with them. Sometimes it feels like you can, though."

"Well, looks like the booths are all we've got," I say. He asks me if I'm sure and I gesture toward the hall. Paul puts his arm around my shoulder and leads on.

"What do you want me to do?" Paul asks. He stands facing me in the dull black cubicle. Two people can come in here, but it's obviously built for one.

"Oh, God," I say. "Whatever you'd normally do. This isn't for me." The wall I'm pushed up against is like a cold hand on my back. His face doesn't look that great in this light, a bare bulb hanging over us, but his body is tense and sweet beneath his clothes. A small stool sits in the corner.

"It's for you," he says, and smiles at me, a hint of hurt in a smile that could bloom into anything. There's a surge of noise, like a subway car straining into motion after a mid-tunnel halt. The partition that separates us from the girl on the other side rises slowly with a mechanized clatter. I can feel the vibration of the rising screen in my feet. I can feel how many times it's been cranked up before.

Her name is Miranda, at least that's what she said when we chatted and chose her in a few moments of friendly negotiation. I see her in pieces as the partition goes up: arched bare feet with bright blue toenails, smooth calves, kind of chunky

thighs, turquoise panties and lace bra that almost match, cute
tits as she immediately strips off the bra. Her hair is in shiny,
almost oily curls around a heart-shaped face. Her lipstick is
bright pink and glossy, her smile seems genuine. She's in
another spare, closet-like room like ours, with a stool and a
shelf full of toys and oils. Paul bought us eight minutes, no
penetration on her. We can do whatever we want, she told him,
although if we get caught she never said that. The digital clock
on her side of the screen, facing us, changes from 0:00 to 8:00.
"Hi," she says wordlessly, pointedly to me. She's done this a
million times. Hell, so has Paul. I suddenly feel like maybe I
should leave them alone. I smile weakly at her.

Paul watches for a moment, smiling, and then glances over at
me. He doesn't know what to do or which want to follow and
neither do I, but, "Do it," I say. He sighs as if someone's
touched him, and turns back to the glass and the girl behind it.
Paul unzips his pants, quickly pulls out his cock. It is completely different how he does it here than when he's done it for
me. Not a striptease, just, boom, his cock. And we're off.

What happens next is a delicious blur of acrobatics. Miranda
immediately hops up on the stool and throws her legs up in the
air. She parts them in a clean, cheerleader "V" – go team! – and
peels her panties off. There is her pussy. Paul keeps stroking,
accepting that I'm OK with this and just going with the fact
that there's a naked woman in front of him. She hangs her head
to one side and grins crookedly, teeth just made for toothpaste,
then puts her feet against the glass. She's spread open, while
I'm all crunched up in the corner. Miranda bends down, holds
each of her ankles in one slim hand. Her knees are bent. Her
wide smile is for my boyfriend, as if she were on her back in
bed, holding her legs open wide for him. I've done that. With a
deliberateness that makes me forget there's only six and a half
minutes left, she slides her slick, pink fingernails along her
ankles, then inside her knees, then inside her thighs. The skin
looks so soft there, like it's nearly liquid.

I really want him. The little clock says we have four minutes
and change. I don't want to get in the way. I keep watching.
Miranda slides down to the floor, places her hands around his
cock and licks the glass in broad strokes, her ass moving as if

someone's fucking her from behind. "Come on," she says, and starts to slap the glass with her hands, as if to pound through it and get to him. Paul laughs, his cock moves up so it's almost flat against the leather of his belt. He's close, but he's being watched, so it's still going to take him a while. I really want him.

"Fuck her," I say. My boyfriend stops, his penis still in the firm, familiar grip of his own hand, and turns toward me.

"What?" he asks. I'm interrupting, all right.

"Fuck her," I say and in two steps I'm there, pressed against the glass, as fully clothed as him. I pull my skirt up roughly, just enough to get to my panties, pull them aside. No strip-tease, just clearing a path. I bring my leg up around him to rest solidly on his flat hip, feeling the leather of his belt against my calf. My leg starts to slide down and he catches it, stares at me for moment. His hand slides down to my ankle, deliberately, so I know as he grabs it too tight, as he pushes my leg back up around him, that he's saying yes.

"God, this is pornography," I say quietly. His cock is rubbing against me now as he fishes in his pocket for the condom that is usually in his wallet.

"Is that good?" he asks, finding it, getting it on.

"Oh, yeah." Arrest me, I think. Better yet, re-zone me. Keep me at least 50 yards away from a school, church, or residential housing at all times.

"Fuck her," I say, which is what I mean. He keeps his eyes on me for one more moment, smiling a little as he finds the edge of my panties and pulls them aside. He pushes in, he gets inside his girl and we both hold in our gasp. As he starts to rock me, all slammed up against the bulletproof glass, I take his face in my hands and push it back up to look at her.

Miranda has taken her cue well, taken it all. She has been behind me, straddling the stool, her face just behind mine but looking down at me. She let us have this together, a point of entry into her. Now, he's all hers again. I turn half to the glass and watch out of the corner of my eye. Miranda scoots her feet up onto the stool's edge and throws her hands up over her head as if welcoming the sun. She presses them against the glass. Her gestures are dramatic but I realize they also help her keep her balance. She's scrunched up now, knees to chest, hands pressed high above us all while I'm spread out against her. She carefully pushes up until she's standing, balanced on the stool. They're both over me.

We're all breathing hard in time with Paul's thrusts, in time with our seconds slipping by. He slides his hand into the cup of my lower back and seals me against him, against his sweaty clothes and one hot bit of bare skin. Paul holds me tight and pushes into me, and into the girl behind me. She's pressed her breasts against the glass and thrown her head back, she's tickling her naked clit with her nails once again. He can pretend I'm her, a girl for pay, a sweet slut, a gorgeous, underpaid nymphomaniac. And maybe also he gets to do it and see it at the same time, as if it's all the same thing.

We don't have much time. I want to see but I want to make him come, so I pull him against me, one hand bracing his ass and the other snaking around the base of his cock, feeling my panties rumpled against my thumb. Paul's mouth falls open and his inhales become shocked, boyish gasps. Miranda drops down so she's squatting on the stool right behind me, as if I could lean back and be held in her slim arms. I barely see her glossy lips, her tongue running over them, then she and Paul move. She's rocking her hips against the air and I know she's telling him *come inside me, yeah baby, fuck me, come, baby, deep inside, that's it, I'm coming with you, yeah, yeah,* and he says it out loud in my ear and moves my head so it's hugged against the side of his neck and he presses his face hard against my shoulder, looking at her, and he comes and comes and comes.

I hold him there as he trembles and I try to suck air back into my lungs. There's a dull thud. We both look up hazily to see the partition coming back down again. Miranda, sweaty and smiling, waves goodbye.

I can barely look at him but I have to ask.

"Good?"

He laughs and stuffs the condom back inside the foil packet, wads it into his wallet again. "Not what I usually get here."

Paul zips back up and wipes his face with the sleeve of his sweater. I'm standing in the centre of the room, a little dazed. It occurs to me that the woman we were just with has a whole life I'll never know anything about. Maybe she likes doing this, maybe it's her ticket, maybe it's hell.

When I look up, he's looking down at the floor, nervous like I just was.

"Did you?" he asks.

"What, baby?"

"Did you?"

"Oh. It's OK."

"Do you want to?"

"Yeah, but, Paul, that was for you. It's cool. Honest."

Sometimes this is true and sometimes it's not. Right now I'm all wound up and confused and we have no time. "Hold on one second."

He opens the door and walks quickly into the hall. I'm scared at first, then I hear him say hello. A woman's voice returns the greeting. It's Miranda.

"I really can't do that," I hear her say.

"You can't?" Paul asks. There is a silence and then more gentle words on both sides. I hear the soft click of high heels retreating, as he pulls the door open with an uneasy metal creak. He steps back in, shuts it behind him. Paul gets the footstool from the corner and smacks it down in front of me.

"We have six more minutes," he says.

"How much did that cost you?" I ask.

"Shut up, baby," he says and presses his whole body against me, from forehead to lips to cock to toes.

"I don't have anything," I say, meaning this is not what I thought would happen today. I thought we would buy keychains and hats with famous logos and then break up. I have no protection on me or in me, and he was only carrying the one condom. Then I'm worried because I've never been able to come standing up, and I sure as hell don't want to lie down on this floor.

"We don't need anything," he says and grabs my leg, lifts it up and slams my foot down on the footstool, spreading me open.

He crumples down in a smooth movement to crouch at my crotch, pulls my skirt up, pushes my panties aside again, and kisses me square on my pussy.

"Use me," he says, and uses one fat hand to pull me against his mouth by my ass. "Make yourself come with my mouth." I can't come standing up. I think this for a minute, then replay the last few minutes in my head and start to move against him as he starts to kiss me there. Jesus, he does this well. He kisses my clit as if it's every part of me, a sweet kiss like on my forehead, deep licks like it's my mouth, then wet, sweet sucking as if on a nipple, as if he sucks my clit to stay alive. I start to moan in the quiet little room. I wonder if a woman has ever been in here before.

Paul pulls away for one evil moment and replaces his mouth with his fingers so he can get out a good line: "You think this is for me. Fuck that. Fuck me, Ann," and with that he dives back into the underworld of my cunt. It works. He does me with his hand and mouth, his tongue lapping at my clit. I like it in here, all dark with the dim blue light, without the other side of the partition glaring through at us. I'm thinking about Miranda, on her knees, how good she was, pounding on the glass and getting to us without one single touch.

I grab his head and rub myself against his lips, his tongue, against his chin. He stops moving his mouth for a minute. Maybe he's surprised. Maybe he's just letting me use his head like a cat uses a scratching post. Paul's my whore for the next few minutes, and he's even paying for it. He begins to lick me again, following my motions. He grips my thighs, then wraps his arms around my hips with a moan and does everything he knows I like, for both of us, and something about being held like that, something about his face smashed up against me in this little room, something about him being my whore, for – I look at the clock – just under a minute, makes it start. I take his wrist and move his hand between my legs so I can feel him inside me as I start to contract around his fingers, as I start to whimper and sound kind of stupid and feel really fucking amazing. I come like a circus, whirling lights and flying through the air, bucking my body shamelessly on his fingers and mouth, hard, rapid, painful. I grab his hair in my hands, hold his head and give him all of it. The clock clicks down to zero and I'm still finishing.

"Oh, my God," I say, panting hard. Paul looks up, his lips and chin wet, a grin of "look what I just did to you" on his face.

"Oh, my God, Paul. Should we get out of here?"

"Let's not find out," he says, stands up and lets me fall back into place. He opens the door and peers out, reaches back for me with his hand, takes it when I give it to him. He leads me out the way we came.

"What was all that for?" I ask him, laughing. We're in the lobby, having made our escape from the cubicle of love. A few men, different types, mill around aimlessly, probably heading up to where we just were. We walk past the newest addition, a bizarre storefront on the first floor that must have sold videos or peepshows before. Two stock boys are pushing a cart full of "I Love New York" paraphernalia through the doorway.

"I don't know. I always wanted to do that. You always wanted to do that. So now we've done it," Paul says. He checks inside the shopping bags to make sure everything is still there.

"There's my problem," I say.

"That's a problem?"

"Yeah. When I like something I usually want to do it again."

Paul stands and looks at me underneath a fake circus bear wearing a clown hat, balanced on a tightrope. We hear all kinds of soft, pre-recorded moans coming from the rows of video booths.

"Well," Paul says brightly, "let's have lots of one-night stands."

"That could be hard."

"I know," he says, looking happy in a conversation with me for the first time in weeks, looking like he used to. "But, I mean, I'm crazy about you. That was fun. We're a lousy couple and we don't want to break up. I want to see other people but I don't want you to," he adds.

"Same here."

"That's very male of you, Ann," he says.

"Ooh," I say. "We could pay each other. $20 for 10 minutes of whatever we want. Pass it back and forth."

"And you won't feel cheap?"

"Well. Maybe. Won't you?"

"Yeah. I kind of like that."

"I know. Wow. This is nuts."

We walk back out into a city that is so lit up it looks like a summer day. We've lit the night up so well that there's no more night.

"Where can we go now?"

"Where do you want to go?"

The unspoken options perch on our shoulders and glare at us, just as our shopping bags and fears weigh us down. Part company or keep going. Call in sick to work tonight, the one thing that is certain for me. Go talk some more or find a place to fuck. An hourly motel, the park, home. I don't know what to pick, so I kiss him, just, boom, my tongue down his throat, tasting myself in his mouth right out here on the street. There's so much to deconstruct and discuss, but after all this I just want to kiss him, just want to do whatever can make us both happy, whether it's OK or not. So I close my eyes and move forward, turning off all these damn lights. We wrap our arms around each other and go back into the darkness.

Progressive Party

Alison Tyler

1

Max and I stood outside the old Victorian, shivering together in the chilly December air. The house was lit with candles and holiday lights, every window sill festooned with festive decorations.

"What's this called again?" Max asked.

"A progressive party."

"And what precisely does that mean?"

"Each apartment has a different theme. You progress from room to room –"

"And from state of arousal to state of arousal?"

From inside the building, we could hear sounds of laughter and the steady beat of rock 'n roll coming from the converted apartments.

"Ready?" I smiled.

"Almost ready –" he said, nodding up toward the sprig of mistletoe dangling right overhead. "Just one more thing." His strong arms came around my body, pulling me close. I could feel his warmth, the heat emanating from the core of his body, and I could feel something else, too –

2

Max's hard cock wanted instant attention. As soon as we entered the front hall of the converted building, I looked around for a quiet space.

"Over there –"

We made our way to the dark corner below a coat rack, where I immediately dropped to my knees and undid Max's fly.

"Pretty baby," Max sighed as I introduced his erection to the warm, wet heat of my mouth. He twisted his fingers in my glossy curls as I bobbed my head up and down. "That's perfect," he groaned, as I kept up the rhythm. I'd have brought him over the brink if a couple hadn't made their way down the stairs right then, reaching over us to grab their coats from the rack. As I quickly stood up, Max fumbled for explanations and for a way to slyly tuck himself back into his pants.

"New strand of mistletoe," Max said, pointing toward the greenery nearby.

"There's a lot of that going around," the lady grinned, nodding towards the open door of the first apartment. "You're going to enjoy yourselves," she assured us –

3

Jasmine's apartment was the first door on the left. Her theme was Retro Hawaiian, and the guests within were drinking from glasses decorated with tiny paper umbrellas. Jasmine and her girlfriend Diva were both clad in grass skirts and bikini tops. Diva's dark skin shimmered with body glitter and Jasmine's plentiful tattoos were on full display.

"Aloha," Diva grinned at me, reaching for my coat. She nuzzled her lips against the back of my neck in a sweet, sultry greeting. Max caught my eye as he gave Jasmine a similar sort of hello kiss.

On one of Jasmine's blue velvet couches, I noticed two feline women in a slinky embrace. The blonde had her hand up under her lover's dress, and her partner moaned and shifted her hips in a restless beat.

"The party's already started," Diva said, "make yourselves comfortable."

"I want to say hello to Sylvan first," Max told me, grabbing me by the wrist and pulling me after him into –

4

Disco Inferno.

That's what Sylvan's party theme was. A mirrored ball spun overhead and the music was straight out of the 70s. Grooving on the dance floor were couples clad in various stages of undress. And right in the centre, were two lovers entirely naked and deeply entwined.

"They couldn't wait −" Sylvan explained.

I leaned back against Max's body, feeling his erection pressed against my ass. His hands came up and began stroking my breasts through the thin fabric of my dress. His fingers pinched my nipples firmly, and I closed my eyes and moaned.

"Maybe we should find somewhere more private," Max whispered.

"Like a coat room?"

"Like a bedroom."

"Let's try down the hall −"

5

But when we got there, we found two couples had already staked their claim to Sylvan's California King. My pussy pulsed at the picture before us − a *moving* picture of four pretty people in a passion play like none other. One well-built man sprawled in the centre of the bed on his back. A striking redhead rode his cock, her legs parted, thighs tight as she worked him. Behind her, a blue-haired minx with multiple piercings was intent on licking the nape of the redhead's neck, moving lower and lower. The fourth member of the party, a well-hung stud with dark skin and razor-cut hair, stood on the mattress with his cock poised right in front of the redhead's parted lips. Between bucks on her lover, she took sucks from this man's glistening penis.

"Oh, man −" Max murmured. "Too pretty −"

"Too busy," I corrected him. "You know. No room at the Inn −"

6

So we headed to the next apartment, where a theme of "Hotel California" awaited us. Plenty of pink champagne on ice and a sign over the door that said, "you can never leave". Based on the erotic atmosphere in the room, I couldn't think why anyone would want to. Max put one hand around my waist and began to move me to the steady, hypnotic melody.

"I like the way you look in that," he murmured, admiring my sleek silver sheath as we danced.

"Do you?"

"But I especially like these," he told me, reaching within the bodice of my dress to tug at the delicate nipple clamps attached within.

I sighed as he pulled, and then groaned as he tightened each clamp, upping the intensity of the experience. My panties were now drenched and when I whispered this fact to Max, he said, "Then let's deal with that, shall we?"

"How?"

"Follow me –"

7

I trailed after him towards the pink-and-white tiled bathroom. Max ushered me inside and then pulled my red satin panties down and waited for me to step out of them. On his knees in front of me, he gently parted my pussy lips and began to lick in long, slow strokes. I closed my eyes and braced myself, surprised when a nearby moan surpassed my own.

"Oh, yes!"

Who was talking? Quickly, opening my eyes, I gazed around the room, finally locking onto the intercom on the wall. Another couple must have been getting frisky near the other pair of this intercom set. Breathless, I listened to the steady build of these nameless, faceless lovers as Max now slipped two wet fingers deep inside me.

"Oh, do that –" the woman urged, and I immediately echoed her.

"Yes, Max," I crooned, "Do that!"

"That?" he asked, wiggling his fingers happily within me.

"Or this –?" he murmured, and suddenly I felt something sweetly vibrating against me –

8

To my surprise and delight, Max had slid a Fukuoku vibe on his finger. Now the soft pad of the toy was pressed deliciously against my clit. Immediately, waves of pure pleasure flowed through me. With my heart racing I had to hold onto the counter of the sink to keep myself steady. Max stood right behind me, still stroking my clit with his magical vibrating finger. When I looked into the mirror, I saw a heat building in my gaze.

"You like that?"

I nodded, unable to speak. The sensation was incredible.

"Now, think about how good that's going to feel when I fuck you –"

A knock on the door stopped our risqué games, and Max and I hurried to fix our appearances and vacate the place.

But where to?

9

"Fire escape," Max said, and we rushed back through Sylvan's apartment. The whole time I was quite obviously aware of how wet I was, how ready to play. My vision blurred as we made our way out of the open window to the fire escape. Here, we could see the beauty of the city, all lit up for the holiday season. But we were more concerned with the beauty of fucking. Max ripped open the button-fly of his jeans, revealing his hard-on.

I bent over the cold metal railing as he lifted my dress in back and slid inside me. I realized that my panties were still on the floor of the bathroom, but then let go of that thought as Max reached again to tug on the nipple clamps. Each pull sent an instant spasm of pleasure that began in my pussy, then radiated throughout my body. When Max brought his vibrator-clad finger to the front of my body, teasing my clit with it as he fucked me in his long, steady strokes, I came.

And just in time, too –

10

"You lovebirds hogging the view?" Danielle asked us, sliding outside with her girlfriend Brandi. While I nodded energetically, Max worked to tuck himself back into his slacks.

"Someone's turned on," Danielle laughed, and Max quickly flicked off the motor of the vibrator and pulled it off his hand. I felt heat rush to my cheeks, but then, as Danielle and Brandi began making out, a different kind of heat assailed me. Brandi tucked two fingers under Danielle's leather collar and tugged hard. When she began to nibble her way down the inside of Danielle's throat, Max nudged me. But I wasn't ready to leave. I watched until Danielle brought her wrists behind her back and Brandi instantly captured them with a set of silver cuffs, running the chain through the railing to keep her lover in place. Time to give them some privacy.

"We haven't been outside yet," he reminded me.

At the end of the hall, a door opened to the rear garden. Max and I made our way out and found a spot on the wooden bench. Max undid his slacks again, and I lifted my dress and climbed on top –

11

When we realized that the hosts of the party were watching us from the windows, that simply added to our excitement. I pushed up on Max's throbbing hard-on, then let myself slip back down. He pulled my dress over my head so that I was naked in the cool night, holiday lights creating a magical multicoloured halo around us. Up and down I pushed, and then Max slid one hand between our bodies to strum against my still-sensitive clit.

I gripped onto his broad shoulders and rode him, squeezing his cock with my inner muscles until I could tell from the look in his eyes that he was almost there. Voices urged us on from overhead, partiers witnessing our lovemaking for their own enjoyment.

"Oh, baby," Max groaned, arching his body as he came. "Oh, yeah –"

I held onto him, riding out the waves, until the two of us reached that far-off place called coming.

12

After we fumbled back into our clothes, Max tricked his fingers through my dark curls. I looked at him and saw the colourful holiday lights echoed in his eyes.

"That's what I call a progressive party," Max smiled at me.

"I couldn't agree more," I sighed, snuggling into his embrace as we made our way back up the stairs and into the further delights of the festivities –

Horsepower

Tom Piccirilli

Cole was coming out of the comic shop on Bleeker Street with a bag full of silver age Fantastic Fours when she caught him from behind.

Terry somebody, Italian last name, he knew her a little from high school. She'd gone goth pretty heavily over the past couple of years. Lots of black and fishnet now, one eyebrow pierced with a chain hanging to her ear, a spiderweb tattoo working itself out of the low-cut collar and up her neck. The city could do it to you.

He wasn't sure if he liked the change, but he let that go for the moment. She stood with two other girls who were much more into the scene, leather and latex and gossamer, dragon tats wrapped around their arms down to the wrists – one real and the other henna. They'd hardly seen any sunlight in the last six months, even now only coming out at dusk. He liked the goth trappings but saw trouble coming as they looked him up and down, giving him the slow once-over. The pudgy belly, the glasses, the sweatshirt, sneakers, holding comic books. They both wanted to be lady death and they did a good job at it, and he knew they wouldn't be able to resist taking a shot at him any second.

There was a war already under way and he had no idea how to stop it. Something about him pissed the new goths off and always had. Maybe it was because he had no real style, too much vanilla padding, totally whitebread. Screaming taxis and family cars with slipping trannies slid past, barging through potholes. One of the lady deaths bent her knees as if she might lunge at him, shove him into traffic. Cole felt sort of weak until a blue '64 Pontiac Lemans GTO 389, the pioneer of the muscle car era, sped by with its dual exhaust bellowing. It gave him some poise back and he almost felt aroused, able to meet their severe eyes now.

Terry Scoletti, that was it. They'd had some good conversations back in Film Studies, sitting side by side in the middle of the class. Peckinpah and Hitchcock and Arthur Penn, film noir, *Vanishing Point, Dirty Mary Crazy Larry, Easy Rider* and *Two-Lane Blacktop*. She found herself a football player and that was about the end of it.

She seemed to remember something about him and cocked her head, blinked a couple of times, thinking back. He could smell a touch of gin coming off her, the others stinking of stale smoke. The dipping sun shed a splash of blood over everyone, pooling at their feet. He could tell by Terry's glittering eyes that something was up, some kind of game being played in there. He was about to be toyed with, which wasn't necessarily a bad thing. One lady death grunted, and then the other.

Hopeful, he decided to wait it out. Terry said, "Hey, how're you doing? Haven't seen you for a while." He nodded, watching, as she became all angles and arches, slinking towards him. He got it now, she was going to put on an exhibition right here, for anybody watching. This was display, this was exposure.

Grinding it into him, pressing at his throat, she was against him in an instant while he stood tightening into stone. "Are you shy?" she asked. The reek of gin was much stronger as she brought her lips up almost to his, the blaring horns growing louder. She let loose with a grin that made him heady. Sometimes it could be like this, seeing old acquaintances out of context. Free of past circumstances.

He knew he appeared almost exactly the same, and maybe he was except for a few threads of silver in his curls, out in front. Terry wanted to have some fun with him, put on a show for the ladies death or maybe, just possibly, for Cole.

Or perhaps it all had something to do with murder. He remembered she had a sister who'd died down in the subways – mugged? . . . pushed onto the tracks? His imagination moved along too fast and he could look into her mind and watch her pulling out a three-inch blade, stabbing him between the fifth and sixth rib, leaving him there on the street because she had to get the rage out. It was an ache he could understand.

Dry-mouthed, he let out a tiny chirp, trying to keep his hands from flashing up to protect his chest. He could see the ladies were voyeurs and had watched this game before. Even this little bit of it was already having an effect. The death gurrls huddled closer, holding hands, their tattoos touching and forming some new picture he couldn't understand. Terry continued to grind on, right there in the street, with businessmen swinging their briefcases and Chinese delivery kids riding by on their bikes.

OK, so it was going to be like that. Terry's blouse was satin and the buttons opened easy, as she slid against his chest a couple of times. They popped open, one after the other, and the hint of her tits made him groan softly, clenching the bag tighter. She was trying to meet his eyes, but he kept staring past her, into the street, waiting for another classic car to come by.

The light had begun fading. She touched the sides of his face and drew him aside. He saw that the web tattoo started at her right nipple and went all the way up. Terry had large, dark areolae. The sight of them made him nose forward, lips parched but his tongue feeling too large and wet in his mouth. She closed in on him, wrapped a leg across his thigh, as she rubbed against his crotch, which was springing up a tad. He probably would've dug this a little more if they weren't out in the middle of the sidewalk, and if two murder gurrls weren't giving him the killing eye.

Or maybe it didn't matter. This wasn't going to work anyway, there was no heat in the seat, no horsepower. Terry laughed, throaty, deeper than he could remember, one hand at the back of his head now and pulling him down. She was holding on to him tightly, had some real strength for such a tiny girl, and he brushed his cheek against her breast. It was the right thing to do and she let out a gasp. She kissed him, both of their tongues working together roughly, even though the make-up, this close up, didn't do anything for him.

There'd been rumours about this sort of thing happening in the Village. A couple of kids just start going at it, right there in a doorway or on somebody's front steps, on the kerb, while the homeless wandered out to watch. The guy left there dying afterwards with his throat cut, the girls laughing. The games had escalated, it seemed. But maybe that was just his naïve perspective – perhaps the world had always meant for him, and failures like him, to croak in the gutter for no reason.

He tried thinking about it but Terry wouldn't let him. "Here," she said. "How's this?" Her hands were claws, capped by two-inch black nails, flecks of red on them like she'd been scratching somebody down to the vein. He let out a hissing stream of breath and she did the same, sort of tugging on him now, leading him. He took four or five steps and she stayed wrapped around him just as firmly. Where were they going? Was she going to toss him into traffic? Taxis kept blaring, mufflers off half the cars in the street, so loud they set his back teeth to shaking. There was no muscle to them.

Terry pulled a funky move, something out of the WWF, spinning until she was behind him, one arm around his waist, jerking him all around. It was a surprise and she kept it going, twining up his back and yanking him once more, as she grooved against him. He almost smiled even though he knew he was being led somewhere he didn't really want to go. She backed off a step and pounced, came into his arms too quickly and crushed the bag in his hand.

"My comics!"

It hit her as if he'd just chopped her in the throat. "What?"

"Listen –"

"Your comics?" There was a titter at the edge of her voice, but it didn't come all the way through. The death ladies tightened their grip on one another until their fingers had grown ashen. "What's the matter with you?"

"Come on, for Christ's sake," he said, realizing he should shut up. "Issue ten features the third appearance of Doctor Doom."

"Issue?"

". . . ten, yes . . ."

Now she was back, all the way, even if her eyes still sparked. If she'd wanted him to die before, as a sacrifice to an indifferent divinity, she no longer did. His value had diminished. It was over, and she buttoned up, confused and ashamed, and even the gurrls became appalled. "What are you, five years old?"

But what could he do? There was a difference between complacency and satisfaction. Opening a vein didn't daunt him, but you had to draw the line. "Jack Kirby and Stan Lee, these are classics, cost me half my paycheck."

"For that kid stuff?"

Of course they couldn't understand, no more than he could see sticking sharp pieces of metal through your body or loving Anne Rice's gay vampires or trying to be the goddamn Crow. You all came to fate on a different curve in the road. Lady deaths one and two were already done with him and marching up the street, fingers splayed as if hoping to find and disembowel a cat. Terry was half-smiling, maybe thinking him a fool or perhaps knowing they were off on tangents but heading to the same place.

He tried again. "Listen. This has age, this has presence. This is twice as old as you or me, it's got wisdom. There's muscle here."

"You need to grow up, Cole," she told him and, surprised as he was that she'd remembered his name, he also sincerely believed her. He remained exactly who he had been, and it gave him some pause.

He took the train back out to his mother's place in Queens and let himself in. She was out as usual, working the night shift at the hospital. He went to the garage and leaned against his father's workbench. The dust had piled up but the tools were still in their proper places. The hedgecutter, saws, levels, hoes, and coiled garden hoses all outlined in magic marker on the peg board.

The old man had moved out five years ago and hadn't taken a damn thing with him. It intrigued Cole that someone could leave an entire life behind and begin a new one – a different wife, with two other kids already. Cole occasionally went by his father's house and peeked in the windows, watching the kids on the couch next to him, laughing, everybody always smiling. It gave Cole a warm but somehow unpleasant feeling. Sometimes he fell asleep in the backyard, head propped against the new siding. He'd been arrested twice but the old man hadn't pressed charges yet.

The sheet over Joe's Mustang hadn't been changed in six months but still smelled of bleach. He drew it off and gazed at the car.

It was a cherry red Boss 429, with 375 horsepower and 450 lb-ft. Sixty-nine, the year that the rivalry between Mustangs and Camaros became well-defined, with street races occurring every night up and down the highways across America's midwest. In 69 the Stang became bigger, heavier and gained in its performance options. Increased height meant a jump in horsepower. Handling was much-improved. The famous running horse in the grille was replaced by a smaller emblem, offset to the right of the grille. There were four headlights now. The interior was more rounded off with two separate cockpits, for the driver and passenger.

He'd almost killed himself with the car before he'd ever driven it. The black depression came down on him at about the beginning of ninth grade, took him low in the guts for three or four days straight and wouldn't shake free. He shut the garage door, started Joe's Mustang up, lay on the cold cement floor near the exhaust pipe and listened to the engine thrum. It made him calm again. About five minutes into it the carbon monoxide got him high and he felt a lot better, shut the car off, puked, and watched the *Nightmare on Elm Street* series on video for the rest of the night.

It was an heirloom. He remembered his brother taking him down to the beach, Joe's muscles rigid in the sun, wet and roiling in the surf with girls in bikinis. Cole would sit up on the sand and watch them in the water, the girls frolicking for a while before Joe led them away behind the dunes. Later, when he and his brother were taking showers in the locker room, the scent of salt and seaweed and manhood all around, Cole would tremble at the thought of the engine. When they got back into the Mustang, the seats too hot to sit on, Joe would lay their damp towels down, and they'd fly out of there.

The first time Cole had toyed with himself was in the back seat, imagining that he was watching Joe in the driver's seat, roaring down Ocean Parkway, some bikini girl working in his lap. Cole had no idea what the hell he was even doing, it started so oddly, just as a way to get back to a place of peace in himself. Ten years old maybe and barefoot, still sort of wishing he was dead but not quite there.

This had muscle. This had age.

Joe had died in the Stang, bolting down Route 25a and dogging it out with a 78 Camaro, 327 intake, Turbo 350 and B&M shift kit. Four in the morning, two miles past the worst of the curves, and they both blew a red light too late. Some baker was off to make the morning donuts, staggering through a left turn in a Gremlin with only one headlight, putting along off a side street. Joe slammed the brakes and spun out, they said, completing three full circles before coming to a stop in a fog of smoking tyres. The Stang didn't have a scratch on it and neither did his brother. Joe's neck was broken.

Cole went inside and made a few calls. It was easy tracking Terry down. Everybody was still in touch on the grapevine, more or less. Three years out of high school and they were all still tearing themselves up about it, eager to talk, to find one another again. It was stupid the way the system did it. Let you spend 13 years surrounded by the same couple hundred kids, then punt you into the rest of the frenzied world. No wonder he had no fucking social skills.

He learned that she lived off St Mark's Place and Third Avenue, around there, but nobody knew an apartment or phone number. Someone said it was over a T-shirt shop, but Cole knew there were about 20 of them on that block so the info was no help. Somebody else said she visited her mother most Sundays, maybe for a family dinner, maybe just to settle her nerves after a weekend of raving. She didn't take drugs and hardly ever drank. There was a whisper that she'd gone a little nuts since her sister was shoved in front of the E Train.

Cole showered, shaved, and dressed the way they used to. Jeans, T-shirt, black riding boots, and Joe's leather coat. It was still in style and always would be. He'd kept the Stang tuned, fuelled, charged. A part of him thought that even if he'd done nothing to it at all, the car would still be ready.

He got in, and it was like he'd never been gone.

The Stang started with a roar, the noise surrounding and filling him from the belly up.

He promised himself he was not going to get out of the car until he had her, and maybe not even then.

Cole prowled the area for two days, skulking along her parents' block, living on drive-through, pissing in the extra-large drink cup, and forcing his bowels to back down. The Stang moved like a shark across the asphalt, heading through the Lincoln Tunnel and down through Jersey, gliding back into the city after the rush hour gridlock had eased.

Sunday, he parked up the street from her parents' place, watching. He saw Terry come up out of the subway at around three and slowly walk along the sidewalk to the front door. She had a fluid grace about her that appealed to him. She'd toned the goth look down a little for Sunday dinner with the folks, but not by much. Cole sort of missed seeing the ladies' death entourage, wishing they were here now to hear the tic of his engine. Terry would probably want to take the A Train back before it got dark, so he waited it out.

She ate and ran, sticking around for barely three hours. She was putting in her time, probably because Mom and Pop still paid her rent, or at least lent her cash when she cried for it. Cole threw the Stang into gear and eased up beside her as she made her way back to the subway station. He paced her for a few seconds until she finally looked over.

"Get in," he told her.

Something like fear in her eyes, but not really. Some wariness and distaste, but mostly cool apathy. Whatever it was, he sort of liked it. Maybe she thought he was looking for revenge for the crushed comic book incident. "No, that's OK."

"I'll give you a lift back to the city."

He had muscle. He had horsepower, wisdom. The ancient dust of lost kings made up the fuel in his tank.

Cole was no longer himself, and could let go of his little boy nature. What he couldn't do, the Stang could do for him. Here, in this cockpit, he had become a man and she somehow perceived it. So what if he needed a little help to get there? . . . everybody needed a boost, a kicker, some extra support.

There was no shame in weakness. The Stang connected him to the ages of warriors, the rituals of maleness. He was complete.

Terry did a little double-take, checking to see if it was really Cole in there. She gave a head toss, her black tangled hair flopping one way, then the other. For a second he thought she might scream for a cop, try to ward him off with a cross, something like that. Scream for any murder gurrls in the neighbourhood to come to the rescue.

Then she sighed and shook her head, berating herself probably, thinking it just more mayhem, and stepped off the kerb.

She got in and he gunned it, letting the tyres squeal but only for a second, the way Joe used to do it. He didn't need a big show, the action happened as part of the car, inside, not out there looking at the red roaring by. She giggled, an unnatural sound for somebody so far into the scene of romantic doom and anguish. It was easy to sense his need.

"You're not thinking of your comic books now, are you?" she asked.

But he was, he always was, the way he thought about novels and movies and everything that mattered when he was younger. Even ten minutes ago. Twenty-one and already he was going grey. He'd be his father in another fifteen years, and he'd already outlasted his brother. You didn't need to dress up like death to find it, all you had to do was start the engine, sniff the pipe.

He had a few wet naps, opened, unfolded them, and started wiping her face of all the powder and wax. The chain between her eyebrow and ear swung wildly. "Hey!"

"I want to see you," he said. He worked at her clothes too, tearing, unbuttoning her skirt. "Get naked. I want to see all of you."

"You're slow to start but, once you do, you speed along."

"Yes."

She mattered but she also didn't matter, right here next to him. He realized he was on the right track now, edging towards a new highway. She fit him perfectly but it wasn't about that now. It was about the place they were going, where they'd been. His heart was killing him, but it wasn't about that either.

The road offered the earth before him, and he thought he might as well make a move for it.

Terry removed her panties, opened her blouse all the way up so he could see the entire tattoo. She had a couple of others, a rose on her hip, a wreath of skulls. There was room enough in the seat for her to turn completely around, show him her beautiful pale ass. Another tat at the bottom of her spine: a face he thought he recognized for a second and then didn't any more. He brushed her with the back of his hand as she clambered around again. Terry reached over and undid his jeans, took him into her hand and began caressing him slowly, with a deliberate and almost familiar touch. She licked her palm and pulled his soul up out of him another half-inch.

"You like this, hm?" She worked him fast for a minute before she let her lips ease along him slowly, inch by inch, keeping pressure up all the way. He wanted to know who the face was, who it was going to be. The Stang screamed. She made gleeful noises, licking, wiping him across her throat like a knife.

He drove like he'd never done before, easily, without a wasted motion, sliding in and out of traffic flawlessly, nobody caring.

"Say my name," he told her.

"Hmm?"

He grabbed her by the hair and hefted her up. She appeared to be growing whiter, the ink of the tattoos standing out even more. He said, "I want to hear you."

"You're the greatest, you're the best, God, I want you, c'mon –"

He held her like that and wouldn't let her get back to it, even though she was struggling now. "Just say it, Terry. My name. Tell me my name."

Her eyes cleared and she understood without judgment. "Cole. You're my man, Cole."

Releasing her hair, he settled back, as she dropped again and continued bringing him to life, switching him into something else. Her naked ass shined against the seat and when Cole checked the rearview, he could almost see Joe back there, watching him as Cole had once watched and dreamed of his brother. He looked around and didn't know where he was any more, and didn't much care.

Terry was a biter, chewing. He finally recognized the face on her back: it was her dead sister. Who had shoved her? Who had been down there in the tunnels for no reason? Where had Terry been that night, and how much anger and provocation had stood between them? How much love? More than him and Joe?

He was ready and shifted, drawing her up with his free hand, the other on the wheel, always on the wheel.

"Here?" she said. "Now? There's traffic. Truckers."

"Come on."

She liked the idea even though it frightened her a little too, and that made it agreeable. They needed more fear at this moment, so that it would last. Maybe she'd never done anything in public with the ladies death watching. Always on the sly, alone, of course, in shadow not on the sidewalk. Or maybe she had started thinking of what would happen next, further down the line, when it was his time. She slinked across him, working one leg over, settling into his lap. She positioned him and slowly slid down, sighing, now hugging him and rocking gently. That's what he wanted, to feel her this close, and closer. And they had to get closer.

Terry kept one hand closed, as if she was hiding something. He could guess. As she bit into his shoulder, he reached over and started tossing her clothes out of the half-open passenger window. He was hard everywhere, with the generations of cool and horsepower riding with him. He hardly had to do anything at all, the Stang took care of her.

Cole kept checking the rearview mirror, waiting, knowing what was coming. It took a while but eventually he saw Joe appear. His brother sat in the back seat, keeping an eye on Cole, watching the world unfolding all over again. Cole couldn't make out the expression on Joe's face – jealousy or disappointment? Probably both, it would always be both.

There was a blur of motion and it took Cole only a second to realize what had happened. She was quick and had practised the move for a thousand hours until she couldn't be seen, slipping something small between her teeth. She leaned in to kiss him and he pressed his fist under her chin and shoved it up tight until her shoulders cracked. He'd been waiting for the move. If he hadn't, he'd be dead.

He slapped her, and her head bounced against the driver's window. "Spit it out."

"Huh?"

Cole slapped Terry again, much harder, and it did nothing but bring a giggle up in her throat. He mashed his lips to hers and could feel the razor blade pressing through her flesh from the other side. They kissed and her lips parted, and then her blood burst into his mouth.

He took it in because he had to and he wanted to, then wiped the back of his hand across his chin. "Spit it out."

She turned her head and spit the razor blade into the back seat.

"Don't try it again," he told her.

"No," she said, "no, not for a while."

Fair enough. It was getting dark now but he didn't put on the headlights. He kicked it up to ninety, still weaving through traffic. She rode and he rode, the engine thrumming, gas gauge more than half-full, staring out at the world descending through the windshield, his neck unbroken, murder just in front, thinking about all the insane and uncompromising curves that lay in wait ahead.

English Lessons

Lee Elliott

Time, time, time, she screamed silently at the indicator light above the door to her prison. Her two students droned on, and Kristi imagined the walls of their tiny booth drawing together until the timid Japanese wool-clad knees touched her skirt. The one that had been talking paused and Kristi smiled and nodded encouragement, oblivious to the conversation. She had learned weeks ago to tune out the hopeless students, like these two women, who just came for the excitement of speaking to a foreigner.

Finally the red light went on, signalling an end to their thirty minutes. Kristi stifled a sigh as she stood up in the carpeted booth, careful to avoid contact with her clients. They smiled, bowed and disappeared, looking as relieved as she felt that their time was up.

Kristi stepped out of the beige booth into a hallway dotted with seven other identical torture chambers, all dubbed *John's Language School*. Students and instructors all sped for the exit, some rushing for trains, others to catch a smoke or a breath before their next session.

A low, welcoming rumble reached her ears as Tom sidled up and said, "Tobacco time – going out?" She nodded up at his dizzying six-foot-three height, so unusual in the sea of shorter heads. "How were the Bobbsey twins today?" he asked as they swept into the hall with the tide of staff and students.

"I've finally learned how to comment without actually listening," Kristi replied, and released her long pent-up sigh.

"Excellent, my child," Tom intoned. "Your next lesson will be sustained visualization. Think of something pleasing and the minutes fly by," he counselled.

Tom had already logged two months at the Kobe language school when Kristi began working part-time there. He became her tutor in the Zen approach to English conversational training and survival. The first lesson was in thinking of the money she was earning, or "yen training". Training then progressed to not thinking at all, and ultimately she hoped to hone her skills in teleportation.

"I'd like to be sitting on a beach with a large bottle of Sapporo," Kristi said as she pulled a wilted cigarette from her tiny pouch. "Got a light?"

"Who's your next subject?" Tom asked, taking her cigarette and lighting it from the tip of his already smoking clove. They had nicknames for all of their students, and discussing their dismal attempts at English conversation helped to pass the excruciating hours.

Kristi brightened. "My favourite student. Shy Adonis is up next," she said. "I like to watch his eyes on my breasts as he tries out new vocabulary."

Kristi enjoyed teaching the younger salarymen who weren't yet completely indoctrinated in Japanese business life. They still clung to lives of their own, and most hoped to learn colloquial English for sightseeing travel to the United States instead of staid business English.

"Have you taught him any pick-up lines yet?" Tom asked, raising one bushy eyebrow.

"He still wants to stick to the manual. Maybe I'll try today."

Teachers at John's Language School were encouraged to teach from an antiquated English guide, but since most of them found out quickly that the sessions were not monitored, they would veer off into more modern usage with promising students.

"Who do you have?" Kristi asked Tom. He pursed his lips and answered, "Housewife hour coming up. I've got two little maids from Motomachi."

"Gigglefest," Kristi commented, and Tom nodded gravely. Idle housewives seemed to take classes only to relieve the day's boredom, since none of them studied or improved on their original mangled pronunciation. The younger ones spent the hour tittering at each other and at the instructor's attempts to get through a lesson.

Lights flickered in the hallway. "Curtain time," Tom and Kristi chimed together. They stubbed out their butts and returned through the rear entrance to meet their students in the lobby.

Kristi's Adonis already sat waiting for her, and sprang to his feet as she approached. His black hair was shaven in back but grew forward thickly from his crown, just brushing the long sculptured sweep of his eyebrows. The haircut accentuated his high cheekbones and surprisingly full lips. Where most salarymen were concave or barrel-chested, he had the full, muscled frame of a swimmer, which even his usual white dress shirt couldn't hide. Although he wasn't tall by Western standards, Takashi stood an inch taller than Kristi's five foot six.

She smiled with genuine pleasure and ushered him into their booth, where he sat opposite her on the built-in carpeted bench.

"How have you been?" Kristi began. She watched his startled gaze travel from her reddened curls and over the black silk tank, down her patterned skirt to the slice of ankle that showed above her black pumps. Kristi was suddenly glad that she had dressed up for the day.

"I'm fine, thank you," he replied cautiously. She saw him grip the primer for safety as he spoke.

"Let's just talk today, OK, Takashi?" she suggested. "Tell me about your plans for your trip to Hawaii."

Panic darkened his luminous brown eyes, but Takashi gave her a tentative smile and plunged in. "I will fly to Oahu on the March ten," he said carefully.

Technically, Kristi should have corrected his error, but she ignored it for the moment. "What do you want to do there?" she asked.

Takashi stammered and looked longingly down at his book. "I want to see the beach and talk to American woman," he confessed.

"Good!" Kristi urged. "What will you say when you meet an American woman?"

"Will you drink cohee with me?" Takashi ventured.

"It's *cof-fee*," she corrected him gently, "but we don't really have coffee houses like you do here. What about saying, 'Will you have a drink with me?' instead?"

"But that is what I said," Takashi answered with a baffled look.

"Don't say 'coffee'," Kristi clarified. "Going out for coffee is not asking for a date. Do you want to go on a date?"

Takashi nodded eagerly for a moment, but then his face darkened again. "I don't know what American women do," he confessed.

Kristi recalled the blunt proposals she received daily from drunken Japanese men who seemed to think that American women did everything at the drop of a fly. At least she could teach one guy how to get a Western woman into bed the right way.

"You could take her out to dinner, go to a movie, or just walk on the beach and talk," she suggested.

"But my English is not so good," Takashi lamented.

Kristi smiled and leaned towards him in encouragement. "That's why you are here." Her movement caused her breasts and hair to swing forward, and Takashi's gaze lingered on her cleavage for a long moment. *Suddenly he doesn't seem so shy anymore*, Kristi thought. *Maybe it's the subject matter*. "Ask me out," she proposed, and quickly added, "for practice."

Takashi flashed an open-mouthed smile, clearly pleased with this idea. Then he frowned just as quickly, as if he was struggling with some inner conflict. Even though Kristi knew he was 25, only a year younger than she was, he seemed to speed through emotions like a child.

Finally, Takashi spoke. "You will tell me if I say something wrong?" he pleaded.

Kristi nodded. Was that all? "Of course," she said. "I will correct your English."

He shook his shock of bangs. "No, not my English," he insisted. "If it is bad to say."

"Oh!" Kristi smiled. "You mean inappropriate?" This sparked an intense shuffle through his English to Japanese dictionary. Takashi brightened again as he read the translation.

"Yes! Eenappropree-ate," he read.

"I will tell you," Kristi assured him. She sat back against the bench.

Takashi scowled, then composed his face and asked, "Will you date with me?"

"Will you go out with me," she coached. He wrote this treasure in his notebook, read it silently, and continued.

"You are very beautiful," Takashi proclaimed.

"Thank you," Kristi answered, and wondered if this was part of the lesson or an actual compliment.

"Do you like Japanese men?" he asked.

Kristi nodded. "Yes," she answered.

"Have you kissed Japanese man before?" he probed, meeting her eyes.

Kristi considered, and decided the question was allowable. "No," she answered.

"I would like to kiss you now," he declared.

So would I, she thought, dwelling on the fine definition of his full lips. Impulsively she said, "Maybe you should, just for practice."

He nodded gravely, and then leaned forward and placed a cool hand on the back of her neck to draw her closer. She thought he would kiss her gently, but as her lips parted he pressed firmly, opening his own mouth and caressing her lips with his tongue. Kristi nearly fell into him as he released her.

"Was that right?" Takashi asked innocently, but she caught a hint of arrogance in his eyes.

"Right," she repeated, stymied now. "That was good."

"Maybe I need practice to make love," he considered aloud and drew his hand softly over the curve of one breast. His hand fluttered, then pinched her nipple. Kristi looked down at the hand that triggered a sudden pulse in her groin. He released her breast, stroked her cheek instead, and lowered his mouth to her erect nipple.

Kristi moaned as he bit through the silk. Her own hands reached for him as he knelt before her and cupped both breasts. She unbuttoned the starched shirt down to his navel, and slid her hands over his solid, hairless chest. Takashi coaxed her to the floor until they both knelt facing each other.

"I want to feel your ass," he whispered into the tendrils of hair tickling her ear. Takashi caught an earlobe between his eager teeth and moved his hands behind her until he cradled her ass cheeks. Kristi couldn't speak, couldn't think of anything but grasping the bulge beating behind his blue wool trousers. She traced the line of his fly, felt the rock hard erection, and descended until she could rake her fingers along the underside of his balls.

"Iro-poi," Takashi murmured into her neck. "Sekushi," he translated, pulling her skirt up from behind. "So sekushi," he added, rubbing both index fingers along the edge of her panties. Suddenly his lips pushed into hers again, and his tongue darted in to lick her own. Kristi felt the answering warmth under his fingers and the throb of his cock under her own hand.

"I want to feel you," Takashi groaned, lifting her again to the bench as he grasped the hem of her skirt with his perfect teeth. She watched the top of his spiky head descend to the place where her black silk panties met the inward curve of her stomach. Takashi pulled them down with supple fingers and his tongue touched the tangle of her pubic hair.

"Eat me," Kristi gasped, arching her back against the wall. A cold rush of air met her pulsing pussy as he backed away to look up into her eyes.

"Eat?" he asked, puzzled.

"Please," she urged, unable to explain in words. Instead, she pushed his face into her wetness.

Takashi paused to absorb this information. Then he smiled and parted his lips.

"I eat you," he said, and fastened his lips to her pink clit, sucking it into his mouth. His tongue gathered the liquid pouring from her as two fingers explored her opening. Kristi lifted her right leg to his shoulder and kicked off her shoe. Without a pause, he caught her ankle with his left hand and drove his tongue deeper to meet his fingers. Then he pulled back just enough to lick the root of her clitoris until it swelled with blood. Kristi bucked under his mouth, and he deftly sucked again and then drew away and released the seal of pressure around her clit. She exploded in orgasm and an urgent moan broke from her throat.

Takashi put his pungent mouth to hers, kissing away her sounds of pleasure. "Please be quiet," he begged. "I need inside you."

She fumbled for his fly and unbuttoned the top of his trousers as he unzipped them, but missed the inner clasp and could only tug desperately at his waistband. Takashi groaned and pulled the clasp open, revealing white briefs and tip of his uncut cock straining to greet her.

"Oh," Kristi crooned. "Let me suck on you." She grasped him as he was standing up, and the skin of his cock slid down to reveal a glistening knob.

"No!" Takashi hissed just as her tongue touched the opening of his cock. "I come too soon," he confessed and snaked his arms around her to lift her away. Kristi reached up to lace her fingers around his neck as they stood. She felt his warmth graze her pussy lips and then sink into her, and he took her ass in both hands and plunged so deep that her feet left the floor. She felt her panties slip down one leg as he rocked in and out.

His cock felt long and slim inside her, so rigid that it bumped the hood of her labia and rolled over her clit as he withdrew slightly, then penetrated again. She hooked her ankles around his waist so that her thighs strained against the taut muscles of his back with each thrust.

Takashi lifted desperate eyes to hers as they kissed again. His jaw hardened and she knew he was trying not to come too soon. She licked his upper lip and whispered, "It's all right."

"Thank you," Takashi sighed as if released from a promise. He clutched her ass cheeks and shuddered through one last push, then withdrew deftly and whispered, "I come now." Kristi crouched over the head of his penis and covered it with her mouth as it exploded. She drank deep for a long moment before she closed her lips over his rod and pulled him into her throat for the last few drops. Takashi took a handful of hair in one hand and urged her gently to her feet. She kissed his lips once and then moved her head to kiss his cheek. Beyond the curve of his damp temple she saw the red light go on.

"The light is on," Kristi said, and Takashi silently sat her down on the bench and pulled up his briefs and trousers in one motion.

He buttoned his shirt before gathering up his manual and notebook. Then he straightened and bowed to Kristi.

"Thank you for the nice lesson," he said formally.

"Your fly," Kristi motioned with a wave of her hand. He looked up in distress. "I mean, your zipper," she clarified, and he blushed and ducked his head. *Is that all?* she thought. *Thank you for the nice lesson?*

"May we continue this lesson next week?" Takashi asked as Kristi stooped to untangle her panties and step into them. She discreetly turned away to rearrange her skirt and felt a tentative hand on her elbow.

"Please continue next week?" he pleaded. Kristi nodded and found her voice.

"Yes, next week. See you next week," she repeated, and he pushed open the door and slipped through. She saw the stray tail of his shirt poking above his waistband and hissed, "Takashi-san!"

He stopped and took a step back inside the door, turning so that she could glimpse his perfect profile again.

"You're doing very well with your lessons," she said briskly, as she tucked the errant tail back into his trousers and hoped he would understand her meaning.

Takashi stood frozen until she withdrew her hand, and Kristi feared she had committed some unforgivable gaffe. Horrified, she moved back and dropped her gaze to allow him a graceful exit.

Instead, Takashi executed a sustained bow, after which he straightened and spoke in clear, well enunciated tones. "Thank you, Kristi-san. You are a very good teacher."

Kristi smiled with relief and nodded her thanks. She managed to follow him into the throng of people in the narrow hallway, and watched his retreating figure until another exodus of students engulfed him. Tom waited for her by the back door.

"How was your Adonis today?" he teased. Kristi sagged against the wall in sudden exhaustion and tilted her head up to find her friend's eyes.

"Oh, my God," she wailed. "I can't go back in there."

"That bad?" He put a reassuring hand on her shoulder.

Kristi shivered. "No – that good!"

Tom raised his eyebrows and lowered his voice. "Oh – your God. I guess he's not shy any more. Shall I call you Venus now?" he joked.

"Tom! How am I going to get through the rest of this day?" she moaned. Tom grasped her other shoulder and leaned in so that their foreheads touched. "I have two words for you, my child."

She wrinkled her eyebrows at him in confusion. "I think I'm beyond yen training, Tom," she complained.

"You certainly are," he murmured. "Two words: private lessons."

Butterfly

Lisabet Sarai

After nine months laying pipe in the Saudi Arabian desert, the dusty concrete towns of northeast Thailand were paradise. Although accommodations were simple, the food was fantastic, and the local people shy but friendly. Our engineering crew was working on a dam near Khon Kaen. Irrigation and hydropower would help enrich the farmers who eked out a living from that salty soil.

Videos and beer were the only entertainment in the little town of Maha Sarakan where we were staying. The beer was good, true, amazingly refreshing after the heat and dust, but my crewmates wanted something spicier. So on our first free weekend, after three weeks on the site, we piled into the minivan and headed south to Bangkok.

When I had arrived the previous month, the airport was all I had seen of that loose and lascivious metropolis the Thais call the City of Angels. My first real trip there was a shock after the tranquil boredom of the northeast. Chaotic traffic, constant noise, mile after mile of grimy cement blocks interrupted occasionally by skyscrapers and the graceful eaves of Buddhist temples.

One of my mates, Charlie, knew the city well. He checked us into a comfortable, ridiculously cheap hotel in the middle of the tourist district. Bewildered and dazzled, I followed him along sidewalks crammed with vendors hawking watches, T-shirts and toys, trying to avoid tripping on the broken pavement.

Beggars with shrivelled limbs extended their bowls in silent entreaty. Blond, ragged-haired tourists in shorts and sandals, slender Thai women in tight jeans and silk blouses, monks draped in saffron, policemen standing stiffly at corners, their revolvers prominently displayed: it seemed that the whole of Bangkok was here on this one street. Meanwhile, an endless line of vehicles crawled by us: tint-windowed Mercedes, sooty trucks, and rickety buses with people hanging out the doors. The air was heavy with diesel fumes, frying garlic, and jasmine. We dined at a quiet restaurant on a side lane, where the young waitress giggled every time we spoke to her. Then Charlie took me off to see what he called "the real Bangkok" – the go-go bars and sex clubs.

I can't say that I was completely enthusiastic. Yes, I admit that I come from the Bible Belt, but it wasn't that. I've been to strip clubs in the States a few times and I simply found them depressing. Everybody looking guilty as they try to have a good time. Drunks acting crude, dancers acting coy, everywhere the desperate smell of dirty money and sexual frustration.

I've been with hookers, too. I didn't enjoy that much, either. It relieved my physical needs, but it left me feeling empty, sour and old.

My job makes it hard to have a real relationship, though. I never know where my next project will be, but I can bet that it won't be in America's heartland. So I read a lot, and seek my own five-fingered companionship. I didn't think I needed what Bangkok had to offer.

We sauntered into the "entertainment plaza". Three stories of indoor bars and clubs surrounded a central court, which was crowded with open-air bars and stalls selling skewers of grilled chicken, fresh fruit, and fried locusts. As we walked along the second-level balcony, bikini-clad girls tried to lure us inside their establishments.

"Come inside," they crooned. "One beer fifty baht. No cover charge." Briefly the woman would hold back the dark cloth draping the door, offering a tantalizing glimpse of flickering lights and bare flesh. "Take a look, no charge, come inside."

The more energetic of these young marketeers would grab us by the hand and, laughing the whole while, try to pull us in. It was all good-natured, though. We'd extricate ourselves from her strong fingers and thank her. "Not now," we'd say. "Maybe later."

"Why not now?" she'd say, stamping her foot in mock anger. "Don't you like me?"

Charlie stopped in front of a doorway surmounted by a blinking neon butterfly. "I came here last month," he said with a grin. "The girls are hotter than average." As if to prove his point, an exquisite creature wearing a fringed bra and a practically non-existent skirt came out to greet us.

"Welcome to Butterfly Bar. Come inside, please." We followed her through the curtains and found ourselves in a space much deeper than it was wide, lit like some disco nightmare. Everywhere, clashing multi-coloured lights flashed, vibrated, spun on the ceiling. Rock music pounded in our ears. Our guide settled us on a plush-upholstered bench that ran along one wall. In a moment, two frosted mugs of Singha beer sat invitingly before us, and we could turn our attention to the entertainment.

The bar that ran along the opposite wall was also the stage. Half a dozen women wearing next to nothing danced there, churning and writhing to the music. Every single one was drop-dead gorgeous.

One wore a bikini bottom made of chain mail, and thigh-high, spike-heeled vinyl boots. Her long hair fell over one eye, Lauren Bacall-style, as she squatted on the bar and circled her hips suggestively.

Another beauty had short, curly hair that looked bleached, and a faraway look. She cupped her perfect breasts absently as she swayed to the beat, sequins flashing from the heart-shaped patch that covered her sex.

Two other dancers were doing a playful lesbian pantomime, grinding their pelvises together and struggling not to laugh. They all seemed so young, despite their salacious behaviour.

Other women, wearing brief kimonos, circulated among the patrons serving drinks, cuddling, or simply chatting. It wasn't long before we had an entourage of three of these little imps. "You want massage?" asked one, kneading my shoulders with clever hands. "What is your name?" asked another. "My name Ao."

"They want you to buy them drinks," Charlie told me. "Whenever a customer buys them a drink, they get five *baht*."

"Is that all they want?" I was overwhelmed by the feminine flood surging around me.

"Well, of course they want tips. And if you like one of them enough, you can pay to take her out of the bar."

"They're prostitutes?" I suddenly felt slightly queasy. The atmosphere was so different from a State side joint, light-hearted and innocent; I didn't want to think about how it might be tainted.

"Well – it's up to them. The bar pays them to dance and to push drinks. If they want to make a private arrangement, it's their prerogative. When they decide to leave for the evening, they simply compensate the bar for lost drink income."

"Hmm." As I pondered this, the music changed, becoming slower and more sensual. Meanwhile, the leftmost dancer stepped down from the bar and the remaining women moved left to new positions. A figure appeared at the right end of the bar.

Something about her caught my attention. With casual elegance she shed her kimono and draped it over a bar stool. Then she turned toward the shrine in the corner near the ceiling. Touching her fingertips together, she brought them to her forehead and bowed, her reverent gesture totally at odds with the environment.

I felt a strange ache in my chest as I watched her mount the steps to the bar, smooth and sure on her stiletto heels. She was taller than many of the girls, slender and willowy. Her long hair rippled around her as she moved, perfectly attuned to the melody and rhythm.

She was a natural dancer. Her fluid gestures held me transfixed. She grasped one of the poles leading from the bar to the ceiling and arched backward until her hair brushed the floor. Waves flowed through her, sweet undulations that began in her pelvis and shimmered up her spine. By compar-ison the other girls seemed clumsy and coarse. She was not trying to entice, it seemed; she was lost in the music. Yet there was something supremely sexy about her performance. I found myself hardening as I gazed at her, turned on for the first time since entering this den of flesh.

As if she felt my gaze she released the pole, turned and looked in my direction. Her red-painted lips curved in a smile of invitation. Her eyes locked to mine, she unhooked her bikini top and let it slide off her shoulders, revealing sweet, small, firm-looking breasts, capped with almond-hued nipples that surely were erect. She brushed her palms over them, closing her eyes as if savouring the sensation. My penis throbbed uncomfortably in my jeans.

The song changed to something more upbeat. She shook her hips, did the same bumps and grinds as the other dancers, but the effect was totally different. She was listening to some inner voice. Every now and again her eyes would meet mine, and that luscious smile would light her face. I found myself holding my breath, willing her to turn again in my direction.

Finally, her set ended. She slipped away into the crowd before I could call to her. I felt a sense of loss totally out of proportion to the situation. Then, suddenly, she was beside me. I discovered that I was blushing.

"Hello," she said, her smile even more intoxicating close up. "You like me? You like my dancing?"

"I certainly do."

"You buy me drink?"

"Of course." She waved over another bar girl. "Mekong coke," she ordered. "And you, mister, you want one more beer?"

"Sure, why not?" I looked over at Charlie, hoping for some guidance. He had one girl in his lap and another whispering in his ear. All three of them were giggling. Charlie caught my slightly desperate glance and shrugged.

"Go for it," he said. "We are. Come on, girls!" He stuffed three five-hundred baht bills in the bamboo tube holding our bill, then headed for the door, one girl on each arm. "Have a great time, Pat," he called over his shoulder. "I'll see you on Monday." Damn him, leaving me alone like that.

I was almost trembling when our drinks arrived. My companion seated herself beside me, her bare thigh pressed against mine, and raised her drink. "*Chok dee*," she said, clicking our glasses. "Good luck to you."

I was tongue-tied with nervousness. Fortunately my lovely friend managed the conversation.

"What your name?" she asked.

"Patrick. Pat."

"Hello, Pat. My name Lek. Means small." For the first time, she giggled in that girlish way I associated with the other women. "It's a joke, because I'm so big."

"You're not big," I said. "At least, not next to me." In fact, she seemed diminutive and fragile beside my six-foot-two, two hundred and eighty pound frame.

She took my hand, and a little shiver ran up my spine. Her skin was smooth and cool. "You have a wife, Pat?" she asked.

I shook my head. "Would I be here with you if I was married?" She doubled over with laughter, apparently finding this hilarious.

"Most men come here have wives. Never mind. You have girlfriend?"

I smiled into her shining eyes. "No, no girlfriend."

"OK, then, maybe Lek can be your girlfriend." Without warning she laid a gentle hand on the bulge in my pants. "You like me, I think."

I swallowed hard, not knowing what to say. "Yes, I like you."

"I like you, too. Maybe we go to your room? You pay the bar five hundred baht, then we can go."

I felt a chill. All at once this had turned into a financial transaction. Still, I wanted her. "What about for you?" I asked. "How much do I have to pay you?"

"Never mind. Whatever you want, no problem." She pulled me to a standing position. "Come on, let's go. I like you a lot."

On the way back to the hotel, I wondered what I was getting into. Lek was nothing like the hookers I had known. Was she just pretending not to care about the money? She chattered away, apparently unaware of my concerns.

My room was cooler than the muggy night outside, but still humid. The whisper of the air conditioning drowned out the traffic noise from the street. As soon as the door was closed and she had slipped off her shoes, Lek was kneeling in front of me working at my zipper.

I tried to make her rise. "No, you don't have to do that." She looked disappointed. "You don't want my mouth on you?"

"Of course I do, but . . ."

"Then let me," she said softly. "I want to." With the hooker, I had to pay extra for a blow job. Lek acted as though I was doing her a favour. As soon as my fly was open, my penis popped out, full and solid as a sausage. She pursed her lips and mouthed the tip, leaving traces of lipstick on the bulb. Then she slithered her tongue down my length, circling the base with her thumb and forefinger while cupping my balls in her other palm. I groaned. It has been a long time since I have known anyone's touch but my own.

"Your cock very nice, Pat," she murmured, in between mouthfuls. She took me deep into her throat and kept me there, sucking hard, nursing my cock like a baby at its mother's tit. I'd never felt anything like it.

Already I could feel the come boiling up in me. I began to thrust, jerking my hips, banging the tip of my cock against the back of her throat. She responded by sucking harder, till I felt that her hot vacuum would literally pull the come out of me.

I wanted to stop. I didn't want to come so soon. I wanted to be inside her, those graceful, muscular legs wrapped around me, when I came. But she wouldn't let me go, and finally, I didn't want her to. I twined my fingers in her hair and pulled her head into my crotch, fucking her face until I could bear it no more. The semen surged up my shaft, filling her mouth and overflowing.

She kept licking me gently as my dick shrank back to its normal size. Then she looked up at me and smiled, an angelic smile made sweetly perverse by the creamy remnants of my come on her lips.

"You like that?" she asked archly.

"What do you think?" I pulled her to me and embraced her, tasting my own bitter fluid on her ripe mouth. "That was amazing, Lek." After a while I released her and looked down ruefully at my limp penis. "Unfortunately, I was hoping to use that to explore some other parts of your anatomy."

"Never mind," she said. "Long night. You lie down there and watch me. You'll be hard again pretty quick."

She was so charming that I couldn't contradict her. I reclined on the bed while she did a little private strip-tease.

She wasn't wearing much, but she made every garment count. Moving to some music in her head, she strutted across the carpet, then turned her back to me. She untied her halter top from around her neck. Then she turned and slowly lowered the hands, gradually revealing to me those luscious little breasts. Her skin was a dusky ivory that reminded me of the erotic figurines carved from elephant tusks that I had seen in Okinawa. Her nipples seemed large in proportion. I ran my tongue over my lips, thinking about having one in my mouth. My penis twitched, already coming back to life.

Next she unbuttoned her miniskirt, shimmied it down to her ankles, hooked it with one foot and flung it playfully onto the bed. Only her panties remained, a black thong that hid the merest sliver of the flesh between her thighs. Looking into my eyes, she undid the ties at each hip. With agonizing slowness, she drew the cloth forward, through her cleft. Then she held the garment out to me.

My hands trembled as I took it from her. It was warm and moist from her body. I held it to my nose, breathing deeply. Her musk was fainter and more delicate than the Western women that I had known, but still strong enough to bring me half-erect.

She posed for a moment, silent and desirable, her gold chain and Buddha amulet glinting between her breasts. Then she came and stood by the bedside, her thighs parted, her hairless mound close to my face. "Touch me," she said. As nervous as a virgin, I reached out my finger and slid it into her folds. She sighed as if in bliss and closed her eyes, twisting her nipples between thumb and forefinger.

Her flesh was slippery and unbelievably smooth. I thought of sun-warmed porcelain, or stones rounded and polished by the river's kiss. My fingers found her clit and massaged it gently. I was rewarded by her soft moans. My cock swelled to fullness as I imagined probing her more deeply.

Lek somehow knew that I was ready. She climbed onto the

bed. On all fours, she presented her ass to me. Her pale, swelling cheeks flowed like sculpture under my hands. I wanted her as I had never wanted any woman.

Fumbling in my pocket, I found a condom and slid it over my now-rampant penis. Then I slipped my fingers back into her cunt, spreading her juices.

Lek looked back at me over her shoulder. "No, not there," she said. "Take me the other way. In the other hole. Like a whore."

Her crudeness, so out of keeping with her earlier manner, shocked me and excited me. I spread her cheeks and placed my forefinger on the crinkled ring of muscle. "You mean here?"

"Yes. There. Like that. You want to, don't you?"

I did. I had never done such a thing, but oh, I had read and I had imagined. I was afraid, though, afraid of hurting her, afraid of the dirtiness of it, afraid of the unknown.

"Are you sure?"

"Do it. Please, now. Fuck me like a whore, Pat."

"You're not a whore, Lek . . ." I began, but I couldn't continue. My cock surged, hardening to pain. I didn't hesitate any longer. I smeared some of the lubrication from her pussy over my cock, until I was as slippery as she was. Then I pressed my knob against that tight whorl, that gateway to the forbidden, and pushed. To my surprise, I slid halfway in, halfway into the tightest, hottest space my cock had ever known.

I grabbed her hips and pulled her toward me, fully impaling her. She sobbed, in pain or delight. From the way she arched her back and pressed herself against my hardness, I thought it was the latter. I began to move inside her. Her muscles gripped me, rippling around my rod. Each time I thrust into her bowels, she moaned, urging me on.

The sensations and the thought of what I was doing fed on each other. I was butt-fucking a beautiful woman. Reaming her. Screwing her brains out with my cock buried to the hilt in her ass. And she loved it, I could tell, from her mewing cries, from the way she writhed beneath me and thrashed her head about until her hair was tangled all over her back.

It lasted a long time. My cock seemed to swell with each stroke. Her passage got tighter and tighter. Finally, I could bear it no longer. With a yell, I rammed myself into her and let the orgasm take over. It tore through me, sweeping away all thought in its path.

When I came back to myself, she was stretched out beside me, stroking my hair. Sweet satisfaction shone in her eyes. "*Khorp khun kha*," she whispered. "Thank you."

"Thank you, Lek." I gathered her in my arms and showered her with small kisses. I had never imagined such generosity in a woman.

We spent the weekend together. The next morning, breakfasting late in the hotel coffee shop, I was self-conscious. Then I looked around and realized that we were by no means the only Thai-foreign couple in the place

She was magnificent company, and a wonderful guide. She showed me the bejewelled Grand Palace and the National Museum. In the Temple of the Emerald Buddha, she lit incense and knelt silently for a long time. I watched, amazed, remembering her reverence in the bar.

We wandered through the weekend market laughing and sweating in the sun, while she bargained for sarongs and cheap jewellery. We toured the canals on a rice barge, ate fiery curry and fried bananas.

And, of course, we made love, a dozen times in a dozen different ways. Finally, I got the chance to sink myself into her cunt, while looking into her eyes. It was clear even to me, though, that she preferred entry via her back passage. I was more than happy to oblige.

On Monday morning, we held hands while waiting for the minivan. All at once I remembered that I had not paid her. I had bought her gifts and given her money for treats, but nothing to recompense her for her time and her physical bounty.

I reached for my wallet. She put her hand on mine. "Never mind," she said.

"But, I haven't given you anything. I have to pay . . ."

"No, no pay, Pat. I'm your girlfriend now. Just take care of me, OK."

I shook off her hand and slipped five thousand baht from my billfold. Folding it, I stuck it into her palm. "You know

I'm going to be gone for the next three weeks. This should help you take care of yourself. I'll see you when I come back, OK?"

"OK, Pat. I miss you."

"I'll miss you too, Lek." The van pulled up and, at the same time, Charlie and the other guys tumbled out of the hotel, looking tousled and somewhat the worse for wear. I kissed her lightly on the lips. "See you soon."

The next three weeks were the longest I had ever endured. The days crawled by in a haze of sunburnt dust. The nights I spent fantasizing, remembering Lek's sweetness and her lust, thinking of new things we would do when I saw her again. I wished that I had a picture of her, but then I knew no photo could do her justice. No photo could capture her dancer's grace, her whimsical sense of humour, her gentleness, or her blazing carnality.

Finally, I couldn't bear it any more. I had to hear her voice at least. I asked one of the Thai members of our team to find the telephone number for Butterfly Bar, and one evening around six p.m., when I figured it would not be busy, I tried calling.

The phone rang and rang. Finally it picked up. "*Kha?*" a woman's voice answered. "Is Lek there?" I asked, miserably aware that I might not be understood. "I'd like to speak to Lek, please."

There was a silence, then the woman laughed. "Oh, Lek, yes, of course. One moment, please."

The line crackled with static as I waited. Dimly, I could hear the thumping beat of rock and roll. I had no idea what I was going to say. I only knew that I needed Lek in some way that was totally new to me.

Finally, I heard a clicking, and then her softly accented English. "Hello? Lek speaking."

"Lek, it's me. Pat."

"Pat!" she almost squealed with excitement. I heard her say something in Thai to someone in the background. "Pat, I miss you!"

"I miss you too, Lek. That's why I'm calling. I just had to hear your voice."

"When you come back to Bangkok?"

"Not until the end of next week. Friday. I'll meet you at the bar, OK?"

"OK, Pat. See you then." There was a pause, filled with static. "Everything good with you?"

"I'm fine except that I wish you were here with me."

"Want me to come up-country to see you?"

I laughed at her enthusiasm. "No, no. I've got to work, and this place would be pretty dull for a gorgeous girl like you."

"If you there, not dull," she said firmly. "We make excitement together."

"You're certainly right on that score, young lady. But no, I'll see you in Bangkok. Maybe we can go down to Pattaya and hang out on the beach."

"Crazy *farang*," she laughed. "No Thai girl goes to the beach. Make us black."

"Well, whatever. Maybe we'll spend the whole weekend in my room."

"Mmm," she sighed. "I like that."

Another moment of staticky silence. Finally, she spoke, so softly I could hardly hear. "Pat? I love you."

"I love you, too, Lek," I heard myself say. I realized I meant it. "See you next week."

The last week seemed even longer than the previous two. Then, when Friday afternoon finally arrived, and I was packing for the trip south, my boss dropped by. He needed me to stay until tomorrow, he said, to supervise the grading of the site. "Can't Charlie do it?" I asked, a bit testily.

"Charlie's sick. Got some stomach bug or something."

As soon as the boss left, I tried calling Lek's bar. This time the phone rang and rang, unanswered. I tried again, around eight o'clock, and again near midnight. No response. I prayed that Lek would not be worried, or angry with me for standing her up.

The grading went like clockwork. I was headed toward Bangkok by 2 p.m., driving one of the company Jeeps. My spirits rose with each kilometre that brought me closer to her. I pulled in at the hotel around six, took a quick shower, and then immediately set out for the Butterfly.

The place was already jumping, full of men in white naval uniforms. Maybe that was why no one had picked up my call the previous night. I sat down with a beer and looked around for Lek. There was no sign of her.

"Hello, mister. Remember me?" I recognized the round face and pixie haircut from my last visit.

"Hello, Ao. Of course I remember." She looked delighted. "Would you like a drink?"

"Yes, thank you." As she was leaving, I grabbed her hand. "One moment, Ao. Do you know where Lek is? The tall dancer with the long hair?"

She shook her head. "She not here tonight, I think."

A bolt of panic surged through me. Did she think I had abandoned her? Had she left the bar with some other man?

"You ask the mama-san," Ao said, pointing to a woman behind the bar. "Maybe she know about Lek."

I picked up my beer and sat down at the bar, inches from the spike heels of one of the dancers. I gestured to the mama-san.

"Excuse me, but do you know where I can find Lek?"

The woman looked me over critically. She was a well-preserved 40, with short-cropped hair and glasses, wearing a fitted hot pink suit.

"Lek buy herself out of the bar tonight. Today her birthday. She want to take the night off, celebrate with her friends."

"Do you have any idea where she might have gone to celebrate?"

"Why? Who are you? You her new boyfriend?"

I blushed, but then nodded. "Yes, I'm Pat."

The mama-san's suspicious manner changed abruptly to friendliness. "Oh, Pat. You call her last week?"

"Yes, that was me."

"Oh, Lek very much in love with you."

My heart did a little flip of gratitude. My dear girl was not angry with me.

"I love her, too."

The mama-san took my hand. "That is so good, mister Pat. She looking for someone to love her for such a long time. Ever since her operation."

Some vague uneasiness gripped me. "Her operation? What was wrong? Is she ill? Did she have an accident?"

The mama-san laughed. "Oh no, no accident. But last year,

she have operation to make her a real lady. No more *katoey*, lady-man. She always want that, save her money for five years to have operation."

"Lady-man?"

"Yes, you know." The mama-san gestured toward one of the dancers, a long-legged, sultry-looking temptress. "Like Nong. Before, Lek a man but look like woman, dress like woman, want to be woman. Now, after operation, she really a woman. No more pretending."

My stomach lurched. I thought for a moment that I would vomit. Lek, sweet, delicate, feminine Lek, was a man! I was in love with a man. I had had sexual relations with a man. The flesh of my penis was crawling, as if loathsome creatures swarmed over it. I was filled with shame and disgust.

"No!" I yelled. I jerked upright, spilling my beer all over the bar. It made a little pool around the heels of the dancer looming over me. She watched me curiously, surprised and shocked by my outburst, wondering what the crazy farang would do next.

"Mister, never mind. Lek good girl. She love you. You lucky man."

"Lucky?" I roared. "She played me for a fool. She defiled me! She's a devil in angel's guise!" I stormed out of the bar. The girls cringed and shrank away from me as I passed.

Without knowing how I got there, I found myself in the shadowy cocktail lounge of my hotel, gulping down a double bourbon. I lay my head in my hands and sobbed. The Filipino band was warming up. I hoped that I would pass out before they started playing their set.

Suddenly there was warmth next to me, and a faint hint of jasmine. Cool, slender fingers touched my arm. I opened my eyes.

"You!" I hissed, jerking away from her hand. "Get away from me, you filthy whore!"

"Pat," she said softly. "Please forgive me. I want to tell you, last weekend, but no time. Always we were laughing, or making love."

A vision of her taut flanks straining back at me. A recollection of the dark scent of her butthole. "Get out of here. Don't touch me, you, you abomination!"

I could see tears gathering in her eyes, making them shine even more than usual. I felt a brief pang of guilt, and something else I could not name.

"Never mind, Pat. You love me. I know you do. Man, lady, lady-man, same-same. All human, all love. Please, Pat."

She looked tiny, suddenly, frail, crushed like a wilted flower. My anger left me, but I still came close to retching when she took my hand. "Look into my eyes," she said softly. "Look at me, and tell you don't love me. Then I go."

I took one last look. Her raven hair shimmered in the multi-coloured bar lights. Her ivory skin glowed golden, stretched firm across her high cheekbones. Wet traces of tears streaked her face, but her lips smiled that same luscious, sensuous, loving smile that I first saw across the room, three weeks, a thousand years ago.

I looked at her, and I wanted her. My cock stiffened even as my gut turned over and tried to expel its contents. I was more terrified than I had ever been in my life. I wrenched my hand away.

"Go away," I whispered. "Leave me alone. I don't love you."

She did not hesitate any longer. She turned on her heels and walked to the door, an epiphany of grace. I bit my lip, and wondered what I had done to deserve this hell.

My work on the dam will be finished in another two months. Meanwhile, I don't bother to go to Bangkok on the weekends any more. Charlie keeps bugging me to join the rest of the guys. He knows that something happened between Lek and me, though of course he doesn't know the whole story.

"Come on, Pat. Forget her. You've got to be a *phee-sua*, as the bar girls say, a butterfly flitting from flower to flower." I just shake my head and turn back to my Orson Scott Card novel.

After this gig is through, I think I might go back to the States. I'll settle down in Cedar Rapids to be near my folks and find some nice girl. Someone blonde, comfortable, totally unexotic.

Then I catch a glimpse of some nymph in the Maha Sarakan market, sarong hugging her hips, jet hair trailing down her supple back and I'm drowning in memories. My cock like granite, my throat burning with nausea, an ache knifing through my chest. Desire, disgust, unbearable longing.

In those moments, I wonder if I'll ever find a place to rest.

Lap Dance Lust

Rachel Kramer Bussel

We pull into the shadowy parking lot in some corner of Los Angeles. I look around the deserted area, wondering where exactly we are, only half caring. Most strip clubs in LA are located in tucked away corners like this one.

I'm a little apprehensive as we walk around to the entrance and part the strings of beads to enter Cheetah's – a strip club, a real live strip club! I've been dreaming of just such a place for years, but have never worked up the courage to actually go, until now. I'd heard that Cheetah's was "women friendly", and from the crowd I can immediately tell it's true. There are plenty of guys but also a decent number of female customers who look like they're having a good time.

My three friends and I take ringside seats along the surprisingly empty stage and animatedly set about checking out each new dancer. Many of them are what I expected – peroxide blonde, fake boobs, very LA and very boring. Some have a spark of creativity and feign a glimmer of interest to tease out one of the dollars we hold in our hands, but many pass right by us or stare back with vacant eyes.

We watch as one girl after another manoeuvres around the stage, shimmying up and then down the shiny silver pole, twisting and writhing in ways I can't imagine my body doing. It feels surreal, this world of glamour and money and lights and ultra-femininity. I look and stare and whisper to my friends. Though I'm having fun, the place starts to lose its charm when I have to get more change and still no girl has really grabbed my eye. I settle in with a new drink and a fresh stack of bills and hope that I won't be disappointed by the next round of dancers.

When the next girls walk out, I'm transfixed. She's the hottest girl I've ever seen. She's wearing cave girl attire, a leopard print bandeau top and hot pants – all tanned skin, natural curves and gleaming black hair. She looks shiny, like she's just put on suntan lotion. She slithers along, making eye contact when she passes us, crawling back across the stage, putting her whole body into the performance. She toys with her shorts, thumbs hooked into the waist, before sliding them down her long legs to reveal black panties. I know that she's the one for me, that I really like her and am not just an indiscriminate ogler, when I realize that I preferred her with her shorts on.

After her performance, I offer her a wad of dollars. "Thanks," she says. "I'm Gabrielle."

"Hi," I say shyly. "I really like your outfit."

"Me too," she giggles, then smiles before waving her fingers and gliding off the stage.

"Oooooh, you like her. You should get a lap dance."

"Yeah, get a lap dance! Get a lap dance!"

My friends are practically jumping up and down in their excitement, making me blush.

"Maybe."

"No, no, you should get one. She's totally hot."

"I know, I know, but let me think about it, OK?" They're so eager for me to lose my lap dance virginity, I'm afraid they may drag me over to her.

I need to get away for a minute, so I go to the bathroom. To my shock, I find her sitting inside, casually chatting with a friend. "Oh, hi," I stammer. "Is this your dressing room?"

She laughs. "No, but it's almost the same quality." I smile at her and then go into the stall, nervous at having spoken to her. When I emerge and begin to wash my hands, she admires my purse. I tell her about it and then take out my sparkly lip gloss. She asks to try some, and I hold it out to her, watching as her finger dips into the red goo. We talk a bit more about make-up and then she says, casually, "Did you want to get a lap dance?"

Did I? Of course! "Yes, I'd like that," I say.

"Great, just give me a few more minutes and I'll come get you."

I practically float out of the door and back to my friends. *I'm going to get a lap dance, and I arranged it all by myself! Ha!* I feel like gloating. I wait patiently, trying not to let my excitement show in a big stupid grin.

After a few minutes, she emerges and summons me, leading me to the other side of the stage, against a wall where I've seen other girls pressed up against mostly old men. She seats me on a plastic-covered couch, then takes a chair and places it a few feet in front of me. "So people can't look up your skirt," she tells me. I smile to thank her for her kindness; it never would've occurred to me. I give her some larger bills, and we talk for a minute or two before a song she likes comes on.

And then, quite suddenly, it starts. She pushes me so my head is tilted back against the wall, the rest of me pressed against the sticky plastic, my legs slightly spread. She stands between my legs, then leans forward, pressing her entire body along the length of mine. She smells like sweat and lotion and some undefinable sweetness, and I breathe deeply. Even her sweat smells good, like baby powder. Her soft hair brushes against my face and shoulders; her breasts are pressed up against mine. Then I feel her thigh against my hand; she's climbed up on the couch with me. This is definitely not what I expected. I've never been to a strip club before, but I thought I knew the deal – I'd seen Go, right? You can't touch the dancers or you'll get kicked out. But what if they're touching you? What about her hand gliding along mine, the outside of her smooth thigh touching my arm, her slightly damp skin setting mine on fire? The look she gives me is priceless: as her body moves downwards and she's crouched near my stomach, I look down and her hooded eyes are on me, her face a vision of pure lust, her mouth slightly open. I'm sure it's a practised look, but it feels as real as any look I've ever received, and it enters and warms me.

I think I know what I'm getting into; I've read all the feminist arguments, the sex worker manifestos. This is just a job and I'm a paying customer: one song, one lap, one transaction. But all of that background disappears, likewise my friends, my family, LA, everyone else in the club. It's just me and her, never mind the music; it's that look as she slides

between my open legs. I swallow heavily. I can't move, and I
don't want to, ever again. I just want to sit here and let her
brush herself against me again and again as I keep getting
wetter. And then her hand reaches up, delicately turning
around my necklace, a Jewish star. It's the sweetest gesture,
and something only another femme would notice or care about.
She gives me a little smile as she does it, and I give her one
back.

The song is almost over, and she gives it her all. Her body
pushes hard against mine, pressing my chest, stomach, thighs.
She's working me so good this huge bouncer walks over and
glances at us suspiciously, but she turns around and gives him a
look that tells him to move along. I like knowing that whatever
she's doing with me is enough out of the norm to warrant the
bouncer's attention. I feel ravished in a way I've never felt
before; it's pure sexual desire, concentrated into whatever
messages her skin and her eyes can send me in the course of
a five-minute song.

When the song ends I give her a generous tip, and she sits
with me for a little while. She takes my hand in hers, which is
delicate and soft, and I revel in her touch. It's tender and
sensitive, and I need this, need to hear her sweet voice tell me
about her career as a singer, her friendship with a famous
musician, her upcoming trip to New York. I need to hear
whatever it is she wants to tell me, true or not. My head knows
certain things; this is a strip club, that was a lap dance, this is
her job. But inside, inside, I know something else. I know that
we just exchanged something special. It wasn't sex or passion
or lust per se; it was more than, and less than, each of those
things. It was contact, attention, and adoration. Call me crazy,
but I think it went both ways.

After we talk, I go back to my friends, but I feel a bit odd. I
know they were watching, but did they see what really happened?

"That was some lap dance."

"Yeah, that was really amazing for your first time."

"She gave you her real name? That's a big stripper no-no."

"I think she liked you."

I nod and respond minimally, still in my own world. For the

rest of the trip, whatever I'm doing, wherever I am, part of me is still sitting on that plastic-covered couch, looking down at her, breathing her scent, revelling in her look.

I haven't gone to any more strip clubs since, or gotten any more dances. How could they ever live up to her? I don't know if I want to find out.

A Cool Dry Place

R Gay

Yves and I are walking because even if his Citroën were working, petrol is almost seven dollars a litre. He is wearing shorts, faded and thin, and I can see the muscles of his thighs trembling with exhaustion. He worries about my safety, so every evening at six he picks me up at work and walks me home, all in all a journey of twenty kilometres amid the heat, the dust and the air redolent with exhaust fumes and the sweet stench of sugarcane. We try and avoid the crazy drivers with no real destination who try to run us off the road for sport. We walk slowly, my pulse quickening as he takes my hand. Yves's hands are what I love best about him; they are calloused and wrinkled, the hands of a man much older than he is. At times, when he is touching me, I am certain that there is wisdom in Yves's hands. We have the same conversation almost every day – what a disaster the country has become, but we cannot even muster the strength to say the word "disaster" because such a word does not aptly describe what it is like to live in Haiti. There is sadness in Yves's face that also cannot be aptly described. It is an expression of ultimate sorrow, the reality of witnessing the country, the home you love, disintegrating around you. I often wonder if he sees such sorrow in my face, but I am afraid to look in a mirror and find out.

We stop at the market in downtown Port-au-Prince. Posters for Aristide and the Family Lavalas are all over the place, even though the elections, an exercise in futility, have come and gone. A vendor with one leg and swollen arms offers me a box of Tampax for twelve dollars, thrusting the crumpled blue and white box toward me. I ignore him as a red-faced American tourist begins shouting at us. He wants directions to the Hotel Montana, he is lost, his map of the city is wrinkled and torn and splotched with cola. "We are Haitian, not deaf," I tell him calmly and he relaxes visibly as he realizes that we indeed speak English.

Yves rolls his eyes and pretends to be fascinated with an art vendor's wares. He has very little tolerance for "fat Americans". Just looking at them makes him feel hungry and feeling hungry reminds him of the many things he tries to ignore. Yves learned English in school, but I learned from television: *I Love Lucy*, *The Brady Bunch*, and my favourite show, *The Jeffersons*, with the little black man who walks like a chicken. When I was a child, I would sit and watch these shows and mimic the actors' words until I spoke them perfectly. Now, as I tell the red-faced man the wrong directions, because he has vexed me by his mere presence in my country, I mouth my words slowly, with what I hope is a flawless American accent. The man shakes my hand too hard and thrusts five gourdes into my sweaty hand. Yves sucks his teeth as the man walks away and tells me to throw the money away, but I stuff the faded bills inside my bra and we continue to walk around, pretending we can afford to buy something sweet or something nice.

When we get home the heat threatens to suffocate us. The air conditioning is not working because of the daily power outages, so the air inside is thick and refuses to move. I look at the rivulets of sweat streaming down Yves's dark face and I want to run away to some place cool and dry, but I am not sure that such a place exists any more. My mother has prepared dinner, boiled plantains and *griot*, grilled cubes of pork. She is weary, sweating, slouched in a chair. She doesn't even speak to us as we enter, nor do we speak to her because there is nothing any of us can say to each other that hasn't already been said. She stares and stares at the black-and-white photo of my father, a man I have little recollection of because he was murdered by the Ton Ton Macoute, the secret military police force, when I was only five years old. Late at night, I am plagued by memories of my father being dragged from our home and beaten as he was thrown into the back of a large green military truck. And then I feel guilty because, regardless of what he suffered, I think that he was the lucky one. Sometimes, my mother stares at the picture so hard, her eyes glaze over and she starts rocking back and forth and it is as if he is dancing her across the small space of our kitchen the way he used to. In those moments, I look at Yves. I know that should anything happen to him, it will be me holding his picture, remembering what was and will never be, and I have a clear understanding of a woman's capacity to love.

We eat quickly and afterward, Yves washes the dishes outside. My stomach still feels empty. I rest my hand over the slight swell of my belly. I want to cry out that I am still hungry, but I don't because I cannot add to their misery with my petty complaints. I catch Yves staring at me through the dirty window as he dries his hands. He always looks at me in such a way that lets me know that his capacity to love equals mine: eyes wide, lips parted slightly as if the words "I love you" are forever resting on the tip of his tongue. He smiles, but looks away quickly, as if there is an unspoken rule forbidding such minor demonstrations of joy. Sighing, I rise and kiss my mother on the forehead, gently rubbing her shoulders. She pats my hand and I retire to the bedroom Yves and I share, waiting. It seems like he is taking for ever and I close my eyes, imagining his thick lips against my collarbone and the weight of his body pressing me into our mattress. Sex is one of the few pleasures we have left, so I savour every moment we share before, during and after. It is dark when Yves finally comes to bed. As he crawls under the sheets, I can smell rum on his breath. I want to chastise him for sneaking away to drink but I know that a watery rum and coke is one of the few pleasures he has for the savouring. I lie perfectly still until he nibbles my earlobe.

Yves chuckles softly. "I know you are awake, Gabi."

I smile in the darkness and turn toward him. "I always wait for you."

He gently rolls me onto my stomach and kneels behind me, removing my panties as he kisses the small of my back. His hands crawl along my spine, and again I feel their wisdom as he takes an excruciating amount of time to explore my body. I arch toward him as I feel his lips against the backs of my thighs and one of his knees parting my legs. I try and look back at him but he nudges my head forward and enters me in one swift motion. I inhale sharply, shuddering, a moan trapped in my throat. Yves begins moving against me, moving deeper and deeper inside me and before I give myself over, I realize that the sheets are torn between my fingers and I am crying.

Later, Yves is wrapped around me, his sweaty chest clinging to my sweaty back. He holds my belly in his hands and I can feel the heat of his breath against the back of my neck.

"We should leave," he murmurs. "So that one day, I can hold you like this and feel our child living inside you."

I sigh. We have promised each other that we will not bring a child into this world, and it is but one more sorrow heaped onto a mountain of sorrows we share. "How many times will we have this conversation? We'll never have enough money for plane tickets."

"We'll never have enough money to live here, either."

"Perhaps we should just throw ourselves in the ocean." Yves stiffens and I squeeze his hand. "I wasn't being serious."

"Some friends of mine are taking a boat to Miami week after next."

I laugh rudely because this is another conversation we have had too often. Many of our friends have tried to leave on boats. Some have made it, some have not, and too many have turned back when they realized that the many miles between Haiti and Miami are not so small as the space on the map. "They are taking a boat to the middle of the ocean, where they will surely die."

"This boat will make it," Yves says confidently. "A priest is travelling with them."

I close my eyes and try to breathe, yearning for just one breath of fresh air. "Because his kind has done so much to help us here on land?"

"Don't talk like that." He is silent for a moment. "I told them we would be going too."

I turn around and try to make out his features beneath the moon's shadows. "Have you taken complete leave of your senses?"

Yves grips my shoulders to the point of pain. Only when I

wince does he loosen his hold. "This is the only thing that does make sense. Agwe will see to it that we make it to Miami, and then we can go to South Beach and Little Havana and watch cable TV."

My upper lip curls in disgust. "You will put your faith in the same god that traps us on this godforsaken island? Surely you have better reasons."

"If we go we might know, once in our lives, what it is like to breathe."

My heart stops and the room suddenly feels like a big echo. I can hear Yves's heart beating where mine is not. I can imagine what Yves's face might look like beneath the Miami sun. And I know that I will follow him wherever he goes.

When I wake, I blink, covering my eyes as cruel shafts of sunlight cover our bodies. My mother is standing at the foot of the bed, clutching the black-and-white photo of my father.

"Mama?"

"The walls are thin," she whispers.

I stare at my hands. They appear to have aged overnight. "Is something wrong?"

"Gabrielle, you must go with Yves," she says, handing me the picture of my father.

I stare at the picture, trying to recognize the curve of my eyebrow or the slant of my nose in his features. When I look up, my mother is gone. For the next two weeks I work and Yves spends his days doing odd jobs and scouring the city for supplies he anticipates us needing. I feel like there are two of me; I go through the motions, straightening my desk, taking correspondence for my boss, gossiping with my co-workers while at the same time I am daydreaming of Miami and places where Yves and I are never hungry or tired or scared or any of the other things we have become. I tell no one of our plans to leave, but the part of me going through the motions wants to tell everyone I see in the hopes that perhaps someone will try and stop me, remind me of all the unknowns between here and there.

At night, we exhaust ourselves making frantic love. We no longer bother to stifle our moans and cries and I find myself doing things I would never have considered doing before;

things I have always wanted to do. There is a certain freedom in impending escape. Three nights before we are to leave, Yves and I are in bed, making love. We are neither loud nor quiet as, holding my breasts in my hands, I trace his muscled calves and dark thighs with my nipples, shivering because it feels better than I could ever have imagined. Gently, Yves places one of his hands against the back of my head, urging me toward his cock. I resist at first, but he is insistent in his desire, his hand pressing harder, fingers tangling in my hair and taking firm hold. In the dim moonlight, I stare at his cock for a few moments, breathing softly. It looks different to me, in this moment, rigid and veined, curving ever so slightly to the right. I part my lips, licking them before I kiss the strangely smooth tip of his cock. His entire body tenses, Yves's knees cracking from the effort. I pretend that I am tasting an exotic new candy, slowly tracing every inch of him with my tongue. I drag my teeth along the thick vein that runs along the dark underside of his cock. My tongue slips into the small slit at the head. He tastes salty, yet clean, and my nervousness quickly subsides. I take Yves's throbbing length into my mouth. It becomes difficult to breathe, but it also excites me, makes me wet as he carefully guides me, his hands gripping harder and harder, his breathing faster.

Suddenly, he stops, roughly rolling me onto my chest, digging his fingers into my hips, pulling my ass into the air. I press my forehead against my arms, gritting my teeth, and I allow Yves to enter my darkest passage, whispering nasty words into the night as he rocks in and out of my ass. At once I feel so much pleasure and so much pain and the only thing I know is that I want more – more of the dull ache and the sharp tingling just beneath my clit, more of feeling like I will shatter into pieces if he inches any further. More. At the height of passion, Yves says my name, his voice so tremulous it makes my heart ache. It is nice to know that he craves me in the same way I crave him, that my body clinging to his is a balm.

Afterward, we lie side by side, our limbs heavy, and Yves talks to me about South Beach with the assurance of a man who has spent his entire life in such a place; a place where rich people and beautiful people and famous people dance salsa at night and eat in fancy restaurants overlooking the water. He tells me of expensive cars that never break down and jobs for everyone; good jobs where he can use his engineering degree and I can do whatever I want. And he tells me about Little Haiti, a neighbourhood just like our country, only better because the air conditioning always works and we can watch cable TV. Cable TV always comes up in our conversations. We are fascinated by its excess. He tells me all of this and I can feel his body next to mine, tense, almost twitching with excitement. Yves has smiled more in the past two weeks than in the three years we have been married and the 24 years we have known each other, and I smile with him because I need to believe that this idyllic place exists. I listen even though I have doubts, and I listen because I don't know quite what to say.

The boat will embark under the cover of night. On the evening of flight, I leave work as I always do, turning off all the lights and computers, smiling at the security guard, telling everyone I will see them tomorrow. It is always when I am leaving work that I realize what an odd country Haiti is, with the Internet, computers, fax machines and photocopiers in offices, and the people who use them living in shacks with the barest of amenities. We are truly a people living in two different times. Yves is waiting for me as he always is, but today he wears a nice pair of slacks and a button-down shirt and the black shoes he wears to church. This is his best outfit, only slightly faded and frayed. The tie his father gave him hangs from his left pocket. We don't talk on the way home. We only hold hands and he grips my fingers so tightly that my elbow starts tingling. I say nothing, however, because I know that right now, Yves needs something to hold on to.

I want to steal away into the sugarcane fields we pass, ignoring the old men, dark, dirty and sweaty as they wield their machetes. I want to find a hidden spot and beg Yves to take me, right there. I want to feel the soil beneath my back and the stalks of cane cutting my skin. I want to leave my blood on the land and my cries in the air before we continue our walk home, Yves's seed staining my thighs, my clothes and demeanour hiding an intimate knowledge. But such a thing is entirely inappropriate, or at least it was before all this madness began.

My face burns as I realize what I am thinking and I start walking faster. I have changed so much in so short a time.

My mother has changed as well. I would not say that she is happy, but the grief that normally clouds her features is missing, as if she slid out of her shadow and hid it someplace secret and dark. We have talked more in two weeks than in the past two years and, while this makes me happy, it also makes me sad, because we can never make up for the conversations we did not have and soon cannot have. We will write, and someday Yves and I will save enough money to bring my mother to us in Miami, but nothing will ever make up for the wide expanse between now and then.

By the time we reach our home, Yves and I are drenched in sweat. It is hot, yes, but this is a different kind of sweat. It reeks of fear and unspeakable tension. We stare at each other as we cross the threshold, each mindful of the fact that everything we are doing, we are doing for the last time. My mother is moving about the kitchen, muttering to herself. Our suitcases rest next to the kitchen table, and it all seems rather innocent, as if we are simply going to the country for a few days, and not across an entire ocean. I cannot wrap my mind around the concept of crossing an ocean. All I know is this small island and the few feet of water I wade in when I am at the beach. Haiti is not a perfect home, but it is a home nonetheless. I am surprised that I feel such overwhelming melancholy at a time when I should be feeling nothing but hope.

Last night, Yves told me that he never wants to return, that he will never look back. Lying in bed, my legs wrapped around his, my lips against the sharpness of his collarbone, I burst into tears.

"Chère, what's wrong?" he asked, gently wiping my tears away with the soft pads of his thumbs.

"I don't like it when you talk like that."

Yves stiffened. "I love my country and I love my people, but I cannot bear the thought of returning to this place where I cannot work or feel like a man or even breathe. I mean you no insult when I say this, but you cannot possibly understand."

I wanted to protest, but as I lay there, my head pounding, I realized that I probably couldn't understand what it was like

for a man in this country, where men have so many expectations placed upon them that they can never hope to meet.
There are expectations of women here, but in some strange
way it is easier for us, because it is in our nature, for better or
worse, to do what is expected of us. And yet there are times
when it is not easier, times like that moment when I wanted to
tell Yves that we should stay and fight to make things better,
stay with our loved ones, just stay.

I have saved a little money for my mother. It started with the
five gourdes from the red-faced American, and then most of
my paycheck and anything else I could come up with. This
money will not make up for the loss of a daughter and a son-in-
law, but it is all I have to offer. After we leave, she is going to
stay with her sister in Petit Goave. I am glad for this, because I
could not bear the thought of her alone in this stifling little
house, day after day. I am afraid she would just shrivel up and
die like that. I am afraid she will shrivel up and die, regardless.

I walk around the house slowly, memorizing each detail,
running my hands along the walls, tracing each crack in the
floor with my toes. Yves is businesslike and distant as he
remakes our bed, fetches a few groceries for my mother, hides
our passports in the lining of his suitcase. My mother watches
us but we are all silent. I don't think any of us can bear to hear
the sound of one another's voices and I don't think we know
why. Finally, a few minutes past midnight, it is time. My
mother clasps Yves's hands between her smaller, more brittle
ones. She urges him to take care of me, take care of himself. His
voice cracks as he assures her that he will, that the three of us
won't be apart long. She embraces me tightly, so tightly that
again my arms tingle, but I say nothing. I hold her, kissing the
top of her head, promising to write as soon as we arrive in
Miami, promising to write every single day, promising to send
for her as soon as possible. I make so many promises I cannot
promise to keep.

And then, we are gone. My mother does not stand in the
doorway, waving, as she might were this a movie. We do not
look back and we do not cry. Yves carries our suitcases and
quickly we make our way to a deserted beach where there are
perhaps thirty others, looking as scared as Yves and I. There is

a boat – large, and far sturdier than I had imagined, for which I am thankful. I have been plagued by nightmares of a boat made from weak and rotting wood, leaking and sinking into the sea, the hollow echo of screams the only thing left behind. Yves greets a few of his friends, but stays by my side. "We're moving on up," I quip, and Yves laughs, loudly. I see the priest Yves promised would bless this journey. He is only a few years older than us, so to me, he appears painfully young. He has only a small knapsack and a Bible so worn it looks like the pages might fall apart at the lightest touch. His voice is quiet and calm as he ushers us onto the boat. Below deck there are several small cabins, and Yves seems to know instinctively which one is ours. At this moment, I realize that Yves has spent a great deal of money to arrange this passage for us. I know he has his secret, but I am momentarily irritated that he has kept something this important from me. He stands near the small bed, his arms shyly crossed over his chest, and I see an expression on his face I don't think I have ever seen before. He is proud, his eyes watery, chin jutting forward. And I know that I will never regret this decision, no matter what happens to us, because I have waited my entire life to see my husband like this. In many ways, I am seeing him for the first time.

Little more than two hours after the boat sets sail, I am above deck leaning over the railing, heaving what little food is in my stomach into the ocean. Even on the water, the air is hot and stifling. We are still close to Haiti, but I had hoped that the moment we set upon the ocean, I would be granted one sweet breath of cool air. Yves is cradling me against him between my bouts of nausea, promising that this sickness will pass, promising this is but a small price to pay. I am tired of promises, but they are all we have to offer each other. I tell him to leave me alone, and as his body slackens against me, I can tell he is hurt, but I have too many things happening in my mind to comfort him when I need to comfort myself more. I brush my lips across his knuckles and tell him I'll meet him in our cabin soon. He leaves, reluctantly, and when I am alone, I close my eyes, inhaling the salt of the sea deep into my lungs, hoping that smelling this thick salty air is another one of those things I am doing for the last time.

I think of my mother and father and I think that being here on this boat may well be the closest I will ever come to knowing my father, knowing what he wanted for his family. My head is splitting because my thoughts are thrown in so many directions. All I want is a little peace, and I never feel more peaceful than when I am with Yves. Wiping my lips with the back of my hand, ignoring the strong taste of bile lingering in the back of my throat, I return below deck to find Yves sitting on the end of the bed, rubbing his forehead.

I place the palm of my hand against the back of his neck. It is warm and slick with sweat. "What's wrong?"

He looks up, but not at me. "I'm worried about you."

I push him further onto the bed and straddle his lap. He closes his eyes and I caress his eyelids with my fingers, enjoying the curl of his eyelashes and the way it tickles my skin. He is such a beautiful man, but I do not tell him this. He would most likely take it the wrong way. At the very least, it would make him uncomfortable. It is a strange thing in some men, this fear of their own beauty. I lift his chin with one finger and trace his lips with my tongue. They are cracked but soft. His hands tremble but he grips my shoulders firmly. I am amazed at how little is spoken between us, yet how much is said. We quickly slip out of our clothes and his thighs flex between mine. The sensation of his muscle against my flesh is a powerful one that makes my entire body tremble.

I slip my tongue between his lips and the taste of him is so familiar and necessary that I am suddenly weak. I fall into Yves, kissing him so hard that I know my lips will be bruised in the morning. I want them to be. Yves pulls away first, drawing his lips roughly across my chin down to my neck, the hollow of my throat, practically gnawing at my skin with his teeth. I moan hoarsely, tossing my head backwards, a gesture of acquiescence and desire. My neck throbs and I know that here, too, there will be bruises. He sinks his teeth deeper into me and I can no longer perceive the fine line between pain and pleasure. But just as soon as I consider asking him to stop, he does, lathering the fresh wounds with the softness of his tongue, murmuring sweet and tender words. Such gentleness in the wake of such roughness leaves me shivering.

The weight of my breasts rests in Yves's hands, and he lowers his lips to my nipples, suckling them. He looks up at me as he suckles, and it is unclear whether this is a moment of passion or a moment of comfort for him . . . for me. And then I cannot look at him so I rest my chin against the top of his head, my arms wrapped around him, my hips slowly rocking back and forth. My cunt brushes along the length of his cock, hard beneath me. I am wet already, and I want him inside me, but I wait. This moment, whatever it is, demands patience. He turns our bodies so that I am lying on my back and slowly, almost too slowly, he draws his tongue along my torso, inside my navel, the round of my belly. He is reverent in his touch and I can feel the tension in my body easing away as I surrender my trust and fear and hope to this one man.

His hands massaging my thighs, Yves places a cheek against the soft, wiry patch of hair covering my mound. And then he is tracing the lips between my thighs with only one finger. His touch is tentative at first, and then it is possessive and insistent as he covers the most sensitive part of me with his mouth, tasting and teasing me with his tongue, that one finger sliding inside me so subtly that I gasp, and clench around him and hear a distant voice begging him for more. It is agonizing that at a time like this, Yves is making love to me in such a manner when all I want is him fucking me so hard that I feel everything and nothing at all. His tongue is moving faster, so fast that it feels like a constant, and then I cannot take it any more.

"Fuck me," I say harshly, and he blinks, looking at me as if he, too, is seeing me for the first time.

"*Oui, ma chère,*" he whispers, crawling up my body, kissing me as he slowly slides his cock, inch by inch, into the wet heat of my cunt.

Yves takes hold of my knees, spreading my legs wide and pushing them upward until they practically touch my face. I rest my ankles against his shoulders and shudder as he pulls his cock to the edge of my cunt and then buries himself to the hilt over and over again. I am intimately aware of his pulsing length; his sweat falling onto my body, into my eyes, mingling with mine; the tension in his body as I claw at the wide stretch of black skin across his back with my fingernails. Tomorrow,

he, too, will have bruises. My cunt loosens around his cock and
Yves groans, hiding his face in my armpit, trying to stay in
control.

"Let go," I urge him.

Then, he is fucking me faster and harder, so much so that I
cannot recognize him, and my chest heaves because I am
thankful. A cry that has been trapped deep in my throat is
finally released and the sound of it is peculiar. It is a sound that
only a woman who has known what I have known can make. I
can feel wetness trailing down the inside of my arm. It is Yves's
tears. My thigh muscles are screaming, so I wrap my legs
tightly around his waist. I am tender inside but I don't want
Yves to ever stop, because with each stroke of his cock he takes
me further away from the geography of our grief and closer to a
cool dry place.

Bacon, Lola and Tomato

Susannah Indigo

The first time Lola found out that Keith had cheated on her, she gained ten pounds almost overnight. *I love you and I will wait for you, my sweet tomato*, his email note had said when she "accidentally" read it on his computer, which was cute, except that he certainly never referred to *her* as any kind of fruit or vegetable. "It's nobody," he offered with a guilty shrug as she sat slurping her second bowl of ramen noodles, "just a way to waste time online and avoid working on my novel."

"I am not a tomato," Lola Maria Estonia pointed out to him, just in case he had forgotten. She flipped her long black hair in the way that made men crazy and wrapped it around his wrists as though she could hold him that way. "But you do always wait for me."

They laughed; she forgave him; they made love; she got up afterwards while he slept and made herself a big bowl of Apple Jacks with raisins and four teaspoons of sugar.

The day Lola found his cell phone bill she discovered the joy of a box of Krispy Kremes, fresh and warm off the rack, half of them eaten directly while she was still in the bakery, the rest of the dozen melting in her mouth on the drive home. It appeared that the *sweet tomato* lived just one area code away and received almost daily calls ranging from ten minutes to two hours.

"I love you, Lola Maria," Keith swore that night when they crawled into their four-poster bed, the same bed they had shared for one year, two months, and twenty-three days. He whispered as he slid inside her and gave the extra soft flesh on her bottom a spank: "*You are the voluptuous overflowing lush root of every desire any man has ever had.*"

This was why she had moved in with him in the first place, because he had the words that could change the way she breathed. But now his words seemed to be adapting to her new body – he used to only call her *my fragile princess, my little girl*.

"I'm sorry I've hurt you," he whispered as they laid in bed with their legs entangled. "Is there anything I can do to make it up to you?"

She hated to think of fighting with him, or worse, to hear him lie again. "I'm *hungry*," she finally answered, sure that more carbohydrates would make her vision of telephone bills disappear into sated bliss. So Keith got up and made her his special omelette with sausage and potatoes, no tomatoes, and for once she ate every single bite on her plate.

Lola Maria Estonia was up to a size 14 from her former size 8 when she finally went to visit the mysterious *tomato*. The sun was growing hotter and hotter as she stood on the sidewalk across the street from the address she had tracked down from the phone number. Lola was so fascinated that she took up more space in the world than she used to, even in the middle of the sidewalk, that she only smiled as the warmth grew under her red leather jacket, newly purchased from the Coldwell Collection in a comfy size for the "plus" woman. She had thrown out all of her old skinny jeans, although Keith had suggested that perhaps she should keep them because she would need them again soon. Lola had just smiled and gone shopping.

It didn't seem that Keith spent much face-to-face time with the *tomato*, because he was usually at home at his computer, or at his part-time job at the bookstore, or out with Lola. She wasn't about to ask Keith any more questions – she just monitored his email and phone calls, as though she was a detective. She also checked up on his novel that he said he was *almost* done with, and realized he hadn't written much of anything in a long time. *Why is it that I live with this man?* she wondered on her bad days, but then she remembered all the words, and how he made love to her with such passion, and how she was *almost* sure he was her soulmate, not to mention a good cook.

The *tomato* came out of the front door of her small house and walked directly toward a Lincoln Town Car that was parked just beyond Lola. "Nice jacket," she said to Lola as she passed by.

"Would you like to have it?" Lola asked in an awkward gesture of friendliness that she hoped covered her desperation to find out more about this *tomato*. She had heard that people did this in some other places – Japan, maybe? – and suddenly it seemed like offering another woman her red leather jacket on a hot summer day was a normal thing to do.

The *tomato* stopped, turned, and laughed, taking Lola in fully from head to toe for the first time. Lola wore a long black cotton skirt, a white shirt with her black lace bra peeking out, and heavy silver jewellery. "Would I like it?" The *tomato* moved closer and stroked Lola's arm, checking the fabric, checking Lola, deciding. "Sure. It looks like a good fit."

"Thank you," whispered Lola in her smallest voice, though she knew she was the one who was supposed to say, "you're welcome." But she could not keep her eyes off the *tomato* – she had long curly red hair down to her waist, large breasts, great cleavage in a tight black tank top, and black jeans that looked to Lola like they were just about a size 14, maybe even 16. She was almost, Lola realized, identical in body to Lola's new look, and if Lola dyed her black hair red, she thought she could almost be her twin.

"My friends call me Cherry," said the *tomato*, slipping on the red jacket. "And you are . . .?"

"Lola Maria Estonia. Can I come with you?" Odd words were flowing out of her mouth, like someone else was writing them – better dialogue, she thought with a sharp twist of spite, than anything she had ever read in Keith's agonized attempts at novel writing.

"Do you know where I'm going?"

Lola couldn't guess, but she knew she wanted to be there. The curves on the *tomato*'s hips were hypnotizing her, and she thought that maybe she wanted to touch them.

"To meet a man?" she guessed timidly. "My boyfriend's in love with you – maybe it's him?"

Cherry *tomato* laughed again, a long rollicking laugh, a laugh that Lola wanted to climb inside of and ride on, knowing it would carry her to a new place. "They're all in love with me, sweetheart," Cherry finally said. "Let's go eat meat."

The steakhouse was wood-panelled with high leather booths, an old-style male bonding place, complete with a private cigar room. Cherry tucked Lola into the booth seat and then slid in beside her. They each ordered the 14-ounce prime rib, baked potatoes with sour cream and butter, no salads, and chocolate amaretto pie for dessert.

"It's just phone sex for me, sweetheart," Cherry explained between bites. "But as soon as I tell them I have long red hair and big tits, they're in love. The attention is great, along with the money. It supports my other passion."

"Keith has phone sex with you? Keith . . . pays . . . for phone sex??" Lola repeated in amazement.

"Keith? I don't remember their real names very well – what's he like?"

"Well, he's really smart . . . and he talks a lot, but I guess everyone must to have phone sex. His words – they're fancy, poetic, sometimes a bit over-the-top – he's a writer."

Cherry scooped up the last bite of pie and turned to feed it to Lola. "Open wide, sweetheart." As it melted in Lola's mouth, Cherry began to kiss her and lick her lips clean. "Yes, I know which one he is, baby," she whispered through the kisses. "I call him 'Bacon' – I give them all meat names, my little joke, but they think it's a macho compliment – he's a bit . . . greasy, isn't he? Doesn't seem like your type."

Lola couldn't imagine why she should care, and could barely remember who he was herself. This woman, this *tomato*, this lovely plump mirror image of herself, was driving her wild with her lips and her fingers running up and down her legs. *Maybe this is why I just keep eating so much*, she thought, *to be worthy of someone like her*.

Cherry's fingers were high up her thigh under her skirt, beginning to stroke rhythmically towards her clit, when the waiter reappeared with the check. "Thanks," Cherry said to him, "we do have to hurry and we have someplace to be."

Lola assumed it would be her bed, or the backseat of the car, or any place nearby where they could continue. "No, sweetheart, I'm an organizer," the *tomato* explained to her on the way out. "We have a demonstration this afternoon. Consider yourself recruited – I promise you'll think of yourself differently after the day is done."

A group of about twelve women had gathered in the park just off of the Walnut Street open-air mall. They were holding signs, and there were hundreds of other people on the mall, most of them barely paying attention to the women. A few of the women were on rollerblades, one was doing tricks on her skateboard, and another had a baby on her hip.

Cherry parked the car and turned to Lola.

"They're waiting for me . . . for us, to start, baby. Take your shirt off."

"What?"

"Your shirt – take it off. Here, I'll help."

Lola decided this was a game, a tease, so she let Cherry unbutton her shirt and slip it from her shoulders.

"Nice, baby, good girl . . ." Cherry was unhooking Lola's bra and kissing her nipples, sucking on them, pulling slow and hard, sending the tingle right down to Lola's toes. "We should get them pierced," Cherry told her between kisses. "That always stops the cops."

"Cops?" Lola pulled away, just as two women with their picket signs approached the car and banged on the window for Cherry. The sign that Lola could see said: TOPFREE! TAKE YOUR SHIRTS OFF FOR EQUALITY!

"Yeah, you know, cops – pigs – that other mostly white meat around here," the *tomato* answered. "Technically, they can arrest us, but they rarely do, as long as we get the girls with the best tits to talk to them."

Cherry pulled Lola out of the car before she could answer, looping Lola's shirt into her jeans belt beside her own top she had stripped off. "You're a goddess," Cherry said as they joined the group on the lawn, "and you have as much right to be shirtless as any man does."

It was hot, and there *were* lots of men on the mall with their shirts off, and nobody looked twice at *them*. Lola watched as all the women around her took their tops off, in awe at the variety of breasts and backs and skin tones.

"They're beautiful," she whispered to the *tomato*.

"Exactly. So why is it that women have to keep their shirts on? Because they can feed babies from their nipples, a purely natural act? Or is it because women are nothing but sex objects to men, almost like pieces of . . . *meat*?"

Lola laughed and stood up a little prouder, her newly plump breasts perking up a bit more. "I've never even thought about it," she confessed.

"I know. Yet if you go out and do it by yourself somewhere, even on a beach, it's a criminal act. Equality for women is my passion, sweetheart, and nothing makes a stronger statement than this."

Lola had to agree as they began their march down the mall. Some people cheered, some booed, and a lot of men hooted and cat-called at them. But no one stopped them – Cherry went in the record shop to buy a CD, and though the manager asked her to put her shirt back on, she said, "No," pointed to a man in the jazz aisle with *his* shirt off, and then proceeded to make her purchase and leave.

"*No*. That's about my favourite word for women." Cherry had big, gorgeous, heavy breasts, and though Lola was trying to think about politics and women's rights, sex was churning between her thighs. "No whining, no fuss, just '*no, I won't*' does wonders."

Lola trailed behind her like a puppy dog, trying to remember if she'd ever said "no" very firmly to Keith or any other man anywhere in her life.

"Hey, T-Bone, what's happening," the *tomato* said to a tall dark-haired man who greeted her near the central water fountain. Lola watched as the man kissed Cherry's hand, never touching her breasts, chatted for a few minutes, and then turned to go into a pizza shop.

"One of my clients," Cherry explained.

"Your client? They come here to see you? Does Keith . . . come . . . see you?" Lola raced over her words as she tried to wrap her mind around the sudden image of Keith seeing her half-naked in a public street mall.

"Bacon? He has. Some do – after I know them for a while, I tell them to stop by one of our demonstrations, it's good for them – seeing me in the flesh raises their consciousness and their cocks at the same time."

Lola stood speechless as she watched a security guard approach the group. He looked them all up and down – one woman was quietly breastfeeding while sitting on the edge of the fountain, others were chatting, some had packages from their purchases, and one woman with lovely brown breasts who looked like she might be 60 or so had pulled some yarn from her fanny-pack and was happily knitting and purling while waiting for the group.

"What do you think you're doing?" the guard said, a bit tentatively.

Cherry held Lola's hand. "Well, *she's* shopping for some new clothes, Afton there is making her granddaughter a sweater, and the rest of us are just relaxing." Cherry's breasts were about two inches from the guard's chest while she was talking, and Lola knew, just knew, that when he put his hands in his pockets it was not to pull out a gun, or even a ticket, but to keep himself from stroking her nipples. "Well . . . I think you should all put your tops back on, ma'am . . ."

"*No*. We can't do that. I know you believe that women and men are equal, right? So if you ask us to do that, you'd have to ask Bratwurst over there to do the same." She nodded toward a stocky brown-skinned man who had his shirt off and was talking with the woman on a skateboard. The guard looked towards him for an explanation.

Bratwurst just shrugged toward Cherry. "She's a *hot tomato*," he said with a wink at the guard.

"Yeah," echoed T-Bone, overhearing as he rejoined the group, pizza in hand. "And she's explained it clearly enough to *me*. Tits just want to be free."

"Well done, meat." Cherry whispered to the giggling Lola, "I train them well." The security guard rolled his eyes and shook his head. "OK, *girls*, just be gone when I come back this way later."

"*No,*" the *tomato* said loudly to his departing back, but he didn't turn back to argue with her.

Lola never saw him again during the afternoon, though she imagined him hiding in shops and peeping at them whenever he could. After the rest of the group left for the day, Cherry dragged Lola into the *Dress Barn Woman* store, saying only, "Let's go change clothes."

In the dressing room, which fortunately had a wooden door that locked and went almost down to the floor, the *tomato* told Lola to strip.

"Everything?"

"Everything. Now. We're going to change clothes – with each other."

Lola pulled off her skirt and her panties and watched Cherry take off her jeans. They stood side by side in front of the mirror and looked at each other, their breasts tanned from the afternoon of sun, their sturdy hips, their matching curves, their long hair only an inch or so different in length – *maybe not twins*, Lola thought, *but definitely sisters.*

Cherry held Lola in front of her and caressed her. "Watch me," she whispered as her hands ran down over Lola's belly and her fingers began to slide inside Lola, who was already soaking wet.

"Watch me watching you," Cherry whispered again, and Lola met her eyes as Cherry's thumb stroked her clit and two fingers twisted deep inside her. "More," Lola sighed, "more . . . more." Cherry slid a third finger inside her as Lola leaned back against her and began to shudder.

"Open your eyes and watch," Cherry said, and she did, and all she could see was feminine skin and beauty and softness and her own trembling legs and Cherry's strong fingers bringing her to the finest orgasm she could ever remember having.

Cherry began to dress her in her jeans and tank top, but Lola protested that it was her turn. "Not yet, sweetheart," the *tomato* laughed. "Right now, I'm hungry."

"For what?"

"Bacon."

"I don't know if he'll be there," Lola said nervously as Cherry drove her home.

"It doesn't matter," Cherry said with a smile, Lola's thigh pressed up against hers as she drove, her right arm draped around Lola's shoulder. "He'll come."

Lola thought maybe she wanted to stay sitting just as they were in Cherry's old-style car for ever, with Cherry wearing Lola's skirt and shirt, minus the black lace bra since it wasn't quite big enough. They could drive around town, calling out new meat names for men, calling out to women to *take their tops off for equality!*, then ride off into the sunset, stopping every now and then to climb in the big back seat and fuck each other into some kind of happiness.

"Check the missed calls on my cell phone, baby, I'm sure you'll find he's around. But tell me, Lola, do you own a strap-on?"

Lola saw Keith's cell phone number on the phone, and tried to care, but she was too busy giggling at the idea of herself with a strap-on. "No, just a regular plug-in vibrator. We've never been too big on sex toys."

Cherry patted her shoulder like a child. "You'll find that Bacon has plenty."

"He does?"

"Yes, baby, check his gym bag that he never goes to the gym with."

The sudden curiosity growing over Lola was stronger than the rays of final evening sunlight piercing through their windows. "What do you do with him, Cherry? Why does he call you?"

"About the same as all meat, baby. They stroke themselves, they fantasize, I fantasize for them, they imagine sucking my tits . . ." she said, guiding Lola's head to that spot, unbuttoning one more button for her to imitate. "Then I almost always have them picture me with my big black strap-on fucking them up the ass, while they do it to themselves with their own dildoes and plugs."

Lola sucked, pressing her head hard to Cherry's breasts, while she felt her wetness almost flow down to her toes at Cherry's words.

"Yeah, I know," Cherry whispered softly to her, "it's hot, isn't it, baby? You can see why I do it for a living."

"He's never asked me for that," Lola said, coming up for air. "My finger there, maybe sometimes, but nothing else."

"And that's your answer, isn't it, why meat comes to the *tomato* – to get what they're not comfortable going for elsewhere. Don't worry, baby, we're here, and Bacon's got everything we need. We'll sizzle."

They took their tops off, even though it was dark, and ran up the stairs to Lola and Keith's place, but found no Bacon in sight. Lola found the gym bag immediately, and couldn't help but laugh at the variety found there.

"Let's greet him with them," Cherry said, starting to lay out a trail of toys from the front door to the bed with Lola's help. "Save these two, baby, that's what you'll need."

They raided the fridge and fed each other in bed; they raided each other and ate, and ate, until the entire apartment smelled like sex, and contentment. The sound of his key in the lock woke them both from their drowsy sexed-out sleep. Cherry jumped out of bed and covered Lola up with the quilt.

"You can't be here!" Keith said as the *tomato* stood in front of him stark naked and greeted him with a kiss. But she felt for his crotch and he was already hard, so she only laughed and walked him carefully through the toy-trail towards the bed.

"Lola will come home!" he tried again, but she assured him that wasn't a problem, and he began to lose track of his concern as she unbuttoned his shirt and kissed him again, hard. When he started moaning, she stopped undressing him, stepped back and said, "Bacon, strip."

He stripped for her, quickly. Lola popped up from beneath the covers and stared. Bacon. Keith was tall and lean, and if Lola squinted at him just right he did look like a piece of bacon – hot, a little slippery, not necessarily good for you, but tasty.

"Lola!" He looked more than stunned, staring at the two voluptuous naked women in front of him, rather like he was watching both his wildest fantasy and his worst nightmare come true.

"Lola, get dressed," he said in his firmest boyfriend voice, trying to regain some control over the situation.

"No," she said, and it sounded like someone else's voice, a strong voice, a voice that could stand up for itself anywhere in the world. "*No, I won't.*"

"Don't sweat, Bacon," the *tomato* jumped in. "We'll fuck *you*, you'll cook for *us*, we'll talk – *grill you* even, maybe. It will all become clear."

Keith smiled, then frowned, but Lola noticed that his cock never went down. "Lola, I barely know this woman . . . nothing she's told you is true . . . you both need to get dressed, and she has to leave."

"*No*," Lola said, this time in the voice of a goddess, a voice that owned not just its sexuality but its freedom, its joy, and the strength of a dozen proud women. She brought out the lube and his silver rocket dildo and held them up to him with a sweet smile. "*No. No more lies.*" She moved towards him and spanked his ass lightly. "Bend over, Bacon."

The Swing

Mari Ness

Hi. Ask a Nurse?

Great. You're like totally confidential, right? Like, totally, really confidential? OK. OK. Yeah. Well, see, this is real embarrassing. Yeah, I'm sure you have, but I don't know that you've heard this one. OK, OK. My wife's hanging suspended from the ceiling, and, she, well, this is the crazy part. She kind, err, superglued her strap-on to her skin, and it's starting to hurt her.

No, this isn't an obscene phone call. Believe me, if it were, I'd be coming up with something a lot less embarrassing.

No, I don't want to call 911.

I don't exactly have a lot of clothes on myself.

Oh, that. Well, the thing is, I'm kinda handcuffed to this chair.

Yeah, you're right. Maybe I should start from the beginning. How much of a beginning do you want?

Well, you see, here's the problem. My wife is *hot*. Seriously, seriously, hot. She's shaking her head right now at me, but I'm telling you, this woman is a fucking sex goddess.

Ma'am, believe me, this is relevant. None of this would be happening if she weren't so hot.

So what this means is, I want to fuck her. All the time. I mean, constantly. And she's fine with this, but she wants variety. Not just the same old missionary position over and over again. And I'm fine with that. But after a few years, when you're having the kinda constant sex that I'm demanding, you're kinda running out of positions on the bed, you know? Yeah, you know. So we're thinking through our options, wondering what we can do to get the variety she needs. We're not really that into, you know, sharing, and some of that S/M stuff – well, it's all pretty cool, but some of it just isn't, you know, us.

Oh, you do know how we feel. Good.

So anyway, we're shopping around, looking for catalogs and stuff, when suddenly we find The Swing. Think capital letters here, ma'am. Really capital letters. The thing's suspended from the ceiling, you see, and from it, either she, or I, can get into any number of positions that we could never reach on a bed. And the best thing of all – the thing can be raised or lowered *even as you're having sex*. I'm talking hot. I'm talking the thing had me so hot that I had to grab her right then and there while we were reading through the catalogue.

Oh, that time was in the kitchen – her up on the countertop. Quick, hard, good. I'm telling you, this woman is absolutely something.

Well, yeah, I'm handcuffed to a chair right now, but that doesn't mean I'll say absolutely anything. Besides which, if you were looking at her right now –

Yeah, I'm pretty tall. But the thing is, you can do the same thing, if you just get up on a stool. I mean, my wife's a bit shorter than me, so when we were going in the opposite direction –

Yeah, I'll get back to the story. So anyway, we bought this chair. Pretty damn expensive, but what the hell – we could easily delay buying me a new car for another couple of years, right? I mean, the thought of having Janice in there – that's her name, by the way, Janice – was just way too much to resist.

Oh. We bought it on the Internet. Amazing site, too. But you can find them anywhere. Another good thing – you can take the thing down quickly if, like, your mother-in-law's coming by, or something. Although we hung ours up in our extra room – the one we told guests was, you know, just storage. Course, we did store things there – a spare mattress, a hardback chair, a softer chair, some little toys and all that –

Oh, you have one of those too? Yeah, great, aren't they?

So anyway, we hang the thing up – having sex like three

times while we're doing it, cause, well, you know, it took some time to find a good stud to put a nail –

Yeah, okay, I'll stop with the bad puns. So anyway, we get this thing hung, and it's *incredible*. I mean, *incredible*. Once she's in it, I can do anything. I can pull her to any height I wanted, screw her up, down, sideways, you name it. She got me to hang in there a few times too, and let me tell you, the feel of her mouth on me when I was suspended – it took the whole concept of blow job to new levels. And the way she managed to angle me so I could watch every single moment of what she was doing – God, I'm telling you, it might be just as well that orgasms like that don't come every day.

Most of the time, though, it was her up in that swing, hanging lusciously down, letting me fondle every single damn part of her skin. For the first time, I could take her from behind – I mean, really, really take her from behind. Pull her up to just the right angle for my knees and so that I could just reach the G-spot and make her start going really wild, you know. I could fill my hands with her while I pushed into her – God, I'm hard again just thinking about it.

No, I can't do anything about it – my hands are handcuffed behind this chair, remember?

And she wore these great little silk things every time we used the thing – although to tell you the truth, since it's just you and me and she's over there suspended from the ceiling, I pretty much prefer her naked. I mean, she was meant to be naked, what with that amazing ass of hers. She's got, let me tell you, the absolutely perfect butt. She keeps claiming it's too fat, but I'm telling you, it's incredible – rounded, soft, meant for fondling and gripping. Sometimes I think I married her for her ass. And now, with this thing, I could have as much of her ass as I wanted. I could have her dangle there for hours, while I sucked and nibbled, sometimes rubbing at her hole, sometimes fucking her with my finger while I nibbled around her butt. It was –

Are you all right?

OK, just wondered about that sound there. Anyway, the thing was, I got totally, totally, into handling her ass, which was not cool, she tells me, because our agreement was variety.

And I'm like, fine, I like variety, but I just have to have more of your butt. And then it occurs to me. There's this one thing that we haven't tried.

Yeah, the other thing. Anal. I get, I gotta be honest with you, totally worked up at the idea. I've never done it before; she's never done it before. She's a little uncertain. But we've got lots of lube on hand, and I say, hey, it's variety, and she's like, OK, and I get her up in the swing and start playing with her tits, just to get her really ready again, until she's starting to moan again, and then she turns to me and says, with this incredible look on her face, you know, I get to do you next.

I'm so involved in her tits I totally miss this. All I want to do is suck at them some more before I move on, but then she raps me a bit with her fist and says, hey, did you hear me? And I look up at that, keeping one hand on one nipple, and say, what? And she repeats it. I get to do you next.

Now, I gotta tell you. I'm feeling really uneasy with the concept, variety or no variety. I mean, yeah, I've heard about guys doing this with their wives – but you, in the sense of jokes and stuff. And well, I never thought Janice had that sort of kink. But she looks as me as she's dangling there, in her little red silk teddy, and she – I swear – wiggles her butt at me. So what am I supposed to do, huh?

Yeah, that's right. I start playing with her breasts again, and then start lubing up her ass. And I do her in the ass, and, you know, it feels pretty good – very tight, very hard, and I come good and hard. It feels great. I give her a long kiss, and help her out of the thing, and then spend more time kissing and fondling her butt, and then, you know, we're going at it on the mattress again.

Six years, next Friday. Yeah, we're kinda stunned about some of these marathon sessions too. But, as I told you, she's hot.

Anyway, I admit it, I totally forget about my end of the bargain, and it's a few days before we head into that room again. By now we're both really horny again, since, believe it or not, there's been nothing since, and I want her, badly. This time, she's got on this black silk thing that shows off her legs, and I'm telling you, if I didn't know how good things were going to get, we would have been using the mattress right then and there. But I start pulling at the swing, lifting it up from the floor, and checking the ropes, watching her rummaging through drawers, wiggling her butt at me. And then she pulls out this strap-on.

And I'm like a bit, whoa, but she's grinning and twirling the thing around, and saying, remember what you agreed to. And I'm stuck, because, after all, she's right, I did agree to this. So she wiggles into the thing, and I'm staring at this strap-on attached to my wife, and I have to tell you, it's, well, quite something.

Honestly, I have no idea what I felt. Something, anyway.

But anyway, she comes up to me wearing the strap-on, and starts kissing me, and of course, my dick starts responding to this – can't help it, really. It's jumping, and I'm starting to jump, and she puts my hand on one of her tits, and that's enough to get me going. I play with her nipple for a bit, and then she breaks away and grabs a bottle of lube from the drawer.

Hey, I say, a bit uneasily. Before you like, get that inside me, why don't we try a few practice runs first? And she says, what do you have in mind, and I say, the same thing I do with you, you know, just rub it over me. Not the sexiest way to put it, I guess, but she seems to get all hot at the idea, so she slaps the belt holding the thing on and goes, yes, and points at the mattress. So I fall on it, and she follows me, and gets on top of me and begins kissing me and rubbing this dildo over me. Which I have to say is pretty weird, but I'm enjoying it anyway, because I can see that she's enjoying the experience. So I flip over on my front, and she runs the thing up and down my butt, and then I flip over again, and she mock-fucks me, moving between my legs, and I have to admit, this is all pretty fun.

There's only one problem – the strap-on itself, you see, which doesn't seem to understand that it's meant to be *strapped on*, and not, you know, wiggling about. Which it's doing. So Janice keeps having to stop, to adjust the thing, or make it tighter, or something. Come to think of it, I'm still not sure if she really put the thing on right in the first place, or if she even got the right one. Maybe she did, maybe she didn't. But the thing wasn't all that controlled. I mean, fine for our pretend leg fucking and all, but if she was really going to fuck me, she needed more control.

No, I didn't say anything. She decided that herself. She finally got up and walked over to our drawer where we keep various things, saying, maybe there's something here that will help this thing stay on better, and in the meantime, I'm just laying back, watching, because during all of this that little black thing she'd been wearing has come off in places, and I have one great look at her legs. So I put my hand down and start stroking my dick again, watching her rummage through the drawer, and I gotta say that I'm wondering if she's going to pull out some other fun toy, or if I'm ever going to get to do her again from behind in the swing again, or if she's just going to keep torturing me all day. But she rummages along, and finally comes up with a small tube of something. I think I can use this as sealant, she says.

Yeah, you can see where this is going.

Fuck, I say, that's *crazy glue*. But it's too late. She's already got the thing on her and it's good and stuck. I'm telling you, what they say about that stuff is absolutely true. It gets you in seconds.

Yeah, you must hear a lot of people saying this. I heard of one girl who glued her eyes shut.

Yeah. So anyway, here we are, me lying on the mattress looking at Janice, who is standing there with a strap-on literally glued to her. And she looks – sorry Janice, but you did – she looks totally ridiculous. Plus, I can see the expression on her face. That thing is not all that comfortable.

Oh come on, Janice. It was not.

Yeah, that's her in the background. She hasn't got much else to do but comment on this.

Anyway, I'm watching her. And I say something dumb.

Never mind how dumb. Let's just say it's one of those typical male comments, and leave it at that, OK? She gets this gleam in her eye as she says, oh really, and she comes over to me, swaggering, with this strap-on thing, and I'm still laughing. So she comes up and suddenly leans against me and with one hand pulls me down to her, so now I'm caught between a kiss and a laugh except that I'm not laughing any more, I'm kissing her, hard, because, damn it, it's laughable, but she's still got a way with her tongue, and the next thing I know, I'm sitting against the hard chair with her on my lap and that damn strap-on pushing against me, not that I care, because she's got her mouth on mine and her hand on my dick and she's rubbing it up and down gently, and I'm so fucking absorbed in this that I totally don't notice that she's also got my left hand, which is why I miss her slipping my hand into one of the metal handcuffs.

Now, I do notice the click. But hey, I've got her hand on my dick, and we've played this sort of thing before. I have a safeword, she has a safeword, and I don't think it's time for that sort of thing yet. So I go on kissing her, and she goes on threading the handcuffs through the back of the chair, and then she grabs my other hand and shoves it into the other cuff, so I'm firmly cuffed to the floor. And I'm thinking – I know it's stupid, but I'm thinking, oh man, I am going to get seriously fucked here. And I'm incredibly excited. She only cuffs me if she's really going to be driving me to my limits. I am almost jumping in the chair, I'm so ready for her.

She kisses me for a few more seconds, and then stands up. I give my hands a little tug – oh, yeah, I'm secure, and I wiggle a bit, just to show her I can. She grins at me, and then slowly turns and wiggles her butt at me. It's pure torture. I try jumping the chair a bit closer, and she shakes her head at me. Screw you, she says. Laugh at me because of this? Well, I tell you what. I'm going up in that swing, and I'm going to fuck myself up there with this thing, and you're just gonna watch. That's it. Nothing more, loverboy. And you're not even gonna be able to touch yourself now to get off. You're just going to have to watch and watch and watch as I get off. Funny, huh?

Now, of course, what I really want her to do is sit on me, even with that damn strap-on, and ride me hard. Or kneel down in front of me and give me a blowjob. Or something. I want her hands all over me. Of course, I'm too dumb to say this. I just say, hey, don't you think we should have a doctor check out that crazy glue?

Yeah, I mean, I thought it was a medically good idea too. She just turns and wiggles her butt at me. Oh, we can play doctor later, she says, as she saunters over to the swing.

I'm telling you, I forgot I was in that chair. I tried to get up and follow her, and of course I got slammed back down. I was a bit worried – usually I help get her into the thing, and I wasn't sure she could do it herself with any safety, but I guess we'd been using it enough that she had no problems. She put herself in so that her breasts were hanging down, and as she got in, one little nipple popped out, looking unbelievably tasty. I started moving my chair forward again. I had to have that nipple.

As I did so, I noticed something about that strap-on. It was one of those double-ended ones, see, with a part that she could insert inside her. Now, given the way she had it glued to her, she couldn't actually get it inside – not without getting a lot more limber, and she's shaking her head at me even now for saying that. But what she could do, see, is rub the edge against her clit. In fact, she was already doing that naturally. I could tell, just from her expression. That wasn't just turned on, that was totally stimulated. And, as she started to pull herself up, I could see, through the straps, that long black dildo working against her, and actually see how wet she was. So there she is, up there, suspended about six feet from the ceiling, and I'm there, moving my chair under her, begging her to come down a bit so I can at least get a taste of the nipple. She just smiles at me, and then manages to pull one hand down around to her clit. Let me tell you, I've been in that thing, and that's a lot harder than it looks. She must have been getting really horny. So she reaches her hand down and over and grabs the dildo and begins moving it back and forth a little –

Are you OK?

OK. Just sounded like you were having breathing problems or something.

Yeah, I can go on.

So anyway, she reaches for the dildo, and she moves it a bit, but she's forgotten something – the damn thing's still glued on. OK, technically it's only the straps, not the actual dildos, but they aren't all that mobile at the moment. I can see it's frustrating her. She gives up on the dildos, and instead, starts using her hand to start playing with her clit. I'm right under her, and I can tell you, it's an incredible sight, watching her play with herself, watching her start to moan and wiggle, watching those lovely fingers move up and down, fast, slow, up, down – I'm literally going crazy. My dick's so hard it's actually purple.

God, honey, I moan. I don't think I'm going to be able to take this any more, I say. You're going to have to come down and suck me. I'm not even sure she hears me. She's just there, taking care of herself, breaking hard, moving her fingers in and out of herself, starting with one finger, then two, slipping them in and out, hard, and then rubbing them against her clit. I can see that she's making this one of her long sessions, drawing this out the way she likes to do when she's torturing me, and God, it's working. I want her, desperately. I mean, I'm literally bouncing in this chair, which is not really a good thing, because my wrists keep hitting the handcuffs, you know, so I finally force myself to stop bouncing, and just sit back and watch. It's one beautiful sight, watching her up there, her eyes closed, her hand moving, her body continuing to move with her rhythm, swaying back and forth in the swing. And that's when the problem starts.

Yeah, problem. This is why I'm on the phone, remember? Here's the thing. As she's touching herself, she starts to come. And I can tell that for her, this is going to be a big one. Maybe because of the pain from the strap-on; maybe because I'm down here, telling her how incredibly hot she is while she's doing this, how much she's torturing me, how much I want her to come down here and suck my balls off or ride me, do something with me, and I know – I just know – that she's going to have to do this soon, because, I'm not kidding, there's a good chance of me getting a heart attack watching this if I can't touch myself and if she's not touching me. I know this has to be making her more intense, because I can tell you, I've been watching her come for years now, and I know the major orgasms when I see them. This was one of them.

She came, hanging up there in the swing, and – I swear to God – her body actually started to shake while the orgasm was running through her. I mean she's bucking up there, her hips gyrating as she comes, and she's shaking hard enough that she actually *flips over* in the swing. Worse, she releases the rope that allows her to go up and down, so it goes *flying* – literally flying up and around and around and ends up *circling* her. I barely even notice. The sight of her breasts quivering during this – and then suddenly the sight of that hot ass flipping around so that it's dangling down, right over me, where I could almost touch it if she was just a bit lower – well, let's say that I was a bit distracted. All I could do was watch that ass as it continued to quiver above me, until finally it stopped moving, and she just hung above me, panting. I could just see her sex peeping through, and it was enough to make me almost come, right there.

And as she's hanging there, she says, fuck. I think I'm stuck. And I'm looking up at her, still hard and say, what? And she says again, I think I'm stuck. So I look up at her.

Now, usually we follow the instructions, and leave that rope attached to the wall, so this sort of thing doesn't happen, but this time, we've both been so involved in what's been happening that we totally forget about this part. Which is a problem.

Christ, she repeats. Neil, I'm stuck.

And I'm like, what do you mean you're stuck? And she says, well, *I'm stuck*.

And that's when I notice it – the rope has twisted around her. And with each arm in a strap of the swing, and her torso supported by another strap, and her two legs caught in a strap – well, at this point, she's not very mobile, especially since the rope that would give her more mobility is *also* wrapped around her. She can't loosen herself, she can't lower herself, she can't even move me. She's just hung there, suspended from the ceiling, with a strap-on superglued to her. And I'm here handcuffed to the chair, right below her, unable to move, looking up right at that incredible ass.

The medical emergency?

I could have a heart attack here. That's the medical emergency.

Yeah, I still had a hard-on, and we're talking painful here. Very painful. If I could have, I would have bent over and taken my dick into my own month just to help things out. But I'm not that flexible.

Well, it was down, but I have to tell you, I'm hard again just talking to you about this.

What'd we do? Well, we always keep a cell phone in this room, so after I managed to get my hard-on down a bit – and let me tell you, with an image like *that* in the room, that was damn near impossible, I shifted my chair over across the floor, bit by bit, and opened the cell phone with my mouth, and dialled info with my nose, and asked for you guys.

Yeah, that's right, I dialled you with my nose. But let me tell you, that's a lot less frustrating than being this damn close to a woman tied up like this and not be able to do anything.

OK, so what, medically, should we do at this point?

Yes, medically.

Well, yes, I do intend to treat my wife to a nice long relaxing hour in a real bed very soon, but what I meant was, do you have any ideas about how I can get out of these handcuffs, so I can get up from this chair, lower her a bit, and totally, completely fuck her to make up for the way she's been torturing me for the last two hours?

What do you mean, you've gotta go to the bath –

Crap.

Honey, I'm sorry, but it looks like you're going to have to hold on for just a few more minutes.

Well, if you think telling the nurse took a while, wait 'til I try explaining this to 911 . . .

The Blood Virgin

Anne Tourney

For Joseph Nunez

The first time you kissed me, your lips tasted of my blood. That slippery cunt-sugar kiss wasn't what I wanted. For years I dreamed of a rough stranger who would break down the doors of my father's castle, pushing me into the shadows while whispering obscenities into my ear. I dreamed of having him deep inside me, pounding at the bloodstone of my isolation. The last thing I wanted was a lover like you, with your dainty forked tongue, and your nipples like little red bullets.

The first time you came to my father's house, I wondered why you wanted to talk to me at all. My father is the one who knows about murder. He's the world-famous poet of abnormal psychology, expert on deviance, violence, and the clotted glue of desire that binds them together. My father would have gladly written an account of your story: the story of his own brutal death.

She didn't bother to knock. Like a draft from the frozen lake that separates my father's property from the outside world, she slid into our house, slipping through oak and steel to get to me.

"Someone's breaking into the castle," my father warned me. "It's a woman. She smells of Easter lilies, with a tang of cunt." He paused, inhaling deeply. "I've always loved the scent of lilies."

My father spoke to me through a transmitter in my left ear. The device had been carved out of a shard of his skull. Years ago he had lost a piece of his cranium after being attacked by a guest in our castle. He had turned the fragment into the perfect telecommunication device, an instrument that fit snugly against my eardrum. That spectral circuitry made us closer than lovers.

I sat at my desk in the library and waited. Spike heels clicked on the stone floor. Maybe this intruder was one of my father's obsessive female fans, I thought, or a witness to one of the slaughters he wrote about.

Before she entered the library, I could smell her – floral, feral. Then she stepped into the room. She was a black blade of a woman, slut and schoolgirl in the same glossy package. Black hair fell to her shoulders, framing her face in sharp parentheses. Her mouth was painted the colour of dried blood. The pouting lips glistened and quivered, true labia blossoming in the centre of her porcelain face. She wore a black silk jacket and pleated skirt. Against all that darkness, her pale skin hit the eyes like a slap.

I asked her what she wanted.

"I want you to interview me."

"I don't do interviews – my father does. Let me call him for you."

"But I don't want your father. I want you." A strange tension seized her face, a flicker almost like panic.

"You don't understand," I said. "My father is a criminal psychologist. He's the one who interviews criminals. I'm just his secretary."

And his research assistant, archivist, and ghost-writer. His hothouse lily and captive slave, I might have added, but I wasn't going to share my bitterness with a stranger.

"Your father wouldn't understand my crimes. *You* would."

With those words she touched the hidden bruise in me. She set her fingertip on my core of rage, and pressed and pressed, until that ache turned into a roaring pain.

"What do you mean?" I said.

"I don't commit the kind of crimes that built this house."

She let her eyes wander along the yards of books that lined my father's library. She was right. Every brick, every exotic carpet fibre, every gleaming inch of marble in our mansion had been bought with the profits of someone's crime. The murderers came to my father, longing to be heard. He recorded their confessions; I transcribed them faithfully and shaped them into the manuscripts that had made my father famous.

"What crimes have you committed?"

"You'll find out if you interview me."

"Are you a murderer?"

She sucked her forefinger in mock contemplation. Then she trailed the glistening fingertip down the neckline of her jacket as she stared at me with her sloe eyes. Something squirmed in the depths of that gaze, something fearful, struggling to achieve form.

"Maybe," she said. "Wouldn't you like to know?"

"Really, my father —"

"No! You!"

She grabbed my wrist. "Please. I just escaped from prison. As soon as they catch me, I'll be sent back. Then no one will hear my story."

"How did you escape?"

"The guards couldn't watch me 24 hours a day."

"I don't know why you came here. I can't help you."

Her lips shivered. "Don't be angry. I need you."

She held out her hand. I looked at that slim white wing for a few moments. Then I took it. Living in my father's house, with him so distant in his locked chamber, I had forgotten the pleasure of touching another person's skin. When the intruder's cool hand clasped my fingers, a trap door banged open in my chest, and my heart plunged into a bottomless well of desire.

"Will you meet me tonight?" she asked.

"I can't. My father doesn't like to be left alone."

Her grip tightened. "Please?"

Please . . .

Please!

I said yes.

She smiled. On the inside of a matchbook she wrote down the name of a club in the city. Neutral ground — no fathers allowed. Then she leaned over and kissed me.

I expected a light peck, but she clutched my shoulders and pressed her mouth so hard against mine that my skull ached. Our tongues danced. Hers held a secret: a stud of glass that bit into my flesh and drew blood. Sugar and rusted tin, the taste of cruel candy. Her nipples were nails boring into my chest. When I cried out, she pulled away, clamping her hand over my mouth.

"Don't disappoint me. I can be very, very dangerous."

She whispered her threat into my right ear, the one without the transmitter. Her velvet adder's tongue caressed my earlobe with each syllable.

My father used to call me – as a term of endearment, believe it or not – his "blood virgin". No matter how many killers' confessions I transcribed, he refused to admit that I could be intimate with blood. He believed that some membrane lay across the psyche that kept the innocent from understanding violent crimes. Breaking that membrane didn't necessarily require killing another person; my father had never broken a law in his life, but he was the high priest of murder. Maybe the rupture came with a flash of insight, a glimpse into the locked chamber. As long as I played deaf, dumb and blind, my moral hymen stayed intact. It wasn't until I entered my father's chamber that the wall of my cell burst, and I saw what murder was: a miracle of transubstantiation, performed in reverse.

I searched the online databases for killers who matched the black-haired woman's description, but I couldn't find anyone like her.

"What did she say her name was?" my father asked.

"She didn't."

"You mean you didn't ask?"

"No."

"When are you going to meet her?"

"I don't think I want to."

I pressed my fingertips to my temples. Inside my skull I felt the pulse of my father's curiosity. Or was it envy, that insistent throb behind his concern?

"Never break an appointment with a murderer who wants to confess. Go talk to her."

My father, Pontius Pilate. He was pushing me towards the chasm of this murderer's desire to explain herself, and he didn't seem to care that I was about to fall. He usually hated to let me leave his castle. I was his Easter lily, his unsullied symbol of eternal life. Now he was urging me out into the night, to meet this seductress who claimed to be a murderer.

I finally gave in.

That night I dined alone, as usual. I couldn't stop thinking about the satin clutch of the murderer's lips, or the pressure of her breasts against mine. Her pebble-hard nipples had left two sore spots on my chest. Every few minutes I would touch one of those tender places, and the room around me would dissolve in a mist of desire. I could hardly swallow my food. When I tried to chew a bite of meat, the flesh tasted of cunt and Easter lilies.

I didn't have anything to wear to a club. My own clothes were drab, penitential. I searched the castle's guest rooms, looking for some sultry gown that a female visitor might have left behind. My father often hosted murderers in our home while he interviewed them, as if his hospitality were critical to their absolution.

In a tiny bedroom in the east wing I found what I was looking for. Years ago, a murderer had stayed in that room. The woman had bludgeoned her father to death in his private study. Afterwards, she drained some of his blood into a chalice and left the cup on a pedestal in her father's sanctuary. Her father continued to communicate with her after his death, speaking to her through the enchanted chalice.

"Blood speaks to blood," the murderer explained. My father showed a strange affection for this monster. He offered her our finest guest quarters, but she insisted on staying in that cramped cell. Knowing she was bound for prison, the murderer had left behind a closetful of evening dresses and shoes. Sequins and beads glittered on black velvet sheaths; iridescent feathers adorned the hems of floor-length satin gowns. I didn't think those seductive clothes would fit, but they slipped over my body as if they had been made for me.

I chose a red satin dress, slit to the spine. I wore it with black seamed stockings and stiletto pumps, wicked grace notes on my feet. As I stared at my reflection, I felt the murderer's spirit stealing through my body.

Pale throat and breasts glowed against the crimson.
Fragrance of lilies, cunt-sugar and crimson.
How could I be a virgin, when I looked like this?

My father keeps a distance from his guests, to protect his
spiritual hygiene. None of them has ever seen him, though
many have tried to push through the scrim that hides him from
the world. He sits behind his curtain like the sacramental host
while, on the other side, his guests hunger for him. His
compassion keeps him separate from the accused. The murderers envy me, living so close to my father. In their fantasies I
have an open audience with the wise judge, who listens to my
confessions with loving tolerance and absolves me with a gentle
touch.

My father once told me that all of their confessions arose from
the same crime, and that those crimes originated with lust.
Desire was dangerous – a threat to the cohesion of the mind.
But my father left me with something more dangerous than
desire. Rage demands a consummation of its own, an orgasm
turned inside-out. The censors will never let you read this, and
my father would hate to hear me use such vulgar language, but
I've come to believe that murder is an inverted fuck.

My father's guards escorted me across the lake. A car met us in
the city. As soon as the driver opened my door, I dashed for the
club. Sheltered by the crowd, I yanked the transmitter out of
my ear and let it fall on the floor with the spilled drinks and
cigarette butts.

The club had more rooms than my father's house. Caverns
led into cubbyholes, which lengthened into hallways that
opened into chapels, and the entire structure – walls, floors,
elaborately moulded ceilings – throbbed with a feverish per-
cussion. Soon my pulse was keeping time with the electronic
drums, and the rooms I explored felt as intimate as the
chambers of my heart. The revellers were lost in their own
obsessions. A man struck matches on his lover's shimmering
tits. His tongue sizzled on her flesh. A line of people waited to
have letters carved into their bellies and breasts, asses and
thighs. By the end of the night, the letters would form a poem.

Did my father know that places like this existed? Probably, but he never would have let me come here. Outside my father's house, hordes of lovers had been meeting for these cherished private games, while he had kept me locked in his castle.

I stopped in front of a stone grotto. Against one of the outcroppings, a woman braced her nude body, her legs wrapped around her lover's waist. His hips joined hers in an urgent undulation, his long black hair swinging in time to his thrusts. As his strokes quickened, her fingers raked purple streaks into his skin. Her moans melted into the cacophony around her, but I could see her lips repeatedly forming a single word: *Please*.

This was a raw ritual compared to the elaborate games I'd seen tonight, but I couldn't tear my eyes away. The black pendulum of the man's hair measured the hours I'd spent alone, imagining this scene. The woman's flushed throat was mine, and her hot mouth was mine, and the brutal grinding of her flesh and bones into the stone was mine. With his hard cock, her lover was battering the buried atom of her isolation; when he smashed it, she would come into being like a newborn star.

Now I knew what my father had been afraid of.

Jagged laughter tore my reverie. The murderer grabbed my hand and spun me around. My skirt rippled like a blood pool.

"Beautiful!" she shouted over the din.

The murderer wore a black mini skirt and cropped T-shirt, so short that its hem skimmed the underswell of her breasts. Written on the shirt in glittery script were the words FUCK US ALL.

"The interview!" I cried. "Where can we have the interview?"

Her forked tongue swept across her lips. That lewd promise was her only reply.

The murderer led me out of the club through a door that opened into a warped funnel of blackness. She dragged me through a passageway under the city, into the echoing sewers that spread under my father's lake. She knew every turn by heart, as if she had spent her whole life in the subterranean tunnels of my world.

When we burst into the open air, I heard wind skidding over frozen water, and I knew we were back at the castle. The ice sheets creaked and groaned, singing the same stern song that had lulled me to sleep since I was a child. But the rhythm was different now; the lullaby had been inverted. The night itself had been reversed – even the constellations of stars were upside down.

"Keep moving," the murderer urged. She was shivering in her scanty clothes.

"Why are we back at the castle?"

"I want you to take me to your father's study."

"Then why did you ask me to meet you at the club?"

The murderer smiled. "I had to bring you here through my secret passage," she said, "or you'd never understand who I am."

She pulled me close and kissed me until my legs turned to water. Her tongue slithered between my lips and tickled the roof of my mouth. My red dress slipped from my shoulders. Her cold fingers crawled across my breasts – squeezing, kneading, as if my flesh held secrets. Our scents rose and mingled, smoke flowers freezing in mid-air.

"Now," she said, "ask me who I am."

When you kissed me that night, I made the mistake of opening my eyes. I wanted to peer into the tunnels of your pupils, into the coils of your brain matter. I wanted to watch the clockworks of your mind, but your face was a glass orb filled with darkness. All I could see was an obsidian opacity. I don't know what scared me more – the fact that your beautiful skull had turned hollow, or that its surface didn't reflect me at all. Even a charlatan's seeing stone would have reflected a white smudge.

Then you slid your tongue into my mouth. Instantly your face was flesh again, your cheeks hot to the touch. You clutched my breasts, pinched my nipples as if to milk blood from the nubs. The treacherous stone in your tongue wasn't a diamond, but a shard of ice, which melted into sweet water. With one moan, I drowned out the nightmare that I'd seen in your eyes.

She whispered her story into my ear.

Three words. That was her history. Three words, and I knew all I could stand to know. If she had told me any more, I would have fallen off the narrow ledge of myself into the void below.

She slid her finger into my mouth, dug something from the hollow under my tongue, and pressed the object into my palm. It was a key made of bone. She didn't have to tell me which door the key would open.

"Let's go see your father," she said.

We ran up the hill to the castle and flew through the massive doors. We climbed the twisting staircase that led to my father's study, ascending so high that the air became too thin for us to breathe, and we had to stop to gulp air from each others' lips. Our hearts banged like lust-drunk birds against the cages of our ribs. We stood in front of the door to his chamber and clung to each other like teenage lovers, our tongues weaving and slapping as we kissed.

Then my father cried out my name.

The murderer's body stiffened against mine. Our excitement hardened into a crystalline rage. We broke our embrace. I pushed the bone key into the lock. As soon as the door opened, the cry stopped. A staggering silence filled the room.

The study was empty. Cobwebs and their listless shadows stood in lieu of objects. I saw phantom bookshelves that held no books, a pair of hovering chairs, and a floating globe that replicated no world I had ever seen. My father's private sanctuary was as bereft as a desecrated shrine. At the heart of this sepulchre stood a pedestal draped in threadbare velvet. On top of the pedestal sat a chalice.

I went to the pedestal, lifted the tarnished cup, and looked inside. A layer of dust shifted on the surface of the fluid. A fissure opened in the dust, revealing a crimson crescent, like a mouth. The thin lips parted. The mouth sighed my name.

"That's his blood," said the murderer.

I screamed.

The murderer snatched the chalice and tipped it onto the floor. Gore rained in clotted gouts. She pulled something out of the cup. It was a carved bone fragment, identical to the transmitter that my father had given me. I took the shard and held it for a long time, watching it float in my shaking hand.

"Go ahead," the murderer said. "See if it works."

I placed it in my ear. Not so much as a whisper seeped through the circuits.

"Do you remember the day he died?" she asked.

"No."

The murderer squatted on the floor, tracing letters in the red liquid: FUCK US ALL.

Her porcelain cheeks were streaked with blood. I sank to the floor beside her. Using her forefinger as a brush, she painted my mouth.

"Beautiful," she said. "Now paint mine."

I did as she said. She caught my finger between her teeth and suckled at the tip. The suction sent a spear of longing through my belly.

"Remember when you came up to this room, the night you told him you were leaving?" she asked. "He said he'd never let you go."

"I don't remember."

"He said you could never leave the castle," she went on. "You were his lily. His hothouse flower."

"I didn't kill him."

"You did, my dear."

"My father can't be dead. How did he interview all those criminals?"

But I already knew. I had ushered the murderers into the castle and led them into the library, where I sat them down in front of the confessional screen. I had set up the tape recorder to record their stories. The criminals believed they were pouring out their hearts to a man, a corporeal being like themselves. But the voice that spoke to them came from a distant part of the castle. The voice came from my father's blood.

When the interviews were over, I transcribed the tapes. I wrote my father's books; I published them under his name. And all the while his blood instructed me, guided me, from the chalice upstairs. Blood speaks to blood.

"You're remembering, aren't you?" the murderer said. "Think back. Do you remember why you wanted to escape?"

She kissed me. Our lips and tongues merged in a slippery knot. Her hands slid under my dress and glided up my thighs, up to the crevice that had never been opened. Her fingers sank into flesh so wet that it gave way to her caress like ectoplasm.

"Please," I whispered. "Please."

She took hold of my shoulders and pushed me onto my back, parting my knees. Her face, as she gazed down at me with lust-dark eyes, was a mirror image of my own longing. I spread my thighs and raised my hips, so that her lily-white hand could dive into my deepest secrets.

Outside the castle, the lake screamed. The ice was tearing itself apart. When the sheets melted to let the lake's secrets rise, my father's remains would bob to the surface. First the small bones would emerge, then the heavier ones, and finally the massive cranium with the star-shaped hole that I made when I bludgeoned him to death.

"Do you remember now?" she asked.

I moaned, tossing my head from side to side.

"You wanted to leave the castle because you wanted to get fucked." She drove her fist deeper. My mind flashed to the lovers in the club, to the scene that my father had always been afraid of.

"Yes," I whispered. "Yes, I wanted to get fucked."

"Did you think it was a coincidence, when you found that dress tonight? You used to pay your father's guards to smuggle those slutty clothes into the castle. You used to lie awake at night, wishing some stranger would break in and deflower you. Like this."

The murderer drove her vicious little fist in and out of my cunt. She had almost reached the hard atom at my centre. My hips pumped up and down in their own frenzied dance – faster and faster, until my inner walls burned. Then her knuckles struck the core of my memory, and I fell into a blood-red seizure.

My body convulsed. Delirium. The stench of burning cunt and lilies filled the room. I saw the crime I had committed. Blood, ribbons of blood, streamed across the walls and ceiling. I danced among the streamers of bright blood. My father cried out to me from the empty chalice.

Then the moment exploded, and memory became a mist.

Minutes passed, or hours. I sat up, shaking, and pushed my hair out of my eyes. The strands were heavy with clots of dried blood. I looked around at the dusty crepuscule of my father's study, at the stains that darkened the floor, and remembered nothing.

I was alone.

You were captured that night and thrown back in prison. I send you letters, but the censors cross out all the parts about blood and memory and desire. I don't know if you read what I've written. You never answer. Sometimes I think I'm writing to myself.

I make sure that you're never left unguarded. I make sure that you're kept in the smallest possible cell, with no sexy clothes to remind you of who you were when you were free. You are not allowed to have lovers in prison, or to touch yourself, or to fantasize about being touched. Prison life will leave you hollow. You will grow smaller and smaller, until you disappear.

My father and I will be safe here, in the house that murder built. Our devotion to each other will prove that you are a liar, that those three words you spoke to me were a delusion of your fractured mind.

I am you, you whispered into my ear.

No. You are the enemy.

Sakura

Diane Kepler

ICHI

It is that magical week when the cherry blossoms are just past
the height of their fullness and their petals begin to flutter
down in a fragrant, pink rain. The streets and avenues are
quieter somehow, and more comfortable, as if wrapped in a
rosy quilt.

The pastel-patterned sidewalk occupies Hiroe as she makes
her way home from school. Her gait is dreamlike. At times she
slows, lingering under the perfumed boughs, lifting up her face
to feel the petals alight. They dot her cheeks and the fragile
domes of her closed eyes. Each contact is like a kiss. She smiles
to herself, imagining the real kisses that are soon to follow.

He waits for her at the temple. Not grand Kinkakuji or
ancient Daitokoji, where the other foreigners swarm like so
many pale moths, but the humble sanctuary that marks the
spot where her lane joins the main thoroughfare. He is burning
incense when she arrives. As always, she is reminded of the
first time she saw him there, kneeling composedly, and, as far
as she knew from her casual acquaintance with Jodo Bud-
dhism, doing everything exactly right.

NI

She waited, on that first day, until he'd finished his devotions.
Waited and then hurried forward as he was stepping into his
shoes back on the wide, wooden verandah of the shrine.

"Ex-cu-suh me, pu-ree-suh," she managed after a great deal

of shifting from foot to foot. For the first time, Hiroe had cause to regret all those notes she kept passing during English class. But he was so beautiful. She had to say something.

When he turned she saw how wide his eyes were and, when he answered in polite, idiomatic Japanese, how elegant his smile.

"I'm sorry, Miss, could you repeat that? I didn't understand."

"A Kyoto accent," she'd whispered to Rei and Asuka at school the next day. "It's as if he'd lived here all his life."

"Is he handsome?" Asuka urged.

Hiroe lifted her chin. "Remember Yuji from the Weiss-Kreuz anime?"

Rei gaped at her. "You mean the tall blond?"

"Exactly. And not only that, he's smart! He's studying history at Kyodai – politics and culture of the Muromachi era. Aunt Setsuko said he knows as many kanji as she does. He's practically a poet."

"How does your aunt know him?"

"That's the very best part," Hiroe sighed. "He's staying at her guesthouse!"

"Right down the street from you," breathed Rei.

"Fifty-four steps," confirmed Hiroe with a nod of her head. "I counted."

Rei and Asuka drew their friend into an exuberant, three-way hug. "Iyaaa!" they shrieked in unison. "You're so lucky!"

"So, does he like you?" Rei prompted, which forced an awkward pause. Hiroe dropped her eyes, scuffing one shoe along the paving stones of the schoolyard. "I don't know. At first I thought no, but then . . . How can I tell?"

"That's easy," said Asuka. "He buys you things."

SAN

"Happy birthday," John murmured as the subway gathered speed. It was a Thursday afternoon, an occasion that had shot up Hiroe's "Favourite Times of the Week" chart ever since she'd met him by chance on his way home from classes and found that their schedules coincided. She'd lain in wait for him ever since.

From his knapsack he conjured a small, flat package, elegantly wrapped in the old style in a square of plum-coloured silk. It was a favourite trick of Aunt Setsuko's, and Hiroe couldn't help wondering if her aunt had taught him or if he'd figured it out himself.

She gave a small cry of happiness and then worked at the knot, concealing neither her eagerness nor her disenchantment when her long-awaited present turned out to be just a book of classical poems, and a used one at that.

How . . . boring, she thought. And how cheap! This was nothing like the extravagant presents from the salarymen who wooed some of her classmates.

John watched her closely and then gave a little grin. "I know, it's not what you expected. But I'm hoping you'll appreciate it some day."

"No I won't," Hiroe pouted, squinting at the elegant type. "Who cares about standing under a straw roof in the rain?" Yet despite her moue of displeasure, she was more happy than not. Finally, after months of waiting, summer slipping into autumn, he had given her a gift. And now, a lucky break. A rude little dumpling of a boy who seemed destined for the sumo ring had wedged himself in on her other side, giving Hiroe the excuse to press up against John, hip to hip and thigh to thigh, so that, whenever the subway slowed, she could lean in to him, pretending it was her own inertia that took her.

The doors closed, the train gathered speed. Hiroe dared a glance at the object of her affection.

"Now a book of love poems," she murmured, with her toes touching prettily and her eyes as round as she could make them, "that would be an ideal gift for a girl like me. Why don't you give me a book of love poems, John?"

He scratched his head, pretending to think. "Uh, because we're not lovers?"

"Yes, we are. I love you, and you're just crazy about me!"

That brought an honest laugh out of him. "Ah, Hiroe, Hiroe," he murmured, shaking his head.

She thrilled at the way he said her name: gently, with each of the three syllables glowing as if lit up from the inside.

"We should take a honeymoon," she declared. It was half a joke, but as always, it was also half serious.

John raised an eyebrow at her. "You're getting ambitious. First you suggested a tryst in the park, then a love hotel, and now an honest-to-goodness trip somewhere? Hm . . ." he pretended to consider, "I hear Singapore's popular. My savings could probably get us to Osaka."

"I have money. I can pay."

He pursed his lips and then twisted them in an expression she couldn't understand. "You probably could at that. Tell you what. Give me a while to pick out a destination."

"How long?"

His sweeping glance was appraising but not unkind. "How about a few years?"

Hiroe went red and looked down at her lap. The book of poems was still there, also red against the blue pleated skirt of her school uniform.

"Maybe in your backward country they have some crazy laws, but –"

He sighed and leaned back against the subway seat, fitting the heels of his palms against his closed eyes. "It's got nothing to do with laws, Hiroe. It's about consent, and the ability to know what you're agreeing to – we've been through this before. And I wish you'd stop asking all the time." He took down his hands and gave her a meaningful look. "Do you have *any* idea what that's like for me?"

"No," she sulked, and this time her expression was real.

John turned toward her then. He put an arm around her shoulders. "Have you ever heard of the Chinese water torture?"

Hiroe was shocked and amazed. He had his *arm* around her! In public, no less – like they were a real couple. She fought to keep her breathing even. Betraying her excitement might dislodge him.

"Most likely some product of another barbarian culture," she said loftily.

"Ah, the youth of today," he sighed and ran a finger along Hiroe's forehead, stroking the roots of her glossy black hair. "Please, allow me to educate you."

"What does this have to do with –"

"Shh," he whispered. "Now lie back."

Hiroe felt a gentle tap on her forehead. She knew it was his finger, but it felt as if a drop of water had landed there. She felt another tap after a few seconds, and then another. Hiroe's head rolled in time to the swaying of the subway car, but somehow he always managed to touch the exact same spot.

"John –"

His opposing hand on her shoulder held her in place. The tapping continued, becoming very annoying very quickly.

"Quit it!" Hiroe twisted away.

He smiled at her. "Terrible, isn't it? The Chinese used to interrogate prisoners this way. They'd tie people down, suspend a water clock over them, and let the droplets fall, just like that, for hours or days. Sometimes people went insane."

He leaned in close and his voice was barely a whisper. "That's what it's like for me when you keep asking all the time."

SHI

Hiroe, entranced by the blossoms, has taken longer than usual on her walk home from school. Yet he is there, at the temple.

He is kneeling with his back to her, as still as a lake in winter. She doesn't dare interrupt his meditation – at least not at first. But after a time, worry steals in. Is he angry that she is late? Did he even hear her approach? It wouldn't do to call his name, but . . .

Carefully, she slips off her shoes and kneels down beside him.

"Why are you here burning incense all the time?" she whispers in the semidarkness.

"Usually it's to ask Amida Buddha for guidance." His measured words rise like smoke toward the wooden rafters. His gaze is also directed upward, until he directs it to her dark and shining eyes. "But sometimes I also ask for forgiveness."

She shivers.

On the tatami mat in front of him, Hiroe sees a bag from Kyobuy, the new department store near the university.

"What's in there?"

"You're a curious little girl, aren't you?"

"Is it a present for me?"

"Perhaps. Or it might be for me. One never can tell."

He rises fluidly, makes a final obeisance to the Buddha image, and then strides to the porch to find his shoes.

"Where are we going?" chirps Hiroe, stuffing her feet into her black tie-ups, usually fashionable but now a nuisance. She lets the laces dangle, clattering down the steps after him.

He strides quickly through the mosaic of fallen cherry blossoms, snow white in the light of the streetlamps. His pace is brisk. She has to run to catch up.

"Where are we *going*?"

"You'll see."

It is in fact a teahouse in the heart of Gion, one that used to host geisha in bygone days. Hiroe is aghast at being taken to such an elegant place in her school uniform, while he's almost unbearably handsome in his khakis and a white button-down. But when she tells him as much, he laughs.

"So I was supposed to have let you go home to change? I'm sure your mother would have just let you breeze on out again."

Hiroe hadn't thought of that.

"Where do your parents think you are, anyway?"

"At Rei's house. Studying."

"Ah, of course." His expression is unreadable and dark somehow. For the first time, Hiroe feels a bit apprehensive.

The hostess seats them in a private room, with a black lacquered table in the centre. There is a view of the courtyard – some greenery and a pond. A heartbeat after the hostess leaves, the paper screen slides back to admit a cheerful woman with a tea service. There are cups on the tray, a pot of steaming water, and a small porcelain bowl with tea itself. As she leaves, John tips her. The yen notes are discreetly folded, but Hiroe realizes this is much more than the average gratuity.

Once their server has padded noiselessly away, John turns to her.

"Well, my dear, we're alone now."

She sits still, wondering what he'll do next.

"Don't you want to kiss me?"

She blinks. It takes a moment for her to realize that he really expects it of her, that he won't move until she acts first. Afraid and yet mesmerized by the beautiful shape of his lips, she slides off of her cushion and crawls to where he sits quite composedly. Her first kiss is delicate – just a brush of his cheek with lips sweetly pursed – yet while he doesn't flinch away, he doesn't kiss her back either.

She draws nearer. She takes his face in her hands. With a thumb on each cheekbone she traces them, traces the contours of his eyes and then closes them. His nose and chin are the targets of her kisses, and then his mouth. When their lips touch he returns the kiss at last. The caress of his mouth is indeed as she imagined: as soft as the petals falling silently in the streets outside, but warmer. There is a perfume to him, too – a wonderful manly scent that she'd never noticed because she'd never come this close. His breath wafts across her nose and her lashes, causing a shiver to course through her, and a stirring, farther down.

His kisses are chaste, gentle. After a time Hiroe tries to speed them into something more passionate, but each time he draws away. She is kneeling to one side of him. He has not moved except to turn his head. The effort of rising to meet his lips is telling. Her thighs quiver with the strain of it. It makes her aware of the growing heat between them.

"Hiroe, permit me something."

She leans against him, the top of her head against the centre of his chest, but she is looking at the tatami mats to one side and not into his lap because she's shy about what has grown there.

"Anything."

She can feel his smile. "Just what I wanted to hear."

He pushes her back and dips a careful finger into the water for the tea, which is still steaming. Fleetingly, he frowns.

"I want you to sit up here on the table facing me."

Hiroe opens her eyes. He is putting the tray with the tea things on the floor, making room.

"Sit? On the table?" It's a preposterous suggestion, as if he'd asked her to eat dinner off a chair.

"Shh. I'm going to give you your present now."

GO

Hiroe shuffled glumly out into the schoolyard. On either side of her, Rei and Asuka chattered merrily, but she couldn't find it in her to join them. The chill winter air nipped at her knees and nose, reminding her that despite these weeks upon weeks of carefully spaced intervals of flirting with John and ignoring him, nothing had changed.

"Keep after him," Asuka advised when Hiroe appealed to them for help.

"You must be like the river," said Rei, who was hopelessly addicted to historical dramas and fond of wise-woman sayings. "The water is soft, but patient. In time, it wears down even the hardest stone."

"Even the *hardest* stone," echoed Asuka, with a grin.

But despite all of Hiroe's efforts, John didn't give in – not when she flirted and not when she cried and not even when she called him one desperate night after her bath.

"John, I need you." Hiroe gripped the receiver with one hand, her other wandering. If she closed her eyes she could imagine him standing there at the common phone in the hallway at Aunt Setsuko's.

"Aren't you worried about your parents hearing you talking this way?"

"Mother's having her bath, and Father's out drinking with his colleagues. I am free to talk to my boyfriend however I please."

A sigh from the other end. "I see. Well, you'd better hang up then, he might be trying to call you."

"You silly . . ." She giggled, tracing the downy lips of her sex through a clean pair of cotton panties.

"Hiroe, I have to go. I have lots of work tonight."

"I can help," she offered, desperate now.

"I doubt it. My assignment is to write a poem in the style of Fujiwara no Sadai."

"I could write it for you! On your stomach, with a brush and ink. Our lovemaking would inspire me."

He laughed out loud. "Yes, I could just see myself untucking my shirt in front of the class tomorrow. I can hear my thesis adviser now: 'Whose is this terrible calligraphy?'"

He'd meant it to be funny, but she hung up the phone in a rage.

RYOKU

Her heart was sore with the agony of yet another refusal. Still, it did not stop Hiroe from drifting past the guest house on her way to school. But when she saw him looking mussed, and as if he'd only just stepped into his shoes, Hiroe hurried past.

"Good morning," he said with exaggerated politeness. His eyes looked small in the morning light and his shirt was wrinkled.

"Leave me alone," she shot back.

"Well, that's quite a change from last night."

"I'm a changed woman," she said airily, "one who'll forget you by taking another lover."

"Taking a lover, you mean."

She quickened her pace. "There are a lot of boys at school who would kill or die to have me." This was not precisely true, but with a bit of advertising, she could probably make it so.

"Hiroe." He stopped walking, and after a few steps she did, too. "I told you to forget this."

"I am."

"No, I mean really forget it." He sighed. "I'm tired of this."

"Tired of what?"

"Of you trying to force everything to be the way you want it. I told you how I feel, so live with it."

She rounded on him angrily. "I'm not going to stop my life just because you feel guilty."

"I never told you to stop your life, Hiroe. I just want you to wait for the right time."

"And you're the one who gets to decide *my* right time? Well, forget that. I'll just find a real boyfriend."

In two steps he was on her, hands on her upper arms.

"Don't do this to be vindictive. All that will happen is you'll wind up getting hurt."

"What do you care?"

Suddenly he turned and pressed her up against the stone wall of the temple. He had an arm on either side and a leg between both of hers. His lips were close and his breathing ragged. Hiroe struggled, aghast. No one could see them now, but someone could turn the corner at any moment.

"Listen!" he said forcefully, and she was compelled to stop moving. "Maybe it's not obvious to you, but I care quite a bit."

They stood that way with gazes locked. Out of the corner of her eye, Hiroe could see the cherry blossoms falling to the avenue, just a few steps away.

"You want it your way?"

"It's not —"

"Do you want it your way?!"

"If that's how you see it, then yes!"

"Fine. Meet me at the temple after school."

He walked off without looking back. Hiroe gazed after him, confused, her throat tight with words that had gotten stuck. The event had to be some kind of victory, yet it didn't feel that way at all.

SHICHI

Naturally, her friends got to hear everything.

"Make sure he buys you something nice," said Asuka, playing the role of auntie. She was only a year older, yet well versed in this type of transaction. She'd given her virginity away on four separate occasions and had found it quite profitable.

"Quiet, you girls!" commanded their teacher, and of course there was no choice but to obey.

HACHI

"You want to give me my present?" whispers Hiroe.

"That's right." He sweeps a hand over the table's smooth, shiny surface. "Go on."

Hiroe gets up, adjusts the pleats of her skirt, and then sinks uncertainly down onto the black lacquer. He is still on his cushion, gazing up at her now. She blushes furiously.

He reaches up to stroke the tender flesh of one calf, to run his hand over her fashionably bunchy sock and slide it down to her ankle so he can kiss the smooth flesh he has laid bare. The other sock promptly follows, and when both her legs are naked, he begins kissing his way slowly up one and then the other, in careful increments calculated to tease. Whenever his lips reach a new level, he pauses long enough for her to draw a breath and then switches to the other leg, starting at the bottom and moving steadily up. At the level of her knees, he feels resistance. Her legs close in on either side of his head, forcing him away.

He sits back.

She's the very image of timidity, there on the table with her eyes closed and her head turned to one side. Her knees are together now and the last knuckle of her middle finger is pressed against her lips. It's almost a caricature, really, and John doesn't know which is stronger, his irritation or his mad urge to laugh.

"Come on. Don't tell me you're going to play the blushing maiden now, after all this."

Her eyes flutter open. "What?"

He sighs and looks smilingly ceiling-ward. "Amida Buddha, grant me the patience to –"

"Oh no you don't," she laughs, ending his prayer with a kiss.

When they finally come up for air, he grins at her. "Ah, there's my impetuous darling."

"I'm not impetuous."

"Of course you are," he says, kissing her knees. "And also predisposed to theatrical displays of hyperfemininity. But you're young and Japanese, so I'll forgive the second flaw."

"And the first?"

He grins. "You'll learn that in time. Want your present now?"

"Yes," she husks, making every effort to look at him directly.

"Then spread your legs."

He leans into her then, bunching her pleated skirt in his hands as his questing lips find the source of her secrecy. Her nether lips are held closed by a thin cotton veil and he kisses her through the white eyelets. A moment later he feels her begin to dissolve. Her legs relax on either side of him. Her hands sink into the pool of his wavy blond hair, combing it out and stroking it as he licks her. The first touch of his tongue tip feels to Hiroe as if one of the cherry petals has alighted at the base of her mons, where the bud of her womanhood would jut if it weren't wrapped in cotton and imprisoned between the pouting lips of her sex. The next touch is a slow, broad stroke of his tongue along her dewy furrow. After two more strokes it's unclear how much of the dew is coming from within and how much from without. But the scent of her guides him. John breathes her in, filling himself with the scent that reminds him of an ocean breeze after the rains in late summer.

A dovelike sound from above encourages John to explore further. His licks are deliberate. No matter how she rolls her hips or presses into him, he keeps his own pace, nuzzling her stiffened bud or nibbling at her sweet lips or pointing his tongue and, only when she is no longer expecting it, pushing it into her cranny.

At last, a pause. He stops to watch her. She is adrift on a cloud-sea of pleasure, with her eyes closed, swaying gently on the table. Tenderly he collects Hiroe from her uncertain perch and gathers her into his arms. It is a sweet feeling to have her there, this warm, heavy, girl-shaped bundle with her temple pressed up against his chin.

He touches her cheek and she nuzzles, catlike, against his hand. He traces the outline of her lower lip – the very fullest, pinkest part. Her mouth opens and, fluidly, his thumb slides in. At the new sensation, her eyes open as well. They follow the path of his digit as he draws it away and glosses her lips with it. So he lets her have it back, and her eyes fall closed once more.

"That's a good girl. Suck it."

Another small sound escapes Hiroe. Her hands tighten on his knees.

"Suck. With that pretty mouth and those cheeks all hollow. Do you have any idea how many times you've shown up in my dreams like this, you little carp?"

She moans for real this time, wanting nothing more than for him to slide his hands down under her skirt, under everything, to touch the very core of her and finish what he has started. All those nights she had lain in her bed, with her own hands wandering through her garden, are nothing compared to the distilled essence of desire that is coursing through her now.

And so her need expresses itself in the movements of her lips. They close upon the narrow part of his thumb and he twists, enjoying the feeling of her tongue fluttering against its very tip – a heady sensation, even without her pert bottom pressed enticingly into his groin. Still, he knows Hiroe is expecting her gift, so he lets the digit pop free and uses his hands to slide her panties down. He tucks the hem of her skirt carefully into its waistband and gazes down at her from above, at her mound and the beautiful thatch of hair that graces it. Hiroe feels open and exposed, but the rustle of the paper bag distracts her.

He takes out an ordinary sea sponge, golden and no larger than his palm.

She wants to ask, tries to, but he shakes his head no, and the movement is transmitted along his jaw and through the obsidian waterfall of her hair. Her eyes trace every movement of the sponge, from the bag, in a low arc past the table, to the floor with its tray and teacups and kettle of water, no longer steaming, only warm. The kettle is as shallow as her breathing. It has a wide opening in the top, large enough for him to dip the entire sponge inside. He soaks it and squeezes just slightly. There is no other sound in the room, in the teahouse, or perhaps in the entire world.

Water is falling in drops now, from the sponge and onto her young and sensate skin. The first two drops, fat and rapid, alight on her stomach and splatter there. He goes back and squeezes out the sponge a little more. The next few drops are slower. They fall on her belly, her mons, and then on her pink and jutting centre. She hisses at the teasing contact. She struggles to get free, beating her stockinged feet against the tatami. But his other arm is locked about her waist and there is no way to free herself without hurting him.

He waits, with the sponge in his upturned palm, until she is finished struggling. Then he turns his hand over and begins again.

The next drop falls exactly where he wants it, and so he braces his forearm against her bent knee and lets the sponge hover there as he watches the subtle interplay of gravity and tension. Hiroe is keening softly in his arms. He soothes her with murmured words. Nonetheless, each tiny impact makes her body jerk. Soon she is digging her nails into the long muscles of his thigh, and of the arm that binds her, her head rolling from side to side. He goes back for more water. Again he lets it drip against her core and again the struggle begins. But after a time, her breathing quiets down. He can feel her heart slowing and, in the tiny movements of her eyes, sense her attention wandering from the sponge between drops. The water is cool now, as it trickles along her slit to the sodden pillow beneath her. She cools as well, and her sighs are frustrated.

"What's the matter?"

"John, I – I don't think I can. . . ."

"Don't think you can what?"

"You know," she says shyly, half-turning to press her cheek into the row of buttons on his shirt.

"You can say it."

A sigh. "Come," she breathes at last. "I don't think I can come like this."

"Well, who said you were supposed to?"

She pulls away to look at him. "But –"

"But what?" he remarks, tenderly untucking her skirt and smoothing her hair into a semblance of order. "Oh, I see. You thought that due to the elegance of the surroundings I was going to, maybe, deflower you here?"

"I –"

"Or perhaps that this was all about your pleasure? That there wasn't something bigger wrapped up in all of this?" John regards her with a bemused expression as he squeezes out the last of the water and returns the sponge to its paper home.

"But . . . you want to." She reaches for that forbidden part of him, and at her delicate touch he springs instantly back to full erection.

"You," he says, pointedly removing her hand, "need to learn some patience."

She regards him with a dark, shifting kind of expression.

"All this time I've waited for you and you're telling me I need to learn patience?"

"All these months of teasing me, you mean."

"Teasing you?" Her expression hardens and she chokes the words out, rising up onto her knees, small fists angled away from her body.

The instant stretches out into a moment and then into a longer time. The dim lighting along the floor etches years into her face and her frame trembles, but it is her eyes that finally enlighten. The pain in them – he'd never seen it before.

He opens his arms then. She is reluctant at first but then comes into that longed-for circle. A kiss and she trembles in every part. A hand beneath her skirt and she sighs. This time he goes directly to her slippery cleft, working her still-swollen nub with a trio of careful fingers until she gasps, until her hands tighten on his crisp, white sleeves and she coats him with her essence, at last turning to muffle her impassioned cries against his chest.

When her eyes blink open, he has another kiss for her, soft as a cherry blossom on the sacred space between her brows.

"Hiroe," he says at last. "I'm sorry. I promise – no more games."

So that when her small hand closes around the hardness that still pulses at the root of him, and when that member leaps in her hand like a fish, he surrenders, at last.

Drift

Christopher Hart

It was a hot summer night and I was at a party in a large, dark garden somewhere, nowhere in particular. The hosts might have called it London, only because they didn't know what else to call it. But it wasn't London. The garden was too big.

It was later summer, everything sighing and dying, the most lethargic and dreamy time of year. BMWs and Jags snoozed and purred on the gravel drive round the front, and round the back, light spilled out from the open windows and across the lawn and caught our champagne glasses as we stood around in the darkness, the air filled with murmurous insect voices. I couldn't even be bothered to drink much, and I never did like champagne. Filled you up with gas, made you feel like you were about to take off. I was very bored.

Then I saw a girl stepping out of the french windows and coming across the lawn. She was striking rather than pretty, in red heels and a figure-hugging long red dress and very white arms and shoulders and long red hair. I hate that look. And despite the loud, loud colour signals, she walked quite shyly, head down. It was obvious I had to go and talk to her.

"You don't have a drink."

"My boyfriend's just getting me one," she said, not even registering me, nodding back inside. Perfect.

She relented a little. "A cocktail of some sort, so he says."

"Ah, so – is he a cocktail waiter by profession?"

She gave me a look and something inside me whimpered. I quite enjoyed it really. "No," she said, very slowly. "He works in LA. Title credits."

I was beginning to like her. "What, you mean the lettering? How to spell Nicole Kidman and things?"

She ignored that one entirely, looked away, and lit a cigarette. I was really beginning to like her. Then she looked back. "And if you dare to say I remind you of Nicole Kidman I'll put my heel through your foot."

"As if," I said. "There's nothing sexy about Nicole Kidman." No response. "So he's out there a lot, is he? In LA? Mixing his cocktails? Leaving you all alone?"

She looked very, very bored. I felt quite perky now. We stood a while longer in companionably mutual dislike, plus something else. Finally she muttered "fuck" and dropped her cigarette and went back inside. She came back with a glass in one hand and a bottle of champagne in the other.

"No cocktail?"

"Seems he's too busy," she said. And then, ah! Like a little beam of light between a woman's thighs, she looked up and smiled. Admittedly it was a smile made up about half and half of unhappiness and malevolence. But it would have to do.

There weren't many guests left outside, and we were at the end of the garden in deep gloom, when the music changed. "When a Man Loves a Woman", of all things. So I slipped my right arm round her waist and laid my left hand on her cool white shoulder and pulled her as close to me as I dared and we started swaying. She didn't resist. Although the way she continued to swig from the bottle while we danced seemed to me kind of detached. I felt myself hardening already and pressed myself closer. She ignored it, continued to swig from the bottle.

Over her shoulder, the other guests all looked like they were in black. And as if they were frozen, not moving, unable to see us back here. I felt suddenly hot. Something was wrong, or very, very right. Something was out of control, anyhow. I leaned down and kissed her. She kissed me back. We were like figures in a painting coming mysteriously to life and beginning to move, while everyone else was still and silent, dressed in black. And so cold.

But her small waist was warm under my hands; hot, even. We kissed and revolved anti-clockwise and nobody saw us, noticed us. We would have been more subtle, teasing, educated in our kisses, if we had pulled back, taken breath, then kissed some more. But we couldn't do that, couldn't pull apart, remained caught; there was only one kiss between us and we couldn't escape.

The first I knew of it, the pressure on the soles of my feet had gone. Like your health, it is not something you notice till it goes. There was no pressure there, just loose, bewildered blood. Her feet too were dangling free in the air, and kicked lightly against mine. We were six inches off the grass, a foot, two feet and rising. We were also drifting dangerously towards the house.

"Um . . ." she said, cautious, English. "Is this . . .?"

I was cool about it. "Gravity seems to have failed us." I didn't feel cool about it all. This was supposed to be a hollow seduction, nothing more. Not this, not now. Not this serious. I kissed her some more. She pulled back again.

"I think this is quite serious," she said, looking down between our feet. We were now above the guests' heads. No one had noticed us yet. But if one of them should just happen to glance up . . .

"They'll see us," she hissed. "And it'll really freak them."

I don't think we cared. There didn't seem to be much we could do except kiss again. I wrapped her in my arms and slid my hand down over her bum, the fabric of her dress cool to the touch but her flesh so warm beneath. Her eyes opened, upturned, beseeching, needy, and closed again. We both opened our eyes again when we bumped up against the side of the house. About twenty feet up. I grazed my knuckles slightly on the brickwork, and the bottle she was still holding clanked noisily.

"Jesus," she whispered.

But it was too late for that. I pressed her against the wall and dropped my hand down between us and pinched her breast so lightly she didn't even gasp, but her eyes flared wide. We began to slide upwards again.

The light was on in the bathroom and we were heading straight for it, like insects illuminated. I loved her face then, and my hand already loved the giving curve of her waist. We pushed off from the wall and floated past the window. Inside there was a girl on the loo and another standing nearby, gossiping. Ideally, I suppose they would have been going for it too, if this was just another erotic dream. But it wasn't.

She managed to lodge the champagne bottle in the guttering, and then we pushed off harder, out over the lawn again, and started to pull each other's clothes off. I had her dress rucked up around her waist and her knickers down to her knees, floating back, my face buried between her thighs, when she whispered urgently about . . .

It was true. I couldn't just drop them, they could land on somebody's head below. I stuffed them in my jacket pocket and she began to unbuckle my trousers. We were drifting towards a tree, a big old copper beech.

Half naked now, we slid in among the covering leaves, which rasped and tickled against our bare hot skin. In another month or two the leaves would brown and fade and crisp but now they were their rich summer copper and soft and generous as skin. We drifted in, scraping our bare limbs on the bark, past caring, wondering if those down below would see the shimmy of the branches, hear the gasps from above.

We draped our clothes over the black branches as we went past, tucked my shoes away in a cleft, but I made her keep the red heels on. Some things never change, even in zero gravity.

For a while I held us steady with my hands on a branch above, and she spread out in front of me on a wider branch and I slipped straight into her, she leaned back taut, unable to fall if she tried, I fucked her in slow steady strokes, and then I let go of the branch and she wrapped herself around me and we rose higher, up through the last thin top leaves and out into the night sky.

There was no wind, or we could feel none. We just drifted. In a hot air balloon you never feel the wind, because you travel exactly at its speed. Maybe that was us. Our discarded clothes lay on the branches below, flirting with the wind, but we couldn't feel it. We rose higher.

Instead of the wind I had her white limbs wrapping around me. The moon was a black disc with a white splinter on its back, and, above the street lights, we could now see all the stars. And looking down, we could still see the guests on the lawn, a vertical view of the tops of their heads and sometimes their feet poking out below. She whispered, "There's my boyfriend," but it was a hollow word now and didn't carry.

Below us the town was laid out like an illuminated map, parks and gardens and cats under the cars. We could see it all. Though in the east already the night was fading away, and before long we'd have to come down. Brush down past the swaying branches, scramble for our cold clothes, nod our goodbyes. But not for now, not yet, not while I was still inside her and she was arched back from me and I leaned down and took each breast in my mouth in turn, not yet, trapped in a dream of flying and no desire to escape or come down at all.